D0726178

For Rich,
as always, for so many reasons.

And for Pamela Musso Costidis,
a courageous, great friend.

PART ONE

The opposite of love is not hate, it's indifference.
The opposite of art is not ugliness, it's indifference.
The opposite of faith is not heresy, it's indifference.
And the opposite of life is not death, it's indifference.
Elie Wiesel, U.S. News and World Report,
October 27, 1986

1

The rainy night air smelled toxic – burnt and bitter – like a house fire a day after being put out, its charred remains smoldering in puddles full of water and chemicals. The thick taste coated her throat. No matter if she spit or swallowed, there was no getting rid of it.

The girl stumbled through the maze of sugar cane stalks. With no moon, stars or light to guide her it was hard to make out even the hand in front of her face. She was barefoot and the muddy, gloppy soil was laden with chunks of limestone that, when stepped on, felt like she had walked on a hidden land mine because of the glass that was still stuck in her foot. The pain would explode and travel like a lightning rod through her whole body, setting even her teeth on fire. As soon as she could stop running she'd try to feel around and pick the pieces out. But that time wasn't now. With outstretched hands, she staggered down the row of thick stalks that towered over her small frame, hoping they would brace her should she run into something.

Or someone.

The terrifying thought made her shake. That, and she'd never been so cold before. She'd grown up in Florida. It never got cold here, even when some front blew in from Canada

3

and all the old people and news anchors started yelling it was freezing and that the orange trees were gonna die. But she was completely soaked and the crazy-assed wind from the crazy-assed storm ripped right through her. It raced through the cane stalks making them whistle so piercingly they sounded like they were screaming. She bit her tongue to stop her teeth from chattering.

It was hard not to yell out for help. There could be someone or something out there beyond all this fucking cane. Yards away, maybe. A home. A gas station. A road that led out of here, wherever here was. Somewhere nearby, cane fields had been torched and harvested. That's what she was smelling and tasting in her throat – burnt sugar cane. Maybe there were people out here. Maybe farmers or migrant workers living in tents or shanties, waiting for the storm to pass and first light to come so they could torch these fields. Maybe someone could hear her, help her, take her in.

Hide her.

But even as she thought it, she realized that was fool thinking. Chances were there weren't. Chances were she was in the middle of nowhere with no one around for miles. Chances were she was out here on her own and the best thing she could do was to take cover in the stalks until the sun came up and those migrant workers showed up by the truckload. Chances were that the only people who would hear her cries for help were the very men hunting her. The faces of loved ones flashed before her: Sweet baby Ginger who still wanted her bottle at night even though everyone said she was too old for one. Luis. He was a bastard – a jealous, cheating fuck. He'd broken her heart more times than she could count. Oh God, how she loved him. Always had, always would. Mami, Papi, Abu, Cindy, Alonzo, Quina Mae. She pushed the faces out of her head. To think of them meant she was giving up and saying her mental goodbyes.

No! No! Pull yourself together!

4

She wiped her eyes and sucked in the sobs. Those men were out there. They would hear her whimpers and hone in on them like vultures listening for the struggling breaths of a dying creature. Right now they were circling the fields she was lost in, trying to GPS her location, swoop in and pick over what was left of her. She tried to focus instead on the scent of pine. Somewhere beyond the stench of wet, burnt cane was the crisp smell of slash pine trees. It was the scent of hope. She was going to make her way toward that. No more mental goodbyes: she was a survivor. So far she had made it farther than the others.

She was still alive.

The cane stalks attacked her face and hands like accomplices as she forced her way through them. Once she hit the clearing where the cane had been burned she could run. Damn the fear and the pain in her foot, she'd run. Of course, she would be exposed in a clearing. The tears started again.

Maybe they were waiting for her to do just that, to spare them the trouble of ferreting her out. Those men – those Crazies – they likely knew these fields. That's why they'd brought her here. They knew which ways led in, which ways led out. And that place – that horrible, horrible place they had taken her to. It was surrounded by so much cane, stalks had started to grow inside.

You can't stay here. Choose! What would be worse? Hiding in a cane field, only to be found and taken back to . . . that place? Or making a run for it? Making a run for one of those homes that might be out there beyond the stalks?

Better to run. Better to go down fighting. Luis would tell her that, for sure. God, she wished he were here. He would cut those motherfuckers into a million little pieces and then force-feed them to each—

'Here, kitty, kitty.'

Her heart stopped. He was behind her. He was gaining on her. Her head darted around. *Where the hell was he?*

5

She dropped to her hands and knees, crawling into the stalks. She felt a searing pain shoot up her leg, the one with the glass in it. She reached down and felt the open flap of skin on her heel, the warmth of her own blood as it ran out through her fingers. The cane stalks were razor sharp. She bit into her hand and tried to shake off the pain. The bad thoughts returned. The faces of her family reappeared.

At least this way the police will know I was here. They'll see all the blood and test it and know I was here. I won't have just disappeared. No one will think I left town, that I ran away from Ginger . . .

But even as she thought it, she knew it was ridiculous. She could completely bleed out in this field and no one would ever know she'd been here, crawling in the dark, trying to hide from her killers. The rain would wash it all away. The workers who tended these fields would step on her grave and, if the Crazies didn't leave her body where they killed her, no one would ever know. And if they didn't kill her here, if they dragged her away to that place to do all the horrible things they had promised to do to her, there would be nothing left in this spot to find at all. Or they could leave her here, chopped into bits and pieces and sprinkled all over, like seasoning, knowing that these fields would soon be incinerated. After the inferno there would be nothing left to find but ash. If the migrants ever did stumble on what remained of her, and if crime scene people like the ones in *CSI* could actually identify ash and bone fragments, then maybe, just maybe, some detective might try and come out here one day and piece together her final moments. He might try to figure out exactly what had happened here. She bit harder into her hand. But that was impossible. Because no one could ever imagine the moment she was in right now. The horror of it was unimaginable.

'You know why the dog chases the cat?'

He was feet away. She could hear him even over the

screaming of the cane stalks. He knew she could hear him, too – he was yelling, but his swampy Southern voice was calm.

Was she crawling toward him or away from him?

"Cause it runs. If the cat don't run, then the dog don't chase. The cat and dog – they can be friends, darlin'. But if that cat, well, if she runs . . .' His voice trailed off. 'See, all you gonna do, darlin', is piss off the fucking dog – get him all tired and shit. So come on out, kitty, before you piss me off. It's just gonna hurt more, bitch.'

The light sliced through the stalks – up, down, over, across. She stopped crawling and tucked herself into a tight, tight ball.

'Maybe that cat's hiding right now. Praying for morning and some Hondurans to come save her.'

The light crossed over to the row directly across from her. She cast her eyes to the ground, so the light wouldn't catch on the whites of her eyes. In her fist she clenched the stalk.

'That would be fool thinking.'

His work boots squished in the mud.

'Dogs have a great sense of smell. There ain't nowhere that cat can hide, 'cause that dog can smell pussy. Oh yeah. And when that dog finds her, well, he's gonna tear her limb from limb for making him work so hard.' He started to chuckle. It bloomed into a frenzied, maniacal laugh.

She put her hands over her ears.

'You seen her yet?' It was another voice. It was the second Crazy, speaking over a walkie-talkie.

'Not yet, brother,' replied the swamp voice. 'But this here's the fun part. This is when we get to find her and teach her why it wasn't a smart move to leave us none. Whoo-wee, we're gonna have us a good time!'

She covered her mouth so he wouldn't see her breath. A loud rumble of thunder sounded.

'Go over by the tractor,' said the swamp voice into the

7

walkie-talkie. 'Make sure she don't get past that and onto the road. We're fucked if we lose her to the road.'

Another rumble. She looked up at the sky. *Please, please, please – no lightning. It'll light up this field like the second coming of Christ . . .*

The swamp-voiced Crazy sniffed at the air. 'But I'm telling ya, I don't think she's got that far, 'cause there's pussy around here somewhere.'

Hot tears ran down her filthy face. There were so many things left to do in life. So many times she'd wished she could start over, because she'd screwed up so many times. Always the big disappointment.

'Dino trackers still find dino footprints, stuck there in mud. Miiillllions of years old . . .'

She rocked back and forth, her body tucked into a tight ball, her hands over her ears. Every day she'd tell herself she'd turn her life around – tomorrow. Tomorrow always came and went. Now she knew she would do it. For Ginger, who deserved a better momma. For her own mom, who worried so much about the way she lived her life. If she ever saw another tomorrow . . .

The light was right in front of her, now, inches from her foot, sporadically slicing through the stalks like the beams of a searchlight would dissect the night sky at the club where she danced. 'How long you think a footprint stays 'round, darlin', before rain runs it off?' It slithered off into the cane, brushing her jeans. The work boots plodded away. *Squish. Squish. Squish.*

Then he turned, ran back real quick, dropped to his knees, and stuck the flashlight in her face. 'Hey there bitch!' he cooed. 'I got her!' he yelled out triumphantly.

Not yet. There was still tomorrow. She threw a fistful of mud and rock at his face and stuck the cane into his eyes. When he yelped in surprise, she leapt up and kicked him in the face as hard as she could. She wished she were wearing her boots. Those would've taken out a few teeth. Then she could stomp on his ugly cracker head with her stilettos and pop those bloodshot, lecherous eyes. But they'd taken her boots.

He fell to the ground and she kicked him in the face two more times before bolting into the stalks.

'Bitch!' he howled.

The clearing was up ahead, she could feel it. The pine was strong. There was still hope. And then, like a miracle, lightning lit the sky, illuminating the path that had been cut through the cane stalks. Jesus had turned on the lights at the right moment and showed her the way out.

'She's on the run!' she heard the swamp-voiced Crazy scream. 'Fuck me, motherfucker, she stuck me! I can't see nothing! You better get the car! Don't let her get into town!'

2

Faith Saunders felt her eyelids start to slip closed and she slapped herself hard across the cheek. Then she lowered the SUV's window and stuck her face out into the rain. She had to stay awake. She had to. It was midnight and she still had a ways to go. Stopping was not an option. Not out here. There was no place *to* stop.

She dried her face with the beach towel she'd found in the back of the Explorer before wiping the fog from the inside of the windshield. On top of all that had gone wrong tonight – and there was plenty – the AC and defroster had stopped working, thanks to the humungous puddle, a.k.a lake, she hadn't seen when she tore out of her sister's development back in Sebring. She sat up straight, stretched her back and leaned on the steering wheel, trying to concentrate through the exhaustion and pounding headache that had been building behind her eyes. Outside it looked the same as it had since she'd left Charity's – wet and flat and black. Endlessly black. It had been at least a half-hour since she'd seen another car on the road.

On its way to wreak havoc on Texas, late-season Tropical Storm Octavius had stalled over a sizable chunk of the Sunshine State, making life miserable for the past two days for everyone in Central and South Florida. Faith had grown up in Miami, and in her thirty-two years she'd seen her share of bad weather and hurricanes – usually they blew in, took down a few trees and power lines and blew out. But Octavius wasn't playing by the script: the storm was expected to continue thrashing the state with rain and fifty-mile-an-hour wind gusts for at least one more day. Most people were smart and had heeded warnings to stay indoors and off the roads.

Most people.

Faith chewed on her lip. She wasn't sure she was lost, she just didn't know exactly where she was. She was supposed to be on State Road 441, only this didn't look like the 441 she'd taken up to her sister's that afternoon. Of course, she'd driven up to Charity's in the daylight, and with no streetlights, gas stations, restaurants, motels or landmarks to help guide her, everything looked different in the dark. Out here there was nothing but acre after acre of farmland and for the last umpteen miles, stretches of sugar cane fields, their bushy, imposing stalks looming menacingly over both sides of the roadway. This was Central Florida, and outside the urban vortex of Orlando and the 140,000-room hotelopolis of Disney, Universal and SeaWorld, the middle of the state didn't offer much more than a handful of small towns, rural farmland, Lake Okeechobee and the Everglades. If you were headed south, like she was, it wasn't until you hit Palm Beach County that you'd start to see life and lights and buildings taller than two stories. The further south and east, the brighter the lights and taller the buildings until you finally hit the neon glow and towering skyscrapers of Miami, where there were sure to be bars open and people out and about, even at midnight and even in a tropical storm. But Faith wasn't in Miami. She was far from it, still way out somewhere in the boonies, trying to get home, trying to stay awake, and trying to forget all the horrible reasons why she was out here on such a horrible night in the first place.

A blinding streak of lightning cut across the sky right in front of her and she sucked in a breath. Her eyes darted to the rearview, to where Maggie, her four-year-old, was asleep in her booster, a thumb in her mouth, her other hand clutching a well-worn, stuffed Eeyore. Faith counted off the seconds in her head. When the boom of thunder came, it was so loud and so intense that she could actually feel it roll through the car. She stiffened, staring at the mirror, bracing for the fallout. Having had to unexpectedly leave her cousins' house had triggered one of Maggie's inconsolable, crazy tantrums and she'd spent the first forty-five minutes of the drive home screaming, crying, and kicking at the back of the passenger seat, finally falling asleep from pure exhaustion. Faith watched as she sucked her thumb harder, her tiny, slender fingers clutching at her freckled nose, her long blonde eyelashes fluttering, threatening to pop open.

She carefully exhaled the breath she'd been holding, reached behind her with one hand and gently rubbed Maggie's exposed bony knee. The two-sizes-too-big pink cowboy boot that had been precariously dangling off the edge of her toes fell to the floorboard next to its mate. 'Cha-Cha', the threadbare crocheted receiving blanket that Maggie never left home without, had slipped down the side of her car seat. Stretching her free hand, Faith found it on the floor and tried to toss it over Maggie's bare feet. It landed instead on her head, completely missing the bottom half of her body and covering her face. Not exactly what she'd intended, but perhaps better, she thought as another jagged streak of lightning lit the sky, so frighteningly close you could almost touch it. Cha-Cha would help mute the thunderclaps and block the wicked flashes that lit the car up like a Christmas tree.

Faith popped the two Advil she'd found in her glove compartment and downed them with a slug of ice-cold Racetrak coffee left over from the afternoon drive up to her sister's. Had she really made this same drive only, what? Ten hours ago? She sighed and looked again at the shrouded tiny figure in the back seat as another round of thunder rocked the car. Even though the fight with Charity wasn't Faith's fault – and it certainly wasn't how she'd envisioned her sister's birthday party ending – she was going to have to make it up to Maggie for the way they'd had to leave tonight, rushing out in the rain with all those strangers watching, her cousins witnessing the mother of all break-downs happen live from their bedroom window. She'd take her to a movie, or skating at Incredible Ice tomorrow. Or maybe she'd let her stay home from St Andrews and they'd bake cookies; Maggie would've missed school anyway if they'd stayed up in Sebring as originally planned. God knows that, after what had happened tonight, Faith could use a Mental Health Day herself.

The memory made her heart hurt. No matter how much she wanted to forget, her thoughts kept returning to her sister's kitchen, to the crowd of gaping, snickering strangers gathered around the makeshift bar at the dinette table watching the family drama unfold as if it was part of the evening's enter-tainment. Charity had chosen the path she'd chosen in life and the man she'd chosen to walk it with, and it was time for Faith to accept that and stop trying to fix her little sister's problems, because she obviously didn't want them fixed. For years, everyone had been blaming Charity's shortcomings on her idiot sloth of a husband, Nick, but maybe it was time to place that blame where it really belonged. And tonight . . . well, tonight was the last straw. Angry tears slipped down her cheeks.

Even cold, bad coffee couldn't get rid of the icky-sweet taste of the hurricanes that Nick had insisted she try when the night was young and the party was in full swing and all was going well. The back of her throat still felt like it was coated in Hawaiian-Punch-flavored wallpaper paste. She

13

looked over longingly at the open glove compartment where she'd found the Advil. Inside, under a pile of napkins, was a stale half-pack of Marlboro Lights. Faith had picked up the habit back in high school, and had been trying to drop it ever since college. It had taken a bout of morning sickness to get her to finally quit the first time. She'd successfully stayed off the sticks for four years, but then came the phone call that changed everything last year and the first thing she'd picked up after she'd hung up was a Marlboro. It was like welcoming home an old friend, something that she definitely needed at the time. Not so much as a tickle of disapproval had sounded from her throat, and in no time she was back on a pack a day. Quitting this time around was proving much more difficult, though, and getting pregnant again to help her try and kick the habit wasn't an option she was ready to consider.

She reached over and slammed the glove compartment shut. No matter how much she needed an old friend right now, she couldn't go there. Not with Maggie in the car. Nope. Jarrod, Faith's husband, had no idea she was still trying to quit, and Maggie could never know she ever smoked. She'd be nominated for Bad Mother of the Year if she lit up with her young daughter's clean lungs two feet away. She anxiously nibbled on a cuticle instead.

The rain started to come down harder and Faith slowed to twenty. She looked at the clock. In six minutes, Charity would be turning the big 3-0. What was she doing at this very moment to celebrate? Was she passed out on the couch? Were Nick's stupid friends still over? Was she having wild birthday sex? That thought made her want to gag. Was she even the least bit upset over how Faith had left?

Originally, the plan had been for Faith to take Charity and her three kids – eleven-year-old Kamilla, five-year-old Kourtney and two-year-old Kaelyn – up to Disney next weekend, along with Maggie, to celebrate Charity's thirtieth. No husbands

– just the six girls and Mickey Mouse living it up in the land where everyone's always happy. Faith had booked two rooms at the Walt Disney World Dolphin Resort well in advance. Ironically, the reservation had to be cancelled by midnight tomorrow – the last minute of Charity's actual birthday – or Faith would have to forfeit her deposit. Of course she'd have to cancel, she thought as she wiped away more tears. There was no way things would be right between them by Friday. They might never be right again.

After ten years of marriage, maybe Nick had wanted to finally show that he cared. Maybe he'd wanted to one-up Faith's Disney trip. Or maybe throwing Charity a party was simply a good excuse for him to have a good time with his friends since Charity didn't have many that he hadn't slept with. Whatever his reasoning, Nick 'Big Mitts' Lavecki, the man who had forgotten his wife's birthday more often than he had remembered it, had decided to throw Charity a last-minute surprise party. Last minute, as in he'd told Faith about it this morning.

'Tonight, Nick?' Faith had looked at the clock above the fireplace in her family room, which was in Parkland, a good two hundred miles from where her sister lived in Sebring. It was ten thirty on Sunday morning.

'Nothing fancy. A bunch of friends, ya know, some beer, food from Costco, like those platters of wieners and chicken nuggets, that sort of crap, and ya know, a cake. I'm gonna get that at Costco, too. A chocolate cake. They can write "Happy Birthday Ya Old Bag" on it.' He laughed. 'Maybe they can put, like, a wheelchair decoration on the frosting or something.'

Faith cringed. 'Really, Nick?'

'No! I'm only fucking with you, Faithey. But I am taking the kids so they can pick out black balloons and Over the Hill plates.' He laughed again. 'Char will get a kick out of that.'

Faith had looked out her kitchen window at the toppled lawn umbrella and the chaise longue cushion that had blown into the pool that was close to overflowing. Jarrod had cocked his head at her from across the table and mouthed *What?* She shook her head at him. 'The weather's pretty nasty, Nick.'

'It's not so bad up here. Everyone says they're coming anyway.'

'Everyone? How many people?'

'I dunno, about thirty or forty.'

'Wow. When did you plan this?'

'I dunno. A week or so ago.'

'Thanks for the notice.'

'Yeah, I thought I told ya. I get it if you can't make it. We live so far away. What's Jar call it up here? Bumfuck?'

Three years later and Big Mitts was still holding onto the comment he wasn't supposed to have heard. 'He was kidding, Nick.'

'Yeah, I know. I'm only busting chops, Faithey. Look, I get it if you can't make it. The weather sucks and it's a long drive. No big deal. Char will understand.'

Of course Nick would understand if Faith didn't make it, because he didn't want her to make it. The kids had probably been bugging him all morning, asking if Aunt Faith and Uncle Jarrod and Maggie were coming to Mommy's party. That's likely what had prompted the phone call. That and Charity would be livid if she found out her only sister – her only sibling – wasn't invited to her birthday party.

'I'll be there,' Faith had said.

What? Jarrod had mouthed again.

'Great,' Nick had unenthusiastically replied.

'Save the couch for me. I'll drive home in the morning.'

'You might be sharing it with a new friend, Faithey.' She hated when he called her that. Absolutely hated it. It was Charity's pet name for her since they were kids, but when

16

Nick said it, it felt like he was mocking her. 'I think T-Bone's already called it,' he added with a chuckle that she knew was accompanied by a smirk.

Most of Nick's friends had nicknames, too: T-Bone, Skinny, Slick, Gator. But they weren't gang members or cops or Mafioso – they were just grown men with nicknames.

'Tell T-Bone he can sleep in his car; I'm calling the couch,' Faith replied coolly.

'Daddy, tell Aunt Faif to bring Maggie!' said a little voice with a lisp in the background.

'Well, if you're coming, bring Maggie,' Nick had said. 'The kids'll all be upstairs, locked in. We won't let 'em come down for the stripper. Promise.'

'You're kidding, right?'

'Yes, I'm kidding. I'm not getting my wife a stripper. At least, not one she'd be interested in watching, although that's a fun idea and it would make her a real fun wife if she was into it. I'll get the kids pizza. And, ah, Jarrod too,' he'd added hesitantly. 'I, ah, hope he can make it.'

Jarrod had stopped mouthing *What?* because he had figured out what *What?* was and he wanted no part of Nick's couch. He slumped down in his seat and hid behind the paper, like a kid in class who doesn't want to be called on.

'Have you looked out a window?' Jarrod had asked as Faith was buckling Maggie into her car seat a couple of hours later. She clutched Eeyore in one hand and a pouch of fruit juice in the other.

'It's her birthday, Jarrod. You know what she's going through. All his friends are gonna be there – probably *only* his friends. Knowing Nick, he'll invite the next mistress. It's only rain; I'll be fine.'

'Since you must've missed it on the news, I'll be the one to tell you that there's a tropical storm happening. That's the first thing. Second, these are not normal people, Faith. This is not gonna be a normal party.'

Jarrod was not a fan of either Nick or Charity's. Faith's sister and her husband ran in completely different social circles: Jarrod was a former criminal defense lawyer and Nick was a scheming petty criminal. His trade was fixing transmissions, but he was always looking for a way to beat the system, score unemployment, cheat the IRS. Aside from the weather and the Dolphins, there wasn't much for the two of them to talk about when they did get together, unless Nick wanted to put Jarrod on retainer. Charity wasn't like that necessarily, but having Kammy so young and marrying Nick had made her completely dependent on him and it had changed her. That's the Charity Jarrod saw.

'You're being dramatic,' she'd said.

'Drama is your sister's middle name. Wait till she finds Nick in the bathroom banging another one of her girlfriends – you'll see some drama.'

'Jarrod . . .' she'd scolded, nodding at Maggie, who'd sat quietly watching both of them, the blonde pigtails on the top of her head flopping about as she followed the conversation.

'Better hide the cutlery,' he'd added.

'You're welcome to come.'

'I've never wanted to write a motion for summary judgment as badly as I do today.'

'I bet.'

'I'd like to talk you out of making a two-hundred-mile drive in a tropical storm is what I'd like to do.'

'I wish he'd consulted me before he planned it,' she replied, 'but I wasn't even on the D list of invitees, apparently.'

'Stay home. With me.'

'Come with us.' She smiled. 'On second thought, that's a terrible idea; you'd be miserable. What are you gonna do all by yourself on a rainy night?' Even as she asked the question the unsettling, queasy feeling roiled her stomach. She hated that feeling. She hated that, after all these months, she still

18

couldn't stop having it. She wondered if she'd ever not get nauseous at the thought of what might happen when she left her husband home alone. She looked away, out the open garage door.

He knew what she was thinking. 'Order a pizza and finish my motion.'

She nodded.

He came up behind her and rubbed her shoulders. 'I don't have a good feeling about this. The weather is brutal,' he said softly, kissing the back of her head. 'You're going up to Orlando next week, anyway. Your sister will understand. We can cook something special tonight, chill out with the rain.'

'I can't miss this party. We'll be home tomorrow afternoon.'

'What about St Andrew's?'

'It's preschool; Maggie can miss a day. And she gets to see her cousins!' she'd added, turning her attention back to her daughter with a big smile. 'That's pretty exciting, right?'

'What's cutlery?' Maggie had asked, as a gust of wind ripped an enormous frond off a Royal Palm. It crashed to the ground outside the garage, steps from where she and Jarrod were standing.

Another streak of lightning cut across the sky, pulling Faith's thoughts out of her garage and back into the moment. In the instantaneous flash of brilliant light she saw the sprawling fields of cane stalks violently twisting in the wind – assembled in tight, neat rows, like a plant army getting ready to march. Then it all went black again.

Where the hell was she? She could only hope that she was still on 441 and not on her way to Tampa. She thought of the creepy zombie game that she and Charity used to play as kids, where you close your eyes and count and when you open them all the zombies are frozen in place, having silently advanced on you while your back was turned.

A cold shudder ran down her spine as she forged ahead into the endless black. She couldn't help but fear what it might look like out there in the middle of nowhere when the lights flashed back on . . .

3

Jarrod was right: Charity did love her drama. Three hours into her party and feeling no pain – thanks to Nick's hurricanes and more than a few glasses of wine – she decided to invite a little in. When she caught him chatting up some young girl in the living room, amnesty was over.

'Why you gotta look at her like that?' she'd demanded in a loud voice when he came into the kitchen to get a beer.

'What?' he'd asked, obviously annoyed.

'That girl. The one in that slutty dress. Why do you have to talk to her, huh? Why?'

'She's Gator's girlfriend. Stop being jealous, Char. I was only telling her I liked that dress.'

'Oh? Not her boobs in that dress? What is she, sixteen? She could be your daughter, you know. You're disgusting.'

'I didn't ask her how old she was. She looks good in that dress. Real, real good. Now if you looked good in a dress, I'd compliment you, too.'

Some mean idiot had crooned an instigative, 'Ooohh . . .'

'What does that mean?' Charity had asked defensively, moving her body in between Nick and the plastic bucket of beers on the counter.

'You know what that means,' he said, reaching behind her

21

LOUTH
6060441

to grab a beer. He poked her in the stomach with his finger. 'Lay off the Twinkies and birthday cake, honey, and one day you'll look good in a dress again, too.'

An embarrassed hush had come over the kitchen crowd. Then one of the Nicknames whooped and laughed. Everyone had heard what Nick said and everyone was waiting for Charity to do something. Throw something. Say something.

No one had been waiting longer than Faith. 'What the . . .?' she'd started to say, turning to Charity, who was standing next to her looking pathetically weak and as challenging as a kitten. Nick had never hit her sister, but Faith had often thought it'd be better if he had. Maybe if she could see the damage he inflicted with his words she'd realize how badly she'd been hurt.

Charity started to cry. She wrapped her arms protectively around her belly, obviously ashamed at how she looked.

It wasn't her place. Faith knew that now. She shouldn't have said anything. She should have realized it wasn't gonna do any good anyway; everyone had had too much to drink. She had, too. But after listening to her sister complain and cry for years, all the pent-up anger bubbled to the surface and spilled out of her like lava from a volcano.

'You know, Nick,' Faith had snapped, 'you got a few tires to spare yourself. Charity, will you please finally tell your asshole of a husband to go to hell!'

But Charity had not told her husband to fuck off or get out or drop dead. She hadn't squeezed Faith's hand and thanked her for her support. Instead she'd spun around and glared at her, her face red, her green eyes on fire. 'You want me to leave him!' she screamed. 'That's your answer! It's always the answer! Stop doing that to me! Stop doing it already! You don't know what's going on here! You're the one who's wrong!'

Instead of Nick, it was Faith who Charity had set on. She was dumbfounded. And mortified. The entire house went quiet.

Even the music stopped. 'I want you to stand up for yourself,' Faith had barked back when she found her voice again. 'I want you to have some self-respect for once. You're better than this loser. You're better than . . .' she gestured around the crowded kitchen, '. . . this.'

It came out sounding awful. She winced now at the memory of all those people staring back at her.

'That's real nice. Fuck you, Faith,' Charity had said.

It got worse. 'These people . . . they're not your friends, Charity. They're *his*. They're pulling you down, making you believe his shit, like you have to take it!'

'Maybe I don't want no different. Have you thought of that? 'Cause my life's not perfect like yours I gotta go change it? It's not good enough? 'Cause my kid's flunking school and talking to pervs on the Internet it's *my* fault, right? I can't find a job in this shit town because I'm the fool who didn't go to college. 'Cause my husband's screwing my friends and I'm not leaving, it's *my* fault? I'm never good enough, never right enough, never mad enough for you, Faith. Stop judging me! You make me feel worse than him!'

She should've walked away then, just said Goodnight Gracie and left. But she didn't. 'So *I'm* the bad guy? I've never said anything like that! All I've done is listen while you cried and bitched about what a jerk he is. If you don't have the balls to leave, I want you to stop letting him talk to you like you're worthless, because you're believing it. I mean, look at you – you deserve better than this! What does he have to do or say to get you to see that? 'Cause calling you fat and stupid on your birthday in front of all his friends who are laughing at you doesn't seem to flip the switch. He wants you to leave – don't you get that? He wants you to leave so that he's not the bad guy for running out on a wife and three kids – and you're not reading the cue cards!'

'Hey,' Nick had said, his hairy face growing dark. 'You're in my house now. You and your tight-ass lawyer husband might think you're better than us, but you're in *my* house now.'

The lava would not go back in. No way, no how. 'That the bank is foreclosing on,' she'd snapped. 'Try paying for it, Nick – then you can call it yours. Try holding a job for more than six months. And while you're trying to be all man of the house, if you want her to work, get your wife a car that can actually make it to the grocery store and back when she needs to buy your fat ass a six-pack. And one last thing, man-up and stop screwing her friends like a total pig. Or at least have the decency to take them to a Motel Six. Hey,' Faith had called across the room, 'Gator! You better keep an eye on your teenage girlfriend over there, because your friend Big Mitts sure is.'

'I never liked you,' Nick replied angrily. 'Or your prick husband.'

Charity had moved next to Nick. He put his hand on her back.

'Get out, Faith,' Charity had said. 'Get out of our house. I want you to leave now.'

Nick reached for Charity's hand and she grasped it. That's probably what smarted the most – even more than the stares and snickers. Every Nickname and his spouse/significant other stood watching as Faith headed straight for the door, calling for Maggie to come downstairs. The terrible moment was made that much worse when Maggie started bawling about how she didn't want to leave. Faith had to physically carry her out of the house, kicking and screaming.

In the chaos and rush to get out, she'd left both her bag and her cell at Charity's. It wasn't until she'd tried to check for directions after Maggie had finally fallen asleep that she'd realized it, but by that point she was too far away to go back. It didn't matter, though. Even if she were two miles down the road, she wouldn't have turned around. She was beyond

24

humiliated – she was crushed. Devastated and crushed. Charity would have to mail her stuff to her – after Big Mitts probably emptied the wallet and sold her cell. The tears were streaming down her face now. She never wanted to step foot in her sister's house ever again.

Something ran across the road then, in front of her car. Faith jerked the car hard right, heard a thump, and swerved off into the cane field, stopping with her headlights pointing into the tangle of dense stalks that were only inches away.

Her heart was pounding. There were no more thoughts of Charity or Nick or the crowd of Nicknames at their door, condemning her as her sister banished her into the rainy night. There was no more feeling sorry for herself or thinking up ways to avenge her embarrassment. There was only one thought on her mind now. Only one.

What the hell did I hit?

4

She squinted into the racing wipers, her sweaty hands clutching the steering wheel in a death grip. It was gone. Whatever it was was gone.

It looked like . . .?

She pushed the thought out of her head before her brain could finish it. It was a crazy, impossible thought. She'd only caught a look at whatever it was for a split second. It couldn't have been a person. Her headlights stared dumbly out into the stalks.

It must've been an animal. A deer. Maybe a dog. People dumped dogs in the Everglades. It was terrible, but they did. She was probably in the damn Everglades. Or even a bear. She'd read about some lady in Orlando who had walked out and found one picking through the garbage in her garage.

What if it's still out there, under the car?

The thought made her want to vomit. The sky lit up. The angry cane army had indeed advanced during the blackout – its stalks hovered menacingly over the hood of the Explorer now, their razor sharp fronds clawing furiously at the metal.

She turned off the radio and tried to listen. It was hard to hear anything over the rain and the scraping of the stalks and

26

the furious beating of her heart pounding in her ears. Nothing. There was no barking, no whimpering. No moaning.

She rubbed her eyes and shook the fog from her head. Had she nodded off? Had she imagined she saw something? There was only one way to really know. She turned and checked on Maggie – who was still fast asleep under her Cha-Cha – opened the door and stepped out into the downpour. She ran to the front of the car on jelly legs, holding her breath as she approached the cane field and the front end of the truck.

Nothing. There was nothing there. Nothing splayed across her hood. Nothing stuck to her grille. Nothing lying on the ground.

'Hello?' she called out into the night.

Nothing yelled back.

She tried to look under the car, but she couldn't see a thing. She stumbled back to the car, her feet sinking in the muddy ground. She climbed back in the driver's seat and toweled off, staring out at the angry cane. She was still shaking, her head spinning. Sheets of rain whipped across the windshield as the wipers raced to keep up.

You must have imagined it.

She slowly backed the car onto the road, holding her breath as she did, every muscle in her body tensed. Her headlights stared at the pull-off where the truck had been. Nothing. There was still nothing there. She finally exhaled.

You're tired, is all. Tired and upset. You're not thinking clearly.

She put the car into drive, watching the stalks where she'd just been as she drove off. The plant army writhed and roiled in the expansive field, beckoning her to come back.

She was scared now – she was physically and mentally exhausted and perhaps nodding off at the wheel. She had no cell and was somewhere in the middle of nowhere, although she was still reluctant to say 'lost' – that word would set off a total panic and she never thought clearly under pressure.

She could feel the fear brewing in her belly, trying to force its way up into her throat, and she tried to swallow it back down, along with the icky sweetness from the hurricanes. She probably shouldn't have had that last drink at Charity's, damn it. It was hard to think straight. She'd felt it when she stood up. She had a quarter of a tank of gas, which should be enough to get her home, but what if she was going in the wrong direction? What if she ran out of gas? Jarrod wasn't expecting her till tomorrow afternoon. No one knew where she was. She was sure Charity hadn't called him to say she'd kicked her out and, 'Oh, by the way, Faith left her cell and bag at my house when she stormed out of here crying.' Charity probably didn't even know that Faith had left her bag behind. She probably should have turned around and gone back, but she'd let pride force her into making a bad decision. She should've stopped and gotten a hotel near Sebring and driven home clear-headed in the morning, but Maggie was so upset and so out of control that Faith had just wanted to go home. That's all it was – she'd just wanted to go home.

A series of bad decisions had led her here; panicking would make things worse. She needed directions, was all. And a phone so she could call Jarrod so someone would know where she was. Maybe he could come find her, get her, meet her out here, take her home . . .

As quickly as it came to her, Faith dismissed the romantic thought of a midnight rescue in a rainstorm by her husband. No matter how mad she was at Charity, she didn't want Jarrod thinking less of her sister. He already didn't like her. If he found out about tonight, he'd be beyond angry with Charity: he would hate her. Nothing would ever change that – he was German and decisive. Although Faith wasn't sure about the future of her relationship with her sister, she didn't want her husband forcing her into making a decision she wasn't sure she wanted to make. If she and Charity did manage to repair things – which they had in the past after some other whopping fights (they were sisters, after all) – Jarrod would always be there to remind her how Charity had treated her tonight, even if he didn't say a word. She would know he knew about the stares and the snickers and the humiliation. And he would be right to wonder why she had allowed her sister back into her life.

She wiped the tears defiantly, this time before they fell. Charity had been there before when Faith had needed her . . . after the phone call that had changed everything. She didn't know all the ugly details, but her sister had been supportive in her own way without knowing exactly what Faith was struggling with at the time or why she was so depressed. She hadn't told her about Jarrod's affair for the same reason he didn't need to know about everything that had gone down at Charity's tonight: Faith had never wanted her sister to hate her husband in the event she decided to forgive him. She'd never wanted Charity to think less of her for staying with a man who had strayed. After all the advice Faith had handed out over the years, she'd never wanted to be accused of being a hypocrite. Damn, her brain hurt from dredging up painful memories and betrayals. She wanted to go home and think things through before she made any more bad decisions. She was getting too good at that.

Then she saw it – the glowing red and yellow sign off in the distance. It was a fast food, or motel sign, she couldn't tell. It was a business of some kind, of that she was sure. She breathed an enormous sigh of relief for the third time that night.

There was life up ahead.

5

Faith followed the glow through the asphalt maze that wound through the cane stalks until she came upon a lone, old-fashioned Shell station with two pumps at a four-way stop in an otherwise remote, isolated area. The station was closed.

She could feel the panic building inside, with the same fever and intensity as the rain pattering on her roof. *Where the hell was she? And what should she do now?* The street sign on the corner said Main Street. OK. Main Streets always ran through the center of a town, right? The thought encouraged her, although she couldn't help but wonder what the rest of the 'town' must look like if this was where the hubbub was supposed to be happening. Then she spotted a road sign with a pointing arrow: SR 441/ US 98.

What road she was on before, whether she was ever really lost, didn't matter any more because now she could find her way home. She followed the sign down a desolate Main Street, past a blinking, swinging streetlight, and finally into what looked like a small, one-street town. There were boarded-up buildings, a closed convenience store, a shuttered Chinese restaurant. A thrift store/hardware store/barber shop, all in one. Another streetlight that was blinking yellow. A medical clinic.

The buildings appeared old and rundown, dating to the forties or fifties, if she had to guess. Most of the signs were hand-painted on the businesses that looked like they were still in business: Chub's BBQ, Sudsy Coin Laundry, Frank's Restaurant. Other businesses were clearly gone and had been for quite a while. It looked like a town that might have had a heyday a very long time ago.

There were no cars parked on the street or in the little lots adjacent to some of the buildings. It was only her in the Town That Used To Be. The wind rocked the street's second and final traffic light. She watched it swing back and forth on the cable like a gymnast getting ready to flip over. A streak of lightning splintered the sky, striking terrifyingly close. Raindrops the size of quarters began to ferociously pummel the car, making it literally impossible to see more than a few feet in front of her. She was in the heart of the storm. There would be no outrunning this rain band or driving through it. She pulled over defeatedly in front of a sign that said 'Valda's Hair Salon', which she couldn't tell was closed for the night or closed forever.

The adrenaline rush from running off the road earlier had subsided. She wasn't panicked now as much as she was mentally overwhelmed and physically exhausted. And discouraged, because even though she was on the right road, she was still a long, long way from home.

Time for a smart decision – maybe the first one of the night. It was probably best to wait out the squall and let the worst of the rain band pass. What she didn't want was to get lost again. Or run out of gas. Or worse, have an accident. There was no one out here to help her. She turned off the car to save gas, raised the volume on the radio so Maggie wouldn't hear the thunder, and settled back to wait out the rain. The bands seemed to move quick; the worst rain should pass through in the next ten minutes.

Faith turned and watched Maggie, still shrouded in her

31

blanket like a ghost, sleeping peacefully in the rearview. Her hand had slipped out the side of her Cha-Cha and tiny fingers – that Faith noticed her cousins had painted a bright pink – clutched Eeyore to her chest. She was definitely out for the night, which was a very good thing, having slept through Faith's run off the road and into the cane stalks, and now through rain that sounded like a million Drummer Boys going at it on the roof. She placed the beach towel over Maggie's bare feet. Watching her sleep made it easy to forget how difficult raising her was at times, although one look at the back of the passenger seat would probably remind her – there was likely a hole in it from the latest tantrum. Maggie's 'fits' were one of the reasons she and Jarrod had decided not to get a new car for a few years – one that would have had GPS; they were waiting for Maggie to grow out of this challenging phase that was looking more and more like a condition.

Faith leaned back against the headrest and closed her eyes. Her brain had no more real estate left for a new worry. And she didn't want to think about Charity's kitchen, or Jarrod's intern, or the snickering Nicknames who would be talking about her in the morning over an Alka Seltzer. Instead, to pass the time, she thought about all the things she had to do tomorrow: she had a stack of purchase orders at Sweet Sisters that had to be signed, then the ad copy had to be written for the paper, and Maggie had ballet at four. If they were going to see a movie, it would have to be before that. There was laundry in the bucket . . .

A loud but muted bang sounded near where her head was resting against the seat, by the window. She sat up with a jolt and looked around. The SUV's windows were all fogged. She wiped the drool from her mouth and looked at the dashboard clock: 1:11.

Thwap!

It was at the driver's side window. Something had hit the window.

'Help me!' a voice said.

Faith's blood turned to ice. There was somebody out there.

It was still dark, but she couldn't hear the rain any more. She wondered if she was dreaming, if this was all part of a dream. Her hand hesitantly moved over the driver's side window, gingerly wiping away the fog with her fingertips. The glass was cold. And wet. Water ran down her palm and up the sleeve of her silk blouse, making her shiver.

Something did not feel right. Something was very, very wrong.

She pressed her face up to the glass to see what was outside.

And the real nightmare began.

6

The girl stood there, her palms pressed flat against the window. Strands of long, dark hair were stuck to her face and neck; a blue leopard-print bra was visible through her dirty, wet T-shirt. Costume dragonfly earrings dangled from her ears. She stared at Faith with deep-set brown eyes that were streaked with heavy black eyeliner that had run down her cheeks. She put her face up to the window, her cracked lips touching the glass. 'Help me!' she said in a raspy voice. Katy Perry crooned on the radio.

Faith jumped back in her seat, smashing her hip into the center console. She looked around the car, but all the windows were fogged. She had no idea what else or who else was out there.

The girl turned to look behind her. Strands of her wet hair whipped against the window. Then she looked back at Faith and slapped the glass again. Her palms were filthy. 'Hurry! Damn it! You have to let me in!'

She wasn't screaming. She wasn't yelling, either. She was talking excitedly, but in a hushed, croaky voice. Faith moved off the center console where she was perched, and wiped the whole window with her sleeve to get a better look at what was outside. The girl's face was inches from her own; she could see the diamond stuck in the middle of her bottom lip, the tiny hoop in her nose. Two more silver hoops pierced an eyebrow. A line of blue star tattoos ran up the inside of her wrist, all the way to the elbow. On her neck was a tattoo of a pink heart wrapped in chains. 'I . . . I . . . can't,' Faith stammered, shaking her head.

The girl made a squealing sound. 'He's coming!'

A man dressed completely in black suddenly appeared beside her, like a vampire who materializes out of a thick fog. He had shoulder-length dark waves that clung to a chiseled, bony face carpeted in gruff that was well past a shadow and not quite a full-on beard. He was slender and tall – much taller than the girl. His long fingers found her tiny shoulder, swallowing it whole, and he pulled her to him. She stumbled back, almost falling, but he caught her before she could. Then he spun her around and bear-hugged her. Her feet dangled in the air behind her when he lifted her up. Faith saw that she was barefooted; her feet, too, were filthy. The man dipped her and kissed her hard on the lips. Then he looked over at Faith and grinned.

It was surreal, as if she were watching a staging of a contemporary take on the iconic V-J day *Life* cover, where the soldier greets the nurse upon returning home from war. She rubbed her eyes. It felt like she was still dreaming.

The rain had stopped; the moon had finally emerged from behind the cloud cover – at least part of it. It was bright yellow, framed by threatening clouds – the kind of moon that called for a witch to fly by. In the distance, flashes of lightning quietly exploded, like bombs being dropped on far-off cities. Her eyes caught on a red-shirted figure running between the trees of an abandoned lot across the street.

Patches of moonlight lit the chunky remains of a building's old foundation and crumbling walls, decades neglected and overgrown with shrubs and slash pines. The roof was long gone. Behind the ruins was a densely wooded lot, beyond that

35

was likely cane fields. Chain-link fencing had once tried to contain the property, but that had long since rusted and collapsed in spots. A man wearing dark jeans, a red shirt and a white baseball cap burst out of the slash pines, emerging on the far side of the building.

Using her hands, Faith furiously rubbed the fog off the windshield behind the steering wheel. The man's red shirt was open, revealing a round potbelly stuck on an otherwise thin frame. When he saw the girl and the man in black, he stopped short, as if there were a line in the woods that he wasn't allowed to cross. He bent over, hands on his hips, obviously trying to catch his breath, while he eyed the two of them.

'No!' yelled the girl.

Faith turned back to her. The man in black had his arm around her shoulders and was walking her across the street to the abandoned lot, to where the red-shirted man was waiting. She was holding on to him and it looked like she was limping. He had his face buried in her ear.

The potbellied guy – who looked like he had walked right off the set of *Deliverance* – ventured out into the street. Faith could see now the bushy patches of hair stuck on his cheeks. Not quite a beard and not a mustache. He was agitated, pacing like an anxious dog trapped behind one of those invisible electronic fences that zap you if you step outside the perimeter. He took off the baseball cap and ran a hand over his bald head. She saw that one side of his face was red and raw-looking.

The man in black brought the girl over to him. She began to wave her arms and clung tighter to the first man. Then the three exchanged words Faith couldn't hear and red-shirt shoved her back at the man in black before angrily walking off. The girl swayed on her feet, as if she might go down, but the man in black caught her and stroked her head. 'We got us a Looky-Look!' shouted the red-shirt, turning to point to where Faith was. He spat at the ground. 'Come on out and play with us, Looky-Look! Don't be shy!' Then he started across the street. The invisible fence was down.

Faith reached with a violently shaking hand for the jumble of key chains that hung from the ignition.

The man in black stepped in front of red-shirt and pushed him with enough force that he stumbled backwards and fell in the street. 'I told you I got it!' he yelled. 'Back off! Don't fuck it up any more than it is.'

Red-shirt scrambled to his feet and, taking the girl by the arm, led her toward the wooded lot he had emerged from. Faith couldn't hear what he was saying, but the girl wasn't waving her arms any more. She turned and cast one last look in Faith's direction. She smiled weakly and nodded. Then the two of them were gone.

It had all happened in a matter of minutes, maybe less. But exactly *what* had happened? Faith could hear her heartbeat pounding in her ears. She turned to check on Maggie, then thought of the man in black and whipped her head back so fast her neck cracked.

He was standing right outside the driver's side window.

She jumped onto the console, smashing her hip again.

He tapped on the glass with a long fingernail. It made a screechy sound.

Faith tried to scream, but fear had completely closed her throat. The only sound she managed was a gurgle. She tried to force the gearshift. It wouldn't budge. The car wasn't on.

His hand went to the door handle. She could hear the click of the metal as he tried to open it.

She couldn't get her fingers around the key, her hand was shaking so hard. Her foot, too. On the brake, off the brake. On, off. Flopping about like a fish out of water. With one hand she tried to hold her knee down.

The man cupped a hand around his eyes and put his face to the window. She saw he had dark brown eyes and long lashes. In his other hand he held a flashlight. He beamed it straight in her eyes, blinding her. Then he moved it down over her body and across the front seat. When he aimed it into the back, his face lit up, like a child who has spotted what he wants under the Christmas tree. He tapped on the glass with the flashlight and pointed.

Faith turned the ignition and the car started. She floored the gas and the engine screamed, but the car didn't move.

The man stepped back into the street, raised a finger to his lips and smiled. It wasn't the full-on freaky grin he wore with the girl. This was a smug, toothless, dark smile that made her skin crawl.

She threw the car out of park into drive. The tires spun with a screech and the Explorer lurched forward. She couldn't see anything – the windshield was fogging again from her breathing so hard. She wiped it with her bare hand, but not in time. The truck smashed into a garbage can.

The plastic can careened along the sidewalk, belching whatever contents it still had left all over the road. She tore off down a street, praying that the road wouldn't be a dead end, or a cul de sac, leading her right back around to where she'd just been. The garbage can lid tore off the top, scraping against the asphalt underneath her car, stuck on something. She made another quick turn. Then another.

The cane army excitedly welcomed her back into the maze, the rustling stalks whispering their false promises of refuge, swallowing her whole as the wind kicked up and the stalks closed ranks on the road behind her.

7

The girl burst out of the woods, hobbling on what remained of her battered foot and a possibly busted leg. She could hear the revving of an engine, the screeching of tires as they spun out, the bang as the car collided with something. *Please, lady, wait! Wait for me!*

She saw the Crazy, standing there in the middle of the street, waving goodbye as if the lady in the SUV was his wife, off to run an errand.

'Stop!' the girl screamed at the Explorer that was hauling ass down the block. But only a squeak came out. In her hand she clutched a chunk of Swamp Thing's face that she had managed to rip off with her fingers.

For a moment she thought she might beat the odds again. Odds that had been against her since she'd first stupidly climbed into the Cute Crazy's car two nights ago to make a little cash. Odds that would've had her dead already, or hanging from that beam in that shack. But she'd made it out of the horrible place that stunk of death, with its walls and floor stained with blood and torn fingernails and its floor of broken glass. A place she knew others had not made it out of. She'd made it across fields in the middle of a storm in the middle of the night. She'd survived being hit by a car as the Crazy Brothers hunted her down. She'd walked on shredded feet. She'd made it *here*. She'd found civilization in the middle of nothing but cane fields. She'd found a lady actually sleeping in her car in a town where there was not a single other soul around. It had to be a miracle. It had to be. She was so close to a happy ending – it couldn't end here. It couldn't end this way. 'Stop! Please!' she barked.

She saw the flash of brake lights and started to cry, but then the SUV turned down a street. Her body finally gave out. It could take no more. She collapsed on her knees, surrounded by garbage, her arms outstretched. Her leg felt like it was on fire. 'Come back!' she screamed.

But her voice barely made a sound. Fear had claimed it.

Swamp Thing was behind her – he wanted his cheek back. She tried to crawl away, but didn't get far. He found her feet and dragged her like a caveman might, back toward the woods. Her fingers clawed at the asphalt.

The last thing she saw before the woods consumed her, and the mud and leaves and rocks filled her nose and mouth and eyes, was the other Crazy – the one she'd thought was handsome when she'd danced for him, with his long, dark waves and his scruffy beard and intense eyes. He had a hard body and strong hands. Hands filled with cash and, as her friend Loni liked to say, green made every guy look good. But the tall stranger hadn't needed much help in that department. Now he was standing in the street, facing the direction where the SUV had driven off. His arms were raised up to the sky and he was laughing. As she was being dragged to the slaughter, he was laughing into the rain. Now she could see him for who he really was, for *what* he really was. He was the Devil, dressed all in black, daring God with his outstretched arms to come down from the heavens and perform one last miracle for His little lost lamb.

But there were no more miracles to be had. Not tonight.

The clouds gathered, seemingly at his command, consuming the moon again, and the biblical rain started up once more, washing away the drag marks that her body had left behind.

8

Faith's heart was pounding so hard, she thought she might actually be having a heart attack. It was hard to breathe. She turned the car down another road. And then another. She was surely lost, but was she far enough away? Had she gone in circles? Were they behind her?

A toddler could read the body language – that man was telling her to be quiet, he was telling her to shut up, putting his finger to his lips. It was a gesture that an annoyed librarian might make to a table of giggly teens. But he'd pointed at the back seat. He'd pointed right at . . .

Maggie!

The thought overwhelmed her and she started to cry as she turned her head to look in the back seat. Maggie was still asleep. Her Cha-Cha had come off her head – probably when she'd hit that garbage can – but she was still clutching Eeyore and her blanket and still sucking her thumb. Her face was buried in the corner of the booster. 'Maggie, honey?' she whispered cautiously. 'Maggie, are you OK, baby?'

There was no response. Faith actually moaned with relief.

What had happened? What had she witnessed back there?

She checked the rearview. The back window was completely fogged.

Who were those people? Where had they come from?

She lowered her window to clear the fog and checked her side view. No one. There was no one behind her. No headlights gaining speed on her in the distance. She listened as the rain and wind rushed in the car. Sweat ran down her face and neck. She reached for her cell phone and remembered she didn't have one.

A million questions rushed her brain: *Where had that girl come from? Were those people watching her when she was asleep? How long had they been out there? Who were those men? What did they want?*

She looked back at the rearview. Still pitch-black.

The events of the last five minutes played over and over again in her head. Each scene demanded to be replayed first, and the images quickly tumbled together, as every detail fought to be remembered before it was forgotten.

Help me! She heard the raspy, hoarse voice, the palm slapping against the glass. She saw those crazed brown eyes, that twitching mouth with an earring stuck in the lip. And one in the nose. And two in the eyebrow. The dirty clothes. The tattoos. She saw the disheveled possessed girl from the movie *The Ring*, climbing through her driver's side window, trying to get in, that's what she saw. She shook her head.

What was wrong with that girl? Why was she like that?

Maybe she was on drugs. Maybe she was drunk.

Was she running from that man? From both of those men?

With that heavy makeup and the tattoos and the piercings, and the dirty bare feet she must have been high. Who would be out like that in the middle of the night in a terrible storm unless they were high on drugs? And that town – it had Faith thinking of every freaky horror movie she'd ever seen.

She looked again at the side view. If someone were following her, she'd be easy to find, even miles away. She was the only car on the road.

He's coming! Let me in! The girl was back in her head. Faith rubbed her temples.

What had the girl meant by that? Was she in trouble? What had that second man, the man in the red shirt, done with her? Where had he taken her? Faith stared ahead into the endless black. There was nothing out here. Nothing at all.

She had smiled at Faith. The girl had *smiled* at her. And that guy in black had grinned. The two of them had kissed. What was that about? It was all so weird. Now that red-shirted potbellied guy – *he* was definitely creepy. And he looked angry. The girl had looked scared of him. He'd certainly scared the hell out of Faith.

She ripped off the cuticle she'd been gnawing on before. Blood filled her mouth. The clock read 1:40.

Again she checked the side view, but there was still no one there. No one was following her. If she'd witnessed something really horrible, something like a rape or an attack or – she sucked in a deep breath at the thought – something even worse, wouldn't someone be following her by now? Bad guys didn't leave witnesses. If they'd been doing something evil to that girl, those two guys would never have let Faith leave. In fact, the guy in black had actually *stopped* the red-shirted man from coming over to her car. Neither of them had a weapon. If they had, surely they would've used it to stop her – *if* they were doing something to that girl, right? So they must not have had a weapon. The thought made her feel a little bit better. Until the next question came at her.

Why didn't you let her in, Faith?

She felt nauseous. Her brain started to sputter out a litany of excuses.

It all happened so fast.

Maggie was in the back seat. She couldn't let a girl like that – a stranger – into the car with her daughter right there.

What if the girl was a robber? What if the cry for help was a ruse to get those other men in the car?

Jarrod used to be a public defender in Miami. He used to tell Faith all about the horrible crimes his clients had been accused of: carjacking, robbery, rape, kidnapping, murder. The insider stories were enough to scare anyone from ever stepping outside their front door. And when he described how criminals thought the twisted things they thought, why they targeted certain people, how they hunted their victims – it was bone chilling. More than one story had involved home invasions that kicked off with a female accomplice: women posing as sympathetic ruses, claiming they'd been hurt in an accident, begging for help on a doorstep while their armed boyfriends waited in the shadows for the unwitting Good Samaritan to unchain the door and let them all in.

She ran her hands through her hair, trying to hold her thoughts together. There was another reason why she hadn't opened the door: she was scared. No, she was terrified.

She finally spotted a sign: **West Palm Beach, 41 miles.** She wasn't just on the right road – she was almost out of the maze! She knew where she was. A car actually passed her, heading the opposite direction. It was the first car she'd seen since she'd left Highlands County. Up ahead was civilization, even if it was closed for the night. A few miles later she saw the golden arches of a McDonalds and a red-and-white neon sign welcoming people to the Sunland Inn. They had a vacancy. From the looks of the empty parking lot they had more than one room available. She pulled in and sat there for a moment, staring at the glass doors of the empty lobby.

The rain had stopped, the band had moved through, but it was still crazy-windy – the air whistled as it forced its way through the cracked driver's side window. She'd go in and tell the motel manager what happened and ask him to call the police. That was the right thing to do. Let the law figure out what had happened back there. But as her hand touched the door handle, her brain fired off one final question.

What did you hit back there?

Faith let go of the handle. *Nothing. There was nothing there.* All the same her hands went sweaty and her heart sped up. She looked around the lit parking lot at the cobra-head lampposts. She'd be able to see the whole car now. The thought filled her with a sense of dread.

You have to look. You have to see. You have to know.

She got out and slowly walked to the front of the Explorer. The wind whipped her hair and she wrapped her arms around herself. She stared at the front end. Her stomach flipped and her knees threatened to give out. She steadied herself on the hood. The bumper was lopsided and dented. Not a big one, but the dent wasn't there yesterday. The grille was dented, too. She'd definitely hit something, there was no denying it.

The garbage can? Maybe it was that garbage can . . .

She ran her hand over a smaller dent on the lip of the hood, as if that might tell her something, like where and when it had gotten on her car.

Maybe someone hit you at Charity's, but you didn't see the damage when you looked in the cane fields because it was so dark.

She crouched down and stared at the grille. She ran her hand over the dented bumper and looked at her palm. It was wet from the rain. Even though her brain screamed at her not to do it, she tentatively ran her hand back up and under the bumper, her fingers exploring places in the twisted, cracked plastic and metal undercarriage that her eyes could not see. She looked again at her palm in the beam of the headlight. There was a dark substance on it this time. It looked red. It looked like blood. She fell back onto the wet pavement.

It was a deer. Or a dog. It wasn't what you're thinking, Faith! Oh God, don't let it be that . . .

She quickly wiped her hand on her jeans and stood up. A tiny, ragged piece of fluff clung to the dented grille. She pulled it off. It was a thin, white material. Maybe from a rag.

Or a T-shirt.

She bit her hand and forced back the scream of horror as the tears started up again.

What had she done? What the hell had she hit back there in those cane fields?

9

The clock read 1:50. Almost forty-five minutes had passed since . . . Faith stared through the windshield at the glass doors of the motel.

They'd ask questions, the police. Some she couldn't answer.

'Where were you, Mrs Saunders? What was the name of the town? We can't send someone out to do a check if we don't know where to go.'

Then there were the other questions . . .

'Mrs Saunders, when this girl was banging on your window asking for help, why didn't you let her in?'

'You've had an accident. You have damage to your bumper and grille. Did you call the police? That's required by law, you know.'

'There's blood on your bumper. You obviously hit something that bleeds. Was that something human?'

She looked desperately around the parking lot and tried to think of the right answers. *I don't know! There was nothing there.*

'How hard did you look? Or did you just leave?'

She shook her head. *There was nothing there.*

'Mrs Saunders, have you been drinking?'

She covered the gasp with her hand. She had had a couple

of glasses of wine, true. And maybe a drink – a seven and seven – but it wasn't that strong. And those hurricanes . . . She tried to swallow the awful, sweet taste but it still wouldn't go down. Yes, she had been drinking, but she hadn't expected to drive. She'd felt fine, really. Maybe a little off when she first left Charity's, but that'd been a couple of hours ago. She remembered her head spinning when she first got out of the car in the cane field to look at the front end. She breathed into her cupped hand. The same hand that had rubbed the . . . *substance* . . . off the underside of the bumper. A wave of nausea came over her and she wiped it furiously again on her pant leg, so hard and fast her palm grew raw.

They would smell it on her breath for sure.

'Mrs Saunders, please step out of the car. I'm going to need you to perform some tests for me. Can you walk a straight line, please?'

They'd make her take a Breathalyzer.

She could refuse, but they could arrest her even if she did. She bit her lip hard, put her forehead on the steering wheel and closed her eyes.

They'd run her license.

When she was a senior at the University of Florida, Faith had been arrested for DUI and leaving the scene of an accident. It was a night out with friends. They were at a party off campus. There was too much beer and too many shots. She wasn't supposed to drive home, her sorority sister was, so she'd partied hard. She was in college – everyone partied hard. Then Regina went home with a boy and told her she'd see her in the morning. It was less than a ten-mile drive back to the dorm. It was late – no one was on the roads, anyway.

The car had come out of nowhere. She didn't actually remember hitting anything at the time – just looking at this sedan that was coming at her, thinking, 'Wow, that guy is kinda close.' So close she could see his eyes, his open mouth,

49

his facial expression. He looked surprised. She'd made it back onto campus with a bent axle and no headlights. The other car had flipped.

'Thank God the old guy was wearing his seatbelt,' the cop who'd arrested her had said when he placed the handcuffs on her. She was standing on the lawn outside her sorority house, crying, her knee bloodied from where it had smashed against the steering column. 'Or else this coulda been real bad, honey. Real bad.'

They'd see the prior conviction. They'd smell the wine and hurricanes. They'd examine the dented fender and grille and take samples of the dark substance underneath the bumper.

Faith banged her head back and forth on the steering wheel as the tears streamed down her face. Jarrod was a defense attorney; he could tell her what the police would think: *If you did it once, we know you did it again.*

'Bond is set at one hundred thousand,' the judge had ordered, while he stared at her over thick glasses, his ancient, oversized brow a mass of judgmental wrinkles. The young public defender who was supposedly representing her actually gasped at the amount. 'Because you, young lady, are a person who cannot be trusted. You left that man out there to die. Left him on the side of the road. By the grace of God, he wasn't killed. So you can't be trusted to do the right thing and you can't be trusted to come back to court.' She'd done a year of probation, a hundred hours of community service, apologized, paid a huge fine and spent eight nights in jail before her disappointed mother finally bailed her out.

She banged her head even harder. It wouldn't matter why she'd called the police – she'd be the one going to jail tonight. No doubt about it. The tears dripped onto her lap. *Oh God, what if she got arrested in front of Maggie? What would happen to her? Would they put her in foster care while they waited for Jarrod to show up?* She envisioned Maggie screaming out for her as they slapped cuffs on and placed her in the back of a police car, its red-and-blue lights spinning across her little girl's tear-stained face, like a scene from a movie. And then Jarrod – looking shocked and disappointed as he stared at her through the jail's bullet-proof glass asking her how she could drink and drive with Maggie in the car. How could she do such an awful thing?

Why did she drink tonight? Why did Charity make her leave when she knew she'd been drinking? Why didn't she get a hotel? Why didn't she listen to Jarrod and stay home? Why? Why? Why?

A series of bad decisions – one after the other after the other. The one smart choice she thought she'd made turned out to be the worst one of all – stopping in that god-forsaken, Twilight Zone town. She looked around desperately. The windows were fogging again, blurring the motel doors. She felt trapped – cornered in this car, in this deserted parking lot, boxed in by her terrible decisions. It was so claustrophobic, she could feel her chest closing. Her eyes caught on a figure moving across the empty lobby of the motel.

You are a person who cannot be trusted.

I don't have a good feeling about tonight . . .

She squeezed her eyes closed. It wouldn't matter *why* she'd called the police; she'd be the one going to jail tonight.

Forty-five minutes had passed since she'd woken up in a nightmare. Since she'd seen whatever it was she'd seen. They were all long gone by now – that girl, with her tattoos and piercings and dirty hands and bare feet, and those two creepy men. It wasn't right to judge, but, well . . . who . . . who knows why they were all out there? No one had a weapon. The girl looked tough. She wasn't bleeding. *She wasn't bleeding!* That was important.

Faith took a deep breath, wiped her face with her sleeve

and put the car in drive while her brain kept throwing around rationalizations.

All three might've been on drugs; they might have robbed you.

She pulled out of the parking lot and onto Southern Blvd.

They could've hurt Maggie. Or worse. God knows what might have happened if you had opened that door. As Jarrod once said, 'It's hard to appreciate the tragedy that would have been when the plot is foiled before the bomb is built.'

She spotted the sign for Florida's Turnpike.

All three of them were long gone from there. And you don't even know exactly where 'there' is, Faith. You'd have to retrace your steps with the police, and they wouldn't do that with you once they'd placed you under arrest. You'd be in custody. You'd be headed to booking. Getting ready to have your mug shot taken and be fingerprinted and then strip-searched in some local Podunk jail.

She set off, heading south. There were a few other cars on the road now. That was comforting.

It was a deer, Faith. Deer can cause nasty damage. You weren't going fast, so it wasn't hurt too badly and it scampered into the cane. That's why there was nothing there.

It was past three when she pulled into her driveway. She looked in the back seat. Maggie was like Jarrod – she could sleep through anything. Faith leaned her head back on the headrest, feeling both intense relief at having made it home safe and overwhelming shame for the same reason. Like a character in a Grimms' fairytale, she had left the haunted forest with all its perils and dangerous, strange inhabitants far, far behind her, and had arrived back at the castle. She took a deep breath and checked her rearview one final time. The rationalizations had worked like shoddy patchwork on a leaky roof: they'd done the job for now. It would hold, but there was no telling for how long.

Then she hit the garage-door button and with a chilling sense of impending dread, watched it close on the night with a heavy thud.

10

'Hey there, honey,' Jarrod whispered, his breath warm on her cheek. 'What time did you get in?'

''Bout three,' Faith answered softly, her face buried in a pillow, most of her head and body burrowed under the comforter, her eyes still closed. The house was freezing; Jarrod liked to keep it like an igloo when they slept.

'Why aren't you at your sister's?' He sounded distracted.

She could smell the fresh scent of soap and his Bulgari cologne; she heard the crisp rustle his jacket made when he checked his cell phone and put it into his suit pocket. Without opening her eyes, she could tell he was dressed for court and probably running late.

'Long story,' she mumbled. 'I . . . I wasn't feeling well; I didn't want to stay.'

'What?' His hand found her forehead. 'What's the matter?'

'My stomach . . . I'm OK now.'

'Did you get sick?'

'I didn't feel well. It's all right, I'm OK.'

She could tell he was checking his cell again. 'You must have some great stories to tell about last night.'

Faith buried herself deeper into the pillow.

He kissed her on the cheek. 'Sleep in; it's early. I got a

motion in Palm Beach, so I gotta run. I'll take Maggie to school.'

'Maggie's up?'

'Up and downstairs and ready to go and, boy, is she in rare form. She actually *wants* to go to school today. Mrs Wackett is in for a treat. Did she sleep at all?' he asked, his voice fading as he moved toward the bedroom door.

'In the car.'

'That must have been some ride home . . .' he said, his voice rising on the word 'some' as he opened the door and headed out into the hall.

She opened her eyes. 'Huh?' The room was dark but for a slice of weak light that leaked onto the carpet where the drapes didn't meet.

'Love you!' he yelled from downstairs. She heard him hurry Maggie into the car, then his garage door opened and shut and he was gone.

When she woke up again the bedroom was still dark. For a few blissful seconds while she lay there tuning in to the day, she forgot about the night before – the party, the fight, the storm, the girl, the strange men. But with just a few blinks, the static was gone and it all came rushing back. And along with the assorted upsetting memories came guilt, accompanied by a heavy, awful, queasy feeling in the pit of her stomach, like she had drunk a shot of glue. She looked over at the clock and sat up with a start. It was already eight thirty. She hadn't slept that late in ages.

Her head throbbed and her body ached. Physically, she felt like she'd been hit by a truck. Emotionally she felt just as drained, like the mornings after she and Jarrod had had an argument and she'd spent most of the night crying. After she'd put Maggie to bed last night she'd finally had that cigarette, along with a generous shot of Stoli, out on the back patio. That was probably a bad idea in hindsight, but she could not sleep when she first got home. She could not calm down. She couldn't turn her brain off. She had reached for the phone a few times, only to put it back down before even punching a number. More than three hours had passed since she'd seen what she'd seen. Then it was four. With every slip of the minute hand, the sense of urgency seemed to wane. *Nine-one-one. What is your emergency? Well, I guess it's not really an emergency any more, Operator, now is it? I'm back home and those people are long gone back into the woods. Where, you ask? I don't have a clue. Make a left at the cane stalk and then drive around in circles for a long time.* The same fear-stoked rationalizations popped back into her head, fighting off the guilt, aided and abetted by the boozy effects of the vodka, which finally worked its magic. She'd gone upstairs somewhere around five, staring at the shadows of the palm fronds that violently danced on her ceiling, courtesy of the patio light that she had forgotten to turn off outside.

She got out of bed now, moved over to the drapes and hesitated, looking at the nondescript light slice on the carpet, her hand on the cord. *What's behind curtain number two, Bob? Show us what she's won!*

Faith hoped it would be sunny and beautiful outside – a normal, enviable Florida day. Bright blue skies, puffy white clouds. She hoped it would look nothing like the day before. A do-over – a symbolic fresh start. But when she opened the drapes her heart sank: it was gloomy and rainy. In fact, it looked exactly as it had when she'd pulled out of her driveway yesterday. The glue shot churned in her stomach. She scanned the backyard below. Everything looked the same as it had twenty-four hours earlier – same lounge cushion in the pool, same pink impatiens in the garden, same swingset in the corner, same toppled-over umbrella.

Everything looked the same. Everything was completely different.

She turned on the TV, raising the volume so she could hear it in the bathroom as she showered. The local morning news was over, so she clicked on *Headline News*. The DOW was up. So were oil prices. A child murder from 1957 was finally solved. Another corporate swindler was indicted. The polar ice sheets were melting faster than scientists had predicted.

No missing persons in Florida. No dead girls found in sugar cane fields.

Downstairs she put on a pot of coffee and scanned the *Sun-Sentinel* – even the sports section, in case the girl from last night was some high school track star who hadn't shown up for practice. There was no mention of any missing girls, in Florida or anywhere else. She felt a tiny bit better, although she knew something that had happened in the middle of the night would not make the morning paper. It might make the TV news, though, and there was nothing there, either. She'd have to keep checking the paper and the Internet and watching the news over the next couple of days. If there was still nothing by Wednesday or Thursday, then there was obviously nothing to worry about. She could officially breathe a sigh of relief and chalk up whatever had happened last night to some weird, unfortunate experience that she hoped never to go through again.

She popped three Advil for the headache that wouldn't go away and downed them with a long gulp of coffee. She still couldn't shake the unsettling, off-kilter feeling. It was a feeling that something was . . . wrong. Amiss. Out of place. Not right. She looked around the kitchen. The milk was on the counter, cereal bowls left in the sink, the toaster was out. But it wasn't the mess leftover from breakfast or the lounge cushion still floating in the pool that was bothering her. Like in her bedroom, everything *looked* exactly as she had left it before she'd headed to Charity's yesterday. The hand-painted canisters she'd gotten on vacation in New Orleans were displayed neatly next to her collection of olive

57

oils and a decorative tin of amaretto cookies. Maggie's artwork covered the fridge: circles made with glued-on buttons, crayoned stick figures, Jackson Pollock-esque finger paintings. Jarrod's shoes and jacket were sitting on a seat, waiting for someone to take them upstairs and put them away. Maggie's toys were spread out all over the family room. Like the backyard, everything *looked* the same, but it was all completely different. It made her think of Maggie's favorite story, *The Cat in the Hat*. It felt like, while she was away yesterday at Charity's, strangers had come in, partied on her furniture and done crazy stuff with her house, then gone and cleaned up and put everything back in its proper place moments before she'd stepped through the door. Everything looked the same . . . but it wasn't.

Faith put the milk away and the dishes in the dishwasher. The 'change' she was sensing was obviously imperceptible to others, instigated by her own Irish Catholic guilt. Hopefully, time would temper the guilt and the unsettling feeling would settle down and go away. After all, the unsuspecting mother in the Dr Seuss tale had no idea what calamities befell her house while she was away and she would never have to know since everything had been put back in its proper place. It was the children who faced the moral dilemma of whether or not to tell her. She looked around her kitchen. Would it really matter what had happened last night as long as everything was put back to the way it was supposed to be?

Then she thought of the Explorer. She braced her hands on the island's sink and stared at the door that led out to her garage. Not everything looked the same as it had when she'd left yesterday . . .

After she'd finished cleaning the kitchen, she headed back upstairs to the laundry room. Her clothes from last night were buried in the hamper where she'd stuffed them, including her blue jeans. Her shirt smelled of wine and beer and smoke and partying and she sprayed it with Febreeze and a glob of Shout for good measure. Then she squirted a mound of the spot cleaner on the dark stain on her jeans and shoved everything in the washing machine, watching as it filled. A fresh start. A do-over.

Then she headed back downstairs.

The house had two garages: a double on one side where her car was, off the kitchen, and a single on the other side of the house, which was where Jarrod parked his Infinity. She hesitated for a moment with her hand on the door to the garage that housed her Explorer and held her breath. Part of her was hoping that last night was somehow a dream. A crazy nightmare that only felt real. Or maybe one that she was remembering as worse than what it actually was. She took a deep breath, turned the knob and flicked on the light. Her heart sank.

The grille was dented and so was the bumper. There were two dents in the hood along with two deep scratches. It was all very, very real.

She ran her hands over the hood, her fingertips following the scratches. On a shelf by the AC handler was a box of rags. She took one, wiped underneath the fender, held her breath again and looked at it.

Nothing. There was nothing there. No blood.

She exhaled. She stuck her head under the car and wiped again – hard. She looked again. Nothing. She scrubbed. The rag was dirty, but it wasn't red. The rationalizations were back.

Maybe it wasn't blood that you thought you saw. Maybe it was grease.

She got up and went over to the driver's side window and looked in. She could see the scraggly streaks inside from where her own fingers had wiped away the fog when she first saw the girl. She traced the glass outside, where the girl had been standing, where she had placed her dirty palms. But like the dark substance under the fender, the handprints that she feared might still be there were gone.

Faith took a deep breath, twisting the rag around and around in her fingers.

Then she took the rag and wiped the glass clean, anyway.

11

'I can pull that out. No biggie. You don't even need a paint job,' said the mechanic with the name patch that read 'Sal'.

'Really?' Faith exhaled a deep breath.

'Yeah. It won't be perfect, like if you got a new fender or nothing. Same with these dents on the hood. I'll pop those out.'

'That would be great. And the . . .?' She pointed at the scratches next to the dents.

'I can wet sand those,' he answered with a smile. 'I'll try compound first. That might work.'

'Well, that's better than what I was thinking.'

'Problem is your grille. You need a new one.'

'Oh.' Her face fell.

'Oh man – you are far too pretty to have such a glum kisser. Listen, it must be your lucky day, 'cause I can probably get that part from a buddy without a hassle. Unless you want it new, because that might take a couple of days.'

'No, no, it doesn't have to be new, as long as it looks the same.'

'It'll look like you never hit . . .?' he said, his voice rising. He was obviously waiting for her to fill in the blank.

'A used part is fine,' she replied.

He nodded. 'You're paying cash, right? You don't want to put it through insurance? That's what you said on the phone.'

'No. My rates will, you know . . . they'll go up. I just want it fixed as soon as possible.'

There was a brief silence. He rubbed his nose with a greasy finger, grinned and said, 'Oh, I get it.'

She shifted uncomfortably. 'What?'

'You don't want the husband to know.' He was looking at her wedding ring.

'You got me.'

'I've heard that before. But it's a shame.'

'What's that?'

'You're married.'

'Thanks, Sal. But you were nowhere to be found seven years ago.'

He laughed. 'I could fix your car for free no matter how many times you banged it up. And I'm very forgiving. Well, if you ever get rid of the husband, look me up. By the way, it's Lou, not Sal,' he said, pointing up at the sign above the garage bay that said: *Lou's Automotive Repair. Fast. Friendly. Dependable.* 'Sal's my brother. He works here, too. And he lives with me. His shirt was the first one I found in the dryer this morning. Don't mix us up if you come looking to take me up on that offer, Mrs . . .?'

'Saunders.'

'But if you're coming in to complain, then ask for Sal,' he added with a robust laugh.

Faith looked around the garage. There was another car on a lift and a dozen smashed-up vehicles in the yard. 'Can you do it today, you think, Lou? And the AC, too?'

'Today? You crazy?'

She bit her lip. She must have looked as desperate as she felt, because he added, 'That husband of yours must be a real unsympathetic character. Accidents happen.'

She nodded. 'I can pay you . . . extra?'

He studied her for a moment before he nodded. 'It's those blue eyes of yours; they'd get me to agree to anything. If you can throw an extra two-fifty my way, I'll drop everything I'm doing just for you. I gotta see if Jimmy has that grille, so I may need you to come back later in the week to finish up. I can't make no promises now.'

'As long as you can get the dents taken care of today, I'd be really, really grateful.'

'So what'd you hit anyways?' Lou was down on the ground, examining the fender, his hands feeling up underneath it.

Her heart began to race. *There was nothing there.*

He stood back up and wiped his hands on his blue work pants. He stared at her, waiting for a response.

'A deer,' she said softly.

He nodded. 'Ouch. Not around here . . .?'

'No. I was up north, at my sister's, coming down 441. But it didn't die. It . . . ran off,' she answered softly.

'Well, don't worry about it none,' Lou said as he walked her back into the office. 'Deer can fuck up a car; you're lucky this one didn't do much damage. She probably wasn't very big. And ya know,' he added as Faith stared out the window, blinking back tears, 'you couldn't've hurt her too bad or she wouldn't've gone and run off on ya, now, would she?'

12

The aroma of chocolate cake baking filled the air outside of Sweet Sisters. Faith could smell it the second she opened the taxi door. It was a scent that normally triggered fond memories of warm kitchens and holidays and baking with Grandma Milly. Today, though, she felt undeserving of such comforting nostalgias. The normalcy of the scent, of smelling it here outside her beloved bakery where she spent a good chunk of every day, made her feel like she had back at the house – anxious and guilty.

She paid the driver and slipped in through the back door, passing the kitchen and heading straight for her office. She could tell from the chatter and bustle that the line was long and the tables were filled, which was good – people were willing to dodge rain and blustery wind for a crème brûlée cupcake and a caramel apple latte. Financially October was going to be a good month, even with Octavius trying his damnedest to drive customers away.

The back office was empty. On Vivian's desk was a half-empty, cold cup of coffee and her makeup bag, but her purse was missing, which meant she was out of the office, but she hadn't gone far. Vivian Vardakalis and Faith had been the best of friends since they were six. They'd stayed BFFs through high school, then were sorority sisters at UF, and now, for the past three years, business partners in Sweet Sisters. Faith knew Viv about as well as she knew her sister and for almost as long – the girl couldn't go too long without lipstick and concealer. She was probably grabbing lunch, running errands, or at the bank. Faith had called her yesterday on her way up to Charity's to tell her that she wouldn't be in till late today, if at all, but she hadn't spoken with her this morning. Though neither of them actually did the baking any more, one of them was physically present at the cupcakery every day. 'It may take a village to raise a child,' Vivian liked to joke, 'but it only takes one employee with his hand in the till to bring down a cash-based business.' She was an accountant by trade. 'If the mice know the cat's away, they play, play, play. And they don't give a shit about over-frosting your three-dollar-and-fifty-cent cupcake so that you make even less profit on a perishable product with a limited shelf-life.'

Vivian knew all about the drama parade that seemed to follow Charity's life around. At different points over the years the three of them had been BFFs, but that was hard to maintain. As Faith's mom had warned a long time ago, friendships in pairs worked fine, but odd numbers meant there was an odd man out. Through high school it was pretty much Vivian & Faith and 'we could ask Charity to come, too!' After college, when Vivian had gotten wrapped up with her husband, Gus, and following *his* life around, Faith and Charity had reconnected. Then four years ago, Nick had made Charity move from Miami to Sebring – or as Jarrod called it, 'Bumfuck' – and the relationship with her sister had changed to long distance. Gus, meanwhile, had gotten a job with Motorola, Vivian had returned to South Florida and the BFF roles rotated positions once again. That was when the idea of Sweet Sisters was first conceived – during a ladies' night out to celebrate Vivian's purchase of a home a mile away from Faith's in Parkland. Too many martinis later, it didn't seem like such a silly idea to start a cupcakery. Two months later, when both of them were perfectly sober, they'd found the perfect location, signed a lease and started the build-out. Today they had a healthy Internet business and were looking at expanding with another store in Fort Lauderdale. The notion of franchising was no longer a pipedream – they both joked about someday giving Starbucks a run for its money. Faith sometimes felt bad that the idea for Sweet Sisters had come to her when the BFF positions had switched. Charity's financial situation wouldn't have let her be a partner, but she might've been able to participate in the business in other ways, and maybe her life would be different right now. Maybe she'd stayed with Nick and put up with his shit because she didn't want to be a single mom and the odd man out in Coral Springs.

Faith closed the door behind her and went to her desk, trying to push all thoughts of her sister from her head. Right now she didn't want to have pity for Charity, in any way shape or form. But there, stuck to her computer screen, was a note from Vivian: *Charity called AGAIN. She has your phone??? And purse?? She said to tell you she's sorry for being a bitch? Can't wait to hear this one! That explains why you're not answering your phone, I guess . . .*

Faith's eyes welled at the memory of her sister standing hand in hand with Nick, watching with the crowd as she wrestled a crying, screaming, freaking-out Maggie into the car in the pouring rain. She wanted to tell Vivian what had happened, but then the rest of the night rushed into the mortifying memory. Leading the charge was the haunting, pale face of that girl. The thick, glue feeling in her stomach was back. And she knew she couldn't tell her best friend that part. She couldn't tell anyone that part. Ever.

Work. Bury yourself in a project. The fervent need to get this off your chest will pass. That girl is OK. Maggie is OK. Everything will be OK.

She wiped the tears before they fell, sat down at her desk

and pulled out the file of purchase orders. After that was the ad copy she needed to write for the *Sun-Sentinel* and the application she had to finish for *Cupcake Wars* – the Food Network baking competition show that she was trying to get Sweet Sisters on. And finally, payroll. That should keep her in the office and her mind busy until the Explorer was ready. There was no way she could talk to Charity today without losing it – either breaking down in tears or screaming like a lunatic at her. It wasn't going to be a quiet conversation, no matter what. While Faith verbally wanted to blame her accident and dented car on her sister, and shift some of the guilt she was feeling onto *her* shoulders, she didn't want anyone to know what had happened last night after she'd left the party – what she had done. Or, more accurately, what she hadn't.

She tapped her fingers anxiously on the desk phone and thought again about calling the police. But what good would that do now? Time had kept ticking on. Those characters, that girl, were long gone. Questions would still be asked by the police that she still didn't have the answers to. And while she'd pass a breathalyzer for sure now, her car was sitting in a repair shop. How would that look? She'd have to explain the accident to Jarrod. And now the cover-up of the accident. Once again, she pulled her hand off the phone. Charity had been so wasted last night, so damn wasted – now she wanted to apologize? All that had happened had happened for no reason? The thought made her so angry her hands shook. Perhaps the best way to handle her sister would be to send her a text from Vivian's phone cordially telling her to please mail the purse and cell back – that she would even send her a check for the postage. Leave it at that. Leave their whole relationship at that. What made her even more upset was knowing that Charity was likely apologizing because Nick was back to being an ass this morning and she wanted to go back to complaining about him and her life. *Just hit the reset button and all is forgiven.*

It's business as usual. Faith looked around the office that, like her home, looked the same as she'd left it on Saturday, but was somehow totally different. *Not today it's not, Charity. Life might never be usual ever again.* On the other side of the wall she could hear the bakers laughing and kidding around with each other. She envied the simplicity of their conversation.

A graduate of the College of Journalism at UF, owning a cupcake bakery was the last thing in the world Faith Saunders would ever have imagined herself doing. She might have fond memories of helping Grandma Milly bake cookies at Christmas, but stirring the batter, pouring in the chips and testing the dough was about the extent of what her grandma ever let her do. Hence, she was lacking some serious culinary skills after Grandma Milly left for, as she called it, 'the big dog park in the sky' – reunited for eternity with the dozens of Boston terriers she'd raised over her eighty years. Faith certainly hadn't learned anything in the kitchen from her mother, Aileen, who couldn't boil water and hadn't inherited her own mother's fondness for baking; cracking open a roll of Nestlé Toll House was asking too much. It was Faith's dad who'd taught Faith the basics so she could survive and snag herself a husband. Patrick 'Sully' Sullivan was a closet cook. By the time Faith graduated high school she could grill meat, roast potatoes, and make pasta. As for dessert, Sully was off-the-boat Irish – he finished off his meals with a Jameson twelve-year-old – so Faith had never had any experience in baking confections. Dessert usually meant peeling the lid off a pint of Ben & Jerry's or defrosting a Sara Lee cheesecake.

Jarrod had thought she was still drunk the morning after that ladies' night out when she told him about her and Vivian's plans to abandon a stalled writing career and a fledgling accounting practice to become bakers. It'd taken her a few weeks and continuous tries with various recipes in the kitchen to convince him she was serious. But when he came around to the idea, he'd embraced it. He was the one who'd actually found the former Payless shoe store property in a strip mall in Coral Springs. And he had been able to negotiate a good chunk of the build-out into the lease, which made the project less financially daunting.

Initially, the plan upon graduation had been to take her journalism degree and become the next Edna Buchanan at some hotshot publication, then use all the fascinating stories she'd reported on as inspiration for the crime fiction novels she was going to write from her and Jarrod's hip Manhattan apartment, as he worked his way up the ladder of some fancy New York law firm. But as Steinbeck once noted, the best-laid plans often went astray, awry or up in smoke: the hotshot publications weren't hiring and Jarrod had decided to go with the Public Defender's Office in Miami. *Time* was gone and New York was out. Faith had waited tables at night and managed a kiosk at the Aventura mall that first year out of school, sending out résumé after résumé, feeling beyond dejected when the phone didn't ring. When the managing editor of the monthly South Florida magazine, *Gold Coast,* offered her a part-time position as a features writer she'd jumped on it, happy to finally be working in her field and hoping to build her résumé so when the market rebounded and the hotshot publications opened their online doors she'd get to do what she thought she'd always wanted to be doing: investigative reporting.

And then she got pregnant.

It had now been eight years since *Pomp and Circumstance* had ushered her out of Gainesville and into the real world. She'd missed her midterms at UF because of the DUI, and for months after that it was impossible for her to concentrate on anything. It had taken her an extra year to graduate and cost her a small fortune when she lost her Bright Futures scholarship and had to take out student loans to finish up. Of course, she'd ended up meeting Jarrod that extra year, so some amazing good did come out of God-awful horrible. In between researching and writing compelling articles for *Gold Coast* that questioned whether the South Florida art scene was suffering from a dearth of true artists, she'd managed to fire off a few chapters of a manuscript that was currently residing in the bottom of a desk drawer. But that's all she had accomplished of the original plan: a few chapters. She'd had a baby, yes, and that was definitely an achievement, but the fantastic ideas for a fantastic thriller had never come to her; a visit to the office from race-car driver Hélio Castroneves was about the most exciting thing that ever happened at the magazine. After Maggie was born, Jarrod had suggested she stay home at least for a couple of years. So she did, and tried to kick off a freelance writing career by penning articles about motherhood for *Parenting* and *Baby Talk* and *Family Fun*. That's when she'd first realized her experiences with child-rearing were altogether different than the average mom's.

As she closed the PO file, Vivian burst into the office. Burst, because Viv could not do anything quietly. She wore lots of makeup, jingly jewelry, oversized purses, flashy clothes, and sky-high heels that you could hear coming a mile away. And even though she'd moved to Miami from Hoboken when she was six, she had a thicker accent than a star on the *Real Housewives of New Jersey*. Vivian smiled at Faith and continued her conversation with Albert the baker through the office wall. 'Fruitcake! That's what she wants!' She sat on the edge of Faith's desk, pointed at the wall, and made a spinning 'He's crazy!' motion with her finger.

'No one's gonna eat that!' the wall yelled back.

'So make one that someone will! We're gonna give her what she wants; it's her frigging wedding! Enough; we'll talk later, Al.' Vivian flipped her long, thick, black hair off a shoulder and said to Faith in a voice that was low for Vivian: 'Just bake the cake, right? If I wanted an argument, I'd go home and talk to my husband. I think you're gonna have to help him with the fruitcake, hon. You can make something tasty – put enough rum in it, nobody will give a shit what flavor it is.'

Faith smiled. 'I'll talk to Al. When's it for?'

'December eighteenth. Cupcake tree with fruitcake cupcakes for two hundred and fifty. It's a Christmas-themed wedding, so you have lots of time to help him come up with something. Soooo . . . I was at the bank with the weekend deposits for the past hour and it was a friggin' zoo! Like everyone picked today to go to the bank. They had a flood with all this rain and all the ugly bank furniture is stacked in a corner. It made me think, ya know, for all the money Bank of America's got, you'd think they'd pick nicer furniture, right? Not Costco shit that peels when it gets wet. So how you doing?'

Faith sat back from the computer screen and rubbed her eyes. 'I finished the purchase orders and the ad copy. I'm gonna take on payroll next.'

Vivian frowned. 'I'll do payroll; I hope you didn't rush back here for that. You look like shit, honey. No offense,' she said, as she reached over and examined Faith's ponytail with a long, red fingernail. 'What's with the hair? You didn't want to do it today?' Vivian was always perfectly dressed, coiffed, manicured, and made-up. Always. Even when she went into labor, she looked hot on the delivery table.

'Do I look that bad?'

Vivian nodded. 'Yes. Well, you looked tired, is what you look. Those circles . . . I can fix them if you want.'

'You're too kind.'

'Please,' Vivian replied with a dismissive wave of her hand. 'So what the hell happened at Charity's yesterday? That's why you're stressed, I bet. And why does your sister have your phone and purse? What is she sorry for? Huh? Don't spare details.'

'Long story.'

'I got time. When did you get back?'

71

'Last night.'

'Last night? You drove up to Charity's and back in one day? What's that about? Oh boy, this is gonna be good,' she said, getting up and grabbing her coffee off her desk. She rushed back and settled a butt cheek on Faith's calendar. 'What did Charity do now? No – what did *Nick* do? Why'd you leave early? What is she sorry for?'

'That's ice, you know,' Faith said, nodding at the cup.

'I know,' Vivian replied, sipping it. 'So what happened?'

'We had a fight when she let him talk to her like she was a nobody,' Faith replied softly. 'He basically called her fat and stupid. I couldn't watch any more, so I left. That's it.'

'What do you mean "That's it"? No way is that it.'

'Like I said, it's a long story. By the end of the night they were . . . holding hands, and I couldn't stay. I said some things that I probably shouldn't've and so did she. It got heated. I took Maggie and left. I forgot my bag in her bedroom and didn't realize it till I was halfway home; there was no way I was going back.' She wanted to tell Vivian everything that had happened in the kitchen but feared she might break down if she did. It was hard to open the door on only one part of the night – all the ugliness that followed wanted in, too.

'And you just drove home? In the middle of that crazy storm that has flooded the bank and ruined the ugly bank furniture and cancelled my brother's flight back from Chicago – and I have to tell you as a side note that he's driving Gus crazy – and you just drove home? What time did you leave?'

'Eleven.'

'Eleven? How long did it take you to get home?'

'Don't ask. I was doing thirty the whole way.'

'No wonder you look like shit. You should've called me; I was up till three with Lyle, anyway. He had a tummy-ache. Gus slept great, though. Why do the kids always want their mommies when they gotta puke? Why's it never Daddy?'

Faith wanted to tell her best friend. She wanted someone

to nod and tell her she was right, that she'd done the right thing by leaving, the thing they would've done too. She wanted to feel better. But she feared that's not what Vivian would say. Or she might say it, but she wouldn't think it. Vivian probably would've opened the door. She would've let the girl in and asked questions later. And she definitely would've called the police, even if she had been drinking, which she wouldn't have been with her kid in the car. She would've told her husband Gus what happened. She wouldn't have had Lou fix her truck. *No.* There were some secrets she was going to have to carry alone. Faith bit her lip. 'Oh no. Is Lyle OK?'

'Oh yeah. Too much chocolate ice cream. Thanks, Daddy. Charity . . . that girl,' Vivian said with a shake of her mane. 'She just keeps jumping back into it. I love her, but . . . I mean, after all you've done to help her and show her that there's a life out there for her without that idiot in it, offering to let her live with you and all. You've got more patience than me; I'd tell her she was on her own after the eighth rescue mission. Maybe when he beats her ass she'll finally leave.'

'Jesus, Viv, I hope it doesn't come to that.'

'Me too. I mean, I love Charity, but I'm thinking that might be the only thing that gets her to see the light. You're a saint, Faith. You're a really good person, honey. And I'm sorry I said anything about your hair; I didn't realize the night you'd had.'

The tears started. So did the wave of nausea that was about to bring up her coffee. 'I'm not feeling so hot,' she managed before running into the bathroom.

After reassuring Vivian she was fine through the door and that she wasn't mad at her, she rinsed her face with cold water and stared at her image in the mirror. Like she said, the woman staring back didn't look so hot. She was pale, her mouth and lips tensely drawn. Circles were visible under bloodshot blue eyes. Normally she would have put on a full face of makeup, but this morning it was only a touch of mascara. She'd pulled her honey-blonde hair into a ponytail this morning, not blow-drying it and styling it like she usually did. Like Vivian said, she looked like shit.

The girl's face was back in her head, staring at her with those crazed brown eyes. The diamond in her lip was trembling. Raindrops rolled down her face, carving pale white rivers in her dirty skin.

Faith shook her head but the image wouldn't go away. 'I'm no saint, Viv,' she whispered at the mirror, wiping her eyes. 'I'm not a good person.'

The woman looking back at her just kept on crying.

13

The playground at St Andrew's was empty. The rain had stopped, but the ground was still a sodden, muddy mess, dotted with puddles you could sail boats in. Faith spotted the forlorn faces on a few of the preschoolers staring out the window at the slides and jungle gym, wishing either they could play on the swings or jump in the mud. Seeing as those faces belonged to boys, the wishing was probably on the side of making mud pies in the sandbox.

She opened the door slowly so as not to take out a kid. Or let one escape. Maggie was sitting by herself playing with a My Pretty Pony. Ms Ellen, one of the volunteer moms, sat at the opposite end of the table watching her carefully while cutting out ghosts from a white sheet of paper.

'Hi there, Magpie!' Faith called out.

Maggie didn't answer. She didn't even look up. She was intensely trying to dress a pony in a Barbie gown. It wasn't working and her face was growing red.

Faith tried again and got the same reaction: none. Not even a tilt of the head to acknowledge that she'd heard her. Ms Ellen looked at Faith, smiled awkwardly and shrugged. More guilt. Faith had wanted to treat Maggie to a movie or to something special today but the time had gotten away from her. Lou had managed to fix her car, but hadn't finished till close to six. She'd had to race here from three towns over to make it by six.

Mrs Wackett, the preschool teacher, was hanging up Halloween decorations around the chalkboard. In her seventies with poofy, marshmallow-colored hair, she had a cherubic face that belonged in an AARP ad. She smelled like rose-scented hand lotion and always wore a bulky purple sweater that she had hand-knit herself. Always. Even when it was ninety. 'Hi, Mrs Wackett,' Faith said softly after Maggie still hadn't acknowledged her. 'How was she today?'

The news, she could tell, wasn't good. Mrs Wackett put her cardboard witch down and went over to the inbox on her desk. 'She tried, Mrs Saunders,' she began with a frown and in a disapproving voice as she looked over at the clock. It was five minutes of six. 'But this is a very long day for her. Very, very long.' She handed Faith a slip of paper with a traffic light on it. It was colored red. 'We tried time-out, but she had to go to the cafeteria with Sister Margaret because she didn't want to listen to Ms Ellen or me. She has been somewhat better since the cafeteria break; I've been letting her do her own thing. She's been working on the pony for a while now. Longer than I've ever seen something hold her attention, so I suppose that's good.'

'I'm sorry. I didn't expect to be this late, Mrs Wackett. I had some car issues.'

'I understand. Things happen,' she replied, but her scowl did not match the words coming out of her mouth. It was like the audiovisual wasn't properly synced. 'We're working on boundaries, like you and I have discussed, and respecting other children's feelings, but Maggie shoved Melanie, one of the girls, and when she was reprimanded she, well, she ran out of the room – right out of the room and down the hall, heading for the exit door. One of the janitors stopped her, thank God. We simply can't have that, Mrs Saunders; she has to be able to listen to teachers and adults. That's why she received a red light today.'

Faith nodded somberly. That's why Maggie had received a red light *today*. The 'get all green lights for a week and pick a toy from the treasure chest' motivational system was obviously not working for her – she got more red than she did yellow and hadn't seen a green since the first week of school.

'Perhaps she didn't get enough sleep?' Mrs Wackett tried.

God bless Mrs Wackett for continuing to try and find a simple, organic reason for why Maggie was . . . well, the way Maggie was. While she had been polite enough not to come out and say it – not yet anyway – Faith suspected that, like most people, Mrs Wackett attributed Maggie's behavioral issues to bad parenting and a lack of discipline and follow-through at home. Today, though, unfortunately her question was right on target. 'We did get home late last night,' Faith admitted, sheepishly.

'Maggie did say that she was at her aunt's house and that there was an argument and she had to leave in the rain. She was quite upset.'

Faith swallowed hard. 'She was, but then she fell asleep in the car,' she replied slowly. 'My sister lives in Sebring, you see, and it was a long drive home. Maggie slept the whole way back. I would have kept her home today, but my husband said she wanted to come in.'

There was a long, uncomfortable pause. *What else had Maggie told her about last night?*

'Hopefully tonight she'll get to bed early.' Mrs Wackett nodded curtly. She didn't have to say what she was thinking: keeping a child out late and then dropping her off at school the next morning so she could be the teacher's problem was not acceptable. Especially not a child with issues like Maggie.

'Come on, Magpie,' Faith said, bracing for the embarrassing fight she knew was coming. 'It's time to go. We have to hit the grocery store.'

Maggie shook her head.

Faith sat down next to her, feeling the judging eyes of both Mrs Wackett and Ms Ellen upon her. 'I like your pony; she's pretty,' she said in a low voice.

'It's a boy!' Maggie gave another vigorous shake of her head, stood and walked over to the toy bin.

'We have to go, Maggie; Mrs Wackett wants to go home. School's over.'

Again the shake of the head. This one was even more defiant. The ponytail whipped about like the stinging tail of a scorpion, hoping to find a victim within its reach. 'No!'

It was the same thing most every day. On red-light days, it was guaranteed. Faith felt her cheeks go crimson. She followed her over to the toy box. 'We have to go now.'

'No!' Maggie screamed.

Next would be the pony, thrown across the room. Followed by half the toy bin. Then the stomping feet, the crying, the pacing of the room like a wild tiger. And then Maggie would go to the place in her head where she could not be reasoned with.

At this very moment, Faith didn't care what anyone thought about her or her parenting skills – she just wanted to go home. She leaned in close to Maggie's ear. 'Do you want to go for ice cream? Huh? Would you like that? Chocolate? You can get marshmallows, too.'

Maggie's face calmed to pink. 'I don't want to go to ballet. I don't like Cecilia.' Cecilia was another little girl who, for some reason, Maggie despised.

'We're not going to ballet; we're going to Publix. You can help me pick out dinner.'

'I want ice cream.'

'OK, then let's go for ice cream, but only if you're good. And we have to go *now*. No screaming. No tantrum. Best behavior.'

Mrs Wackett shook her head in disappointment.

With Maggie's hand firmly in hers, Faith walked to the door. In Maggie's other hand was the My Pretty Pony. 'I'll bring the pony back tomorrow, OK, Mrs Wackett?'

Mrs Wackett nodded. 'How's therapy working out, Mrs Saunders? Is she still going?'

Faith nodded. 'Very well, thanks. See you tomorrow.'

Then she and Maggie walked out the door and across the dark parking lot as the sad-eyed boys looked on from the other side of the window, waiting for their parents to come for them.

14

'I don't like her,' Maggie said as she licked her cone and played with her pony on a table outside the indoor gym at A Latte Fun. 'She's a mean lady.'

Faith sighed. 'Why? What makes Mrs Wackett so mean? I think she's very nice.'

'She put me in time-out.'

'Did you do something bad to that new girl?'

Maggie shrugged. 'I pushed her.'

'Why?'

'She called me a mean name. And she pulled my hair.'

Faith frowned. 'She did? When was that?'

'When I pushed her.'

'Well maybe you shouldn't have pushed her, and then maybe she wouldn't have pulled your hair and called you a name.'

Maggie's face grew dark. 'She shouldn't call me names. That's not nice.'

Faith sighed and sipped at her water as she watched Maggie draw circles in the puddle of ice cream that had dripped on the table. She had the face of an angel – creamy white and round, with a sweetheart chin, apple cheeks, big, pouty pink lips and light blue eyes, that often looked like they were off dreaming about somewhere else. Her unkempt blonde hair had natural highlights that women would pay big bucks for at a salon. She didn't like Faith to brush it, so it was usually up in a pony or pigtails. A splash of sprinkles across her nose completed the look.

The diagnosis, if one wanted to call it that, was 'developmentally delayed' – an evasive, catch-all condition that made Maggie sound stupid, which she wasn't. Most of the time she knew what she was doing was wrong, but she did it anyway. 'Poor impulse control' was the name of that symptom. Then there was her 'short attention span', her 'forgetfulness', 'anxiousness', and, of course, her 'anger management issues'. She'd hit some developmental milestones right on time, but not others: rolling at three months and sitting up at six, but she never crawled and she didn't walk by herself until she was almost fourteen months. She lacked some fine motor skills, but mastered others without any apparent difficulty. The behavioral problems, which were the real worry, began after her second birthday. Maybe earlier, but Faith and Jarrod hadn't seen the signs – no parent wants to think their child is different from other kids. It was only when Lyle, Vivian's son, who was almost a year younger than Maggie, toddled up to Faith with his sippy cup and asked for 'mo moke, peez' that she started thinking something might be wrong with Maggie. She hadn't yet said a word. Not 'mama' or 'da-da' or anything and she was two and a half. She'd point if she wanted something, and shake her head if she didn't, so they knew she understood and that she wasn't deaf. In hindsight, what made it both ironic and sad was that stay-at-home-mommy Faith had been churning out articles for the parenting magazines, writing pieces like 'Important Milestones for You and Your Baby' and 'Why Crawling Is So Important' and didn't realize her own kid was missing all the marks – and for that she still felt incredibly guilty. In her defense, as she had assured other moms in her articles, most every developmental milestone was scaled: kids 'usually' started walking 'between nine and eighteen months', and babbling 'around twelve to eighteen months'. She herself had written advice like: 'But don't worry if *your* baby doesn't start right on time. Every child learns to walk at his or her own pace. Some children skip crawling altogether and go straight to walking!' She hadn't seen the problems because she hadn't wanted to. She'd wanted to hold out to the absolute last second hope that Maggie was just in the bottom of the milestone class, and that everything would eventually work out fine.

Then the head-banging started.

That particular milestone wasn't in the 'What to Expect' books. At least not to the extreme that Maggie did it. Walls, floor, high chair – anything that was in proximity to her head was in grave danger whenever she got frustrated, which, by the age of three, was often.

Pediatrician #1 suggested putting Maggie on Adderall, a drug for hyperactivity, after a five-minute exam. But drugs were something Faith couldn't see putting a three-year-old on. After garnering a few other second opinions, none of which were consistent and all of which subscribed to medicating toddlers, she'd found Dr Michelson, who explained that ADD or ADHD – or whatever acronym it was that might be causing Maggie to put holes in walls with her head and jump into pools even though she couldn't swim – couldn't be accurately diagnosed until a child was six or seven. He'd suggested a gluten-free diet, occupational therapy, and patience. Lots of patience.

The circle drawing turned to palm smearing. And for the grand finale, Maggie giddily smacked her hand into the ice cream, so it splashed back up on her clothes and hair. She started to walk around and around the table, shaking her head. Dancing to music no one else heard.

Faith grabbed the stack of napkins from her purse. 'Did you run away from Mrs Wackett and Ms Ellen? What did we talk about?'

'No running.'

'That's right, Forrest – no more running.' Maggie might have taken too long to learn how to walk, but once she did, she went straight to running and never stopped. Jarrod had nicknamed her Forrest Gump because she didn't stop until she got tired, which was . . . well, never. Faith handed her the napkins.

Maggie's face went dark again. The napkins fluttered to the floor. 'Don't call me Forrest Grump.'

Faith tried not to laugh.

'It's not funny.' Maggie smashed the ice-cream cone which she still held in her hand face down on the table and crossed her arms. Jarrod had named that look the Incredible Sulk.

Faith had seconds to defuse the bomb. 'You're right; no one should call you names,' she said, picking up the napkins. 'That's not nice. Please wipe your hands.'

'Like Melanie.'

'That's the new girl?'

'It's an ugly name.'

'Why don't you like her?'

'She called me a name.'

'What was that?'

'She said I was a weirdo and that no one wanted to play with me 'cause I play weird.'

Faith felt something stab her heart. She crushed the empty water bottle with her hand. 'That's not nice. I understand why you got upset, but you can't hit her.'

Maggie turned to run off to the ball pit, then stopped midway and ran back. 'Are you mad?' she asked, looking at Faith strangely, her head cocked.

'I'm mad that someone said something mean to you. And that you won't listen to me or Mrs Wackett.'

'You was mad yesterday,' Maggie said slowly, as if she wasn't sure she should proceed. As if there was another thought floating around in her head and she was toying with throwing it out there by testing the temperature. 'Really, really mad . . .'

Faith swallowed hard. Perhaps it was the guilt hangover that was making her paranoid. Maggie had been asleep the whole time in the back seat – she'd checked on her. 'What are you talking about?' she asked, hoping to disguise the anxiousness in her voice. 'Are you talking about at Aunt Charity's? When we had to leave Aunt Charity's? What are you talking about?'

Maggie squirmed in her shoes uncomfortably and looked around the gym.

'Yes, I was mad at Aunt Charity's,' said Faith. 'My feelings were hurt, the same way yours were when Melanie called you a name you didn't like. Do you want to talk about it?'

'I don't like it when you're mad,' Maggie said, her eyes wide and tearing up, her lip puffing. 'You're scary, Mommy.'

But before Faith could pull her close to ask her what she meant by that, the tears were gone and she was off running, squealing with delight as she dove into the ball pit face-first.

15

She was in bed when she heard the rumble of Jarrod's garage door opening, followed by the chirp of the alarm being unset and the slam of the door. Then the rattle of pots being manhandled and cabinets opening and closing. The ding of the microwave. A plate clinking when it hit the sink.

'It's me!' Jarrod finally called out, in case Faith was hiding in a closet, frying pan in hand, waiting to give it to the ballsy burglar who was busy fixing himself a snack before heading upstairs to raid the jewelry box.

'Hey there, honey,' he said with a smile as he came into the bedroom eating a Yodel a few minutes later. He walked over to the bed and kissed the top of her head.

'Hi, yourself,' she replied, muting the TV. 'It's almost eleven. You've had a long day.'

'Did you get my text?'

She nodded.

'We wrapped twenty minutes ago.'

'Did they settle?'

He nodded. 'The wife broke. She was what was holding everything up. She wanted the beach condo in Hollywood and my client didn't want to let it go. But money always talks; he stroked Mrs Valez *numero uno* a check for three hundred thousand, signed over the house and half the pension, and that was it.'

'Oh,' she replied softly. 'Is there a number two waiting in the wings?'

'We'll see,' Jarrod answered charily, realizing too late that he had walked into the wrong neighborhood. He was a divorce attorney with a practice that thrived on the break-up of relationships and sometimes he forgot how his flippant comments could sting. 'How was your day?' he asked, stripping off his tie, trying his best to turn around and get out of the conversation.

'It was OK. How many years was this one?'

'Sixteen. No kids, though.'

She nodded absently, watching TV that had no sound. Faith had often wondered if there was a number in marriage that a couple could make it to where they were finally safe from divorce. A buoy to swim for. Ten? Twenty? Fifty years? After Jarrod left the PD's office for what was supposed to be the civil practice of family law, she realized that no number was magical, no marriage was safe, and that there was nothing civil about divorce: when someone wanted out, they could be as emotionally ruthless and cold as the gun-toting stranger who wanted your watch. Before Jarrod began to dismember relationships for a living, Faith was a much more romantic person, a naïve person, believing in forever and always. She used to think that she and Jarrod would be different from other couples, that they wouldn't have to rally back from the stresses that put more than 50 per cent of marriages under because they wouldn't put themselves in a position that required a rally. She used to think that if she just observed her vows, if she did all the things she promised she would, that one person alone could hold the whole marriage together. When his intern, Sandra, called crying and distraught last year, two days after the firm's Christmas party, she'd guilelessly thought it was a wrong number, that Sandra had somehow

86

dialed her boss's house by mistake – maybe a butt dial or she had hit the wrong name in her contacts. She kept telling her to calm down and speak slowly, even soothingly calling her 'honey' because she was having a tough time understanding what the girl was saying, which turned out to be quite true – she had a tough time understanding how her husband could sleep with his twenty-four-year-old law school intern when everything about their marriage had looked and felt perfect to her. It was like living on a sinkhole – the ground had given way that morning without warning, and in a five-minute conversation it had swallowed life as she knew it whole. There was no proverbial crack in the dam, no pre-existing, marriage-threatening conditions that were exploited by a sexy intern on a mission to snag herself an associate's position and maybe a husband of her own. Even Jarrod couldn't offer an explanation for why he'd cheated – only an apology. He kept promising her their buoy was still out there, somewhere, but she couldn't see it.

'We're good,' Jarrod said kissing her on the head again. 'No worries.'

She nodded. 'Are you hungry?'

'I had something downstairs. I see you went to Pasquale's.'

'I picked up a stuffed shell for you. Maggie had ice cream.'

Jarrod shook his head and went into the closet to change. Ice cream for dinner usually meant a red-light day.

The news at eleven started and she turned on the volume as the comely anchor excitedly started to list the night's upcoming top stories. The Explorer was back parked in the garage, the laundry was cleaned and put away, and UPS would be delivering her cell and her purse by 10:30 the next morning. This was it – the last newscast of the day to assure her that everything not only looked like it had yesterday before she had left for her sister's, but that everything was actually OK.

'A fiery crash on I95 kills three people on their way home

from a Christian retreat and shuts down lanes on I95. We also have a breaking story that is coming to us live out of Loxahatchee. The body of a young woman has been found in a canal in western Palm Beach County . . .'

Faith sat up. So did every hair on her body. Her heart clenched.

'So how was Maggie today?' Jarrod was back, standing in front of her and blocking the television while he removed his cufflinks. 'Do I want to ask?'

'Red light.'

'I figured.'

Behind him, the anchor started talking about the doomed retreat.

'What happened?' Jarrod asked.

'She ran outside of the classroom; shoved a girl; wouldn't stay in time-out – take your pick.'

He frowned and blew out a measured breath. 'Did you call Dr Michelson?'

'We're seeing him Thursday.'

'The therapy's not working.'

'I wouldn't say that; it takes time.'

'If medicine will make her better . . .' he started.

'Not till she's seven.'

'What is with that number, Faith?'

They'd had this conversation before. He knew her answer, but continued to ask the question, hoping she'd come around. Hoping that, as she saw Maggie fall behind academically and socially and watched her emotional outbursts grow worse, she'd ease up on the anti-drug stance. While Jarrod was well intentioned in his belief that medicating Maggie would help her be like the other kids, there was no guarantee it would. No one knew exactly what was wrong with her yet, much less how to fix her.

'Her brain is still developing and she hasn't even been officially diagnosed with ADD. Putting her on psychotropic drugs right now to chill her out would be to make life easier for us, not her.'

'You took psych back in college, Faith. Medicines are always being tweaked and improved; maybe things have changed.'

'Her issues are difficult for the people who have to work with her all day long, so you don't have to worry about it. I didn't complain about my day or hers; I simply told you what happened.' She tried not to sound abrupt.

'They'll ask her to leave St Andrews. That one was a favor.'

'Then we'll leave.'

He sighed and walked into the bathroom. She had won. Again. It didn't make her feel good.

She watched him go. Since the affair, he gave in to her on most everything, especially on matters that concerned what was best for Maggie. Other men might buy their wives expensive jewelry or a car to say they were sorry for cheating. Her present was control. And an acquiescent husband.

'So how was your sister? What happened last night?' Jarrod called out from the bathroom, trying on a new subject.

Her stomach flip-flopped. She'd rather debate how best to treat Maggie's emotional issues. But before she could answer, the anchor was back on TV, struggling to contain a mega-watt smile behind a concerned frown, all set to deliver the tragic, breaking news coming out of a wetlands preserve in western Palm Beach County.

16

A field reporter in a yellow rain slicker stood before a cluster of flashing police cruisers. 'Trudi, I'm at the Grassy Waters Preserve, a nature preserve and park in West Palm Beach, where a few hours ago a couple out walking one of the nature trails made a grisly discovery. The nude body of a woman was found in the water, right off this path behind me. Because of the tropical storm, the Preserve didn't have many visitors over the weekend, and that might be a blessing, as it could have been a child who made this discovery. Police have confirmed that the body is that of eighteen-year-old Desiree Jenners of Wellington, who was reported missing Saturday night by her family. Detectives are not releasing details on the cause of death, other than to say that the body had been in the canal less than a day, and that this is, in fact, a homicide investigation.'

Faith clenched the sheets beside her.

'Desiree was last seen leaving the Wal-Mart where she worked with a white male believed to be her ex-boyfriend, Owen Walsh. Detectives with the Palm Beach Sheriff's Office are asking the public for help in locating Walsh, who has an extensive criminal record and an outstanding warrant out of Miami-Dade County. If you have any information about the disappearance of Desiree Jenners or the whereabouts of twenty-five-year-old Owen Walsh, please contact the Palm Beach Sheriff's Office.'

It was like watching a horror movie: she wanted to throw the covers over her head so she wouldn't have to see what she knew was coming next. But she had to know. She had to. She twisted the sheets around and around her wrists, so that they bound her to the bed.

The split-screen picture of a smiling Asian girl and her dog and the mug shot of a stocky, brooding redhead appeared on the screen then with the names DESIREE JENNERS and OWEN WALSH. Faith exhaled and fell back into the pillows. The emotional roller coaster had recovered from another drop. But as quickly as it had come on, the feeling of relief was palliated by the realization that she'd been checking Internet newsfeeds all day and had seen nothing about any missing girls in Florida. Nothing at all. Not even the mention of this girl Desiree, who had apparently gone missing for several days before her body was found.

Were all missing people reported missing? And did all persons who were reported missing make it on the news? She knew the answer: obviously not. Just as every crime didn't make the news, neither did a report on every person who didn't come home. Newscasts would be two hours long and newspapers would be a lot thicker.

If pretty, unimportant Desiree Jenners from the upscale town of Wellington didn't make the news when she went missing, why would the disappearance of a tattooed, pierced, probable drug addict raise eyebrows? The answer was, it likely wouldn't. Ignorantly believing no news was good news, Faith had kept wishing all day long for tomorrow to get here so that she could know for sure that the stranger from last night was fine.

The smiling anchor was back, along with the weatherman who wanted to talk about the beautiful weather pattern that was finally moving into South Florida. Faith watched as he and the anchor chatted cozily about what they would be doing outside with all this newfound sunshine. Now she understood that no news was simply that – no news. It didn't mean the girl from last night was safe; it didn't mean she wasn't. What it meant was that Faith would probably never know what had happened to her.

Jarrod walked out of the bathroom at that moment and she unwrapped her sweaty hands from the tangle of sheets and turned off the TV and her bedside light.

She'd never know who the girl was, or where she came from, or why she was out there, barefoot and limping in the rain with those men.

17

'So was Charity surprised?' Jarrod asked as he turned off his light and climbed into bed.

Faith nodded somberly, her thoughts still on Desiree's smiling face alongside that of the man who had likely murdered her and left her body to rot in the water. 'Yes,' she answered softly.

'Why'd you come home last night? Everything OK?'

She could tell by the hesitant yet cheery way he'd asked the question what he was really worried about – that she'd maybe popped back without warning to see if he was home alone. That she still didn't trust him after all these months.

'Charity and I had words so I left.'

'A fight?'

'No, just words. She was all smushy with Nick and that was hard to watch, considering what an ass he's been to her. There was no room at the inn, anyway: T-Bone and Gator and God knows who else were camping out on the couch; I wasn't in the mood for a slumber party. And I had things to do at the bakery.'

She'd decided not to bare her soul about the argument with her sister. She didn't want Jarrod throwing verbal darts at her for the next however-many Christmases they were together. She'd navigate the relationship with Charity by herself.

'Have you talked to her today?'

'We texted.'

'Everything all right?'

'It will be.'

She didn't want to talk or explain any more tonight. She'd relived it too many times in her head already. She just wanted the day to be over. Octavius was gone, but the breezy weather remained. Through the crack in the drapes, a sliver of light shone on the ceiling. She watched the shadows of the palm fronds dance about, writhing in the wind. She could hear them rustling outside her window. It reminded her of the cane stalks and she shut her eyes and rolled over on her side.

'Was everybody drunk at this party?' Jarrod asked quietly.

He was a skilled litigator, ensnaring many a witness with his cleverly worded questions. She knew where he was going, what he was really trying to ask. 'No,' she replied simply.

He moved closer to her in the bed, wrapping his arms around her cozily, spooning her body. He was only wearing underwear. He kissed the back of her neck. 'I missed you last night,' he said softly. His warm hands rubbed her outer thigh, pushing her nightie up, feeling the curve of her hip and the softness of her waist. His fingers delicately traced a line from her belly button up to the fold of skin underneath her breasts, then back down again. Up, and back down. Each time his fingers ventured a little bit further in each direction, tugging at her panties, sliding them down inch-by-inch off her hips.

Before Sandra, she loved having sex with Jarrod. When he looked at her a certain way, with his head cocked, his piercing green eyes saying things she once thought were only meant for her to understand, he could make her wet from across a crowded room. He was mischievously handsome, with tousled sandy-blond curls to go with those magnetic eyes, defined cheekbones, a boyish, broad grin. Physically he hadn't changed much from the days of playing college base-ball: he still had the V-shaped body of an athlete, his muscular chest hairless and cut in all the right places. He ran several times a week and went to the gym. But it was his sultry, smooth charm that Faith had always found made him even more attractive – the appetizer to the physical entrée. It was an *honest* charm – he made friends easily and won over juries because he was the successful, handsome and all-around great guy that most people couldn't believe they had the incredibly good fortune of being friends with. He could be sexy on a phone without trying when he was asking what her plans were for dinner. He could make her do things in bed she shouldn't want to do.

They were supposed to be OK after the affair. It was out in the open. It was over. It was a mistake. It was time to move on and get back to where they'd been. And that included making love with the passion and intensity and frequency that they used to.

Her panties were off now. His hand had moved up over her breast, cupping it in his hand, his fingers caressing her erect nipple as his tongue found her ear. She could feel his penis through his underwear, hard against her naked buttocks. He gently flipped her over on her back and climbed on top of her, his mouth finding her breasts as his hand slipped between her thighs.

Her body still wanted him. When he touched her, physically she still responded. The problem was her brain – it couldn't seem to get past the betrayal and her own stupidity in not seeing it coming long before the dirty details of his three-month affair were divulged to her on the phone by his lover. She hoped that would happen in a matter of time, that the brain and body would reconcile on the same sexual plane that they used to exist on. She hoped that in time, if she physically forced it, she would love him the way she used to. She knew that other women in the same situation withheld sex as a form of punishment, but when she had made the decision to stay in the marriage she had also decided that wouldn't be her. She wouldn't be a bitter wife waiting to passively-aggressively express her anger in the bedroom. She would, in fact, be the opposite. She would do what he wanted when he wanted sexually to show him what a great wife she was, what a great wife she always was, what he had almost lost forever when he screwed that bitch. Her body was the compliant traitor. In the meantime, her brain could go somewhere else for twenty minutes.

She grabbed the curls on both sides of his head with her hands and pulled him up off her breasts, pulling his face close to hers, holding it inches from her own. She couldn't see his eyes in the dark, if he was watching hers or if they were closed. She wondered if he ever wondered what she was thinking. She felt his warm breath on her skin, his lips parted, his mouth waiting for her to make the next move.

'I love you,' he said then.

The grandfather clock began to chime downstairs. Tomorrow was finally here.

She pulled his head down, putting his mouth to hers and silencing him, as her body arched into his, like it had done so many times before.

18

Two weeks later Nick was out.

Actually, since the bank had initiated foreclosure proceedings and no one had done anything to stop them, eviction was imminent, so Charity and the kids were out, too. Charity, however, didn't want to be out with her husband. According to the order of protection, she didn't want to be within five hundred feet of Nicholas Lavecki.

He'd hit her. She'd hit him first, but he'd hit her back, and that's what finally did it. After a night out drinking with the Nicknames, Nick had passed out on the futon and Charity had gone through his cell, something she probably should've done months, even years, before. Nick didn't lock his phone or try to hide it; she'd never looked because she didn't want to see for herself what everyone else knew was going on.

While Nick was passed out, Charity cleaned house. She read the texts from the multiple women and saw the pictures. Then she went looking and found the gambling chits in his sock drawer, and the credit card statements from the Visa card she never knew he had – most of the charges were made at bars and strip clubs. They were drowning in debt.

When he came to, she had out the Louisville Slugger. She'd finished off a bottle of wine herself. She got in one round, and then Big Mitts got in his. Kamilla called the cops. Both of them went to jail – which is where Charity had called her from. It was the first time they had spoken since the birthday party. Charity got out first, thanks to Faith, who'd wired the bond money. And Charity got the first restraining order, thanks to Faith who'd hired the defense attorney. When she got back home from the hearing she saw the Notice of Eviction taped to her front door. That's when she found out she was going to be homeless.

Her sister was in no state to put her life back together. All she could do was cry and count down the days she had left in the duplex while her three kids tried to figure out what to do about dinner.

Numerous times over the years Faith had asked Charity to come stay with her, but that was not an option now, for a number of reasons. In order for Charity to successfully break away from Nick and her life in Sebring she needed a long-term plan, not a short-term solution. Emotionally she was weak: Nick had gutted her self-esteem, so that she was unable to see a future without someone in it supporting her – that someone being him. So from the moment she stepped away from her old life she had to be invested in her future – emotionally, physically, and financially – not camping out on her sister's couch, irritating her brother-in-law, wallowing in self-pity, biding time till Nick came calling. She needed her own life and she needed to see she could be successful at running it. With Vivian's help, Faith found a modest, three-bedroom apartment in Coral Springs near the bakery and within walking distance of the middle and elementary schools. Their mom agreed to give Charity her old Jetta, as the bank was going to repossess Charity's mini-van once they found it. She set Charity up to work at Sweet Sisters when the kids were in school, and found a low-cost daycare down the street from the bakery for the little one.

And she footed the bill for it all, on the understanding that

Charity would be responsible for at least a portion of her monthly bills until she got on her feet, however long that took. All she had left to do was physically get her sister down to South Florida before Nick came back around. The day after wiring the bail money, she drove to Sebring, rented a small U-Haul and in a single morning she and Kamilla packed up the kitchen, the kids' stuff, and Charity's closet, loaded everything in the U-Haul, and headed back down to Coral Springs, with Charity following right behind her. She took the Turnpike up and back, avoiding 441 and the rural back roads. With any luck, she would never have to drive on them ever again.

Faith was a month shy of her nineteenth birthday when she'd left home for college. She had never returned. Oh, she'd gone back for Thanksgiving and Christmas and summer breaks, but she never boomeranged back to the nest after graduation, like most of her friends had. But when she'd walked out the door of her childhood home in Miami Shores that sweltering August morning in 2001, she had no idea that she wouldn't be back. She probably wouldn't have left if she had, because the thought of leaving her home and her family forever would have been too overwhelming; even though she was aching for independence at that age, she was still a homebody. On that day Charity was sitting at the breakfast bar in sweatpants and a Nirvana T-shirt eating a bowl of Captain Crunch, watching Faith load the car. Their mom couldn't get off work, so Vivian's parents were taking them both up to UF. Once the last bag had been thrown in the trunk and she'd reclaimed her favorite jeans from the back of Charity's closet, she'd returned to the kitchen, patted her sister down for anything else of hers that she might've tried to 'borrow', kissed her goodbye, and . . . that was it. There was no fanfare. No mopey tears or drawn-out clutching, lamenting when the two of them would be together again. She'd just driven off, hand waving out the window, watching in the side-view mirror as her house and her mother and her sister got smaller, never understanding at the time how nothing would ever be the same. Because she had no idea she wouldn't be back. She was looking forward to the future, not missing the past as it waved goodbye to her.

Now here was Charity, back in her rearview, behind her in the U-Haul, a sullen Kamilla beside her in the passenger seat, staring out the window. Torn from her home and her friends without notice, it might be years before Kammy smiled again. Faith couldn't see the tears rolling down Charity's face – just as she couldn't that day she'd left for college – but she knew they were there. Because unlike Faith – who, when she'd left, had always thought she would return home – Charity knew she wouldn't. This part of her life was over.

'I'm hungry, Aunt Faif,' said a small voice in the back seat. It was her niece, Kaelyn, who'd been so quiet, Faith had almost forgotten she was in the car. Strapped in another car seat beside her was a sleeping Kourtney – or 'Mistake', as Big Mitts liked to affectionately call her. Charity called her Boppy.

'Hey there, sugar,' Faith said into the rearview. 'I was thinking that I need to get gas. Did you have any lunch?'

Kaelyn shook her head.

'Then let's get you and Boppy something to eat. I bet Mommy and Kammy are hungry, too. How about a burger? Do you like McDonald's?' Crazy question. Charity wasn't much of a cook. Her idea of a balanced diet was Burger King for lunch and McDonald's for dinner. She followed a semi off the Turnpike and into a Shell station.

Kaelyn nodded. The little girl was so polite and sweet. Just about the same age as Maggie, they were buddies whenever they got together. Her front teeth were missing, and she had chubby, freckled cheeks and a mop of light brown hair that ran halfway down her back. Unfortunately, she looked a lot like her father.

'All right. Let's gas up first and then we'll grab some grub.'

'I don't want that. I want a burger,' Mini-Mitts said softly. 'Please.'

Faith smiled. 'Grub is another word for food. Aunt Faith was trying to be funny.'

'Oh,' replied Kaelyn, rubbing her nose. And obviously Aunt Faith wasn't succeeding.

Faith pulled the Explorer alongside a pump and Charity pulled the U-Haul in behind her. 'Let's gas up and then get the kids some food, OK?' Faith said, walking up to Charity's open window. 'Boppy's still asleep. Will she get up soon?'

'Not if you keep driving,' Charity replied absently. Now Faith could see the tear streaks and the swollen, bloodshot eyes.

'You OK?'

Charity nodded.

'Well, I saw a sign for a McDonald's up ahead. I know the kids didn't have lunch. Viv is stocking your fridge at the apartment, so you'll have stuff for the morning. We can grab a pizza tonight. I doubt anybody wants to cook.'

She nodded again. 'Whatever. I'm not hungry.'

Faith squeezed her sister's hand. 'It's not an ending, it's a beginning.'

Charity wiped away another tear as it slipped down her cheek. 'Thanks.'

'How's Kammy doing?' Faith asked. 'Kammy, are you doing OK?'

Kamilla didn't reply and Charity rolled her eyes. Faith was happy she wasn't in that car.

She gassed up both cars and headed into the station. On her way in, she held the door open for an old guy in a battered coat and high-top sneakers. She could smell the beer as he passed. 'Watch out,' he mumbled angrily as he shuffled past. She wasn't sure whom he was talking to. Then he turned around.

101

'They know what you did!' he yelled at her. Bits of spittle sprayed the air.

'Excuse me?' she asked, taken aback. She still didn't know who he was talking to.

He squinted at her. 'You better run, young lady. Better get in that car of yours and get the hell out of here!' He sniffed at the air and nodded his head, as if there were a person standing beside him. He lowered his voice to almost a whisper. 'Your fear gives you away; I can smell it. You stink of nasty secrets!'

'Skipper . . .' yelled the clerk from across the store. 'Come on. Leave the lady alone.'

'When you give them the pound of flesh they come for, it's gonna hurt.'

Faith shook her head as the man stumbled out, still mumbling. 'Everybody pays. We all pay. Can't get out of paying when the devil wants his due . . .'

She watched through the glass doors as he made his way across the lot, muttering to himself and gesticulating as if he was in a heated argument with someone right beside him. She wanted to make sure he didn't walk over to the cars.

'Don't listen to him,' said the clerk. 'He's an old, sick geezer. Drinks too much. I think he's got something mentally wrong with him. Comes around all the time, telling us how we need to be preparing for the end of days. He's harmless – really.'

Faith nodded uneasily. She picked up a pack of gum and a couple of candy bars for the kids, searching through her purse for her wallet as she walked to the counter. 'I need a pack of Marlboro Lights, too. I'm on pumps five and six,' she said as she dug out her AMEX card. 'The U-Haul and the black—'

When she looked up to hand her card to the clerk, she froze. Everything – her hand, her words, her thoughts. Everything stopped in its tracks. She stared at the poster behind the clerk's head.

'We don't take American Express. Do you have another card?'

Faith looked at him blankly. She didn't understand what he'd said. Not a word. Her knees began to shake.

'Another card?' he asked, pointing at the AMEX in Faith's still-outstretched hand. 'Do you have another card, ma'am?'

It was a handmade poster, like one you might see stapled to a telephone pole or a tree, advertising a garage sale or a found cat. But it wasn't anything as innocuous as that. On this poster was a smiling photo of a girl with dark brown eyes and long, dark hair.

'Do you want to pay with cash?'

On her neck was a tattoo of a pink heart wrapped in chains.

'Ma'am? Hello there? I can't take this card. I told you.'

It was not just any girl. It was not just any poster.

Handwritten in block lettering above the smiling face of the girl who had asked for her help weeks ago in the rain was the word **MISSING**.

19

She had finally stopped thinking about that night. After checking the papers and Internet for days and finding nothing, she'd figured everything was OK, that there was no need to keep worrying.

'Who is that girl?' Faith asked the clerk hesitantly.

'Huh?'

'That girl. The one in the poster,' she managed, pointing. 'The one behind you. Who is she?'

The clerk looked behind him, as if seeing the poster for the first time himself. 'Um, I don't really know. I mean, I don't know her personally. I've seen her before, in here. Her mom lives around here, I think. She works at the Animal. Not her mom, you know, but Angel.'

MISSING
Angelina 'Angel' Santri, 19
5'3, 110 pounds
Missing since Friday, October 17

'The Animal? What is that?'

'Animal Instincts. It's a club, you know? Like a gentlemen's club?' He chuckled because she kept staring at him. 'It's a strip club. She's a dancer there. Her mom, I think, asked my boss if she could put it up. The lady might've worked here once – not Angel, but her mom. Worked the register, ya know?'

Faith shook her head. *No, I don't know!* she wanted to yell at him. She stared at the poster: *Missing since Friday, October 17.* The weekend of Charity's birthday party.

'You know her?' the clerk asked.

'No, no . . .' she replied quickly. 'I don't know her.'

He pulled the poster off the wall. 'You sure? Want to look at it?'

'No.' She stepped back from the counter. 'She looks like my friend's kid. That's what I was thinking, but it's, ah, it's not her.'

He thrust it at her. Like a timid animal, she slowly approached his outstretched hand, her eyes catching on the handwritten words on the bottom of the poster.

Our sweet Angelina was last seen at the club Animal Instincts on Friday, October 17. Angel is the loving mother to 2-year-old Ginger, who misses her mama more than anything and wants her to come home! She was last seen wearing jeans, a white T-shirt, a black hooded jacket and black boots. She has a tattoo on her neck of a heart in chains, blue stars on her arm, and a snake around her left ankle. If you have any information about our Angel, please call

407-669-4322. $REWARD$ OFFERED

'We don't take American Express, so, ah, do you have another card?' he tried again while she was reading, a slight edge of impatience to his voice. 'If you need to use the ATM, it's over there.'

Faith nodded, laid the poster on the counter and put her purse down on top of it. With trembling fingers she dug through her wallet. Receipts, business cards and pictures spilled onto the counter and the floor before she finally found her Visa card.

'What's taking so long?' Charity asked in her ear. Faith jumped, knocking over a display of gum. A dozen packs of Trident spilled on the floor. The clerk sighed heavily.

'Jesus Christ, Charity! You scared me. I'm just paying,' she said, bending down to pick up the gum and her receipts.

'I scared you? Who'd you think I was?'

'I don't know, I . . . there was a man at the door who said something,' she started to say.

Your fear gives you away. You stink of nasty secrets.

'I'm a little . . . I had to get him another card, is all.'

The girl's face flashed in her head, staring at her outside her window. She saw her say the words *Help Me! He's coming!* Her cracked lips touching the glass, the streaks of dark eyeliner running down her cheeks.

'Why? Is everything OK with your card?' Charity asked.

The clerk handed Faith her receipt. She signed it quickly. 'Yes, it's fine.' She had to get out of the store; it was hard to breathe. It was hard to think. She shoved the gum packs back into the display box and grabbed her purse.

'Who's that?' Charity asked, pointing at the missing poster on the counter.

'No one . . . she's . . . it's no one,' Faith replied dismissively as she headed for the door.

'Oh . . .' said Charity, following her.

'She's not nobody, that's not right,' Faith said as she pushed open the door, holding it for Charity. 'She's a girl who is missing. I, ah, I was just looking at the poster. The guy was showing me the poster. I thought she looked familiar, but . . .' her babbling tapered off as they walked back to the cars.

'How would you know anyone from . . .?' Charity looked around the parking lot. 'Where the hell are we, anyway?' Besides the Shell station, there was nothing else around.

106

'I don't know. I don't know where we are,' Faith replied. She ran her hands through her hair. Her thoughts were racing. It was all she could do to keep it together. She had to get home. She had to think. Think about her next move. *What should she do? What should she do?*

Charity laughed wryly. 'I'll tell you where we are, sis,' she said, putting an arm around Faith's shoulders. 'Bumfuck. Isn't that what your husband calls nowhere? How the hell would you know a girl that's gone missing from the middle of nowhere?'

20

Faith woke up the next morning with the sun in her eyes. The curtains were open. There was an egret perched on her balcony with a powder-blue sky and wispy white clouds as a backdrop.

She arched her neck to get a look at the clock and fell back into the pillows: it was almost eight o'clock. Downstairs, Jarrod was telling Maggie to hurry up. She smelled brewed coffee wafting up from the kitchen. On her nightstand was a mug, a banana, and a bottle of Tylenol. She touched the mug. It was cold.

For a brief second, everything seemed OK. Then it all came barreling into her mind, sabotaging the deceptively beautiful day outside. She closed her eyes and lay there for a few minutes.

'Let's go, Maggie,' Jarrod was saying. 'Stop watching TV and help me find your backpack, please.'

'Where's Mommy?'

'Sleeping. We have to go; I have court. And I have a very important phone call I have to take.'

'I want Mommy to take me.'

'I don't think Mommy is feeling well this morning; she was up very late with Aunt Charity.' He sounded annoyed. 'We gotta go, sweetheart. Damn it – where are your shoes?'

The house banged and clanked as plates hit the sink and doors opened and closed in the search for Maggie's shoes and backpack. Maggie whined; Jarrod groused. Finally she heard the chirp of the door alarm sound and the house fell quiet. After a few more minutes Faith sat up, popped two Tylenol and downed them with the cold coffee. God, her head freaking throbbed.

Yesterday she'd dropped off Charity at the new apartment, and that took longer than she'd thought it would. The keys weren't there and they'd had to wait for the property manager. Then Vivian had come over with Maggie and Lyle to see Charity, and the kids were all playing and everyone was talking. They'd ordered pizza and opened a bottle of wine. That led to another bottle or two. When she'd finally gotten home, it was past nine and she had to put Maggie to bed, then Jarrod had come home and . . . well, there was no time. She'd run out of time to make the phone call.

She got dressed and texted Vivian that she wouldn't be in till later on in the morning, maybe after lunch. Then she grabbed a notepad and a pen from the office and a basket of dirty laundry. She'd put in a load, make a fresh pot of coffee, sit down with her pen and paper at the breakfast bar and make that call to the police. She could even drive up to the department if she had to, to make the report, if they wanted her to. She headed downstairs. *OK. What department? Where was she yesterday when she saw that poster?* Nowhere. Bumfuck, Charity had sarcastically called it. She tried to remember the exit off of the Turnpike. She'd have to Google the Animal nightclub where that girl Angelina worked, was all. Then she'd call the police in that town and ask to speak to missing persons.

She heard the sound of the TV in the family room as she hit the second landing. Jarrod must have forgotten to turn it off.

'. . . still developing. Palm Beach detectives aren't releasing much information, except to say that the body was in fairly advanced state of decomposition. The young mother and aspiring artist had been reported missing two weeks ago by her family . . .'

Faith stopped suddenly on the stairs, laundry basket in hand. She leaned against the wall. She couldn't see the TV; she could only hear it. The family room was off the kitchen. Although the volume was low, the horrible words the reporter was saying echoed off the cathedral ceilings as though he were broadcasting with a bullhorn – at least that's how she heard them. Her heart started to race and she tried to tell herself not to jump to conclusions, not to think the worst, even though she knew that the worst was already happening.

'. . . after she failed to come home from work as a dancer at a nightclub in West Palm . . .'

She put the basket down and tried to cover her ears. Her shaking legs advised her to run. *Get out before everything changes! Leave before they say her name!* She frantically looked around the living room below for an escape route, as if that were really an option.

But there was to be no escape. Not from any of this. She thought of the creepy encounter with the man in the gas station and his prophetic Doomsday admonition: *Everybody pays. Can't get out of paying when the devil wants his due . . .*

She felt the life drain from her legs and she slumped against the pretty faux-painted wall, trapped right where she was as the reporter prattled on about the horror of it all.

21

The day her father died was also beautiful.

It was a Saturday. Faith woke up that May morning and looked at a cloudless, cobalt blue sky and thought: 'Beach day!' She was seventeen, summer was weeks away, she'd landed a job at Abercrombie and Fitch, and the boy she'd privately adored had asked her to the movies that night. Then her mother called and told her to take Charity and drive to the hospital and meet her there. Her father was having chest pains and had driven himself to Baptist. Faith got into the car, forgot how to back up, and took out the quarter panel on a mailbox. She cursed the sun because it was too bright and she couldn't see.

When the doctor came out of the ER treatment bay she knew what he was going to say. Perhaps it was the terribly uncomfortable look on his face that gave it away, or the slow shake of his head when his eyes met her mother's in the waiting room as he walked toward the three of them. Faith just knew. She wanted to stop time then. Just stop it, like a witch in a movie could cast a spell to suspend people in a moment. Because once the doctor opened his mouth and actually uttered the words, 'I'm sorry, but we did all we could,' there'd be no going back. It would be real. There would be no return to when everything was OK and life was normal. Faith divided memories into two categories after that moment: Life Before and Life After.

Now she sat on her stairs, not wanting *this* moment to end – when she could still believe that everything was going to be OK because she didn't know for sure that it wouldn't be. Relishing the fleeting final seconds of Life Before. Like that moment in the hospital, she really wasn't prepared for what was coming, even though she knew what that doctor was going to say when he opened his mouth. And no matter how many times since Charity's birthday party she might've tried to imagine the worst-case scenario about what had happened to the dark-haired girl in the rain, her brain couldn't imagine . . . this.

The door alarm chirped off the garage. 'OK, I'm done with my phone call,' Jarrod called out. 'Did you find your shoes, Maggie? Were they upstairs?'

Faith froze.

'. . . detectives are trying to piece together her last hours . . .'

Jarrod sighed as he walked into the family room. 'Did you even look for your shoes?'

'Daddy . . .' Maggie said softly. She was in the family room. *Maggie was in the family room.*

'And you shouldn't be watching this crap; the news is never good. I have to be in court, honey. So let's find those shoes of yours—'

'Daddy, I know who that lady is.'

'What lady?'

The reporter continued: '. . . again, they have just released her name. She has been identified as nineteen-year-old Angelina Santri . . .'

'Her,' answered Maggie.

Her legs weren't strong enough to run, so Faith tried to crawl back up the stairs, back to her bedroom. The doctor was coming out of the treatment bay. He was taking off his latex gloves. She heard them snap against his skin. She smelled

112

the odor of hospital disinfectant. He was shaking his head. *Don't say it, Doctor! Don't change everything!*

'The lady on the news?' The irritation was gone from Jarrod's voice. It had been replaced with confusion. 'That lady? Her? You know her?'

'Yes.'

The laundry basket slipped down the beige carpeted stairs. *Bumpity, bumpity, bump.*

'How do you know her?' Jarrod asked.

'That's the lady mommy wouldn't help,' Maggie answered softly.

PART TWO

The most ominous of fallacies – the belief that things can be kept static by inaction.

> Freya Starke, *Dust in the Lion's Paw: Autobiography 1939–1946*

22

Jarrod heard a thud. He looked over to see the laundry basket toppled by the foot of the stairs, dirty laundry splayed all over the wood floor. He knew that Faith was there, somewhere, listening. He turned back to Maggie. He felt as if someone had punched him hard in the stomach, but he could still breathe and the pain hadn't set in yet. He looked back at Maggie. 'What? What did you say?' The question rushed out of his mouth.

Maggie looked anxiously over at the pile. 'The lady wanted Mommy to help her, but she wouldn't open the door.' Her thumb went to her mouth.

He turned to watch the TV. The caption under the photo of a smiling young woman with dark hair and dark eyes and a neck tattoo said ANOTHER MURDER IN THE CANE FIELDS. 'What do you mean? I'm not getting you, honey. Take that thumb out of your mouth and tell me what happened.' He gently pulled her thumb away.

'There was a mean man there. He was waiting for her outside. He wanted to hurt the lady, but Mommy wouldn't open the door.'

'What door? The door to the house? Here?'

'No, Daddy. The *caaarrr dooooorrr*,' she replied dragging out the word.

'The car door . . .' he repeated, his voice trailing off.

'The lady was scared. Then the mean man took her away and she was crying.'

'Who was crying? Mommy?'

Maggie lowered her voice to a whisper. 'The lady.' She started to pick at the white balls on her reindeer dress. 'I felt bad 'cause she was sad. I don't want Mommy to get mad again . . .' her voice trailed off.

Jarrod knelt down next to her and put his hands on her delicate shoulders that already looked like they bore the weight of the world. 'Mommy's not going to get mad, Maggie. No one's going to get mad. When did this happen, honey? Can you remember?'

Maggie shook her head.

'Tell Daddy. Don't worry about Mommy; she's fine. She's upstairs. Tell me what you saw. Tell me when this happened.'

'Aunt Charity's birthday.'

'When you drove up with Mommy to see Aunt Charity for her surprise party?'

She nodded.

'When did this happen, when you were driving to Aunt Charity's or back home at night?'

'Night.' Her bottom lip ballooned out. 'It was dark and I was scared.'

'Was this after you got mad and kicked the seat?'

She nodded again. The lip was quivering.

Maggie had her issues. She had problems in school but that was because she wouldn't keep her ass in the chair and listen, not because she wasn't smart. Was she defiant? Yes. Emotional? Yup. Hyperactive? That was what his money was on. But with all of her challenges, Jarrod knew lying was not one of them. She could tell tall tales sometimes, though. She was only four and young kids saw things differently than adults did. So what was fantasy and what was reality? Was this story she was telling him pieced together in her brain

118

from movies she'd watched? Stories she'd heard? Video games she'd played? Maybe she'd seen this girl's face in the paper or on the news before? He rubbed his chin. Faith had never mentioned anything like this to him.

'Maggie, you need to be very clear. The lady on the news – you're sure *that* was the lady you saw that night coming home from Aunt Charity's? You're positive?'

She nodded.

'And she asked Mommy to help her? You're sure?'

'Yes. She banged on the window, Daddy. She was all wet, 'cause it was raining out and I don't like thunder. But Mommy wouldn't open the door. She told the lady, "No!"'

'Then what happened?'

'Then the mean man came and he took the lady away and she looked sad.'

'What did Mommy do?'

'Nothing.' Maggie paused and looked down at the floor, as though she were ashamed to say it. 'She watched him take the lady away.'

'Did you say anything to Mommy?'

Maggie shook her head. Tears rolled down her cheeks now. 'The man told me not to.'

'Wait, wait, wait – you spoke to the man?' He wiped her apple cheeks with his big hands.

'He told me not to say anything,' Maggie replied, putting her finger to her lips and making the shush sound. 'He said to shush.'

Jarrod shook his head. He could feel the anger rising inside. A paternal, oversized anger at the idea that a strange man had frightened his daughter. 'Did he touch you? Did this man touch you, Maggie?' He was yelling now, but he couldn't help it.

She shook her head. 'He pointed his finger at me.'

'And what did Mommy do when the man told you to shush? When he pointed?'

'She drove away.'

'She left the lady there with the scary man?'

Maggie nodded. 'I'm sorry, Daddy.'

'You don't have anything to be sorry about.' Jarrod grabbed his daughter and hugged her tight, something he should have done a minute earlier. He dropped onto both knees, stroking her hair, inhaling the scent of her. He was overwhelmed by a sickening feeling that he was lucky to do this – like the man who misses the flight that he heard has crashed. 'I have to talk to Mommy about this,' he said into her shoulder.

Maggie shook her head. 'She's gonna get mad.'

'No, she won't. Did you talk to Mommy about what you saw? Does she know you saw the girl?'

Maggie shook her head and looked at the ground again. 'She'll be mad, like she was at that lady. Mommy made her cry 'cause she was mean and said no. She yelled at me to go to sleep and stop kicking. I didn't want her to get mad at me for being 'wake, so I closed my eyes and 'tended to be sleeping, but I was only 'tending.'

Jarrod felt his heart clench up. The punch to the gut had knocked the wind out of him, and now the pain was here and it was worse than what he was expecting. Whatever story Maggie was telling was not made up. Whatever it was she thought she saw *had* happened. And that scared the shit out of him. Because the story in and of itself was terrifying. And the ending . . . *Another murder in the cane fields.*

He ran his hand through his hair, trying to think clearly. Well, the ending was horrific. Perhaps the puzzle pieces were not fitting perfectly, perhaps Maggie had mixed some facts up, but it didn't matter – a picture was starting to form. A half-hour ago, he'd been frustrated about being late and thinking about court and the conference call he'd had to take out in the garage. Now everything seemed . . . trivial. Inconsequential. While he didn't know exactly what had happened that night, he did know that the pain from the invisible punch he'd just taken was going to be excruciating. He looked over at the dirty laundry, spilled emblematically all over the floor.

'I have to talk to Mommy,' he repeated.

Maggie shook her head defiantly. 'No!'

'Yes. I have to find out what happened.' He stood, picking Maggie up in his arms. She buried her face in his neck. 'Faith?' he called out, walking over to the living room. 'Faith, I gotta talk to you about something.' He rounded the corner, stepping over the blue jeans and towels that lay on the floor.

And there she was. Sitting on the second landing, leaning her head back against the wall. Like Maggie, she, too, was crying. They faced each other for what seemed an eternity and he knew for sure that this was gonna be bad. Really, really bad.

'Jarrod,' she said in a weak, small voice. 'We have to talk . . .'

23

'You think that if I got an artist to come in here, Maggie, you could tell him what the man looked like?' asked the super-sized homicide detective. Slumped shoulders, listless blue eyes, and a drawn, intense face betrayed his cheery inflection and contradicted the widely held belief that fat people were supposed to be jolly. Detective Bryan Nill looked like a man who had been on the job for a long time, even though he didn't look that old – late forties, if Faith had to guess. He looked like a man who had seen a lot of unpleasant things as a detective – and then had the frustrating bureaucracies of a police department to deal with at the end of a shift, which probably caused him more grief than the dead bodies he found and the killers he hunted.

Maggie looked at Jarrod, not Faith, as they sat around a conference table in an interview room at the Palm Beach Sheriff's Office, where they'd been for over an hour. It was the three of them and two homicide detectives: Nill, who was obviously the lead, and Tatiana Maldonado, a Latino in her early thirties with an exotically pretty face. Soft brown eyes betrayed the tough persona she tried to work.

'Do you think you can help the detectives draw a picture of the man, honey?' Jarrod asked.

Maggie nodded shyly, clutching her Eeyore.

'How well did you see the man? Because we don't want the police to draw the wrong picture,' Jarrod added.

'Excuse me, Mr Saunders,' broke in Nill, 'I know you used to be a defense attorney, but that's not your job here.'

'Sorry, Detective,' replied Jarrod tetchily. 'But she's my daughter and today my job is to make sure I protect her from being even more traumatized about this than she already is.'

Nill shook his head. 'No one wants to upset your daughter, Mr Saunders.' He looked over at Faith. 'Or your wife. They've both been through a traumatizing event, it sounds like. But, see, we don't even know what role this man played in what happened to Ms Santri – we just would like to find him and talk to him.'

'I can draw him, Daddy,' Maggie offered, picking up a notepad and a pen. She started to scribble something so intensely the pen tore into the paper.

Detective Nill chuckled. 'Why don't we leave the drawing to Officer Cuddy? He's pretty good at what he does. And if you don't remember something, like your daddy says, then that's OK. You tell Officer Cuddy you don't know.'

'He was skinny. And he had girl hair.' Her nose scrunched and her lip curled in distaste. 'And he was mean.'

Detective Nill nodded. 'Well, it looks like you're ready for Officer Cuddy. You'll like him. I'll get him in here so you two can become friends.' He looked over at Faith. 'And your mom, too. She's gonna help us with this drawing. It's gonna be a joint effort so we can get the best picture possible. Who's that on your dress now? Donner? Blitzen? Big Foot?'

'No! Rudolph!' Maggie squealed, delighted to have stumped an adult.

Nill smacked the side of his head. 'I should've known by the red nose. 'Course that's the exact color and shape of my pop's noggin. Could be him.'

Maggie frowned.

'I'm kidding, kiddo. A little bad humor. You must be getting excited for Christmas; you're sure into the spirit with that dress.'

But Maggie was off and running to try out the other chairs at the table, which had toys and games on it that Faith had brought from home. 'I want an American Girl doll,' Maggie said.

'And I want a Porsche,' Nill shot back as he lumbered over to the door. 'Hope Santa gives us both what we want. You are a ball of energy and the holidays ain't even here yet. Don't nobody give that kid sugar, Maldonado,' he called out to his partner as Maggie spun herself around on a chair, using the table to push off on. He stopped at the door and looked over at Faith again. 'You certainly got your hands full, Mrs Saunders. You'll be OK with this, right? You said you got a pretty good look at the guy yourself?'

Faith nodded.

'I'll have your daughter work with Cuddy first, then you. That way whatever you saw, you saw, and we don't taint what she saw. I'm sure you'll be able to give a better description than your four-year-old, but then again, your daughter seems pretty smart. We'll try and maybe find a mug shot off the sketch. Because Maggie's so young, I don't want to give her pictures of other men to look at before she works with the artist – that might influence her memory. Or at least, that's what the argument's gonna be, if and when we do find this guy. Nowadays ya gotta wear a lot of hats,' he said, pointing to his head. 'Ya gotta think like a lawyer. Those defense attorneys love it when we give them an opportunity for confusion later on. They jump all over that and mess up a perfectly good case – right, Mr Saunders?' He smiled before cracking his gum and walking out into the noise and bustle of a police station at midday.

The door closed behind him and all went quiet again. Maggie spun at the table, Detective Maldonado worked on paperwork and Jarrod stared straight ahead at nothing and no one, his fists clenched in front of him. Faith put her head in her hands. It was as unnervingly quiet as the hour-long car ride to the police station had been this morning . . .

24

Jarrod tried to wrap his mind around what Faith was saying. She was sobbing and it was hard to understand what she was telling him. Or perhaps it was because the story she was telling him was hard to understand.

'So you fall asleep in this town that you're not sure is really a town while you wait for this tropical storm to pass. The storm that closed airports for two days?'

'I was waiting for this rain band to pass, not the whole tropical storm, Jarrod. I fell asleep. Not for long, forty-five minutes, an hour . . . I don't know. When I woke up, she was standing there.' She ran her hands through her hair. 'You're treating me like one of your witnesses again. You're cross-examining me!'

'In the rain?' he asked.

'It had stopped raining.'

'What did she look like?'

'She had black hair and was all wet,' said Maggie.

'And tattoos,' Faith added. 'And piercings. In her nose and eyebrows. She was . . . I was scared. She looked crazed.'

Jarrod shook his head.

'It was one o'clock in the morning. I had my child in the

car. I had *Maggie* in the car. I had no idea where I was. What would you have done?'

'I like to think I would've opened the door.'

'Yeah, well, you're a man. You're not a woman, lost in some deserted, weird town in the middle of nowhere.'

He nodded. 'Exactly,' he said quietly.

'That's not fair,' she sobbed. 'It happened so fast, I didn't know what to think. Then that guy was there and I thought, I don't know, they were going to rob me or something. The girl, I'm just saying, and forgive me if it sounds mean, but she didn't look like Cinderella.'

Jarrod nodded. Faith was right – that jab wasn't fair. If she had opened the door and had let that girl in, it could have been a whole different tragedy. It might've been *his* family on the news today. The thought was too over-whelming to imagine, which was why he was being sardonic.

'I'm sorry,' he said, reaching over to stroke her leg. 'You're right. You're right. I'm glad you didn't open the door; God knows what could have happened. What I'm not getting, Faith, is why you didn't call the police after all this. You just said you thought this girl and this man might have been trying to rob you.'

'I didn't have my cell. And by the time I got home, it was hours later. There was no point . . . I didn't see any point. They would be long gone. I mean, what were the police gonna do then?'

'Where was your cell?'

'I left it at Charity's.'

He rolled his eyes. 'What about the girl, Faith? She was still out there.'

'I didn't think she was going to be killed, Jarrod!'

'A four-year-old knew enough to say something.'

'*After* that girl's face made the news, not before. Maggie never mentioned anything to anyone about her before this morning.'

He patted Maggie on the back. 'Go upstairs and play in your room while Mommy and Daddy talk, please.'

He waited until she was gone and he'd heard her bedroom door shut before he starting talking again, his voice low. 'Wait a second . . . don't go blaming a four-year-old for not stepping up to the plate. She said she was scared that you were gonna get mad at her.'

'Well then, why didn't she tell you without me there?'

'Now who's not being fair?'

She nodded fretfully. 'What I'm saying, Jarrod, is that until this girl's face showed up on the TV – until anyone *knew* she was dead, no one thought anything was wrong. And you're right: I shouldn't put this on Maggie. She's a kid. *I* didn't think something was wrong – wrong enough to call the police when I got home two hours later. Nobody knew this girl was even missing. There was nothing on the news about her before today. Have you heard of her? Did you see anything about a missing girl from Palm Beach? No.' She swallowed hard. 'There was no reason to think something bad had happened to her out there . . .'

He blew out a measured breath, tapping a finger against his temple, trying to think. The puzzle was still missing a few critical pieces, but he thought he knew what they were and why they were missing. He thought about last night and the empty wine bottle he'd found buried deep in the trash when he got home. He'd taken it out and put it in the recycle bin, along with the six or seven other bottles he'd found since the recyclables were picked up last week. Then he'd carried Faith upstairs off the couch in the family room and he'd put her to bed. Ever since his mistake with Sandra, her drinking had gotten worse. She'd always had a sturdy liver and a high tolerance, but she was much worse since last Christmas – and he was the one to blame, so how could he say anything? He was the one who'd strayed for some reason he himself still couldn't explain, much less justify.

He'd broken her heart. He'd devastated her. And he'd almost broken up the family that he would sooner die for. She had every right to find a way to cope until he could prove to her that he'd changed – that Sandra was a stupid fling who meant nothing to him. That she *could* trust him again and that their marriage *could* be exactly as good as it was before the affair. So he didn't say anything and he didn't judge her – he just came home a little later than he otherwise would so that he didn't have to see it, so that he didn't have to say anything. Because Faith was a good woman – she was a kind, loving, generous person. She was a great wife and an amazing mother to a little girl who could drive the patience from a saint and make any parent second-guess their parenting skills. And he had fucked it all up. *He'd* fucked it all up. So the reason for his silence was not because he was willing to accept her excessive drinking, but rather it was a decision based in logic: if their marriage improved and he was a better husband and everything went back to the way it was before his stupid mistake, then Faith would be happy again and she would stop drinking. If P then Q logic. He knew what she wasn't telling him about that night; to even ask her if she'd been drinking would be insulting. Because if she was, he was the reason. In a way, he was the one responsible for . . . this. So he didn't ask. He knew the answer anyway.

'OK,' he'd said, resigned. 'We have to go to the police now.'

'Yes, yes, of course,' she replied quickly.

'You'd better get dressed. I'll call the Sheriff's Office and find out who's handling this. I have to let my office know I won't be in today.'

Faith headed slowly up the stairs and he headed down. He wanted to grab her and hug her and hold her tight, tell her everything was going to be OK. But he didn't. For some reason he couldn't. When he got to the bottom of the staircase, he carefully stepped over the laundry that lay scattered on the

129

wood floor. Upstairs, he heard the door to their bedroom close behind her.

He waited a minute, staring hard at the floor. Then he picked the dirty laundry up, stuffed it back into the basket, and got rid of it all.

25

A comedy of stupid errors. A succession of stupid lies. Like dominoes, one set off the other until they couldn't be stopped.

Faith couldn't tell Jarrod about the second man.

He was a litigator. He was board-certified in both criminal and civil trial practice, was ranked in the top tier of trial lawyers by *Chambers Global*, and last year had been named as one of Broward County's best trial attorneys in *Think* magazine. Faith's father had been a lawyer, too – a general practitioner who was never afraid to go to court. She'd lived with lawyers her whole life and they all shared certain character traits. First, they were quick to react – forming opinions as the facts came in, constantly crafting and revising a closing argument in their heads. Unlike a doctor who'd listen to all of a patient's symptoms then run some tests, and then run some more before delivering a diagnosis, a lawyer was always ready to make a closing. Second, they could think on their feet, already forming their next three questions before the witness had finished answering one. And third, lawyers don't back down. Even if you showed them documentation that water was wet, they would successfully argue it's not, burning your hand with a slab of dry ice to prove their point. But it was the criminal defense attorneys who held a particularly dangerous skill: they could focus in on some weird, seemingly innocuous fact and somehow spin a whole argument around it – changing the paint color to match the speck of dirt they'd managed to spot on the wall. They could turn a character witness into a prime suspect in the minds of jurors just so they could create reasonable doubt.

Faith knew Jarrod was forming those opinions, phrasing his questions, crafting that closing as she was telling him what had happened while they sat on the stairs – he couldn't help himself. She could feel the anger in him swell and saw his body tense when she related certain parts. Because he already knew the ending: the girl was dead. What he didn't know was how she got that way. He didn't know the *story*, so he wasn't sure where the plot points were. She'd proceeded carefully and delicately, navigating through his sighs and comments and emotional interjections like she was driving through a field dotted with landmines. There were things he did not need to know – namely, that she'd been drinking that night, that she'd had an accident, and that she'd had the car fixed. She had to describe the landscape without blowing herself up.

He was mad at himself: mad that he hadn't gone with her to Charity's; mad that he hadn't insisted she stay at a hotel and not on her sister's couch; mad he hadn't bought her a new car with GPS. Then his mad had moved to others: Nick, for having a party during a tropical storm; Charity, for letting her drive home in it. Anger then turned to relief that nothing had happened to his family, that it wasn't their bodies being carried out of a cane field this morning.

Finally, the anger and indignation and relief subsided and the ginormous wave of shock was pulled back out to sea, exposing those landmines embedded in all the muck. Then came the questions. It was what he did best, after all.

'Why did you leave? Why didn't you stay at a hotel? You say this girl looked dangerous – did she have a weapon? Could you hear with the windows up? Why didn't you try to run this guy over? Did he have a weapon? Did you ask Maggie if she was OK? How did you not know she was awake?'

The questions came like rocket fire – often he didn't wait for a full answer before moving to the next one. He wasn't trying to discredit her, rather, he seemed to blurt out questions as they came to him, like a stream of consciousness, and because they were coming from a lawyer, thoughts came out in the form of questions. Her story was being dismantled before it was even finished being told. Her every action or inaction was being called into question. He hadn't found it yet, but he would – that damning speck of dirt on the wall.

That was when Faith decided at the last second to avoid another landmine, turning right before she ran over it.

'So this guy,' Jarrod had said, his hands clasped before him as he sat on the stairs, 'when he tried to open the car door, what did the girl do? Was she just standing there?'

Maggie was the first to respond: she nodded.

'She didn't run away?' he asked.

Maggie shook her head.

Faith shook her head, too.

'And when he pointed and told you to shush, where was the girl? Still standing there alone?'

Maggie thought for a moment, then nodded again.

As it turned out, from her limited vantage point in her car seat coupled with the fogged windows, Maggie could not see across the street. She never mentioned the creepy *Deliverance* guy. She never spoke about how he'd taken the girl back into the wooded lot with him. And that was because, Faith realized, Maggie didn't know he was there. She'd never seen him.

Faith had looked at Jarrod at that moment and a sickening thought had come to her: if he was looking at her this way now, barely masking his disdain for her silence and inaction, if he was doubting her claim that she did not think this Santri girl was in danger when he believed only *one* man was involved, what would he think of her if he knew there was another?

That was the speck of dirt.

Faith had sat on the stairs of her pretty house, looking at the family pictures that lined the walls, following them down into her living room, at the corner where she and Jarrod always put up the Christmas tree, at the couch where they'd made love dozens of times, at the front door, the threshold of which he'd carried her over when they moved in. Memories of the life they used to have before Sandra rushed back. It was a life she wanted to believe they could have again. A raw fear gripped her then – the realization that this could all be over. Forever. He'd walked away before. He'd taken up with that girl and emotionally left the marriage when things were perfect. Now, if they weren't, if she wasn't, why would he stay?

Why would he stay?

And she panicked.

Faith wasn't histrionic. She didn't love *Real Housewives*, she didn't like confrontations. She wasn't like Charity. But Jarrod had never looked at her the way he'd looked at her today. It was a look that betrayed what he was thinking: *I don't know you right now. I don't like you right now: what you did, what you didn't do. You are not the person I thought I knew.*

He looked at her as though she were a stranger.

Until the phone call that changed everything she'd never fretted about The End before. She and Jarrod had had fights over the years, but they were nothing major, nothing that would have readied her for that phone call. Jarrod was her first real love. He was her life. She would follow him wherever he wanted to go, not because he was the head of the house or the breadwinner, but because she thought he had all the answers for them both. She thought he held the secrets of their future together, and she trusted him implicitly with it, never doubting that he knew where to take them, how to invest financially to get them there. Even after Sandra, when she'd abruptly realized that her trust had been misplaced, that it *could* all end and that she'd have to take charge of life on her own, she . . . couldn't. It was like she was a newborn, with arms and legs that were useless for all practical purposes: she didn't know where to go, how to get there, how to do it on her own. And no matter how much she hated him for cheating, no matter how much she wanted to tell him sometimes to take his stuff and get out because he had ruined everything, she couldn't. Because she didn't know a life without him. She didn't want to know a life without him, as pathetic as that sounded. So she'd decided to stay and try to forget all the disturbing, intimate things that her brain had imagined he'd been doing with that woman for months while she was at home playing stupid. She'd decided to hope it didn't happen again.

Maybe it was crazy, panicked thinking, but if she'd admitted there was a second man out there who had physically taken the girl into the woods, she knew Jarrod would never look at her the same again. For all intents and purposes, in his eyes, it would be as if she'd killed that girl herself and it would truly be The End of their marriage. If she could go back and redo that night, make different decisions, call the police, face the consequences of drinking too much at a party because she was upset – she would. In a heartbeat she would.

But she couldn't.

So in a split second she'd made another decision, one that might prove every bit as stupid as the others. And that was to say nothing about the second man – at least nothing about him to her husband. It wasn't a lie – it was just not telling him everything.

It only officially became a lie a few hours later when they were at the police station . . .

'Mrs Saunders, did you see anyone else on the street besides this, ah, this man dressed in black?' Detective Nill asked, while Detective Maldonado took notes. The chair creaked under his girth as he swiveled to face her. 'Any other possible witnesses?'

She'd thought that they'd interview her and Maggie separately and without Jarrod. She really did. Just her and the detectives, like she'd seen on *Law & Order*. And she'd thought that at that time she'd tell the detectives about the *Deliverance* guy. She'd then let the detective know that she wanted to keep that information from her husband and why. The detective would understand, she could sit and look at mug shots for the second man and that would be it.

But that wasn't reality. That didn't happen and, again, the best-laid plans went awry. The interview was conducted in the conference room with everyone present: the two detectives, Maggie, Faith and Jarrod. And it was recorded.

She looked over at her husband, who was watching her intently from across the table, as the detective waited for an answer to his question. She was about to make it all official with an on-the-record lie. Not a dodge, or a half-truth, or a fudge, but a *lie*.

Another one.

Her hands were melting and her mouth went dry as cotton. She tried to think of the best way out of this mess, but the whole truth and nothing but the truth was not going to work. Not at this moment. She'd have to drive back up to Palm Beach tomorrow and make another report with the detectives. She'd have to explain her decisions to Detective Nill later, and she'd do whatever it was the detective needed her to do then: look at mug shots; work with an artist; make another recorded statement, detailing why she had not been completely truthful. But at this moment, at this very moment, her marriage – her whole life – was at stake. She had no choice but to lie.

Faith had looked at Nill when she answered, avoiding Jarrod's stare. 'No,' she said quietly. 'I didn't see anyone else out there that night, Detective.'

26

'Can I ask, Detective Nill, how did this Santri girl die?' Jarrod asked as the five of them left the conference room and made their way to the lobby of the police station. 'Has the autopsy been performed yet?'

'The autopsy is set for this afternoon, Mr Saunders. I'm heading over to the ME's in about twenty minutes.'

'But it is a homicide, without question?'

Nill nodded grimly. 'Oh yeah. There's no question.'

'And the cause of death . . .?' Jarrod tried again.

The detective stopped walking, holding Faith and Jarrod back with his arm, while he motioned for Detective Maldonado to keep walking ahead with Maggie. 'Angelina Santri's murder was particularly gruesome, Mr Saunders. There was evidence that she was tortured. Without going into too much detail, her body was mutilated. As you well know, this is a story that is already generating interest with the press. I suspect it will soon garner even more.'

'Why's that, Detective?' asked Jarrod. 'Not because of Maggie?'

Nill shook his head. 'I'm sure the press is gonna want to be all over your adorable daughter, especially if we do nail a suspect because of her cooperation, but that's not what I think is gonna set off a feeding frenzy.' He lowered his voice. 'This is not official, Mr and Mrs Saunders, and it is not for public consumption, so if it gets out before we're ready to release it, I'll know exactly who the source is. Let me be frank: for reasons I can't yet discuss, I don't believe Angelina Santri is this guy's first victim.'

Faith gasped.

'First?' asked Jarrod, incredulously.

'There are others. As many as three other women, possibly. You and your daughter coming in here today, Mrs Saunders . . . well, it's the first break we've gotten, I gotta be honest. Now we have a face to put out there, to see if the general public can recognize him. Maybe we'll get lucky and get a name – hopefully before this psycho picks another victim.'

Faith grabbed Jarrod's arm.

'Daddy!' Maggie yelled from the doors that led to the lobby.

'Mrs Saunders, tomorrow morning we'll take that drive back through the vicinity where you say you were that night. It's been several weeks, so I'm not expecting much in the form of evidence, but I'll have a crime scene team go over the area once we identify where it is.'

She nodded anxiously. Her face had gone the color of paste. She did not look well.

'I'll be going, Detective,' said Jarrod. 'I'd like to be involved.'

'That's fine,' he replied as they stepped through the doors and waded into a bustling PBSO lobby at lunchtime, filled with uniforms, lawyers, civilians and probably a few criminals, there to pick up reports or meet with detectives.

'Thanks for coming in,' Nill said, patting Maggie on the head. 'You've been a big help on this, Little Lady. You're a real hero; doing the right thing ain't always easy.'

Behind the detective was a glass case that ran almost the length of the wall. Inside was a corkboard full of posters from the Florida Department of Law Enforcement (FDLE), the FBI, DEA, Customs, US Marshal's. Some of the posters had mug shots, some had color photos of missing or endangered children. Some were murky pictures of suspects snapped by surveillance cameras, like bank robbers, and others were artist renderings. There were so many they were thumbtacked on top of each other.

'Is this a bad man, too?' Maggie asked, pointing at a sketch, then another. 'And this one?'

'Don't you worry about those boys,' Detective Nill said, turning her attention away from the case. 'No sense in giving you more faces for your nightmares.'

'Daddy, what's a hero?' Maggie asked coyly.

'Don't be silly. You know what a hero is.'

'She's someone who's brave,' offered Detective Maldonado. 'And like Detective Nill said, she's someone who does the right thing.'

'Like Superman. Or a Powder Puff girl,' explained Nill.

Maggie made a face.

Detective Nill feigned exasperation. 'What? You never heard of them? They were the bomb when my girls were little. They used to fly around fighting crime in their little pink capes. "Just like you, Daddy!" my kids would say. I loved that. "Just like you . . ." How about Kim Possible? She was big, too. Her and her mole-rat friend saving the world from villains.'

Detective Maldonado shook her head. 'You're showing your age, Detective Nill. Your girls are almost in college. Try Elsa and Anna from—'

'*Frozen*!' yelled Maggie.

'Now we're talking,' said Detective Maldonado, holding the door open. 'And it's Powerpuff, Detective Nill, not Powder Puff.'

'Ain't that what I said? Time sure does fly,' Nill said with a sigh as the Saunders family walked out of the station. Dad was holding the kid's hand, while wife/mom/star witness was lagging three steps behind. The body language wasn't hard to read: Faith Saunders had been the odd man out all day, even

139

with her own kid. 'Maldonado, you'll be trying to remember your kids' favorite shows one day, trying not to sound so old.'

'That will be interesting, indeed,' she replied. 'Because the shows I'm gonna have trouble remembering haven't even been made yet.'

'You're too young to be a detective,' he scoffed.

'You think we might have a face?' she asked, watching the family herself as they stepped into the parking lot.

He looked down at the folder in his hand that held Cuddy's sketch. It was as detailed as a photo. 'I do. I can only hope it's good enough to get us a name.'

'Do they know we're looking at a serial?'

'I told the parents. They're pretty flipped. Mom went albino on me. She's taking it hard.'

'She doesn't seem as cold as she sounds; I'm having trouble accepting why she didn't come forward earlier. She's holding back.'

'Oh yeah. But she's got a lot of shit on her plate,' replied Nill. 'Sounds like her and her kid were almost victims number five and six. That'll shake someone up. And there's trouble in paradise with her and the hubby, I think. Let's cut her some slack.'

'That kid really is brave,' Maldonado said softly.

He nodded, watching as the family got into an Infinity and pulled out of the parking lot.

It would not be long before the whole world agreed.

27

There are others.

Jarrod gripped the steering wheel hard and stared straight ahead at the back of the blue semi he was behind on I95. He tried to concentrate on the traffic, but he couldn't get the detective's words out of his head.

Others.

As many as three women.

It was now hitting him exactly what the detective had been insinuating: this guy might be a fucking serial killer. *A serial killer.* His wife and his four-year-old had not just witnessed a girl fighting with her boyfriend – they had very possibly witnessed a girl in the clutches of a serial killer. And they might well have witnessed her final moments before she was . . . *tortured*. Before she was *mutilated*. Before she was *murdered*. That thought was making his hands shake, which was why he was holding the steering wheel so hard.

Maybe we'll get lucky and get a name . . . hopefully before this psycho picks another victim.

Jarrod looked over at Faith, at the back of her head – she was blankly staring out the passenger window. *My God, it could have been her*, he thought. This guy might have gotten in the car and pulled her out – *tortured* her, too. *Mutilated,* was what the detective said. *Mutilated.* The word had many meanings, none of them good. Cut open? Dismembered into pieces? Disemboweled? Jesus Christ. The graphic images inundating his brain were making him nauseous. 'Thank God . . .' he said aloud, without intending to.

Faith didn't look away from the window. 'What?' was all she quietly asked.

'Thank God,' he repeated softly. 'Thank God you didn't open the door.'

He could hear her sniffling and even though he couldn't see her face, he knew she was crying. He reached over and awkwardly stroked her hair.

And Maggie . . . *Jesus, what would that man have done to a child?* His brain couldn't even go there. He had represented horrible people as a public defender in Miami. Mostly fuck-ups and drug addicts who made poor decisions because they were brought up in Shitsville with no role models and were beaten as kids and raised by gangs. But in those five years he had represented a handful of truly evil individuals – people who had no bleeding-heart excuse for being so fucked-up: psychopaths, sadists and sociopaths who enjoyed inflicting pain on others. Those people were why he got out of Miami, out of the PD's office and out of criminal defense altogether. Being too good of a trial lawyer, going up against neophyte prosecutors who were still cutting their teeth in a courtroom, had resulted in him having an epiphany one day after celebrating another not guilty verdict with his home-invader/aspiring-rapist client: some people should never, ever be allowed to live in free society. Politically, morally, he opposed the death penalty, but quietly he acknowledged there were a few select people who deserved it. Scum that the world would be much better off without – human killing machines who, without conscience, hunted fellow humans for the thrill of it, not the necessity. Even a life sentence offered limited protection – anyone they were to come in contact with inside the system was at risk. And heaven forbid their sentences were ever reduced, thrown out, or commuted and they were released . . .

The thought made his blood run cold.

He checked the rearview, where Maggie sat in her booster, watching a DVD with her headphones on, remaining remarkably and uncharacteristically quiet. The car ride home from the police station had basically been the same as the ride up: silent and filled with tension. Faith continued to stare out the window, thinking about God knows what.

Yes, thank God she didn't open the door. Thank God. But why hadn't she called the police? Why hadn't she told him what happened when she got home that night? The next morning even? He thought he knew the answer, but he suddenly wanted to demand she answer the question. That she say it aloud, admit that she had fucked up, that she had been driving drunk, so that he would know, like he might with a wayward teen or client, that she'd at least learned from all this. So that he would know there was a *reason* she hadn't done anything for that girl. To know for sure she was driving shit-faced and was sorry for doing it would be strangely more comforting than believing she was apathetic.

He looked over at her again. He wanted to ask her. Ask her if she was drunk. The pressure in the car might be relieved a little, just by asking the question. Maybe she'd answer him, and maybe they'd talk – actually talk. Or yell. He'd take that – hell, he'd even welcome an argument. He looked back at the semi. He noticed it was a different one than the one he'd been behind for the last ten miles. When had that happened?

An overwhelming feeling of sadness mixed with shame came over him and he swallowed the confrontational question back down. Truth was, they didn't talk much any more. They said words and exchanged pleasantries, and they definitely didn't argue. All that was on him. It was the fallout from his mistake. He deferred to her on most everything and he didn't argue,

143

because he owed her that. *Repairing a relationship after an affair takes time*, a friend had advised him – a friend who should know. *Rebuilding trust can take years and the slightest misstep – a sprinkle of doubt is all it takes – will crush whatever relationship you've managed to build up right back down. So be patient and be on your best behavior.*

He stared at her beautiful honey-blonde hair. It fell just below her shoulders, but it used to cascade down her back in beachy, sun-streaked waves. He used to bury his face in it when she was sleeping and her back was to him – to smell the Freesia-scented shampoo she favored, mixed with her perfume, Ms Dior, and . . . *her*. He used to love to smell her, to breathe her in, because he couldn't seem to get enough. He shook his head. The pressure in the car was too much to take.

'He's still out there,' he announced suddenly.

Faith turned away from the window and looked at him.

'This girl's body has turned up and now that sketch is gonna come out with his face on it and he will put it together,' he said quietly, matter-of-factly, as though he were talking to a client who he was strategically trying to get to cough up the truth – a truth that he could live with defending. 'The detective is talking about three other murders they think this guy has committed, which makes him a serial killer, Faith. The detective is right – the press is gonna eat that up and that sketch is gonna be everywhere. And when the media finds out that a four-year-old is the eyes behind that sketch, Maggie and you will be everywhere. I don't want it to happen, but it will. Because that's the type of story that people are interested in.'

She started to tear up again.

'Even if no one recognizes that sketch in the paper or on the news – or wherever the hell it is they put it – *he* will. Because he's looking to see when he finally makes the papers. And he's gonna know who helped the police sketch it. He knows there're witnesses and now he knows they're talking. Two witnesses: my wife and my kid. It won't be hard for him to figure out the rest – name, address, phone number—'

She turned back toward the window, crying again. 'If you're trying to scare me, it's working.'

That's what he wanted to do. He'd wanted to scare her into admitting an answer to the question he was afraid to ask. He wanted to impress upon her how terrifying this whole thing was. How devastated he would be if he ever lost her to a madman. If he ever lost her, period. But the whole thing kept coming out wrong, like everything else he'd been saying for the past ten months.

So he clenched the steering wheel even harder and stopped talking and he didn't finish the most disturbing fact he had hoped to scare the truth out of her with.

And that was that serial killers don't like witnesses.

28

Gemma Jones looked at the thumbnail-sized sketch that was on the front page of the local section of the *Sun-Sentinel*. She looked back up and peeked outside her cubicle at the young man seated in his glass-enclosed office down the hall. The blinds were closed, but the door was slightly ajar and she could see him talking on the phone at his desk.

Damn it if that sketch didn't look like Derrick.

But Derrick Poole? No way. He was . . . too quiet. Too boring. Too smart. Too cute. Too . . . well, everything and anything that made up a normal guy who you might want to take home to your mother. Who you actually did want to take home to your mother – if only he'd ask.

Gemma chewed on her pen cap. Wasn't that how it worked out in true crime books? Wasn't it always the quiet ones? The smart ones? The ones no one ever suspected? Bundy was a handsome law student. Rader was an usher in his church. Scott Peterson was a father-to-be and sold fertilizer for a living. She rolled the pen cap around in her mouth. *Police seek ID of suspect in rape and murder of Palm Beach dancer.*

Killers don't work at debt consolidating companies, do they? They don't help people put their financial houses back in order. Gemma's useless bachelor's degree was in English,

146

but Derrick – his was in accounting. Accountants weren't murderers. Lawyers, doctors, postal workers – yeah, they could gut their own moms, but never accountants. They were too anal, too precise. They knew the odds of getting caught and found it too risky. Never wanted to make a mess. She chuckled to herself, because the thought of a neat, anal-retentive murderer somehow struck her as funny.

Derrick was polite, sweet, quiet. If she thought he was a psycho, she never would've sat next to him in the lunchroom, wearing her nice perfume and her sexy blouses, hoping he'd ask for her number. She would've known there was something odd about him.

But the one thing every true crime book she'd ever read made clear was – you never really do know. Two weeks ago, coincidentally or not, Derrick had shaved off that not-quite-a-beard-thing he'd been growing on the lower half of his face. His lunchroom explanation? 'It just wasn't working on me. My mom didn't like it.' Gemma had thought it incredibly endearing that a twenty-nine-year-old man still cared about his mom's opinion. She tapped her pen on the thumbnail-sized sketch. The murder suspect had a beard. The dancer had been dead for a while, according to the article.

She peeked over her Formica cubicle again. He was standing next to his desk, talking on the phone. Damn. And he was cute, too. Not in an obvious way, but more like a sophisticated way – like a painting that you look at for a while and realize the subject in it has nice features. You warm to it. You start to like it, appreciate it. And you wonder why it was you never thought the guy was hot at first glance, when it's so bloody obvious now. Tall, Dark and Not Obviously Handsome – that was Derrick Poole. She watched him as he spoke on the phone. His easy smile, dressed in a crisp white button-down and shiny blue tie. With that gruff on his face and his long hair that he kept slicked back in a low pony, he had a rebellious, bad-boy look about him. Now he was clean-shaven, but even sexier. An accountant by day and a rock star when the sun went down. The dress shirt and tie came off and he jammed on a bass guitar shirtless, his carved chest covered in colorful tattoos, none of which said 'Mom'. The fantasy made her smile.

Or an accountant by day and a murdering rapist by night.

Sad. There was no way she wanted him to ask her out now. Well, ask, yes, but she couldn't say yes until she found out for sure that he wasn't a murderer. She'd have to call the police. They'd do all their police things – background checks and fingerprint checks and DNA checks, she supposed – and either confirm or deny that he was the guy they were looking for.

If he was a rapist, well, that made no sense, because she would've given it up to him without a fight. And if it all turned out to be a case of mistaken identity – which she was 95 per cent sure it would be – and Derrick had a doppelgänger out there with a mean streak and a taste for strippers, well, that was kind of sexy. Not that he *was* a murderer, but that her sweet, harmless Tall, Dark and Not Obviously Handsome *looked* a little bit more like a bad ass and a little less like . . . an accountant. He looked like a guy who was accused of murder, and that somehow made him tougher, heartier, meatier, sexier, manlier. Without, of course, being an actual murderer. It was like having the cake without all the damn calories.

But first she had to make sure that was what he wasn't. No sense in getting Momma Jones's hopes all high when he might be headed to the electric chair. After the ribbing she took on the last loser she'd brought home, she wasn't suggesting a Sunday dinner with the family until her badass accountant's name was cleared. She'd have to try and keep her name out of this, too. No one else in the office was staring at him strangely, or doing double-takes at the morning paper. If Derrick should find out that she was the one who'd called the police and told them he looked like a murder suspect – well, she was pretty sure he wasn't going to want to start a relationship. There would be some serious trust issues that would be hard to get past.

Gemma folded the local section, tucked it under her arm and grabbed her cell off her desk. She smiled at Derrick as she walked past his office. He was still on the phone, but he smiled back. She could feel his eyes on her as she walked down the hall and stepped out of the building.

It was all rather thrilling, she thought giddily as she lit up a butt. A little bit of workplace drama to make the day pass faster. She sat in her car and dialed the number that was in the paper.

'Palm Beach Sheriff's. Homicide. Detective Evans speaking. Can I help you?'

'Yes. Um, Detective Nill, please. He's Homicide.' Ooh – that was fun.

'Hold.'

The line went completely silent. Not even elevator music. That made sense – you were calling a homicide unit; everything about it screamed serious. It'd be inappropriate to be caught humming along to Hall & Oates. Gemma flipped down the cosmetic mirror and checked her smile and her breath.

'Homicide. Detective Maldonado.'

'Detective Nill please.'

'Can I ask what this is in reference to?'

'The picture in the *Sun-Sentinel* this morning,' Gemma answered, lowering her voice to a whisper even though no one was around. She tried to contain her excitement.

'I can help you with that. Do you have information?'

'Well, I work with a guy who looks a lot like that sketch. The one of the guy who murdered that stripper.' She flipped the mirror back up and her heart stopped.

Derrick Poole was standing outside her car window.

And he didn't look very happy.

149

29

Leonard Dinks. Derrick Poole. Fred Hutchings. The Guy from My Gym. The Guy in the Mustang Next to Me This Morning. My Ex When You Look at Him a Certain Way in the Bathroom Light.

Detective Bryan Nill scanned the growing list of leads in Angelina Santri's murder that Tatiana had left on his desk. There were 82 'persons' already on it – some of whom didn't actually have a name, only a vague description, like The Guy in the Mustang Next To Me, which, thankfully, also came with a tag number. Cuddy's sketch, along with an article about the murder, had been published in the local papers from Orlando to Miami three days ago and the phones had been ringing ever since.

Bryan sighed and dunked a cruller into his coffee. Even though Cuddy was PBSO's best artist, kooky IDs were always a risk when you ran with a sketch or a blurry video surveillance shot. In a potentially high-profile murder like this, every lead needed to be followed – even the kooky ones – lest the killer actually turn out to be that guy in the Mustang and you failed to check it out and the nut goes and offs another girl. 'Followed up,' though, meant pulling DLs, running histories, doing interviews – slogging through time-consuming bullshit – even though 99.99 times out of a 100, what wound up happening was you wasted a lot of hours and manpower hunting down the guy in the Mustang that someone had sworn on the grave of their mother looked 'just like' the bad guy in the sketch, only to find he looked nothing at all like him.

With four dead girls he had no time or manpower to waste. But with his only lead being an artist sketch based on the observations of a four-year-old and her cagey mom, he couldn't afford not to follow up every tip. Unfortunately, while he saw the potential for high-profile here, the sergeant and the PBSO brass, to date, had not: there was no task force, no squad room full of detectives running down tips with a corkboard full of timelines, maps and crime scene photos on the wall behind them. It was him and Tatiana Maldonado and that was it. And he was lucky to have her – she'd moved from Special Investigations to Homicide two weeks ago. Rather than have her sit around and wait for someone to die and a new case to come in, after Santri's body had been found his sarge had agreed to lend her out to assist with all the slogging and get her up to speed with the squad. Fortunately, she'd spent two years in the Crimes Against Children Unit of the Special Investigations Division and another two in the Financial Crimes Unit, so she had experience as a detective. Unfortunately, she had no real experience in homicide – only a couple of symposiums in forensics and legal procedure. But a warm body was a warm body, and the two of them got along just fine. In the mornings she brought him a cup of Dunkin' Donuts and a cruller, which was very nice. And it certainly didn't hurt none that she was only twenty-eight and easy on the eye, even though she tried her best to downplay that with boyish ponytails and minimal makeup. Sports jackets, slacks and buttoned-up blouses attempted to hide a nice figure. She went by the nickname 'Totts', which Bryan thought sounded dangerously close to 'Toots' and 'Tits' – especially in

151

an all-boys squad, where most of the detectives were even older than him. He liked Maldonado, although it was a bit long. Maldy sounded too much like Moldy. For the time being he was sticking with calling her 'Maldonado', 'Tatiana', or simply, 'Hey'.

He sipped at his coffee and scanned through the file Tatiana had prepared for him on Leonard Dinks, age 47, from Deerfield Beach. She'd written notes all over it in neat, girly handwriting:

Dinks, Leonard Christopher. DOB: 4/22/62. Truck driver for CF Freight. White male. 5' 5". No priors. Wife is Susan Dinks. She says he wasn't home the night of 10/18 and didn't come home for a week after that. He was 'evasive' with her when she asked where he'd been, because he was supposed to drop his load and be back 10/20, but not home till 10/23. Said first thing he did when he stepped in the front door was wash his clothes and 'the laundry room smelled real bad after that, like something had died in there'.

Bryan looked at the DL. Lenny was too old and too bald to be a viable suspect, but hair grew, there were wigs, and everyone knew the people at DMV tried to take the most unflattering license photos possible. The guy could look younger in person. He might not turn out to be the Cane Killer, but the weird comments from the wife deserved a closer look, regardless. He put Lenny on the stack of remote suspects for Maldonado to handle. She could pull the rest of the crap that was missing, fill in the blanks, visit with Mr and Mrs Dinks, write the report and he'd clear it. If she turned up anything interesting in her investigation, he'd revisit.

Bryan didn't yet have a task force. Not even a corkboard. He had a large cardboard file box that contained the unsolved homicide case files of three women: Silvia Kruger, Emily Foss and 'Jane Doe'. The bodies of Kruger, twenty-four, and Foss, twenty, both convicted prostitutes, had been discovered in the cane fields of western Palm Beach County in 2013. Kruger had danced, too, down at some dive in Miami and, for a time, at Mr T's off Gun Club Road in West Palm. 'Jane Doe' was an unsolved 2012 homicide Bryan had stumbled on that actually belonged to the Glades County Sheriff's Office, Palm Beach County's 'neighbor' on the other side of Lake Okeechobee: the charred torso and pelvis of an unidentified female had been found in torched cane fields southeast of Moore Haven. He looked at the brown accordion file he'd started on Angelina Santri. Inside that were the gruesome crime scene and autopsy photos, the ME's report, and Cuddy's sketch, along with all the preliminary reports and witness interview sheets from interviews conducted to date with friends, family members, co-workers and Maggie and Faith Saunders. Angelina Santri's murder brought the body count in the box to four.

Maybe.

Bryan wasn't 100% positive that the same man had killed each girl, but it sure as hell was looking like it – to him, anyways. He wasn't sure when you got to officially call a spate of brutal murders the work of a serial killer. So far the powers that be at PBSO were holding off on any such designation. Bryan was thinking – hoping, actually – that Santri's murder might be the one that forced his sarge and LT and the rest of the brass to see what he was seeing – that four dead, mutilated women all found in cane fields over the past twenty months was not some freaky coincidence. Twenty-three years on the force, seventeen as a detective, nine in homicide, and Bryan had never worked a serial killer. He'd handled multiple murders committed by gangbangers and husbands who went rogue on their families, a couple of serial burglars, and when he was in Sex Crimes, he'd worked two serial rapists, but no serial killers. It wasn't just him – his department

153

hadn't worked any, either. Mark Felding, the serial killer known as Picasso, had held and killed some teenage runaways out in Belle Glade in 2009, but FDLE – the Florida Department of Law Enforcement – had worked that case with a task force that was out of Miami and PBSO had been there to offer assistance after Felding turned up dead.

Contrary to what countless thriller novels and TV shows like *Criminal Minds* would have you think, serials were actually rare, although Miami had certainly had its share in recent years: Cupid, Cunanan, Picasso, Black Jacket, the Tamiami Strangler. But Miami was a pit – it attracted nuts. Andrew Cunanan had actually driven down to Miami from Michigan, killing four people on the way before he found Versace walking back to his SoBe mansion. Palm Beach County, though, was some fifty miles plus north of the pit. It was on the Treasure Coast and was known for its reserved affluence and old money. When people thought of Palm Beach, they thought of the Kennedy compound, Worth Avenue, and Mar-a-Lago. Polo ponies and socialites. The county's median age was 41.7, although in some cities – especially during snowbird season – you'd swear that number was closer to 70. The median income was $52,806.00 – the highest of any county in Florida. In the tony town of Palm Beach, it was $174,889.00. That was income, not net worth. There were some really rough parts of Palm Beach, like Riviera Beach, Royal Palm, Belle Glade, and parts of Lake Worth, but, generally speaking, violent crime was manageable and murders were relatively rare outside those areas.

Not that Bryan wasn't busy: Riviera Beach had a gang problem and domestics didn't only happen in bad parts of town. When his cell rang in the middle of the night there was a good chance it would be because a drug deal had gone bad. Plus, with the Great Recession, desperate people did desperate things, and robberies and home invasions didn't always end pleasantly. He was carrying a caseload of seventeen homicides in various stages of investigation and litigation, and they filled every minute of his forty-hour work week and then some. Most weeks he actually put in an extra ten or twenty, not for the OT his department wasn't paying anyway, but because he was a bit of a control freak who hated loose ends. He had a fear of dropping dead on the way to work one day and the guy who had to take over his caseload bad-mouthing him to the boys in the squad at his funeral over the way he'd left his files. He took a long sip of his coffee. And he had no reason to go home at five nowadays, anyway.

Seventeen homicides on his plate and only three unsolved: Kruger, Foss, and now, Santri; Jane Doe still belonged to Glades County. In March of 2013, Silvia Kruger's nude body had been found in a cane field in Lake Harbor, a small town east of Clewiston, the sugar capital of the US. She'd been shot point-blank in the heart. She'd been identified through her fingerprints – her head was found in a nearby drainage ditch three weeks later. She'd been sexually assaulted, both vaginally and anally, and she had ligature marks on her hands, ankles and torso. Four months later, in July of 2013, Emily Foss's partially charred body was discovered by migrants in a torched cane field off of Hole in the Wall Road, just north of Canal Point. She'd been stabbed multiple times and was missing both of her hands, one of which was found in a neighboring cane field a few weeks later. She, too, had been sexually assaulted. Emily Foss's rape had been so brutal, both her uterus and large intestine had been perforated. After Foss's body was discovered, Bryan did a search on ViCAP – the FBI's Violent Criminal Apprehension Program database – and learned that the remains of an unidentified female had been found in September of 2012 in a torched cane field off SR720, just southeast of the county seat of Moore Haven in Glades County. Jane Doe's torso had been burned so severely, it was impossible for the ME to determine cause of death or if she'd been sexually assaulted. The ME also couldn't place a date on when she'd

155

died, or even how long she'd been in the field. The rest of Jane Doe's body, including her head, had never been recovered.

Now there was Angelina Santri. Her partially nude, decomposing body had been found in the cane fields southeast of Pahokee in the village of Pelican Lake. She'd been strangled with her own bra, her T-shirt pulled up and over her face, concealing, at first, the mess that was once her face. She'd been brutally beaten with what the ME speculated was a garden tool, likely a cultivator. Her driver's license was on the ground underneath her body, which was how she was identified. She'd been tortured for a period before she was murdered – there were healing burn marks, likely from cigarettes, on her buttocks and shards of glass in the bottom of her feet, in various stages of healing. She'd likely been killed elsewhere and the body dumped where it was found – decomposition was progressed, but was not as advanced as the ME would have expected, considering the body's exposure in the cane fields. She had a dislocated shoulder and a hairline fracture in her left femur. The Achilles tendon on her left foot had been severed. She, too, had been sexually assaulted.

Four dead women – each murdered a different way with a different weapon, found in different locations, miles, and even counties, apart from one another. That was one way to spin it, which was why Bryan didn't have either a task force or a corkboard yet. Or four dead girls, all prostitutes or exotic dancers, all sexually assaulted, at least two of whom were tortured, their bodies discarded in remote cane fields that were either burned or set to be burned. That was how Bryan was spinning it.

Unfortunately, no connection had been discovered yet between any of the girls. Foss and Kruger didn't work the same corners, or even the same towns. Bryan didn't know who Jane Doe was, much less where she came from or if she was a prostitute, and Angelina Santri had no priors for prostitution, although it was known that, for a hundred bucks, the girls who danced at the Animal would perform more than a lap dance. The girls all lived in different cities, there was no evidence they knew each other. But the real, unspoken reason for why there was no PBSO/FDLE posse of detectives and special agents hunting the vicious murderer he'd nicknamed The Cane Killer, was because his victims were all prostitutes and strippers. If there were four dismembered coeds from the University of Florida, or four dead tourists or four dead housewives from Boca Raton, a task force would already be up and running. Prostitutes, however, made for perfect victims, which was why they were a favorite of serials. Gary Ridgway had killed twenty of them and dumped their bodies in and around the Green River in Washington before a task force was formed. Like disposable razors, prostitutes came cheap and by the dozen. They had an inherently dangerous job they engaged in with sometimes inherently dangerous people. Many were drug addicts. No one noticed if one went missing from the pack because no one cared.

While arguably all three murders might be unique in style, method and execution – most notably in the different weapons used and the cause of death, which was atypical for a serial – there was one constant: the lack of physical evidence. No prints, DNA, hair, fiber, fluids, semen left behind. And no witnesses.

Until now.

The recent break with the Saunders mom and her kid was unbelievably fortuitous. Now he had a description and a sketch of the person last seen with Santri when she was alive. True, the mom was holding back on something and the kid was only four. Neither was perfect, but Bryan had never met a witness who was. Point being, if he could turn that sketch into a living, breathing suspect, well that would be . . . a very good start.

He brushed the cruller crumbs off his tie, took the paper-thin file of the next lucky shmoe off Maldonado's pile and flipped it open.

Then he sat back in the squeaky desk chair and thoughtfully stroked his generous chin.

The photo on Derrick Alan Poole's Florida driver's license looked an awful lot like Cuddy's sketch.

30

Bryan skimmed through Maldonado's notes:

Co-worker tip. Thinks Poole looks like sketch in the paper. Works as an accountant??? at Debt Destroyers in Lake Worth - a 'loan consolidation' company. Tipster's name is Gemma Jones, age 25 D/O/B: 6/4/88 - wants to remain ANONYMOUS. POOLE, DERRICK: white male, age 29, Height? 'Tall, maybe 6 ft. Probably more.' Dark hair. Had 'goatee-thing going on' but recently shaved - another reason she thinks something's up. She seems OK - a little too into being a witness; excited over the whole homicide thing - but I took the tip over the phone, so who knows?

Maldonado had already had the analyst run a DAVID (Driver And Vehicle Information Database), along with a printout of Derrick Poole's DL, which were both in the file. There was also a detailed CLEAR National Comprehensive Report, which listed any real property and vehicles owned by Poole, utility services in his name, phone numbers associated with him, creditors associated with those phone numbers, aliases, past and present addresses, deed transfers, warrants and traffic citations, possible arrests, and possible court dockets. Thankfully, Derrick Poole was not as common a name as, say, Bob Smith, or else there might have been a dozen reports in the file. But there was only one: he was twenty-nine and currently resided in West Boca Raton.

Bryan put the DL photo, in which Poole wore black, hipster, horn-rimmed eyeglasses and was clean-shaven, next to the sketch. If you could see past that, there was a strong resemblance. At 6'0", the height was on the mark and the hair color was right. He had bony, pronounced facial features – 'chiseled' would probably be a good word, like Faith Saunders had said and Cuddy had drawn. As for hair length, it was slicked back in the photo, so it was hard to tell, but hair grew and got cut all the time, so that didn't mean much. He was a good-looking guy, which threw Bryan off. Not that he hadn't arrested good-looking guys before or that comely people couldn't be murderers, but Poole looked neatly handsome and clean-cut – almost boring. No gang affiliations, or militia connections. A registered Republican. He looked at Maldonado's notes again. The guy was . . . an accountant?

He carefully read through the CLEAR report. Poole had lived all over the state. First Florida DL issued out of Deltona, Florida in 2001 when he was sixteen. Changed addresses to Haines City, Florida three months later. Tallahassee in 2003, presumably for college at Florida State. Then a stint in Atlanta, Georgia from 2008 through 2010. In November of 2010 he'd returned to Florida, living in Wellington, and in January of 2012 to the address he currently resided at in West Boca. He didn't own any property. No lawsuits. Had a couple of traffic tickets, one of which was a speeding ticket in Martin County which he hadn't paid and his license had been automatically suspended as a result. Nothing remarkable at all, except an alias of 'Derrick Freeley' and a star marked on the DAVID next to 'criminal record.' Bryan looked at the FCIC/NCIC criminal history.

160

Poole had a sealed juvenile record out of Haines City, Florida.

Fortunately, from a law enforcement perspective, sealed did not mean expunged. Expunged meant really hard to get, sealed meant not so hard to get. Haines City was a small town with a cooperative police department. Bryan called up the Criminal Investigations Division, spoke with the lieutenant, and in less than an hour, the duty officer was faxing him a copy of Poole's arrest report.

Bryan read it as it came over the fax. Then he called Maldonado. She picked up on the second ring.

'What's up?'

'I need you back here. Something interesting came up.'

'I'm eating lunch.'

'Lunch? What time is it?' Bryan squinted to look at his watch. He was turning fifty in a couple of months and that just sucked. Next thing to go would be the hearing. Hopefully not the hair – his dad still had a full head. It was white as snow, but it was all there. 'What are you, like in middle school? Who eats lunch at ten thirty in the morning?'

'Me. I'm hungry. Don't judge.'

'What are you, pregnant?' he joked.

'You're not allowed to ask me questions like that,' she fired back with a distinct Spanish accent he had not heard before.

'Whoa now. I was only kidding. Where'd the Sofía Vergara come from, Maldonado? You OD on *Modern Family* last night?'

'She's Colombian. I sound nothing like her. I'm Cuban. My father floated here on a raft and a prayer, you know. You're mixing up your Spaniards.'

Bryan took the phone away from his ear a little and made a face at it. 'OK, then. I see why you need to eat something, Maldonado, because you're cranky and I don't want to get sued because I pissed you off with a joke. Just get back here when you're done so I can go over this guy you left on my desk.'

161

'I told you, you can call me Totts, or even Tatiana.' She still sounded irritated. He could hear her crunching on something in the background.

'OK,' he answered.

'We're not TV cops,' she added sullenly.

He rolled his eyes. 'You are in a mood.'

'It's been a bad day.'

'Wanna talk about it?' he asked clumsily. He'd known the woman for two weeks. He didn't want to know her life, necessarily, but he sensed she wanted to tell him.

'No,' she replied testily. Now she sounded surprised *and* irritated.

The Woman Whisperer he obviously wasn't. 'OK, then, well, what I just found out might make your day better. Or at least take your mind off your troubles,' he tried. 'Where are you, anyway?'

'Picchu Palace.'

'Oh . . .'

'What?' she asked defensively, as she crunched.

'I got food poisoning there once,' he replied with an evil smile. 'Enjoy your lunch, Maldonado.'

Then he popped the last of his cruller into his mouth and hung up the phone.

31

'Poole,' Tatiana said, waving a fry about as she stood at his desk. 'I knew that's who you were talking about. He's intense looking.'

'You're only saying that 'cause I showed you the arrest report. I thought he looked boring,' replied Bryan.

'Just this morning I would've said that vacant stare of his makes him look kinda dull, but now that I know he pushed his own grandma down the stairs, it's looking a little twisted. A little Charlie Manson in the early days, actually.'

'After he tried to rape her.'

Tatiana made a face as she read the charges off the arrest form: 'Attempted murder, agg batt, attempted sex batt, animal cruelty. How old was he?'

'Sixteen. The story I'm getting outta that report is that he was living in Deltona with his mom. Dad had abandoned the family when Poole was four. That's what the shrinks are probably gonna say fucked him up, Maldonado, if it turns out that this is our guy. Mark my words: "Daddy left and everything went to shit in my world. I had no father figure." Then in January of eleventh grade he gets sent to live with Grandma in Haines City. What does that tell you? Tells *me* Mom couldn't handle him.'

'Or something happened to her,' Tatiana speculated. 'Maybe Mom went nuts, had a drug problem, ran off, had a health problem, died, got remarried.'

'Nah. Keep reading. It doesn't say nothing about her being in jail or rehab or a nuthouse. It says, "He went to live with his grandmother at his mother's request." That means he was a problem she couldn't handle. You worked Crimes Against Children; you know kids get pawned off on grandparents all the time because the parents can't control them. He's there for three months, going to high school, probably creeping the cheerleaders out with those Charlie Manson peepers. He can't get any from any of them, he gets frustrated, so he goes for Grandma.'

Tatiana looked up from the report and cocked an eyebrow. 'That's definitely not in there,' she said. 'That is pure speculation.'

'Then he drowned her poodle in the pool while she watched. Name was Princess. There's your animal cruelty. *That's* in there.'

'Rape is a crime of rage, not passion.'

'True. But I've been doing this a long time, and I'm willing to bet some *dinero* that our boy didn't fit in at his new high school, grew more and more frustrated and angry with everyone, especially the girls, and got bad grades. He made no friends, and took his pent-up anger out on Grandma, who probably looks a lot like his mother, who he privately detests. Couldn't get to Mom, so the intent transferred to Grandma in the heat of the moment.'

Tatiana put the report down. 'That's an awful lot to reach at from an A-form and a couple of reports; not sure if I'm with you. So what happened? He's obviously out and about in society now. And he's a CPA, so he somehow managed to get his grades up that you just speculated he was failing.'

Bryan shrugged. 'According to the close-out memo, the attempted sex batt charges were dropped. Grandma wouldn't testify about the rape attempt; she wanted him to get help for what she thought was a drug problem. So they pled him to the agg bat, which was a felony, because they didn't need her cooperation to go forward on that. They dropped the animal cruelty. He was sentenced as a Youthful Offender to the Orange Youth Academy in Orlando – a high-risk juvenile facility. He spent two years there. Came out a new man with a GED and a new name: Derrick Alan Poole. That year the case was sealed so he could start fresh.'

'The arrest is under the name Derrick Alan Freeley. Where'd he get Poole?'

'Look at the victim list.'

She took the arrest form back, and flipped it over to see the victim/witness list. 'No way! "Linda Sue Poole" – the bastard took his grandma's last name. Talk about passive-aggressive when plain fucking aggressive doesn't do the trick.'

Bryan shrugged. 'Can't do anything to stop a name change.'

'I bet he's not invited for Thanksgiving dinner at Grandma's.'

'I don't think she's hosting any more holiday dinners; she's in an institution with early-onset Alzheimer's. To his credit, Linda Sue was a relatively young grandma when he tried to get funky with her.'

Tatiana made a face and reached for another greasy fry. 'Sorry – not much of a comfort. How'd you find that out?'

'I ran a CLEAR, found the address, called the home. She's been there four years.'

'So much for proving your "transferred intent" theory; Grandma's not gonna remember sonny's name now, much less if he groped her on her way down the stairs twelve years ago.'

'There's always Mom, Maldonado. Maybe she'll talk to us. I ran her, too; she lives in Phoenix. Moved west in 2003 – a month before Derrick got out of lock-up. Interesting, eh?'

Tatiana nodded thoughtfully and looked down at the arrest form. 'Grandma? Yuck. I haven't heard that one before, and I've heard a lot of shit.'

'I'm liking this guy, the more I read, Maldonado.'

'Totts,' she said.

He nodded.

'A lot of what you're thinking, you didn't read – you made up,' she said.

'It's called profiling. What matters right now is this guy looks like our sketch and he used to live in Wellington, which kisses up on the cane fields of Belle Glade and is close to a couple of our dump sites. He's got a violent sexual criminal history with women, and he kills animals, which is a classic manifestation of a psychopathic personality disorder.'

'So what now?' she asked, crumpling the French fry bag and tossing it across the desk into a waiting wastepaper basket.

'We gotta keep looking at the other names on the list, to be safe and thorough. I'm gonna pull whatever I can on Poole: school records, work history, and whatever I can get from that Youth Academy. Then I'll head back out to the Animal, see if anyone recognizes our boy in a photo lineup, sit up on him a few days and see if maybe he takes us somewhere interesting. Serials sometimes revisit their crime scenes,' he added.

Tatiana frowned and looked at the file box that he had written CANE KILLER on in big block letters. 'A serial, huh? You really think that's what you got going on?'

'I do. And until Amandola assigns you your own caseload, it's what *we* got going on.' George Amandola was the lieutenant who headed up homicide.

'What does he think about the idea that this guy might be a serial?'

'Another body might do it for him.' Bryan shifted in his seat and tapped his pen on the file box. 'Are you, ah, doing better?'

She stared at him for a good couple of seconds. He wasn't sure if she wanted to bite him or hug him and he immediately regretted caring enough to ask the question. 'You sounded upset, is all,' he explained, putting his hands in the air in a show of surrender. 'Sorry for asking.'

'Yes, thanks,' she finally replied. 'I only had a bag of fries and about ten tortilla chips for lunch, thanks to that last comment of yours, so I'm starving.'

'Trust me, in about three hours your stomach will be thanking me. Actually, since it won't know how sick it could have been, it will take feeling well for granted. I'll take you to lunch.'

She raised an eyebrow.

'When you're in a better mood. In the meantime, they got spicy Fritos and Entenmann's chocolate-chip cookies in the vending machine down the hall.'

She passed him the arrest form. 'You wanna do a photo lineup with the kid and mom, then? Get a positive ID on Poole?'

'I'm worried about confusing the kid: she's so young. This guy looks radically different in his DL. She's already gonna be an easy witness for a defense attorney to discredit; let's not give them more ammo with a faulty ID.'

'So whatta ya want to do?'

'A photo lineup with mom. If she IDs, we build a solid case against Poole. Then we do a live lineup with the kid if we think she's strong enough to handle it.'

'Do you think mom will ID? She's definitely holding something back about that night.'

Bryan put the report into a manila folder, slid it into Santri's accordion and put the whole thing into the file box. 'Maybe she's just feeling guilty because of the outcome, what happened to Santri,' he replied thoughtfully. 'Maybe she's got a few reasons of her own why she didn't come forward till her kid spoke up. I think she'll ID, though. Because now she knows what happened to this guy's last victim. I'm sure she doesn't want to be responsible for what happens to his next.'

32

Even though Faith knew detectives were planning on running the sketch in the papers from Orlando on south, she was still startled to see it staring back at her from the front page of the *Sun-Sentinel*'s local section, right underneath the headline:

POLICE SEEK ID OF SUSPECT IN RAPE AND
MURDER OF PALM BEACH DANCER.

And even though Jarrod had predicted that the case might grow larger than the local section, she wasn't prepared to see that same sketch on the news. Or hear the reporter inaccurately portray a 'thirty-two-year-old Parkland woman and her four-year-old daughter' as witnesses to Angelina Santri's abduction and murder. While they weren't specifically named and there wasn't a map to their house appearing on the screen next to the sketch, she immediately thought of Jarrod's frightening admonition: *He knows there're witnesses and now he knows they're talking. It won't be hard for him to figure out the rest – name, address, phone number . . .*

She took a long sip from the flask that she'd filled with Ketel One and stared blankly at the *Cupcake Wars* supplemental application on the computer screen that she'd been working on for over an hour. She had three lines completed so far. It was hard to concentrate on anything. But she hadn't been to the bakery since Angelina's body was found and things were piling up and she couldn't leave everything on Vivian's plate. Without knowing what was going on, Vivian had been very understanding, telling Faith to take as much time as she needed, but that tolerance couldn't – shouldn't – last indefinitely. They had a business to run. A growing business, actually. The realtor had called yesterday to tell Faith that he'd found the perfect location in Fort Lauderdale near the beach for Sweet Sisters' second shop. She was supposed to head out there this afternoon to take a look at it with him.

She felt like a sneaky teenager, drinking on the sly in her office at ten in the morning on a Thursday. She knew how it would look if anyone found out. But no one had any idea the pressure she was under. Her nails were bitten to the quick, her hair was coming out in the shower. She was smoking almost a pack a day, even though she told herself she was still trying to quit. To calm what felt like every frazzled nerve in her body, she reasoned that a shot of something to take the edge off was better than popping a fistful of Xanax, like a lot of ladies on the car-pool line did on a daily basis. It was just less accepted.

A girl was dead and she was responsible. No matter how many ways she'd tried to talk herself out of that account-ability before Angelina Santri's body had been found, it wasn't working any more. The horrifying realization was slowly wearing away at her paralyzed conscience and physic-ally breaking her down, much like waves can reduce a rock to sand by crashing violently and continuously into it. Piece by piece, her life was in danger of falling apart. Then there were all the lies she'd told. And the ill-thought-out lies that followed to cover up the lies that got her in trouble in the first place. Guilt had invaded her sleep, manipulating dreams into nightmares – even when she couldn't remember the dream itself, she'd wake hearing the girl's raspy whispers for help. And her makeup-streaked, crazed face somehow managed to appear in every dream she could recall, even if it was only a face in the crowd. In last night's nightmare, Faith had reached to open the car door, only to hit the lock purposely with her hand, watching as the girl screamed and the *Deliverance* man pulled her out of sight. She'd woken up screaming herself, feeling his mutton chops scratching against her cheek, his breath smelling like sodden earth, his arms wrapped around her own body, pulling her back into the abject darkness with him.

It was actually Jarrod, though, trying to hold her as she thrashed about in their bed, punching out at invisible demons. He was trying to comfort her, to tell her it was only a nightmare, that it wasn't real. He'd asked her to tell him what the dream was about, to tell him what was going on with her, but she'd pushed him away and gone into the bathroom. She couldn't tell him. It was too late.

It was too late.

The plan had been to tell Detective Nill everything when they went out to the scene: the presence of a second man in the woods, the fact that she had been drinking and feared getting a DUI – even the accident. She would tell him everything. She would explain why she was so reluctant to come forward: first for fear of being arrested; and then second, for fear she would lose her husband and her family. That was the plan. But Jarrod had come along. He was in the car with her and the two detectives as they drove down streets that looked much less threatening than they had that night. The cane fields that had menacingly towered over both sides of the roadway, claustrophobically boxing her into a dizzying asphalt maze, had been cut and burned in some stretches; the road signs that she couldn't seem to find in the driving rain were seemingly everywhere. Then they had found the town – Pahokee. It had two stoplights and definitely had seen better

170

days in years past, but with people milling about and businesses open for business, it didn't look so much like the small, creepy, Stephen King town she remembered it being. And the modest houses they passed that fed off Main Street – one after the other, with cars in the driveways and swing sets on the front lawns. She hadn't seen them that night. It was a neighborhood she had driven through. Small, yes – concentrated within a few short blocks – but it wasn't a completely abandoned city like Chernobyl, infested with zombies. In the daylight, the reality of it all was jarring: she only felt more ashamed of her inaction and insecure of her perceptions. And Jarrod was right there beside her and the detectives the entire time – listening, jotting notes, asking questions, taking pictures alongside crime-scene techs. It was almost like he was a PD again, working up a case for one of his defendants. The plan was aborted at the last minute: she'd swallowed the confession that was going to make her feel so much better.

She heard Vivian's jingling jewelry and the clicking of her heels down the hall. She quickly poured a shot of the Ketel One into her coffee and tucked the flask in the bottom of her desk under a pile of junk. Vivian probably wouldn't care, but since she didn't know what the hell was going on, she just might.

The door opened. 'There you are!' Viv began with a broad smile. 'Linda told me you were back here! Where've you been, girl?'

She tried to smile back, but the tears had already started. She put her head in her hands. Jarrod and she had both agreed not to discuss 'the incident' with anyone. Maggie, too, was instructed not to say anything to her classmates, cousins, or teachers. Until they knew how the case was going to play out in the courts, in the press, it was best to keep silent. But the weight was suddenly too much to carry.

'Faith! Honey! Oh my God! What's the matter? Is it Maggie? Is she OK? Is it Jarrod? Are you guys OK?' Vivian was on her knees in front of her, embracing her in a huge hug.

'I have to tell you something,' Faith started. 'It's really bad, Vivian. It's . . . oh my God, so bad . . .'

'Is it cancer? Is someone sick?' Vivian asked, hugging her even tighter. 'Tell me, Faith!'

There was a knock on the office door. 'Mrs Saunders?'

'Not now!' Vivian yelled impatiently. 'Whoever that is, not now! Go away!'

'I'm sorry, Mrs Vardakalis,' replied the young voice ruefully. 'I'm really sorry to bother you, but there's ah, there are detectives out here. And they want to talk to Mrs Saunders.'

33

'We think we have a suspect,' Detective Nill said after his partner had closed the door to the office.

Faith stared at him. She was seated at her desk. The *Cupcake Wars* app was still on her computer, waiting to be completed. The purchase orders in the folder underneath her coffee cup had yet to be placed. Her legs began to shake. She thought of that time in the hospital. Another Life Before moment was about to pass. Everything, she sensed, was about to change. 'Already?' she asked, taking a long sip of her coffee.

'I want to show you some pictures,' began Detective Nill, pulling up a chair in front of her desk. He looked carefully over at Vivian, who had backed away from the conversation and was standing in a corner.

'Faith, what's this about? Should I call Jarrod?' Vivian asked worriedly.

Faith slowly shook her head.

'Maybe you want to do this alone?' asked Detective Maldonado.

'No. She can stay. I'm just gonna look at pictures, right?' Faith said, smiling weakly, her eyes locked on the folder in Detective Nill's hand, the one he was about to open.

Detective Nill shrugged. 'As long as . . .?'

'Vivian Vardakalis,' answered Vivian.

'That's a mouthful,' quipped Detective Nill. 'As long as Ms Vardakalis doesn't say anything while you're looking at the photos.'

Vivian shook her head and backed further into the corner.

The detective then opened the folder and placed it in front of Faith on the desk. 'I want you to take your time and look at them carefully and tell me if you see the man who was with Angelina Santri that night.'

And everything changed.

Six 3×5 close-up photographs of different men – perhaps mug shots or driver's license photos – were lined up next to each other. All slim, white males between the ages of twenty and thirty-five with dark hair. She recognized him right away. She felt her chest tighten and her heart start to race. She watched her trembling finger point at the middle picture, top row. 'Him. This guy.'

'This is the man – you're sure? Number three?'

'Yes, that's him. His hair was longer, and he had that facial gruff I told you about, but that's his face. That's him.'

'Who is that guy?' asked Vivian apprehensively from the back of the room.

'Are you going to show this to Maggie, too?' Faith asked. Underneath the desk she clenched her hands together to get them to stop shaking.

'Maggie?' Vivian whispered, confused.

Detective Nill looked over at Vivian before answering. 'We may do a live lineup with her at a future date.'

'Is this the guy, though?' Faith asked, her voice cracking. 'Is it him? Is this your suspect? Or is it one of the other ones? Did I pick the wrong guy?'

'Does the name Derrick Alan Poole mean anything to you, Mrs Saunders?'

'Derrick . . . Poole? No,' she replied.

'He's from West Boca. Lives off of Yamato in The Shores of Boca Raton. Are you familiar with that complex?'

'No. Well, yes, I know where it is, but . . . West Boca . . . that's right here . . . that's right here . . .' she murmured. West Boca was a large, unincorporated community west of the City of Boca Raton. The Shores of Boca Raton was a housing development off Yamato and 441. It was north of Parkland by maybe five miles. The fact that this man was living only five miles away from her was not just a disturbing coincidence – it was a terrifying one.

'It's not too far from here, that is correct.'

'Did someone see the sketch and recognize him?' Faith asked.

'Oh my God! The guy who killed that dancer in the cane fields!' Vivian exclaimed. The name Angelina Santri had meant nothing to her, but she obviously knew the story everyone in town was talking about this morning – the story that had everyone speculating about the identity of the two Parkland residents who had witnessed the poor young mother's abduction and murder.

Detective Nill ignored Vivian's comment. 'We've gotten several tips from people who think they recognize the person in the sketch. We're investigating them all.'

'So what happens now?' Faith asked. She took another long gulp of her coffee. 'Will you arrest him?'

The detective was slow in replying. 'We're still conducting our investigation.'

'But I've identified him – so you're going to arrest him, right?'

'We don't have probable cause yet to arrest him for murder. Further investigation has to be done to tie him specifically with Angelina's death.'

Faith dug her ragged nails into the chair's arms. 'Wait . . . this is crazy. So he's out? He lives, like, twenty minutes from here, you're telling me, and he's free? And he's gonna stay free? That's crazy. That's just crazy. What about the murders of those other girls you were telling me about? Can't you arrest him for those?'

'Other murders! Oh my God!' cried Vivian. She tried to cover her mouth with her hand, to take the outburst back in, but it was too late.

Nill looked over at Vivian, then back at Faith. 'Like I told you before, Mrs Saunders, and I'll advise you, as well, Ms Vardakalis, that information is not being made public yet. I'm not at liberty to discuss what stage of investigation we're at with possible related cases.'

'So he's just walking around until you do that? What about me and my daughter? My family? Does he know about us?' Faith asked frantically, looking at Detective Maldonado, hoping for a different answer. She was trying not to lose it, but her voice was rising.

Vivian hurried over and rubbed Faith's shoulder. 'It's gonna be OK, honey.' But she didn't sound very sure of herself.

'He told me not to say anything, so I didn't,' Faith muttered. 'He warned me with his finger. I was scared, so I didn't say anything. Now . . . now . . . oh, God. He's gonna know who I am, where I live! Who my daughter is!'

'I don't believe Mr Poole is aware that he's a subject of an investigation yet, Mrs Saunders,' replied Nill somberly. 'He obviously doesn't know that you've identified him, yet. The tip that came in about him was anonymous. I doubt he knows he's being looked at as a possible suspect.'

She thought of Jarrod's warning once again. She heard the reporter's excited voice in her head from last night's newscast, recklessly reporting that there were actual witnesses to Angelina Santri's abduction and murder. The reporter was a breath away from saying her name. She looked off at a spot on the wall. 'But he will, Detectives. I'm married to a former public defender; I know how the law works,' she said jadedly.

176

'He'll have a right to know the witnesses against him, and that will mean he will know my name and my daughter's name. And you'll have to give it to him. Isn't that right, Detectives?'

34

Bryan Nill put down his binoculars and thoughtfully stroked his chin. Through the front window of the townhouse, he could still see the bright flicker and flash of colors emanating from Derrick Poole's living room TV, although without the binoculars he couldn't make out the faces on the screen any more. Or the expressionless face of Derrick Poole, who sat on the couch like a lump, watching it.

Just like he'd done every night for the past five nights.

Except for work, the guy never went out. No one ever came over. He microwaved dinners and did bills on his computer. He played video games, watched primetime network TV every night and went to bed before the news at eleven. He didn't have a dog, or if he did, he never walked it and Bryan never saw it. He didn't play loud music. He took his garbage out on Thursday mornings and put the can back in the garage that night. He drove a tan Honda Accord and didn't go over the speed limit. If the past five days painted an accurate picture, from the outside looking in, Derrick Poole was as uninteresting as you might think a number cruncher would be.

The positive ID by Faith Saunders was huge – but it wasn't enough for probable cause on a murder charge. Just being the last person seen with a girl before she turned up dead, in and of itself wasn't a crime. It was really interesting. It was thought provoking. And it might be damning in the court of public opinion. But it wasn't enough to slap cuffs on the guy. In order to do that Bryan needed more, which was why he was sitting outside Poole's house with a burger in a bag, a six-pack of Red Bull and a pair of binoculars.

The ID was probably enough, though, to obtain a search warrant for Poole's townhouse and car. Once inside, of course, the hope would be to find boxes filled with damning evidence, a closet converted into a torture chamber, and body parts from the other three women who'd turned up dead and missing a couple of their original pieces – but the chances of that happening were pretty slim. The chances of finding much of anything, Bryan feared, were pretty slim. If the guy was a serial killer, he was smart, calculating, and organized. He had successfully abducted and murdered three women over the course of a year without anyone noticing and without leaving so much as one scrap of trace evidence behind. His head-scratching screw-up on the fourth was not disposing of two accidental witnesses. Chances were a killer that disciplined was going to be very careful about not keeping a treasure trove of evidence around his pristine, attached townhouse in posh West Boca that would implicate him in jaywalking, much less murder – especially seeing as he knew he had left witnesses out there. Chances were he had a secret place many miles away from here where he'd held his victims and done his evil deeds. A kill spot that was sure to be filled with damning evidence.

That's what Bryan really wanted to find.

Rather than jump in and get a warrant right away and tip Poole off that they were looking at him, Bryan had decided to set up on the townhouse and gather intel for a few days before the guy had any idea he was a suspect. The hope was that Poole might unwittingly lead him to where he was hunting his victims from, or where he had stashed the missing body parts, or where he was actually keeping that torture chamber of his that Bryan feared truly did exist. He didn't have much time – probable cause to believe 'the object of the search was likely be found at the place to be searched', i.e. the townhouse, had the potential of growing stale the longer he waited and a judge might not issue a warrant. And, of course, once Poole knew that he was on law enforcement's radar, any of the intel Bryan had hoped to gain through surveillance – Poole's habits, routes he travelled, places he visited, and the people he associated with – would be corrupt and of little or no value.

And then there was the more immediate risk that a tactical decision to wait on a warrant presented: if Poole figured out he was a suspect before Bryan got a warrant, he could destroy whatever evidence might have existed in that house. So while Bryan sat outside with his dinner and binoculars watching *Criminal Minds* on Derrick Poole's flat screen, the smart, calculating killer could be in his bathroom flushing incriminating pictures of his victims down the fucking toilet. And the worst part of that nightmare scenario was, Bryan would never know. He reached for the binoculars again as he pounded his chest to get that last bit of burger to go down. Just the thought that the case could already be compromised was giving him a serious case of agita.

So he'd given himself a week. One week to find out all he possibly could about Derrick Alan Freeley Poole without him knowing anyone was asking. Or watching. He and Maldonado had re-interviewed witnesses on all four cases to see if there was any link between the victims and Poole. There was none. They'd shown Poole's picture around at the Animal, but that hadn't jarred any memories. No one could say for sure they recognized him, although the two bouncers who were working the night Angelina disappeared did say that they had seen a person matching Poole's description with a ponytail hanging around the parking lot. Bryan had pulled cell records and looked at texts. Nothing stood out. The next step was

180

contacting Poole's mom in Arizona and visiting his grandma in the nursing home, but Bryan wasn't expecting much from either of those interviews, either.

It had been five days so far and he was beginning to think either he had it all wrong or Poole was playing him, because the guy did *nothing*. Maybe everyone and their brother had told him he looked like the person in the sketch and he couldn't help but agree himself when he saw it, so he figured someone must have jabbered to the cops and he was gonna lay low. Or maybe the girl who had called in the tip – Gemma Jones – had told him she'd tipped off the police. Bryan and Maldonado had visited her at her apartment yesterday, only to hear her now claim 'bad lighting' in the office had made her think Derrick looked like that sketch, because he didn't and she now knew that 'he could never hurt a fly anyway'. Then she worried if he would ever find out she'd called in a tip. It wasn't hard to read between the lines – Gemma Jones and Derrick Poole were dating. Or hooking up. Or whatever it was you call it when young people fool around.

The investigation was at a standstill: surveillance wasn't yielding anything of interest, possibly because it was already compromised, and the clock was ticking down on getting that warrant. Bryan popped open another Red Bull and settled in for one final long night of doing nothing. A week was too long; he had to move soon.

It was frustrating. He knew Poole was his guy. He just knew it in his substantial gut.

The frightening reality might be, though, that he would never be able to prove it.

35

Fucking Gemma.

Derrick watched in his rearview as the car pulled out behind him. He knew they were following him. He'd first noticed them yesterday: black Taurus, dark windows, hanging two cars back, trying not to look obvious.

He knew Gemma had yapped to the cops the day that sketch had come out in the paper: sitting there in her car smiling like the cat that ate the canary with the newspaper face-up on her lap, the picture of his face staring up at her. Then she'd seen him standing there, and that smug smile had crashed and burned. He'd asked her about it when he was fucking her in the bathroom at work two nights later, after everyone else had gone home.

'Hey,' he'd said. 'You think that sketch they're running in the news looks like me?' He couldn't see her face 'cause he was going at her from behind, but he'd felt even her tits tense up.

'What sketch?' she'd tried.

'The one in the paper that's sitting in your top desk drawer.'

'I didn't even know I'd left a paper in there. I must have stuck it there by accident. I never look in that drawer. I don't even read the paper usually. What sketch?'

Blah, blah, blah. The lying diarrhea poured out in stumbling sentences. It was a good thing he couldn't see her face, because he wanted to stick his fist in her mouth so he didn't have to listen any more. 'Cops are looking for a murderer,' he'd replied softly.

'Oh,' was all she managed.

'And a rapist,' he'd whispered in her ear as he came.

That sketch was everywhere now. It was weird seeing his face on the news, like some cartoon comic book villain. He'd wondered and worried how many people besides Fucking Gemma might have recognized him and called the cops. There couldn't be many. Most people didn't notice when he walked into a room, and they didn't remember when he left it. He kept to himself, never talked to the neighbors. He went to different grocery stores each week and never frequented the same restaurant or club twice. Debt Destroyers only had thirty employees and he was the entire accounting department. It wasn't like it was for the guys on the floor, or in HR or Sales who had to schmooze with clients and employees alike. Paychecks were direct deposited; no one knew anyone in accounting.

He was eating breakfast when he first saw the sketch in the morning paper. It made him throw up. For two seconds he'd thought about leaving town – chucking what he could into a suitcase, hopping on I95 and getting the hell out of Dodge. But that would make him look guilty. It was only a drawing; it wasn't a photo. If they had his name, they'd be at his door, he reasoned, not asking for help from the audience. He'd decided to carry on as if everything was normal.

By the time he got to work that morning without being taken down by a SWAT team, anxiety had turned to anger. He'd warned that mommy not to say anything. There were no other witnesses; it could only be her: Blondie. He could have cut her and her little kid into a thousand pieces and scattered them into the cane fields like Profe had wanted to do, but he hadn't. He'd stupidly cut her a break. He'd been a nice guy.

That was the last time that would ever happen.

Fucking Gemma. She wouldn't say shit about him to anyone ever again. But the damage had already been done – that's why that Taurus was behind him.

It was like they read his mind and knew the gig was up. Blue lights exploded in his rearview, followed by the whoop of a siren. He pulled over into a CVS parking lot, threw the Accord into park and reached for his wallet. His hands were shaking and that pissed him off.

There was a tap on the glass. 'Hands where I can see them please, sir.'

He put his hands back on the steering wheel.

'Lower the window, please.'

'You said not to move my hands,' he replied.

'Step out of the car, please.'

Derrick lowered the window and tried to explain. He held one hand up. 'You said to show my hands, that's all I was saying. What's this about, officer? What did I do?'

She was pretty, but plain. Spanish, he figured, like every other person in South Florida. Long dark hair pulled into a ponytail. She wore slacks and a fitted jacket. A gold badge hung from a chain around her neck.

'You didn't signal, sir, when you turned onto Jog,' she answered, matter of factly.

'Oh, OK. I guess I forgot. Look, I'm sorry. I just got out of work right down the block. Can I promise not to do it again?' he tried with a smile. He pushed his glasses up on his nose.

'I'm afraid not. License and registration.'

He handed them over.

'Please step out of the car, Mr Poole,' she said without even looking at the license.

'Sure.' His legs began to shake, too. He opened the car

door and stepped out. 'What's this about? Is this really about my blinker?'

'Why are your legs shaking, Mr Poole? Are you nervous?' she asked, almost tauntingly.

He dropped the smile and stared at her. He could feel his blood pressure rising. *I'll make you shake, bitch* was what he wanted to say. He could feel his tongue trembling and he clenched his teeth together. He heard the crunch of footsteps approaching.

'Hi, Derrick,' said a heavyset man in dress slacks and a jacket as he walked up. A gold badge hung from his fat neck, too. 'I'm Detective Bryan Nill with the Sheriff's Office. You've already met Detective Maldonado here.'

'What's all this about?' Derrick finally demanded, his eyes still locked on the female detective whose neck he now wanted to snap.

'Well, sir, you did commit a moving violation; that's why we pulled you over,' Nill replied. 'And you are driving on a suspended license, which is an arrestable offense, so you've got some problems, son.'

'My license is not suspended.'

'I assure you it is.'

The female detective had broken from his stare, so he turned to the fat detective. 'But that's not why you pulled me over.'

'I want to talk to you about an investigation that Detective Maldonado and I are conducting. It's probably a misunderstanding, but we thought you could help us clear it up.'

'Wow. What kind of investigation?'

'A murder investigation.'

'A murder?' he exclaimed. 'Whoa! What?'

'You look an awful lot like a person who was last seen with a young lady before she turned up dead,' Detective Maldonado said.

He couldn't look at her again. The way she spoke, in that teasing, know-it-all way, was like listening to nails scratch a

185

chalkboard. The fat detective pulled out the sketch that had made him throw up in his kitchen sink.

'Looking like a bad guy and being a bad guy are two different things altogether, Derrick,' Detective Nill said easily. 'And I recognize that. I got a lot of guys who look like this sketch, tell you the truth. I gotta ask them all the same thing. Can you tell us where you were and who you were with on the nights of October seventeenth, eighteenth and nineteenth?'

'The seventeenth, eighteenth and nineteenth of October?' Derrick repeated.

The female shone a flashlight into the back seat of his car and took a nosy peek in the window, her hand cupped around her eyes. 'That was a Friday night, a Saturday and a Sunday,' she piped in. 'It was only a few weeks ago, so it shouldn't be that hard, Mr Poole.'

'If we can verify that information, then we can be on our way and you can be on yours,' said Detective Nill. 'We'll be sorry for wasting your time.'

Derrick tried a smile again. 'Are you kidding me? I can't remember what I had for breakfast today.'

'Oh, I bet you could if you tried real hard,' replied Nill.

'Maybe you can tell me, Detective.'

The fat one stared back. He looked a little stunned.

'I've seen you, you know.' Derrick knew there was nothing he could say that was going to get them to leave him alone. He also knew they didn't have shit on him or he'd be in cuffs right now. Maybe they were hunting down every slob who looked like that sketch. Maybe they weren't. It sure as hell felt like all eyes were on him and only him, and he wasn't going to give them any nails to put in his coffin. 'I'd like a lawyer,' he added before either detective found their voice again.

Fatty raised an eyebrow. 'Whoa, Derrick. What do you need a lawyer for? We just want to ask you a few questions. Same thing I gotta ask the other fellas. All you gotta do is tell me where you were and who you were with. Once I clear you, you won't see me no more.'

Derrick shook his head. 'I want a lawyer. Now you can take me in, you can write me a ticket, or you can let me go, but unless you want to talk about the weather or how the Dolphins are doing this season, I'm gonna exercise my right to remain silent, lest anything be misconstrued against me. Sorry.'

He didn't think they'd let him leave and he was right, so he wasn't surprised when they cuffed him and called in the cavalry. Five minutes later a half-dozen cop cars showed up. He stared out the window of the back seat of the cruiser that was going to transport him to jail, knowing that his every breath was being recorded. He watched as the cops towed his car, so they could search it later with the warrant they were sure to get.

And he thought to himself that when all this was over, after he had bonded out of jail on a bullshit driving with a suspended license charge, after he had had a chance to calm down and think things through, he was gonna have to pay Blondie a little visit.

Maybe next time she'll listen to a killer when he tells her to shut the fuck up.

36

'Anything on the car?' Bryan asked, popping a piece of Nicorette into his mouth as he headed up the stairs that led to Poole's master bedroom. After Audrey left him he'd started smoking again and he'd still managed to gain seventy pounds. Then his internist had told him two of his arteries were clogged and his blood pressure could not be controlled without a pill: he had to quit smoking. And eating. He'd gained another thirty since putting down the smokes and he still couldn't breathe. He pulled the phone away from his mouth so Tatiana couldn't hear him sucking wind.

'We found fibers,' Tatiana replied. She was at the PBSO crime lab with Poole's Honda Accord. 'In the trunk. Also on the passenger-side floorboard and into the seat cushion.'

'How many?'

'Nine in the trunk, and another dozen in and around the front seat. Red and black. Maybe they'll match Santri's jacket. That would place her in his car.'

'Santri's jacket wasn't ripped. But we never found her panties or her jeans.'

'Her bra?' she tried.

'It was leopard print. T-shirt was white.'

'What about that piece of fabric Crime Scene found out in the lot in Pahokee?' she asked.

Now that was interesting. Crime Scene had done a sweep of the area where Faith Saunders had claimed she saw Santri and Poole, including the wooded lot across the street. Because almost three weeks had passed since the encounter, there was no way of knowing what was evidence and what was a beer can that had been sitting there for years. So they'd seized everything – including a torn, not-so weathered piece of plaid fabric that was found in the wooded lot near a felled tree.

'That's a thought, Maldonado. Let's see if we can match those fibers you found to that fabric. If it looks good, we'll send it out to FDLE to see if they can pull DNA. It was out there in the elements for a while, not sure what we'll get.'

'Tell me you found a torn plaid shirt in Poole's closet,' said Tatiana. 'That would be a trifecta: fibers in trunk to fabric in woods to shirt in suspect's closet.'

'The trifecta would actually be fibers under victim's finger-nails to fabric in woods to ripped shirt splashed with victim's blood hanging in Poole's closet. But that's not happening on either end. There's nothing here, Maldonado,' Bryan said with a sigh, looking around Poole's neat, minimalist-styled bedroom. Framed movie posters decorated white walls, like they did downstairs – the guy was obviously a movie buff. TV show and movie memorabilia from *The Walking Dead*, *The Office*, *The Godfather*, *Criminal Minds* filled free-standing shelves. Everything was in its original packaging and arranged as if on a store shelf. The closet, too, looked like it was staged: ironed clothes – all arranged by color – spit-shined shoes. The top shelf was a little more cluttered. There was an assortment of sports equipment and memorabilia: tennis rackets, golf cleats, baseball gloves, a football, pads, hats, lacrosse stick, soccer ball. Even ice skates and roller blades. Looking at him, you wouldn't take the guy for an athlete. No way. Not only because he was an accountant. He was tall and lanky, almost scrawny on the upper chest area, and with those glasses and boring, practical car, you wouldn't think there was enough testosterone running through those veins to fuel an interest in playing every sport imaginable. Plus, Bryan had watched him do nothing but play video games for the last five days. He fingered the equipment. Most of it looked like it had never been used. There was a separate section in the closet for signed jerseys – hockey, football and basketball – that were preserved in plastic. Boy, the shrinks would have a field day with this guy.

'Are you done over there?' she asked.

'Not yet; they're packing up downstairs. If he ever had anything here, Maldonado, he got rid of it as soon as he knew we were on him.'

'Did he bond out yet?'

The DWLS charge was only a misdemeanor. It let them cart Poole off to jail, but it definitely wouldn't keep him there for long. 'I'm sure by now. Nobody was here when we got here with the warrant. I had the place secured by uniforms before we even took him down at CVS, in case he called someone to move shit while he was locked up. No one's shown up. Probably waiting on us to finish up here, 'cause he knows we ain't gonna find anything anyway, Maldonado.'

'Stop beating yourself up. Surveillance was the smart decision,' she said.

'Thanks. The fibers are something, at least. I'll take anything at this point to put her in that damn car. That would be nice.'

'What about three strands of her hair?' Tatiana offered.

'You're shitting me.'

'In the trunk. And no, I would never do that.'

'You have Santri's hair in Poole's trunk?' He caught himself smiling for the first time today.

'Well, the lab will confirm if they're hers, but they're long and dark and one is purple, which, if I remember correctly, matches the color of the streaks she had in her hair. And that would not only place her in his car – it would place her in his *trunk*. Now what the hell would she be doing back there?'

37

Everything suddenly seemed brighter. This was big. Really big. There weren't many explanations for how a dead girl's hair got in someone's trunk that didn't involve her head being in there with it. And if the fibers in the car matched that patch, it would at least place Poole in the same woods that Angelina had disappeared in: It would corroborate Faith Saunders' ID. And it might be enough to charge Poole with murder.

'Now for the not-so-good news,' Tatiana replied hesitantly.

Bryan felt his chest tighten and he got ready for the punch that he had a feeling was gonna take his breath away. 'I knew my high was too good to last. What was that? Ten seconds?'

'I just got a call from Carl Edmunds over at Riviera Beach PD. They got a girl, the name's Noelle Langtry, age seventeen, who's been reported missing. She lives with her mom at Southern Court, a mobile home park. Mom says she went missing three days ago. Teens run away all the time, but what makes this interesting for us is the kid dances at Sugar Daddy's. Mom says she lied about her age to work there – she's a high school dropout. Because of her age she might get more attention from the cops and the media than your average missing stripper. Edmunds saw your flag in the system; they routed the call to me.'

'Three days ago? That was Saturday.' Three days ago he was sitting outside Poole's townhouse till eight in the morning. *Fuck*. 'Was she working Saturday?'

'Yeah. Did her shift, got off at one. Never went home. Apparently that's not too crazy, cause Mom waited two days to report her missing, but no one has heard from her since. Her car was still parked in the back lot.'

Fuck, fuck, fuck. If it was an abduction, it couldn't be Poole. It was that simple. Or that complicated. If this girl turned up dead in a cane field, then it couldn't be Poole. Bryan was watching the house the whole night and the guy was home the whole time. That would mean he was looking at the wrong guy. He wouldn't be the first detective to try and make the suspect fit the crime. Was that what he was doing here?

But Faith Saunders had ID'd. There was a long purple hair in the trunk of Poole's car. Derrick Poole refused to give an alibi, because he obviously had none. There were a lot of pieces missing to the puzzle, but he did have a couple. He just wasn't sure yet where they fit.

'You still there?' Tatiana asked. 'Did you hear anything I said?'

His brain was jumping the gun, imagining the worst-case scenario and trying to fix it. Maybe this Langtry girl had gone missing for the usual reasons strippers and prostitutes went missing: drugs, pimps, boyfriends. It didn't mean she was a victim. And it didn't mean she was a victim on *this case*.

'Oh, I heard it,' he replied quietly, starting down the stairs. He had to let out the crime-scene techs who'd thoroughly combed through the townhouse and found nothing.

'This probably has nothing to do with us,' she tried. 'You want me to take a ride out to Sugar Daddy's and see what they know?'

'Nah. I'll head over there after I'm done here. I'll talk to you later,' he replied quickly.

A discouraging thought came to him as he sat at the

breakfast bar completing the disappointing inventory of property taken under the warrant for the return that had to be filed with the court tomorrow. Maybe he was looking for a serial killer because he was *hoping* for a serial killer. Something that was more important than just a regular homicide. Something that would make him more important than just a regular detective. Something that would make life exciting and him exciting and maybe get Audrey to notice him again.

It was hard to think this way, but he had to be honest with himself. Especially if the case against Poole started to fall apart – or, more fittingly, the pieces never came together to form the picture he wanted to see. Maybe he'd been building this Cane Killer case up, trying to make it something it wasn't so that he wouldn't have to think about how his own life sucked. He could be the rock star of the detective world. At least in Palm Beach. He could make headlines and be asked to speak at conferences and maybe write a book about the experience. Like a bullied teen who dreams of social revenge one day – he'd be someone special again and he'd show her.

He'd gained a hundred pounds since Audrey blindsided him fourteen months ago and asked for a divorce. Before that awful day, he'd taken two-week summer family vacations with her and the girls to family places like the Grand Canyon and the Smoky Mountains. On weekends he'd held garage sales, and washed both the car and the dog in the driveway of the house he'd worked real hard to buy in Boynton Beach, while he waved hello to neighbors he'd known for years. He went out to dinner with other couples, and joshed the guys in the squad who were on wives number three and four.

Now he lived in an apartment that was a few miles from the Key West-style two-story Audrey had once called her 'dream house'. He'd pushed himself and the budget to buy it for her just so he could see that smile on her face – the one that made his insides glow. Most nights he ate dinners that came from a microwave or a local takeout on his rented sofa. He could count the pieces of furniture that were in his apartment on his fingers. He saw his kids on Wednesdays and every other weekend. He tried to see them more, but they were always so busy. The girls were seventeen, and he wasn't sure if it was their age or his size, but they weren't excited to see him any more when he showed up at school to surprise them at lunch or after school at their softball games and lacrosse practices. The twins used to think he was so cool, that what he did was so cool – now they were embarrassed when he hugged them in public. He rang the bell at the house he worked overtime to buy, and watched as his former neighbors avoided saying hello to him as they washed their cars and their dogs in their driveways, because, as Audrey had explained, 'It's awkward for everyone, Bryan.' Twenty-two years and she just didn't love him any more. It wasn't her and it wasn't him. It was as simple and devastating as that.

'We're done here, Detective,' called out Styles, the crime-scene tech, from the front door.

Bryan stood up and looked around the empty kitchen. He felt incredibly lonely. 'Me too,' he replied quietly, gathering his papers and his bag.

It was unmanly to cry, even when no one was around to see.

So he never did.

38

Faith took a cart and waded into the crowded supermarket, politely dodging a woman who was peddling samples of the Publix Apron Recipe of the Day. She had forty-five minutes to grab shampoo, toilet paper and something to cook for dinner, and then shoot back to pick Maggie up from ballet. Sometimes the teacher let the parents into the studio to watch the dance the girls had learned that afternoon, and if that was the case today, she only had thirty-five minutes.

Even before the 'incident', Maggie was funny about ballet class. Sometimes she didn't want Faith to stay, practically pushing her out the door at drop-off, proclaiming she could 'do it herself', and other times she demanded Faith stay and watch, even though mommies weren't actually allowed in the studio itself during class. Most moms sat around the lobby chatting amongst themselves or reading. Despite Maggie's protests of independence, usually Faith did too, but today she figured she'd get shopping out of the way so she didn't have to drag Maggie into the supermarket during dinner hour. Also, the truth was, she didn't want to sit and chat with anyone. She didn't want anyone looking at her for too long. She looked like she was about to crack, and if any of the moms started talking about something cute their kid did for them, or asked how Jarrod was, she might melt into a puddle of tears. And if anyone were to bring up the Palm Beach dancer or speculate as to the identity of the two Parkland witnesses to her murder – she would surely shatter into a million pieces. Right there, right then. That's how emotionally fragile she felt. She could only keep trying to get through each day, hoping that perhaps with time she'd be able to figure out a single solution to the mounting problems in her life: one that could lift the crushing weight of guilt that affected her every thought, but yet not cause the implosion of everything else in her life. Because she couldn't figure one out, she'd done nothing. As she'd already learned, that could be worse than doing something.

She headed off to the shampoo aisle and checked her watch. Hopefully she wouldn't catch traffic on University on her way back to ballet. No matter Maggie's mood at drop-off, she'd absolutely, completely panic if Faith wasn't waiting with all the other mommies when the studio door opened at the end of class. Her anxiety level the past three weeks had been at an all-time high, understandably. One minute she was very clingy, the next minute she ran from Faith as if she were a complete stranger. Usually that happened when Jarrod came home or walked into a room, so Faith wasn't sure if she was playing up to him or playing Faith while she waited for Daddy to come rescue her. She might be 'developmentally delayed', but like all kids, Maggie instinctively sensed weakness in her parents and exploited it to her advantage. She was four and not mature enough to realize, though, that the weakness she was exploiting, wasn't just going to score her a cookie from Daddy that Mommy wouldn't let her have – it was actually wearing away at an already compromised spot in the fabric of her parents' marriage. As much as it killed Faith to watch her little girl, her baby, run from her to Jarrod, it probably killed Jarrod to watch his daughter run from her mother, even if he was at the receiving end of her affection. Faith didn't know where she stood with

197

her daughter, so she could only stand still, waiting for Maggie to give her a sign, watching as she ran – to her sometimes, away from her others. Meanwhile, the stress that filled the house was like carbon monoxide, silently, insidiously, poisoning all three of them, but since they couldn't smell it, taste it, hear it, it was easier to pretend everything was going to be OK. No one argued. No one sniped. No one yelled. And no one talked about the 'incident'. They got up and did all the things they were supposed to do for the day and went back to sleep as the poison continued to fill the house.

The store was abuzz with beeps from the scanners and registers, and overhead announcements from the deli counter and bakery department. On her way to the paper products aisle, she decided on dinner: spaghetti and meatballs. Something quick and easy. She picked up a package of pre-made meatballs from the meat department and headed over to the pasta aisle, grabbing a box of Apple Jacks off an end cap and two cans of chicken stock off another. It was impossible to come out of a Publix with only the original amount of items you came in for. Jarrod was even worse. She'd send him for milk and he'd come back with half the store. And usually no milk. She smiled to herself. And he always came back with Ben & Jerry's Chubby Hubby – her favorite ice cream. Always. She rubbed her eye to stop the tears before they started. She couldn't lose it in Publix.

Bam! Her cart smacked right into another cart.

'Oh, I'm sorry,' she began, 'I wasn't paying atten—' She stopped in mid sentence.

Standing right in front of her, his cart blocking hers, was the man in black.

'That's OK,' he replied with a smile, pushing his glasses up on his nose. 'Accidents happen.'

She began to shake all over.

'As long as you say you're sorry and promise never to do it again,' he said.

Faith looked dumbly around her. The rest of the shoppers carried on as if nothing had happened. People checked prices and ingredients. She heard someone laugh raucously from the next aisle over. The manager urged customers on the overhead system to pick up fresh fried chicken in the deli department.

'Excuse me,' said a woman as she made her way past the two of them. Sitting in the front basket, protected from cart germs by a pink fitted cart Snuggie, was a chubby baby sucking on a pink rattle and fussing.

'Cute,' said the man in black, waving at the baby.

Faith opened her mouth but not so much as a squeak came out.

'Thank you,' said the mother. She shook the rattle at the baby, pushing the cart forward with her elbows.

The man put his finger to his lips. 'Shhhhhh,' he said as the pair passed. But his eyes never left Faith's.

With the cart clenched in her hands, Faith backed up and into a shopper.

'Ouch! Excuse me,' exclaimed an elderly man: Faith had run over his foot with the cart. His wife glared at her.

'That man, there, he, he's a . . . he took a girl . . .' she started to say. She'd finally found her voice, but it was soft and she did not even recognize it as her own. She pointed instead.

The old man was rubbing his foot. 'What did she say?' he asked his wife.

'Just say you're sorry,' snapped the wife, angrily. 'You ran into his foot and he's diabetic.'

'I'm sorry,' she said, 'but that man . . .' she began, pointing.

The man in black was gone.

The wife shook her head. 'Rude,' she said loudly. Then she led her husband away by the elbow. He limped past Faith, pushing the cart until they disappeared around a corner.

Faith reached for her cell phone and tried to think who to call. Jarrod? Detective Nill? Vivian? The aisle was empty now.

It was her standing there all alone with her phone in her hand, her mind paralyzed with fright. She couldn't even think. She left the cart and hurried out to the main aisle. A dozen or more checkout lines snaked their way around display bins full of holiday favorites: gravy, candied fruits, canned pumpkin. Thanksgiving was in a week. Her eyes searched everywhere, but he was gone.

Someone touched her shoulder. 'Faith!' said a cheerful voice. 'It's been a while—'

She jumped in her skin.

'You OK, Faith?' said the stranger she was supposed to recognize. 'You look a little pale.'

Faith shook her head, and with her hands over her ears, ran through the crowded supermarket checkout line and out the automatic doors as if the devil himself was hot on her trail.

39

'Please, mister. Please! I won't say nothing, just let me go. I just want to go home. I want to see my mom . . .' said the once pretty girl with a whimper. She awkwardly clutched the bars of her crate.

Ed squatted before her and cocked his head.

'I won't say anything, swear to God I won't!' she pleaded.

He shook his head. 'We all know you don't mean that, darlin'.'

'I do! I do!'

'You don't! You don't!' he mocked, in the same snivelly voice. He was getting a headache. He didn't have as much patience with them as Derrick. If they played good cop/bad cop, he always assumed the role of the bad one.

'I have a mom who needs me, mister. She's sick. I have to take care of her. I'm all she has.'

'I had a mom, too,' Ed replied. 'Everyone has a mom. Don't make you special.' He lit a cigarette.

'I won't say anything!'

'I've heard that before.' He looked around the candlelit room and sighed with annoyance. He thought of the blonde bitch as he fingered the lock.

'I want my mom!'

201

Ed studied her for a long, long moment. 'How old are you . . . ah, what's your name again? It's like a Christmas carol, right?'

'That's right, mister, it's Noelle. Noelle Marie. My mom is religious, you know. She believes in God. We're both very religious!'

He rolled his eyes. 'Not working in that place, you don't believe in God none.'

'Seventeen! I'm only seventeen!' she cried.

He nodded. 'That is young. Youngest yet. You got a whole life in front of you. Soooo . . . I'll tell you what. You convinced me to take a chance on you . . . kind of. Let's play a little game. It's called Trust Me. I'm gonna see how good you are at keeping your word. If you're better than the others, if you're honest, maybe I'll let you walk out of here. 'Cause being honest means a lot to me. I've been burned before. And it hurts.'

'I won't burn you! I'm not like other girls. I'm very loyal,' she whimpered. 'I'm not like the others. I can keep a secret. I've kept the worst kinds.'

'Now *that* is interesting. Well, I suppose it's not fair to judge you by the sins of the sisters who have come before you. I'm not *loco*, you know? I'm not unreasonable. So I'm gonna take off those cuffs 'cause they probably hurt and I'm gonna open up your crate and then I'm gonna go out, Noelle. I'm gonna walk out that door. And I want to see if you're right *here*, right *here* in this box when I get back. I might be gone five minutes or five hours or five days. But if you are right *here*, right where I left you, when I get back, then I'll know you can be trusted and I can let you go. We already had our fun, you and I. If you don't tell nobody about it, and I don't get in trouble none, then I can live with us keeping a secret.'

She nodded, crying. She looked away from the wall that was in front of her, but he knew she had seen the manacles and tools. He knew she had a pretty good idea of what might have happened to those lying, disloyal sisters who came before her. 'I'll be right here. You can trust me, mister. I swear.'

'We'll see now, darlin'. But you can't move so much as an inch out of your box. That's your den, ya hear?'

She nodded furiously.

He did as he had promised and opened the padlock on the crate and she held out her hands. He unlocked the cuffs and rubbed her raw wrists. He kissed her on the head. 'Now don't disappoint me, Noelle With The Name Like Christmas. I'm expecting big things from you.'

Then he got up, blew out the candles and left.

To her credit, it was almost two hours before he saw the front door slowly start to open. He checked his watch. If it was him in there, he'd've hightailed it out the second the room cleared, but then again, Ed knew what he was capable of. He stubbed out his cigarette before she could spot the glowing ember in the otherwise pitch-black darkness. He watched with a grin through the night-vision scope on his crossbow as she looked frantically around. Then she took off down the rickety front porch steps like a bat out of hell in nothing but a shirt. He let her get to the edge of the cane field, then took her down with an arrow to the leg.

'No! No!' she screamed as he picked her up and slung her over his shoulder.

'Ain't no one gonna hear you, darlin'. No one. You're all the same, you know,' Ed groused as he headed back up the creaky steps and kicked the door open.

'I'm sorry! I'm sorry! I won't say anything!'

'Can't trust the lot of you. But this time *I* did the lying, so don't feel too bad, darlin'. You see, I was gonna kill you anyway,' Ed said as the door closed behind them and the blackness enveloped them. 'I was just gonna make it hurt less.'

40

Bryan felt like he'd been summoned to the principal's office.

With her brow furrowed and her lips pursed, Elisabetta Romolo, the Palm Beach County Chief Felony Assistant secretly nicknamed Maleficent by the defense bar, was either listening intently to what he was telling her or she was growing increasingly annoyed at what she was hearing. She wore chic eyeglasses that matched her dark eyes, and a pantsuit that was a lot more expensive than the average prosecutor could afford. Bryan didn't know labels, but her glasses said Prada and her purse had that Burberry plaid that Audrey used to salivate over when they went shopping at Sawgrass and passed the outlet. Her long black hair was pulled into a pony that hung like an accessory over her shoulder. Most men would say Elisabetta Romolo was pretty – unless that man was charged with murder and she was his prosecutor. Or that man was the lead detective in a murder case and she was the prosecutor.

'The hairs in the trunk are Santri's. Labs came back yesterday. The fibers in the car match the patch of fabric found at the scene in Pahokee,' Bryan continued when she hadn't said anything. 'But we can't find the shirt or clothing where the fibers came from.'

Elisabetta blinked twice. 'And you have two witnesses that place Poole with your victim: Faith Saunders and her daughter.' She looked down at the police report in front of her. 'Her four-year-old daughter.' She sighed. 'I hate kids. As witnesses,' she added after a second.

'Yes. It's circumstantial, and I wish we had a murder weapon, but taken all together, I feel it's powerful.'

She tapped on the ME's report with a long red fingernail. 'But that's all you have in that trunk, Detective. Considering the violence that was committed to Angelina Santri's person, one would expect more. From her person and in that trunk.'

Bryan nodded. 'Maybe she wasn't placed in the trunk after she was dead. Maybe it was before. Maybe he knocked her out then transported her to Pahokee in the trunk before she was bloodied up. She escaped, saw Faith Saunders sitting in her car, was led away on foot and then was taken to where she was killed.'

'Wasn't her body found in Belle Glade?'

'Yes.'

'Well he didn't force her to walk to Belle Glade from Pahokee. So how did her body get to where it was ultimately found? It was transported. And by that point she would have been a muddy, if not bloody, mess.'

'I know what you're getting at. The body was likely tarped or wrapped, that's why there's no other trace evidence,' he replied testily. It felt like he was being grilled by Poole's defense attorney.

'Or she was transported some other way or in some other car, Detective. Don't get me wrong, I like the hairs. They're strong, and they place her in his car. But a perfect case they don't make. I have to be honest, the strongest evidence you have is also your most troubling – your witnesses. Now let's talk about this mom who you described to me as skittish, Detective. Why did she wait two weeks to come forward? And only after her kid spoke up? That's not encouraging. That tells me – no, that tells a jury – that either: a) the interaction that she saw between Poole and Santri was nothing to be alarmed about, which doesn't bode well for our case and doesn't jive with what her kid said; b) she's a cold-hearted bitch who had better things to do than call the police and help this woman; or c) she's covering something up.'

'How about d? She was scared shitless of this guy and worried he was gonna come find her.'

She nodded thoughtfully. 'With good reason. He did.'

'That was no accidental meeting in Publix, Elisabetta.'

'Of course not. It's very disturbing. But there's not enough for tampering.'

He shook his head. 'I can't arrest a guy for shopping in the same store as a possible witness against him in a case that hasn't even been filed. He told her to watch where she was going with her cart. The message worked, though: I think the lady's close to having a breakdown.'

'Understandably. He knows where she shops; he surely knows where she lives. Your sketch worked, Detective – your case has caught the eye of the media. Soon enough everyone will know who Faith Saunders is.' She sighed again and tapped on a gory crime scene photo. 'Still, waiting two weeks to open her mouth makes *me* skittish about her, Detective. That means a lot is riding on this little kid. It's not just me who doesn't like them – sometimes a judge won't even let them testify. They notoriously make unreliable witnesses. Which makes me ask you: Why didn't you get a positive ID on Poole with Maggie Saunders?'

'I thought we may want to do a live lineup with her. I didn't want to confuse her with mug shots of other men and an outdated picture of Poole. I realize the mom is weak.'

'You know that if the kid doesn't ID Poole, you're screwed, right? That'll be hard to recover from, especially with a mom who we can both agree doesn't make the best witness. The hairs? Poole will argue they transferred to his jacket when he hugged the Santri girl goodbye – who, heads up, he's gonna argue was a willing prostitute. Then he put his jacket in the trunk and headed home himself. There are too many innocuous explanations, Detective.' She paused for a long moment. 'Or more insidious ones. Maybe he'll argue *you* planted the hairs – make the suspect fit the crime.'

Bryan felt his face grow hot and his temper flare. He pointed at Poole's juvi report that she'd had her fingernail on. 'You've seen his history,' he replied quietly. 'You know what we're dealing with.'

'Inadmissible, but interesting. Let's talk about those other murders you were telling me about. Do you have anything that connects him to those? Anything at all?'

He shook his head. 'Like I said, same victim typology, same general dump area. Different manners of death, but mutilations in three cases. And all the bodies were clean: no trace evidence.'

Elisabetta nodded thoughtfully. 'The four-year-old as a witness is what makes the Santri case newsworthy, and with the case in the news, there's a chance you might get some more people coming forward with information. Of course, the frightening suggestion that there might be a serial killer at work in Palm Beach will get the phones ringing, too. But I don't think that's a good angle to go with if it can't be proved, Detective.'

The principal had just reprimanded him.

Bryan did not like Elisabetta Romolo, even if she was one of the best ASAs in a courtroom. They'd worked together on a robbery case years ago, back when she was just starting at the State Attorney's Office and a lot more humble and easygoing than she was now. He couldn't remember the particulars, only that she was quiet and sweet and had nice legs. Then, as the rumors told it, she got married to a rich, dickhead defense attorney, was cheated on, and turned evil. She took half of the dickhead's riches in the divorce – which was how she could afford to dress so nice – and the dickhead lost his half to the IRS once he went to prison for tax fraud after an anonymous birdie called in a tip about his offshore accounts. Bryan knew it wasn't easy to be a woman in law enforcement, or a prosecutor working alongside a male-dominated defense bar and judicial bench. But once it's proven you can play ball with the big names, there was no reason to be a bitch to everyone with a penis, including the very detectives who were supposed to help you make your case.

Without another word, Elisabetta stood, walked over to the door and opened it. He doubted she would be the one leaving her own office, so he gathered his Santri case file. The meeting was apparently over. 'What's next?' he asked as he slipped the file into his Cane Killer box. 'What else do you need to move on murder charges on this guy? Whatever it is, I'll do it; I'll get it done.'

'We'll do a live lineup with the kid. Let's see if she IDs, too.'

'OK. If not?'

She shot him a look over her chic glasses. Her fingers were wrapped around the door that she held open for him, her talons impatiently drumming away on the wood. She nodded at his file box. 'Then perhaps Poole is not your man and there's a reason you can't find additional evidence to link him to one murder, much less four, Detective. Because there isn't any.'

41

'You're sure that's him? The man holding the number five?' Bryan asked gently. Inside he was jumping with excitement. The little girl hadn't even hesitated. The whole thing had taken two minutes.

Maggie nodded and rubbed her nose. 'Yes. He made the lady cry,' she relied softly, staring into the glass at the five dark-haired, clean-shaven men dressed in black, who he'd feared would look too much like identical brothers to a nervous kid.

'OK,' Bryan said into the phone. 'Five can step back.'

'He can't see me? Because he'll be mad,' Maggie said quietly.

'No, honey,' replied Tatiana. 'None of them can see you.' She patted Maggie's back. 'Good job, honey.'

'Good job coming in here today and being so brave,' Bryan quickly added. Derrick Poole's attorney lurked in the back of the room somewhere, quiet enough to be momentarily forgotten, which was what he wanted. 'Why don't you and your dad head over to the vending machines by my office and I'll catch up with you all in a few minutes?' he said, ushering Maggie and Jarrod to the door. Jarrod, being a former PD, knew enough about the rules to say nothing. He took Maggie's hand and they walked off together down the hall.

'You told her she was picking the right guy,' Richard Hartwick, Poole's attorney, began to complain when they had left. He had the eyes of a basset hound – they sort of sagged into his long face and long mouth. Even after an acquittal, the man looked overwhelmed with sadness.

'Please, Richard,' Elisabetta curtly answered. 'She'd already picked the right guy. And you're pissed because that makes not one, but two witnesses who have positively identified your client.'

'Please, Elisabetta,' Hartwick snapped back, picking up his briefcase. 'One of them is four. And identified him doing what? Hanging with a girl who later ended up dead? Your victim was known for engaging in consensual extracurricular activities both at work and outside of it. Let's just say maybe she decided to do that with my client. They had their fun and he sent her on her merry way and never saw her again. That's unfortunate for her. My client was shocked to learn of her demise.'

'Really? Then why, Richard, has he suddenly decided to grocery shop at my witness's local Publix, where he coincidentally ran into her the other day with his cart? Do I look stupid?'

'I know you would love to pop him on something, Elisabetta. So I know it's killing you that he didn't threaten your witness, so you could at least have the pleasure of arresting him today. But he didn't and you can't and so we are both going to walk out of here now. Call me when you have a case.'

'What the hell were they doing in Pahokee, Richard?' she called out as he walked toward the door. 'Please. Joyriding in a tropical storm? That's a little far from Boca and Riviera Beach, don't ya think? And how long was their little consensual tryst? Two days?'

Richard turned back around. He was slightly taller than Maleficent but despite that and the angry words that he was saying, he looked rather small beside her. 'Your problem,

Elisabetta, is that your witnesses aren't witnesses to a crime,' he snapped. 'They didn't see your victim being forced anywhere. They didn't see a weapon. They didn't see him brutalize her. If they did, it's not in those reports. And if they did, it would be in those reports.' He turned to look at Bryan Nill. 'I know that you might be trying to make a case against him for some other random homicides you got out there, Detective Nill, hoping to package him up like some wireless bundle, thinking your case will sound better that way, but that ain't happening either. You have nothing but random homicides, so don't go trying to alarm the Palm Beach natives by yelling serial killer at the TV stations because, be forewarned, I will be ready to respond with a defamation suit.'

'Don't tell me how and what cases my detectives should investigate,' warned Elisabetta sharply before Bryan could start yelling himself. 'That threat only rouses my ire more.'

Hartwick scoffed and headed back for the door.

'And you still have those unanswered questions that a jury is going to want an answer to, Richard. What the hell was he doing in Pahokee?' she yelled.

'I'm not going to help you make your case, Elisabetta,' he fired back, his hand on the door. 'You get to figure out the whys, the whos, the wheres, and the hows. All I can offer are words of advice before you let that famous temper of yours get the better of your prosecutorial judgment: remember that your standard of proof is beyond and to the exclusion of every reasonable doubt. Good luck meeting *that*.'

42

'Are they going to arrest him now?' Faith asked anxiously, looking across the parking lot at the glass double doors of the police station. Every time they opened she held her breath until she saw the face of the person walking out. He was in there somewhere. The frightening question was: *Was he coming out?*

Jarrod sighed and shook his head. 'I don't know, Faith.'

They were standing between her Explorer and his Infinity, back by the trunk in the far end of the lot, near where the cruisers parked. Maggie was already strapped in her booster in Jarrod's car with the AC running and a DVD of her favorite movie, *Frozen,* so she couldn't hear them. Detective Maldonado had given it to her today as they walked out.

Faith absently stroked her hair. 'There's something you're not saying, Jarrod. What did the detective say after Maggie identified him? She did identify the right person, right? Derrick Poole?'

'They don't hold up signs with their name on it, honey. Detective Nill did indicate she picked the right person. I spoke with Elisabetta after. There are problems.'

'Who's Elisabetta?' Faith asked flatly, trying hard to rid her voice of the sudden surge of jealousy at the familiarity with which he said another woman's name. A woman she did not know.

'The prosecutor: Elisabetta Romolo. I knew her from when I worked in Miami. I had a client with a case in Palm Beach, as well. She was his prosecutor.'

'Oh. What did she say about this case?'

'She thinks she needs more.'

'What? They have her hair in his trunk, that's what the detective said!'

'Yes, but the hair strands in and of themselves are not enough. They can be explained away. They have these black and red fibers that they found in the car also, that they've linked back to a piece of material found at the scene in Pahokee, but the DNA they pulled on the fabric doesn't match this guy Poole.'

'But we saw him there with that girl! Maggie and I both!'

'It's not the ID. They believe that it was this guy that you saw out there. Problem is, you didn't really see him do anything bad, is what Elisabetta said. You didn't see him hit her or brutalize her or drag her off. You didn't see a weapon. She said "Help me", and she was crying, but then he kissed her and she walked off with him. His behavior in and of itself is not incriminating. You yourself said you didn't think he was going to hurt the girl, that's why you didn't call the police. That's how Elisabetta knows the defense will spin it. Being the last person seen with a stripper-slash-prostitute who ends up dead isn't enough for a murder conviction – you still have to prove he's the one who killed her. And once they arrest him, the speedy clock starts to tick, so they only have one hundred and eighty days to bring him to trial. That's six months. If they don't have enough evidence, and drop the case hoping to find some more, the clock keeps ticking anyway. And if they go forward and lose . . . well, double jeopardy will prevent them from going after him again. The state gets one bite at the apple and if Poole's a serial killer, if he's responsible for the murders of those other three women, then they don't want to screw up the only case where they have at least some evidence that ties him to one of the victims. Because, as I understand it, they have nothing else on the other three except a similar type of victim – prostitutes and strippers – and a cane field as a final resting place.'

'So he's gonna walk out today?' she asked, staring tearfully at the door.

'Until they get more, or Elisabetta has a change of opinion, I'm afraid so.'

For some reason it felt like he stuck a pin in her heart when he said her name. Jealousy was the last ingredient she needed to add to the problem right now and she was mad at herself for even feeling it.

'It's a matter of time before they find something more on this guy,' he added when she hadn't said anything. 'They're not giving up on him, Faith; I'm sure they're gonna pick everything in his life apart to find the smallest bit of shit they can to use against him. And listen, I've seen prosecutors try and make a case with less, sometimes successfully, but because of the other murders he's suspected in, I'm sure they want to exhaust every investigative lead before they rush into charging him. And if they can't find anything else, they might still go forward. They did it in Miami with the Lynne Friend case – took them almost twenty years to seek an indictment against the husband and they didn't even have her body. Proving murder when you don't have a body is a lot tougher than what they have here.'

Faith nodded. Lynne Friend was a woman in the middle of a divorce who disappeared back in 1994 after telling her fiancé that she was headed to her ex-husband's house to pick up a support check. They found her car with the purse and keys in it, but no blood or other signs of foul play. On the same night she went missing, the Coast Guard had stopped a boat seven miles off Miami Beach that they'd thought was drug smuggling. Officers had witnessed the two men on board drop a rather large something off the side of the boat. When they finally caught up to the speedboat, which raced away, it turned out the guy driving it was Lynne Friend's ex-husband. Eighteen years later, without any new evidence or a confession, prosecutors indicted Clifford Friend for first-degree murder. This past summer they got a conviction, even though Lynne Friend's body has never been found.

He reached for her hands. 'You're freezing and it's seventy out. What's that about?' he asked with a smile. He pulled her to him and she didn't resist. 'It's gonna be OK,' he said, hugging her. 'This will all work out. Thank God you and Maggie are OK.' She felt his biceps tighten, his large, warm hands pressing against her back, squeezing her close.

It was the first time in weeks that he had hugged her and it made her feel . . . worse. She wanted to feel his strong arms wrapped around her, enveloping her small body in his, protecting her from the monster that might be walking out those doors at any moment. She wanted to hear his heartbeat and smell his cologne and feel his muscles through his starched dress shirt. She wanted to lose herself in his embrace as she had many times before. But at the same time, she didn't deserve it – him wanting her, protecting her, accepting her. His arms felt like a crushing vise of guilt, sucking the breath out of her. And then there was the intern. Had he hugged her like this? Held her close? Told her things would be fine? She doubted that he had just fucked Sandra for three months without one embrace, without whispering something sweet in her ear. The girl had said she loved him, after all.

She pulled away. 'I have to get down to Fort Lauderdale. I have that appointment with the realtor. You'll take Maggie to school?'

He nodded. He looked hurt and confused, which made her feel worse, and yet better.

'Tell Mrs Wackett I'll pick her up about four. I should be done by then,' she added. 'I'll take her to the park.'

He moved to leave.

'This is all very heavy. It's very heavy,' was all she could say.

'For both of us,' he answered softly. 'Keep it . . . together, Faith. It will all work out.'

It was the perfect moment to tell him about the lies, to trust him, to take a step that any therapist would probably tell her she had to take toward forgiving him for the affair and now forgiving herself for her own failures. But she only managed a nod before hurrying to her Explorer.

Because her focus was back on the two glass doors of the police station and the dark-haired person dressed in a black suit who'd just walked out of them and into the brilliant Florida sunshine.

43

'It's twelve hundred square feet and it was a sandwich shop, so it has a small kitchen built out already, which is fabulous. I think it's got a lot of potential for a cupcake bakery.' The real estate agent's strappy sandals were cute, but they needed to be re-heeled. As she swept across the room to show Faith the details of the mostly empty space that smelled of old fryer oil, the metal clicked on the ceramic tile floor like a woodpecker going at a tin can.

Faith nodded absently.

'And you can't beat a Las Olas location,' she continued cheerily, gesturing toward the plate-glass window that looked out onto Las Olas Boulevard, a tree-lined street filled with cafés and boutiques that ran from downtown Fort Lauderdale to the beach. The window and door, however, were covered with brown butcher paper to prevent people from looking into a vacant store and seeing it was actually vacant. 'It will give your shop the visibility it needs.'

There was a long pause while the realtor waited for Faith to say something.

'Forty-five dollars a square foot is . . . well, that's a lot of cupcakes I have to sell just to make the rent.' Her voice trailed off into a whisper as the sentence finished up. There was a substantial tear in the butcher paper and she could still see the many passing tourists enjoying an ice-cream cone, pushing strollers, window shopping. As they passed, a few of them approached the window and put their faces against the glass where the tear was, trying to see what was inside. She kept waiting for Derrick Poole's face to suddenly appear, his hand cupped around his eyes as they scanned the room for any sight of her. She moved behind a pole.

'You said you were hoping for something that was on Las Olas . . .? Faith? Has that changed? Because forty-five is the going rate. You're gonna find that strip malls downtown or on the beach are in the same price range. Now if you want something on Federal, that's further north and in a changing neighborhood . . .'

The realtor prattled on, but Faith had stopped listening. It was hard to plan for the future with any enthusiasm when her future was so uncertain. 'I'm sorry, Jackie, but I . . .' she said when there was another pregnant lull and it was obvious she was expecting her to say something. 'I, ah, I . . . my mind is not in it today. I'm distracted, is all. It's not your fault.'

She looked away from the window and around the abandoned sandwich shop. An Izzy's Monster Subs specials board still hung over where there was presumably once a refrigerator case. Chairs were stacked atop a couple of lonesome two-tops, as if the place was closed for the night, not for forever – as if there was a chance someone might come in, rip down the butcher paper, fire up the grill and flip the closed sign back over. The space would go on, yes, but Izzy's Monster Subs would not: Izzy had broken the lease and left town, presumably taking the refrigerator case with her. If Faith didn't rent the 1,200 square feet, someone else would and put in a candy shop, or a wine bar, or a pet boutique. A wave of desolation came over her. Anything could be reinvented; anyone could be replaced. And it could even be made better than it was before.

It was time to call Detective Nill and tell him about the second man. As much as she didn't want to see what was happening, she couldn't keep closing her eyes, saying it didn't happen just because she didn't see it. The fibers found in Poole's car that matched the fabric patch found in the woods could be from the second man – the man wearing the plaid shirt who'd taken Angelina into the woods with him after she screamed, 'No!' In fact, they probably were. It was time to finally be honest about what she had seen out there that night, both with herself and with the detectives. It was time to come clean and fix this incredible mess that seemed to surround her, that touched every aspect of her life, and as the lies piled up, consumed her every thought. She had to make it right, whatever the consequences to her own self might be. She had to do what she could to get Poole and his partner/friend off the street, not just so she could sleep at night, but for the other women who the two of them might hurt in the future. No, no, no. Use the right terminology. Open your eyes and see it happening. The word was *kill*. The other women those two men might *kill*. She thanked a disappointed and perturbed Jackie and told her she would call her sometime during the week, as she followed her out the back door of Izzy's and into the alley.

She walked to Las Olas, where her car was parked, trying to ready herself. She lit up a cigarette, inhaling deeply, waiting for the nicotine to hit her bloodstream, do its magic and calm her. Everything would soon change for her. She had no idea what Jarrod would do once he found out about the drinking and the lies and the second man. Like Izzy, he might very well decide it was time to move on, that there was nothing worth saving here and it was time to shut the doors and start anew someplace else. With someone else. She swallowed the lump caught in her throat. If that were the case, they would likely split custody of Maggie. She'd affirmatively decided to stay with Jarrod after the affair because she didn't want to raise Maggie in two houses, she didn't want to kiss her daughter goodnight over the phone or not see her on a Saturday because it was 'his' night. She didn't want to go to bed alone herself and wade back into a strange and scary world of dating. She didn't want to date. She didn't want things to change, so she had swallowed her anger and gone on, but now . . . now she couldn't control the change. Now it was she who had caused the damage. The direction of their relationship, of her future, of Maggie's future was in Jarrod's court. *He* would decide if it was over, *he* would decide if she would be a part-time mother, tossed back like an unwanted fish into a dating pool full of divorcees and bitter women who had failed at a relationship.

Lost in her thoughts, she had walked past her car at some point. In front of her was the Royal Pig Pub. Waiters were clearing tables outside from lunch and setting up for dinner. She looked at her watch. It was two thirty. The restaurant's plate-glass doors were being wiped clean and she could make out the large full bar, the monstrous TVs that hung everywhere. Next door was a Starbucks. The iPhone in her hand had grown slippery as she rubbed her sweaty fingers against the rubber case. Liquid courage to make the call she was about to make did not come in the form of a Frappuccino; she wished it were caffeine she craved. And lunch, she told herself. She hadn't eaten.

She ducked into the 'gastro pub & kitchen' and walked up to the elevated, enormous rectangular wood bar that was the center of the restaurant, which looked a lot more like a pub than a kitchen. Giant flat-screen TVs filled every imaginable inch of wall space and sports games played on each one. The place felt abuzz with activity, although there was really no one there – a few scattered souls around the bar and those finishing lunch in booths. She found a spot in the far back, away from the prying eyes of those who might have reason to peek in the clean windows to see who was inside.

She pulled up Detective Nill's number at PBSO and got it ready on her screen, placing the phone on the bar in front of her. All she had to do was press the green send button.

She was almost ready.

But first she ordered a Stoli and cranberry.

44

Most people remember the moment they knew their spouse was the one. The first kiss that took their breath away, that moment they saw fireworks, that very second when they thought, 'I could have this man's children.'

Faith didn't.

It wasn't that their first kiss wasn't a magical moment. It wasn't that she didn't know Jarrod was the only one for her the first time they made love.

She just didn't remember it.

The Salty Dog Saloon on University Avenue was half-empty. It was midnight on a Thursday and the young, raucous UF college crowd was thinning out a little earlier than usual. It was mid-term week and for a good chunk of students there was still Friday to get through. It was October 20, 2005.

'Hey there. What's your name?' The guy with the mop of curly blond hair and red cheeks who was suddenly sitting beside her at the bar asked.

Faith studied her happy neighbor on the stool over. He was cute: tall, lean, really muscular, as far as she could tell from the tight T-shirt he was wearing. He looked like a biker, she thought. Not a Harley biker – a bicycle-biker. No . . . maybe a surfer, with those salty, bleached highlights, although the beach was hours away from land-locked Gainesville. Judging from the color of his tan, he was definitely from Florida. Maybe California. What he definitely wasn't was Italian, which was her type. She ignored him.

'No, come on, what's your name?' he asked again. 'You look bored.' He cocked his head quirkily and rested it in the palm of his hand, his elbow on the bar. But his head slipped off, and he almost smashed his chin on the bar.

'You look drunk,' she replied.

He looked around and nodded. 'My friends left me. That's sad. I have no friends. And we were so close, all of us. They're like brothers to me. Come on, what's your name?'

'Faith' she answered.

'No shit! 'Cause ya gotta have faith!' He started singing loudly and pathetically off-key. He didn't sound anything like George Michael. Not even close.

'I've heard that one a thousand times before,' she said. 'If you're not gonna be on key, at least be original.'

'OK, OK. Reach out and touch faith!' he tried, again nowhere near the right key. If she hadn't heard those lyrics a thousand times, too, she wouldn't have known it was a song he was trying to sing.

'That's the Depeche Mode version,' he said with a smirk. 'You want me to sing the Marilyn Manson one? I'm really good. Thank God I don't look like him, though. He's scary.' He shivered.

'It's the same song,' she replied, smiling.

He slapped the bar. 'That makes three songs with your name in it! There're no songs with my name in it. You're so lucky.'

'You're good. For someone who's bombed. I'm surprised you can remember the lyrics.'

'I'm not bombed, I'm Jarrod,' he replied with a sweet chuckle.

Definitely not Italian. She smiled anyway.

'Do you go to UF?' he tried. 'What's your major? Let me guess – arch-e-ology!' he declared with another chuckle that was a lot heartier. It was a joke that obviously only he got and one that he found hysterically funny. 'You look like you could use another drink, Faith. One more! Whatever she's drinking,' he yelled across the bar at the bartender. 'Whatever "Ya Gotta Have Faith" over here is drinking.' Then he looked at her drink, reached over, picked it up and examined it. 'It's pink, whatever it is. Make it two! And hit all her friends, too,' he added, looking around the bar. 'Did your friends leave you, too? That's sad. We're a lot alike, you and I – we've both been abandoned.'

'You want to buy my boyfriend a drink?' she asked.

He looked around the bar again and smiled coquettishly. 'Boyfriend? I don't see one of those. Nope.'

'He's in the bathroom, but he'll be back. Then you'll be in trouble – he drinks Scotch.'

The surfer made a face that looked like a two-year-old who had tasted spinach for the first time. 'Scotch? He must be, like, *old*.'

'I like old. And he likes expensive Scotch.'

He shook his head. 'No way. If there was a boyfriend, he wouldn't leave you alone for a second – you're too pretty. But to be sure . . . bartender! *Three* shots of Scotch! What's a good Scotch? I'm not a Scotch drinker. I don't think this place even has Scotch,' he announced as loudly as he had sung. 'No one here is old enough to drink Scotch; they're not old enough to even drink, bunch of freshmen. You have to be a grandpa in a sweater to drink that shit. Chivas, right? That's what my grandpa would drink. You're not a freshman are you? I didn't mean to insult you.'

Faith's friends had cleared out a half-hour or so before. God knows where any of them were now. There was no boyfriend. But a free drink with a cute boy who was making her laugh couldn't hurt.

He smiled at her and toasted her Seabreeze with his beer as the bartender laid out three shot glasses on the bar and reached for the Chivas. 'You're a good man, kind sir! Keep 'em coming till one of us falls down! I hope it's not me. But if it's my new, beautiful lady friend, here, don't you worry: I'll carry her home!'

She woke up the next morning in a strange bed, naked and tangled in white sheets. The blond surfer whose name she couldn't remember was sleeping next to her, his bare ass sticking out from underneath an army-green comforter. She sat up with a start. Where the hell was she? Her head hurt so much. She wrapped herself in the sheet, ran into the bathroom and threw up. She rinsed her mouth out in a sink that was coated in bathroom slime. She spotted a couple of toothbrushes resting precariously in a plastic cup from Checkers on the Formica counter, which was dotted with amber cigarette burns, next to combs and hairspray and different bottles of men's cologne. On the toilet tank was a fish bowl. There was an inch of water in the bowl and a poor fish somewhere in the murky water. On the floor were piles of abandoned towels and men's underwear. She opened the mirrored medicine cabinet, ignoring the partied-out image looking back at her. Trojans, KY Jelly, Gillette shaving cream, aftershave. She bit her cheek. She was in a guys' apartment. Guys' – as in plural. Oh God . . . was she in a frat house?

How much had she drunk? Enough that she had gone home and obviously had sex with a man she didn't know. She didn't even remember his name. What was it again? It wasn't Italian – she remembered that much, but that was about it. She pulled the sheet tighter against her and looked around the bathroom for an exit other than the door. She felt like such a slut. It didn't matter how high up it was, if there were a window, she would've already been out it.

She had to get out before whatever his name was and his frat brothers woke up, before anyone saw her face. Hopefully there were no pictures or video. She quietly opened up the bathroom door.

'Hey there,' he said with a lopsided smile, rubbing his head. He was standing in front of her, completely naked. 'I'm Jarrod. And I hate to ask this, but . . . what's your name again? I know there's a song about it. Mandy? Cecilia?'

She'd been too embarrassed to run out. He had not asked her to leave. So she'd stayed. He went downstairs – after putting on a pair of shorts – and had come back with coffee, two bagels and a bottle of Tylenol. He asked if she wanted to watch a movie. It was a Friday, but she had no class, so she'd said yes. One movie led to two led to a *Godfather* and *Rocky* marathon. They ordered pizza and ate dinner in his room. They had sex and this time she remembered it. And when he kissed her, she definitely saw fireworks.

She learned his last name was Saunders and he was in his second year of law school and wanted to be a litigator. He had a brother and a sister, and he'd grown up in Illinois. His family still lived around Chicago. He went to Purdue for undergrad on a baseball scholarship, but after he tore his rotator cuff and baseball didn't work out, he wanted to get out of the cold, so he picked UF for law school, but he had taken a year off to work for his dad before starting and he knew for sure he didn't want to end up back in Chicago. He had broken up with his girlfriend of a year a month earlier. He hated peppers. His favorite food was Italian. He was German-Irish, so he loved Oktoberfest and St Patrick's Day, which was his favorite holiday. He wanted to move to New York. His favorite baseball team was the Chicago Cubs and he loved the Dolphins but couldn't explain why, because they sucked and they sucked every year and they would continue to suck until he died. He loved dogs and wanted to get a German shepherd and name it Dante when he got his own place.

She finally went back to her apartment Sunday morning and they'd been together ever since. She and Jarrod were the exact opposite of how it should happen. They were the poster children for how not to start a successful relationship. She had stayed that day to prove she wasn't a drunken slut – that, in fact, she was in control of the situation. A *Sex in the City* chick, who could have wild sex with a stranger without regret, although she never had before. He likely had not forced her out the door because he'd wanted to prove he wasn't a jerk. Last month marked nine years that they had been together. Seven years ago, on a freezing cold beach in Key West three days after Christmas, with a breathtaking sunset behind them, she'd promised him forever – for better or for worse, for richer, for poorer, in sickness and in health, through good times and through bad, to love and to cherish, till death do they part. He'd done the same. And when the notary pronounced them man and wife and his soft, warm lips met hers, the sky erupted like it was the Fourth of July.

The bar at the Royal Pig was packed, every table was taken, waiters and waitresses hurried out of the kitchen with platters of food. Dinner hour was in full swing. When had that happened? She craned her neck to look past the bartender – it was dark out. The sun had long since set. She couldn't remember how many vodka cranberries she'd had and she didn't want to. She pushed the last drink back, which was still half-full. She felt proud of herself for doing that – leaving before she had finished.

Then she grabbed her iPhone off the bar and slipped it in her purse.

It was time to head home.

45

'Mr Saunders? It's Irma Wackett over at St Andrew's. Um, no one has come to pick up Maggie and it's now six o'clock . . .'

Jarrod stared at the clock on his computer. It said 6:03. Outside his office window it was dark. It felt as if someone had sucked all the oxygen from the room and he took an extra breath before responding. 'OK,' he replied slowly, while simultaneously texting Faith: **Where are you? Are you OK??** 'I'm on my way right now, Mrs Wackett. I'll be there in fifteen minutes. My wife must have lost track of time.' He slammed his laptop shut, grabbed his briefcase and hurried out of the office, ignoring the wave of a partner he passed in the hall.

That was it, he told himself. Or he tried to, initially. Faith had probably gone back to the bakery and gotten caught up with paperwork or personnel issues or chatting with Vivian. Or her sister. The three of them were like teenagers: they could stay up all night chatting and still have something new to say to each other in the morning. The reason she wasn't answering her phone was because it was dead. She had forgotten to charge it. No big deal.

But then he'd called the bakery and the girl working the counter said Faith wasn't there. Then he got ahold of Charity who told him that Faith hadn't been in the store all day and that she'd been trying to reach her since lunch, but Faith hadn't picked up or texted back. By the time he reached Vivian on her cell, as he was walking into Mrs Wackett's room, and she told him the same thing, panic had set in.

Maggie was sitting by herself at a table in the classroom clutching a My Little Pony. Her backpack was on the tiny table in front of her, all packed up and ready to go. Her bottom lip was quivering, her blue eyes wet with tears. She ran to him as soon as she saw him. When an annoyed Mrs Wackett, with her purse on her shoulder and her hand on the light switch, started to lecture him about the time without even inquiring if everything was all right he ignored her, scooping Maggie up in his arms. When she suggested that Maggie might feel emotionally abandoned because her parents were ten minutes late for preschool pick-up for the first time he still ignored her as he headed for the door. But when she flat out told him that she was concerned that it was really a continued lack of discipline and structure like this that was causing Maggie's behavioral problems, he asked her when and where she had received her degree in psychology. Then he angrily told her that Maggie would no longer be her problem to worry about, because she wouldn't be coming back.

He raced home, hoping to find Faith cooking in the kitchen with some weird excuse as to why she had forgotten to pick up their daughter. Or lying on the bed, sleeping off a terrible migraine. But the house was empty; she hadn't been there all day. His mind raced with horrible possibilities. He called Detective Nill and left a message that he couldn't get in touch with Faith and that he was concerned and to please call him. Despite Mrs Wackett's snippy, judgmental observations about Maggie's fear of abandonment, he had the neighborhood babysitter come over to feed her dinner. Then he got in the car and went out looking for his wife.

Over and over and over his mind returned to the PBSO parking lot. To the question she'd asked him, her eyes filled with tears: *Are they going to arrest him now?* He had given her the legal reasons why Poole wouldn't be, hoping that they would explain away her anxiety: the law dictated that he couldn't be arrested, that there was not enough probable cause. And it was going to be OK, because the law was there to protect everyone, defendants and citizens alike. To reassure her, he had put his lawyer hat on, as though he were calmly arguing in front of a judge that one of his clients was not a danger to society when, as the man's defense attorney, he clearly knew he was.

Derrick Poole was as dangerous as any of the murdering clients he had argued for freedom for in the past. But in this instance he had no control over whether the man stayed behind bars or not, because the decision to charge him was not in his hands. When he secured a client's release from jail – on bond, or through an acquittal, or dismissal of the charges – he knew the last person in the world that client would come hunting for was the man who had gotten him out. As a defense attorney, he had nothing to fear personally when a murderer was set free.

Now he had everything to lose.

To assuage Faith's fears, and reassure himself that all would be fine when Poole walked out those station doors, he'd mistakenly placed his trust in a system he personally knew was fucked up and broken. Instead of barricading her inside the house with Maggie and manning the windows with a shotgun, he had let her go to a meeting with a realtor while he'd taken Maggie to preschool and he'd headed off to a meeting, as if nothing was wrong. As if there wasn't a distinct possibility that a suspected serial killer might come to hunt down the only two witnesses that could directly connect him to a murder victim. He'd been in denial himself. And now he hated himself for it. He was supposed to protect his family. And he'd done nothing of the sort. Now Faith was missing. And the first person he thought would know something about that was the last person he hoped she would be with: Derrick Poole.

As he raced north on 441 toward Boca, his cell rang.

'Detective?'

'Mr Saunders. I just got your message.'

'Where is Poole?' He tried hard to sound calm.

'Mr Saunders? What's going on here?'

'Do you know where he is? I haven't heard from Faith; I can't find her. And I'm, I'm going a little crazy here. I called you to see if Poole was under surveillance, because I'm thinking bad thoughts here.' He punched the console.

'Whoa, Mr Saunders – Jarrod – listen to me. Calm down. Your wife, she left a message on my voicemail this afternoon. Said she needed to talk to me about the case, but when I called her back, I got her voicemail. I've been trying, but I think her phone's off. I haven't been able to reach her.'

'Where's Poole?' Jarrod demanded. The detective sounded way too normal. Way too calm, in light of what he'd just told him. 'Do you people have any idea where he is?'

'He's at home. We're watching him, Jarrod.'

'I'll see about that.'

'Wait – where are you?' Now the detective didn't sound so calm.

'I'm pulling down his block right fucking now.'

'You're at his house? Jesus Christ, are you kidding me? Jarrod, drive away. Your wife is not there. She's not. Poole's been with his attorney all day. He just pulled into his house with a pizza a half-hour ago. You need to keep driving.'

'Where is she, Detective? Why is he out? Why haven't you arrested him? And why can't I find her?'

'Jarrod, I can hear the worry, but I assure you she's not with Derrick Poole. It's only eight thirty. You can't even file a missing persons report yet. Give it a few more hours, call some friends and see if she's with them. Maybe she went for a drive. Maybe . . .' he hesitated. 'I don't know.'

'What is it? I can hear it in your voice, Detective.'

'Are things OK at home?'

'Excuse me?'

'I sense things maybe aren't so good at home. I'm sorry if I'm being too forward with that observation. I'm in the middle of a divorce, so maybe I'm feeling things that aren't there.'

Jarrod said nothing. He nodded at the phone.

'I know you're both under a lot of stress, especially your wife.' There was a long, deliberate pause. 'I'm gonna be honest: I think Faith was drinking when she called me. I think maybe she's out somewhere, maybe at a bar with some friends, maybe blowing off some steam. Could that be it, Jarrod? Has she done that before?'

'Oh,' was all Jarrod could manage. He looked out the window. The lights were on at 2330 Nightingale Lane. So was the TV. A man stood by the window looking out, half his body obscured by drapes. Jarrod drove past.

He promised the detective he would keep him advised of the situation. Then he headed back toward 441. When he got down to Fort Lauderdale he cruised the streets looking for her Explorer on Las Olas, or in one the many parking lots that shot off it. He couldn't find her car, although it could be in a parking garage, he thought, as he passed by the downtown hotspots of Timpanos, The Royal Pig, Yolo, Vibe and Grille 401. People spilled from the restaurants and bars onto the sidewalks. The area was jumping for a Tuesday.

He found the space that she'd looked at with the realtor. Then decided to retrace what likely was her route home. Maybe the detective was right and she had stopped off at one of the dozens of bars and restaurants that lined Las Olas. Maybe she'd had a drink with lunch because it had been a bad day. Maybe she'd had an accident on the way home.

Impending disappointment replaced abject fear. He had pulled off the Sawgrass Expressway onto Coral Ridge Drive in Parkland, and having found no sight of her, was preparing to turn around at the light and try a different route when the call came. He didn't recognize the number, but he knew who it was before he even heard her voice.

'Jarrod?' she asked in a small voice as soon as he picked up.

'Faith! Thank God! Where have you been? I've been so worried!'

She started to cry hysterically.

He pulled over to the side of the road and caught his breath, even though he knew what she was about to say was going to take it away again. 'Honey, what's the matter? Faith, where are you?'

'I'm . . . I'm in jail. I've been arrested, Jarrod, for DUI. They took me to jail . . .'

46

Thanksgiving used to be Bryan's favorite holiday. He'd get up early, put on a pot of coffee, and clean out the turkey while he watched the *Today* show and lead-up to the parade. Then he'd fry a slab of bacon and start sautéing the celery, onions and mushrooms for the stuffing, while he popped the pumpkin pie – that he always added his secret shot of Baileys to – into the oven. The house would fill with the best smells. Audrey always vowed to sleep late on Thanksgiving, but the aroma of everything that was The Holidays would waft upstairs and get under her nose and lead her to the kitchen. He'd already have her cup of coffee waiting and the parade on the TV. Everyone was happy: the whole gang at *Today*, Fudge the beagle, Audrey, and the girls – who would both start shrieking as their favorite balloons crossed the screen. And then Santa . . . well, he was The Bomb. He'd finish it up in front of Macy's and it was official: Christmas was coming. The family and friends would start to arrive around three, the bird was devoured to the bone by eight, Christmas carols on the piano started at nine and no one left before midnight. When the twins turned twelve, the four of them had even gotten into the Black Friday madness – leaving the huge mess for the morning and hitting the malls when the last guest left.

This year Audrey had the girls, Fudge, and a boyfriend the girls referred to as 'John Something'. Bryan had made a small turkey, but it was only to get the smell in the apartment. He'd watched half the parade before putting on a Batman movie. Tatiana had asked him to her aunt's house, and his brother had asked him to come up to Jersey. But he'd said no to both, thinking the day wouldn't be so bad. He was wrong.

So he went for a two-hour walk that nearly killed him, ate his turkey with a salad and watched another Batman movie. Then he'd dragged out the old photo albums that Audrey used to keep – before pictures were on SD cards and cellphones and computers. She didn't want any of them when they split. After defiling a few of them with a Sharpie and scissors, he'd taken out his anger on a boring white wall in his boring, rented apartment with his fist. That hurt. When the joy of blacking out Audrey's eyes in vacation photos fizzled like a dying firecracker and the excruciating pain in his hand subsided to an annoying throb, he decided steps had to be taken before he found himself sitting on the floor in the dark flicking a light switch on and off, fantasizing about boiling Fudge on the stove. He was *that* close to the edge of going crazy. He wanted his life back – the life he and Audrey used to have – and short of barging into his old living room and plopping himself down at that Thanksgiving table that he'd fucking paid for, grabbing a knife and going at that turkey and Audrey's new boyfriend, he couldn't make it happen. Of course, forcefully reclaiming his seat at the dinner table wasn't going to give him back his life – it was going to land him in the slammer. He'd been trying to get a grip on his feelings since Audrey had asked him to get out, trying to figure out – like the detective he was – a solution to their problems, trying to figure out why things went wrong and a way he could get back into his house. And he just had to come to terms with the fact that wasn't gonna happen. In fact, with a new boyfriend at the holiday table, the idea of reconciliation was looking more and more remote. It was time to stop crying in the shower and blaming the water for why he was all wet. He had to face what was happening, accept that he couldn't stop it and plot his revenge.

So he took out all the old photos of himself from those photo albums, back from years ago when he looked good – tan and muscular and somehow taller. Then he cut Audrey out of all of them and covered the fridge in pictures of the self he wanted to be again, and vowed to make a comeback. It was an early New Year's resolution, and it might take him a year to lose that hundred pounds, but by the time Audrey called to tell him that she was going to be the next 'Mrs John Something' he'd be back and she'd be sorry she ever told him to leave. And he would be happy to tell her to go fuck herself, snidely commenting as he closed the door on her once-pretty face that she needed a booster shot of Botox and some rejuvenation down south because both her mug and her vagina were starting to sag.

The lonely house stunk of turkey and the pumpkin pie that he'd actually chucked in the garbage so he wouldn't break his new resolution. Since he would no longer allow himself to find comfort in the company of a meatball hero or a six-pack of Heineken, he decided to get out and do something constructive.

Strip clubs were like hospitals and 7-Elevens – they never closed. Not on Christmas and not on Thanksgiving. Animal Instincts had opened at noon and wouldn't shut its doors till four in the morning. They even served free turkey dinners and pumpkin pie with a paid admission. Bryan still wasn't expecting to see fifteen cars in the parking lot, though – it was Thanksgiving, after all. And it was . . . well, the Animal. While he was no connoisseur of strip joints, the Animal could best be compared to a Rodeway Inn: convenient, cheap, and sometimes clean – adjectives that also applied to its dancers.

Bryan was confident that the pickups and SUVs in the

parking lot were all locals. No one was throwing bachelor parties on a major holiday, and at nine at night the tourists should all still be sitting around their in-laws' tables, finishing pie and coffee with the family, maybe even planning out their strategy for how to attack the malls come midnight. He knew that's where he'd've been if it was up to him. On that annoying thought, he pulled his taped hand, which was probably fractured, out of the gallon-sized Ziploc bag of ice. Argh. Not only was he probably gonna have to sit in the ER on a major holiday weekend with all the food-poisoning victims and morons who almost blew themselves up when they attempted to deep-fry a frozen bird, but he was probably gonna have to pay some outrageous amount in co-pay fees, and probably spend six weeks in a cast. And he was definitely gonna have to fix the fucking hole in the wall. He popped two more Advil, dried off his hand and thought of the line from the movie *Animal House*: 'Fat, drunk and stupid is no way to go through life, son.' And he wasn't even drunk when he'd challenged his apartment to a duel.

The hope was to show off Poole's picture and maybe find someone who was at the club the night Angelina disappeared. Or someone who might remember he was hanging around for a few days looking creepy before her last show. Maybe someone saw something, heard something. Like his pop, who was a detective in the Bronx for twenty years, had taught him: *Retrace your steps from the beginning if you want to figure out where it was you tripped up*. It was worth a shot – he didn't have anything to lose and no place he had to be. And he didn't sleep much any more, anyway.

He recognized the same bouncers working the door, the manager, the waitresses, dancers. He'd interviewed them all before, and when he spoke with them again, they all told the same story. He was about to get to work on the thirty or so guys sitting around the stage ogling a dancer who was twisted like a pretzel around a metal pole when he spotted a bartender he hadn't seen before. She was topless and top heavy, her arms and chest covered in tattoos. While Bryan knew no one on the squad was gonna feel bad for him interviewing topless waitresses and strippers, he still wished the girls had their clothes on. He didn't want them thinking he was getting a free peek, so he strictly focused on their eyes, which looked all the more awkward since he was overweight, the AC wasn't working, and he was sweating like a pig at a barbeque while he asked his questions.

'What can I get you?' the bartender asked, sighing when she saw his badge and folding her arms across her ample chest.

'It's not like that,' he started. He couldn't help but notice that the tattoos were all of dead musicians and actors: Jimi Hendrix, Marilyn Monroe, Elvis. 'I'm not a Narc and I don't care what's going on in the back room. I'm working the homicide of Angelina Santri; she was a dancer here.'

'I knew Angie,' she answered, nodding. The defiant body stance relaxed and she started to wipe out bar glasses with enviable biceps the size of most women's thighs. 'Nice kid. Real nice. I think she had a baby. Damn shame.'

'When was the last time you saw her?'

'The last night she worked – the night she disappeared. I made her a sour-apple martini when she got off.'

'Really? The manager gave me the time sheets of everyone working that night; I thought I'd talked to them all. What's your name?' he asked.

'Amber Kurtz. I wasn't working; I popped behind the bar to help out when it got crazy. I was waiting for Elvira – another bartender – to get off work, 'cause she was crashing at my house and we were going out after she was done.'

Bryan pulled out the picture of Poole. 'Do remember if you saw this guy that night?'

She took the photo and stared at it under one of the bar's backlights. 'Yeah. I saw this asshole. He was sitting at the bar.

He was definitely here when Angie danced. He was watching her like a time clock.'

Bryan felt his heart speed up. This would not only definitively place Poole at Animal Instincts the night Angie disappeared, but it would have him *watching* her. 'Did he say anything?' he asked excitedly. 'You said he was an asshole. Why's that? Did you see him with Angelina later?'

'No, no, no, he didn't say nothing. And I never saw him *with* Angie. Actually, now that I'm thinking about it, it was his friend who was the asshole. He made a comment about my tits. Just a dickhead comment. This guy,' she said, pointing at Poole's picture, 'told him to shut up.'

Bryan frowned. 'Friend? How do you know they were together?'

''Cause they was laughing together, and, well, they were together. You just know.'

'Crown Royal, splash of ginger,' said a customer on the stool over. Amber stepped away to make the drink.

'Did you get his name?' Bryan asked when she came back. 'Of the friend. Did you get his name?'

She shook her head. 'Nope. Didn't get a name on either of them. Ten,' she said to the guy, who handed her a crumpled cluster of bills. She made a face and shook her head as she counted out the cash.

'How'd they pay?' Bryan asked. 'This guy and his asshole friend?'

'Cash. Like most everybody in this place, but they left me a lot more than two bucks,' she barked at the back of Crown Royal's head. She rolled her eyes. 'They were pretty generous. I think the nicer one, the guy in the picture, was dressed in black. He paid with a fifty and left me a twenty for just a couple of beers. That was a surprise.'

'You still got it? The fifty?'

She made a face.

'Some people keep high bills.'

She shook her head. 'Not me. They go to pay the rent.' She tapped on the bar. 'Oh yeah. And then I saw the two of them outside when me and Elvira was leaving. They were in the back lot, standing there, just hanging out talking, like they was waiting for someone to come out. That someone was probably Angie, now that I think about it, you know, after all that happened. And here's some fucked-up thinking, Detective. I remember thinking to myself, "If I got twenty for a beer, he's probably gonna drop a few presidents for some pussy. Too bad I'm gay and don't like dick, 'cause that's one lucky bitch."'

47

It started to make sense. And now he was wondering why he hadn't seen it before, the picture in the hologram that had been there all along: *What if Poole had a partner?* That would explain the fibers being found in and around the passenger seat – fibers that matched the ripped piece of fabric found in the woods that had DNA on it that didn't come from either Poole or Angelina Santri.

Serial partners were extremely rare, but they did happen. Angelo Buono and Kenneth Bianchi, the murdering cousins who were the Hillside Stranglers; friends Charles Ng and Leonard Lake who'd murdered as many as twenty-five people – including infants – at a makeshift dungeon in Northern California; the psychopathic husband and wife team of Fred and Rose West who ran the Gloucester House of Horrors; drifters turned lovers Henry Lee Lucas and Ottis Toole who, at one point, had jointly confessed to killing as many as 108 people; Lawrence 'Pliers' Bittaker and Roy Norris, the sado-masochistic Tool Box Killers. Traditional manuals and treatises on homicide investigation didn't really cover serial killers, because serials only accounted for about one per cent of all homicides. Serial partners were rarer still. The very limited investigative resources on serials that Bryan had found barely touched on the concept of partners. But from what he had read, he knew partners could be even more depraved than 'regular' serial killers. The psychology behind it was weaved into the relationship itself, like in a business partnership, marriage or friendship: the 'you jump, I jump' kind of thinking emboldened people, made them more courageous, more likely to do things they wouldn't normally do if they didn't have someone in their corner backing them up and egging them on. In the case of criminals, that sort of thinking made them even more dangerous. One misogynistic psychopath with a vivid imagination and no conscience was bad enough, but when you threw in a second, the crimes such a pair could come up with were truly unthinkable. Encouraged by their partner, each fed off the frenzied reactions of the other, fueling a sinister competition of showmanship. The relationship between serial partners would need to be as intimate as that of a marriage or business partnership due to the dangerous secrets that each kept about the other. Murdering minds don't just find out they think alike over a beer. If Poole had a partner, it would mean they were friends, lovers or relatives.

Amber Kurtz had given him a description of the man she'd seen with Poole: white male, average height, slim build, 'older than the guy in the picture, maybe forty, forty-five' wearing a white long-sleeved shirt and dark jeans or slacks. She thought he might have had crooked teeth and gray, fuzzy mutton-chops. He wore a black, cowboy-type hat and tinted eyeglasses, so she never saw the rest of his face. When she realized that she might be describing a man connected to Angelina's brutal murder and that this was the first the cops had heard of him, she got very nervous and the generic description that could apply to half the male populace, save the muttonchops, stayed disappointingly generic. She hemmed and hawed about working with a sketch artist.

At about midnight, as malls across America were kicking off the start of the Christmas shopping season, Bryan left the crowd at the Animal and headed due west. Starting with the cane field in Lake Harbor – a remote little town of 200 people on the southern banks of Lake Okeechobee where Silvia Kruger, the first suspected Cane Killer Palm Beach victim was found – he returned to each crime scene. Maybe the connection was where the bodies were dumped. Maybe there was a common intersection or road or rest stop. From Lake Harbor, he headed over to the ditch in Belle Glade where Kruger's head was later recovered. Then he went north to where the brutalized body of victim number two, Emily Foss, was discovered in the cane fields in Canal Point, another isolated town of 525 souls, that was surrounded by not much else but sugar cane. At each crime scene he stopped, got out, walked around, tried to get a sense of . . . *why here?* He left and went on to the next without having an answer.

In and out of the cane fields he drove, down long, empty stretches of road, shining his spotlight into cane so thick sometimes he couldn't see through the stalks. The sugar cane harvesting/processing season for the Palm Beach's 180,000 acres of sugar cane kicked off October 1 and ran through April, so some of the fields had already been torched and harvested, leaving vast stretches of nothingness that seemed to go on for miles. After Canal Point he headed south to the cane fields outside of Pelican Lake, an unincorporated village southeast of Pahokee where Angelina's battered body had been found. Considered a mecca for registered sex offenders and predators, according to the FDLE Sex Offender website, Pelican Lake had more than thirty registered sex offenders living within a one block radius of each other. Yuck. Bryan had checked each of them out thoroughly before he'd focused in on Poole as a suspect. But now that he was looking for a partner, he'd have to check them all again and see if there was any connection to the good-looking accountant from Boca.

It was four in the morning when he cruised down the empty

streets of downtown Pahokee, and pulled in front of the hair salon on Main Street where Faith Saunders had parked that night. Across the street was the overgrown lot where crime-scene techs had found the piece of fabric. Pahokee was a town that had shone back when Big Sugar ruled the Everglades. But once phosphorus run-off fell out of favor, as did choking off parts of the River of Grass, towns like Pahokee and Canal Point dried up. The jobs left and so did most of the people. He thought of the Everglades Regional Medical Center, a hospital opened with much fanfare in 1950 and abandoned without any in 1998. Overgrown with foliage, its innards picked over, stripped and vandalized, it could now be the setting for a *Walking Dead* episode. Sadly, the same could be said about many of the town's modest homes and small shops: Pahokee had one of the highest foreclosure rates in the state. People had up and left during the Great Recession and had not come back when the government said it was all over.

Bryan sat in his car, sipping his coffee, and thought about things. The folks in Pahokee who had stayed and stuck it out were not out shopping at some mall on Black Friday. Civilization was more than forty miles away. Last month, he and Tatiana had knocked on the door of every open business on Main Street to see if anyone had surveillance cameras, but not one single business had. None of the town's five red lights had cameras, either. Out in these parts your alarm was a Rottweiler and your method of protection was a shotgun.

He'd been out here in the daylight, walking the streets and the wooded lot with Faith and Jarrod Saunders and the crime-scene techs, but everything was so very different at night. He looked out the window, as Faith did that rainy night. It must have been terrifying to wake up and see a woman banging on your window and asking for help, out here, in the middle of nowhere with no cell phone and your baby in the back seat. Shit, he might've had a fucking heart attack himself. He knew what Tatiana and Elisabetta thought, and yes, the lady was squirrely, but he felt bad for Faith Saunders. He thought they were being a bit tough on her *because* she was a woman and if they were in her position they would've done more. Being judgmental was a defense coping mechanism for them. *Walk a mile in someone else's shoes*, was what Bryan thought. Hindsight's always twenty-twenty and everyone likes to think they'd be the fucking hero in the crowded movie theater being shot up by a nut in a Joker costume. But that's not how it is when you're scared and taken by surprise. In the weeks that he'd known her, Faith Saunders had aged a dozen years. And knowing Poole was out there, walking around, even if he was under surveillance, and that he knew who she was and where he could find her – well, that would make anyone paranoid. So he couldn't blame her for acting wiggy and he couldn't blame her husband for flipping out and trying to hunt down Poole like Jack Ruby when the little woman didn't come home on time. But the reality that Bryan could see and hear even before Faith Saunders got popped for DUI two nights ago, was that the lady had a drinking problem. And he was pretty sure she had that problem before poor Angelina Santri woke her from her slumber, although the mounting stress that followed from that night was sure to have turned a perhaps manageable pre-existing condition into a full-blown disease. His first guess out of the gate was that she was three sheets to the wind driving home from her sister's in Sebring and had stopped to sleep it off after she got lost. But she had denied, denied, denied touching more than a glass of wine. And until she wanted to admit it, ain't nobody was gonna get her to 'fess up, including her husband – who either saw what was going on and didn't want to say anything, or didn't want to see anything so he didn't have to say anything. Bryan could sense the tension in that marriage the moment the three of them first sat down in his office to tell him what had happened on that drive back from Charity Lavecki's, and having been through a storm himself the past year, he could tell it'd existed

245

for a lot longer than one morning. Something was bubbling under the surface of their good-looking Ken and Barbie marriage. The encounter in Pahokee was the external pressure that was gonna force the gunk up and out.

He turned off the engine and got out of the car. The air smelled like damp earth and night-blooming jasmine. He walked across the street and, using his flashlight, waded into the wooded lot where the techs had found the fabric patch. The earth simultaneously crunched and sunk under his shoes. There was a sort of makeshift path that had been carved out through the overgrown jungle of shrubs and plants. He held the flashlight in one hand and the other up to protect his face from branches and palm fronds. And he swallowed the fear that was trying to creep up in his belly. He was never this daring, or this stupid, before Audrey left. She'd always talked about how worried she was about him as a cop, so he never took risks, which wasn't that difficult to avoid once he went to Homicide, seeing as his victims were already dead by the time he got on scene. Now he felt like Mel Gibson's character in *Lethal Weapon*: crazed, apathetic, lost. Not only did he not care, he dared bad things to happen. From risking a bad diagnosis at the doctor's because he ate and drank and smoked too much, to being attacked by a bear or a snake or a fugitive in the Everglades at four thirty in the morning, he . . . did things. He didn't want to die, he just didn't care if he did.

He found the downed Live Oak where crime-scene techs recovered the patch. They'd also found an array of other crap that people had dumped out here over the years: plastic bottles, paint cans, candy wrappers, beer cans, liquor bottles, cigarette butts. This lot was probably a refuge for bored teenagers looking to get stoned or drunk or lucky. He sat down on the log, flipped off his flashlight and listened to the night.

He was not alone.

Somewhere in all that blackness out there were the unsettling sounds of night creatures going about their business. Snakes, raccoons, squirrels, lizards slithered and snacked and scurried and built, maybe watching him watch them. Probably wondering what the fuck he was doing out here. He imagined poor Angelina, perhaps crouched beside this very log. If she actually died here, Mother Nature had taken whatever forensic evidence the body might have yielded back into the earth. The thought was sobering. Bryan had stood in the exact spot where people had passed too many times in his career.

Angelina had likely been murdered somewhere other than the cane field where she'd been found. So where was the kill site? After the ME washed down her muddy feet to do the autopsy, he'd discovered deep gashes and puncture wounds to both soles and removed pieces of rock and shards of broken glass – injuries he theorized were sustained from running. The severed Achilles tendon was likely punishment for running and to make sure it didn't happen again. Angelina had been missing for over a day before Faith Saunders saw her with Poole, barefoot and limping. Bryan figured she'd been held somewhere during that time period, and maybe escaped, which would explain the injuries to her feet. While the ME could not determine exactly how long Angelina had been dead before she was found, due to the advanced state of decomposition, he could say with certainty that she wasn't in that field for two weeks. There just wouldn't have been as much left of her as there was. Exposed to the elements and the Florida heat, decomposition is rapid. That meant he, or perhaps *they*, had kept Angelina somewhere for an extended period of time, where she was tortured and raped and they could take their time with her, maybe punish her for running away.

If she was being held somewhere and escaped before she saw Faith Saunders, then that place couldn't be very far from the log where he was sitting. A matter of a couple of miles, at most, was how far she could have gotten running barefoot through cane fields. He thought then about Noelle Langtry, the missing

Sugar Daddy's dancer who he'd been hoping would turn up alive, because if she was breathing then that meant she wasn't a Cane Killer victim and Derrick Poole wouldn't have an alibi for the night of her disappearance supported by the lead detective investigating a murder case against him. But she hadn't turned up alive. Or dead. Now that he knew it was possible Poole had a partner and that they might be storing their victims at a secret location, and that that location might be within a couple of miles of where he currently sat . . .

He stood up and shook his head. The idea that a young girl might be out here somewhere, alive, strung up, caged or shackled, maybe being tortured or raped at this very moment was too much. By the time Homicide was called in on a missing persons case, the search parties had been organized and found what they were looking for. Noelle Langtry's name had been entered into NCIC/FCIC – the federal and state criminal information databases – as a missing person, but there were no search parties combing the back alleys and tenements near Sugar Daddy's, or the streets near the trailer home where she lived. And there was certainly no army of volunteers walking the 180,000 acres of sugar cane out here.

The hint of sunrise began to warm the black skies to deep purple. The nocturnal wildlife, sensing dawn, had scurried off to find a safe place to lay low. Nothing had attacked him. He went back to his car, scratching at his legs, which itched like a bitch, probably from the hordes of mosquitos that had been feasting on them. Blech. At least he hoped it was from mosquitos.

He got back in his car, popped three more Advil and headed for home, winding his way down dirt roads with the spotlight still pointing into the cane fields. He was about to turn onto Lucky Bottom Road when he spotted the rooftop of what looked like a barn set back off the road. It was buried under a mop of foliage. Like the Everglades Regional hospital and what remained of the tourist attraction Gatorland in South

Bay off of US 27, the existence of long-abandoned structures was not uncommon out here. He wouldn't have seen it in the dark. And if he hadn't been looking, he wouldn't have seen it at all. Something told him to stop.

He pulled over and up a long dirt drive that led into what looked like it was once a parking lot, made impassable now by shrubs and underbrush. At the mouth of the lot was a metal swing-arm gate with a rusted NO TRESPASSING sign attached to it. The lock on the gate was broken. He pushed it and it opened with a groan. He aimed his spotlight at what he saw was not a barn, but a deceptively large one-story cement-and-wood building that was deeper than it was wide. The light caught on a faded painted sign that hung above a front door. The wood had broken and fallen off, so only part of the sign was visible:

IVE GATOR WRESTL

The adrenaline rush he'd experienced talking to Amber Kurtz at the Animal was back. He wasn't exactly sure what he'd stumbled on, but he just knew that it would prove important. His blood turned as cold as the plastic bag of ice water sitting on his passenger seat and he shook off the ominous feeling that was making his knees shake as he pushed past the metal gate and waded into the thick tangle of underbrush that threatened to swallow him whole.

48

The windows and doors were shuttered with plywood. The railing on the front porch had fallen off. A battered screen-door frame, long missing its screen, lay on the ground beside the railing. Another sign was next to it. This one was metal. He wiped the dirt off with the sole of his shoe and shone his light on it:

FRESH STRAWBERRIES, SUGAR CANE
SOUVENIRS

It had been a store of some kind – a souvenir stand. Judging from the sign above the door, they probably had alligator-wrestling shows in the back, like Gatorland used to. Or maybe panther exhibits. Indian artifact archeological 'digs' in piles of sand for the kids. Guessing from the look of the building, it was built in the forties or fifties – back when people took road trips to Florida for their honeymoons and airboat rides through the Everglades. Mom and pop stands sold what they could: pies and fresh fruit, pink flamingo ashtrays and preserved alligator jaws. Bryan could practically hear the tinkle of wind chimes and groan of the wood planks on the porch as rambunctious kids – happy to finally get the hell out of the family station wagon – raced inside to see what fifty cents in souvenir money would buy them. There were a lot of those establishments surviving around the state, but this one evidently had suffered the same fate as Gatorland: a lack of honeymooning tourists who gave a shit about airboat rides through the Everglades and took the kids to Disney instead.

There was a rusted padlock on the faded red door. He tried it, but it was locked. He went back to the car and got a crowbar and a hammer. He probably should get a warrant, but for what? A creepy building giving him a creepy feeling in the pit of his large stomach? That was grounds for a case of heartburn, not probable cause for a search warrant. Obviously the place was abandoned. Tracking down an owner would be near impossible. He stuck the crowbar in between the lock and the loop and whacked it with the hammer. The lock broke open and fell to the floor.

He pushed open the door. It creaked like a haunted house. Inside, it was completely black. Outside, the sun was struggling to make an appearance, but the shuttered windows were going to keep the daylight out anyway. He could feel his heartbeat pulsing in his temples now. His daughter, Hilary, was a fan of *The Walking Dead*; they watched it together on Sunday nights when it was his weekend. All he saw in his head right now were zombies – smelling him in the dark and searching out a snack. Waiting for him inside could be a colony of crack addicts. Or rats. Or snakes. Or nothing – just the remains of an old-fashioned business that had died a slow death thirty years earlier, after Walt Disney and his princesses had replaced alligator-wrestling and live mermaid shows at the WeekiWachee.

The door closed behind him with a bang. He was in a tight hallway that smelled old and awful – like mildew and dirt and old house and fermented skunk. He waved his flashlight about, trying to orientate himself, one slice of room at a time. His hand hurt like a bitch – he'd aggravated it whacking on the crowbar, even though he'd hammered using his left hand. He stepped out of the hall, and shone the light on a wood counter, behind which was a large pot-rack-thing suspended from the beam above with a couple of empty hooks still attached. He unsnapped the Glock strapped to his side. If he had to shoot, he'd have to use his left hand. Fuck. And in the dark, no less. Sweat poured down his face and back. He ignored the voice in his head telling him to go back.

He turned a corner into what felt like an open, spacious room. He took a step and fell about two feet, landing, thank God, on his ass. But everything hurt. His legs felt like they had knives in them. Before he could appreciate what he'd fallen into, or how badly he was hurt, he smelled it: a horrible, putrid, rotting stench. He recognized right away what it was. It was death.

He scrambled to find his footing and stand. His right hand was throbbing, but now he felt a sharp pain in his left and looked down, flashing his light. The cement floor glittered with broken glass. Blood ran down his palm. He shone the light around him – he had fallen into a short, wide pit of some sort, which was carpeted in broken glass. What remained of a metal railing surrounded it. He moved his flashlight around the walls of the pit and sucked in a breath.

He jumped up and reached for his cell with shaking hands. He hit the button – no service. Then he dropped the phone. He could feel blood running down his ass and his legs. He must have cut himself on the glass shards, even through his pants.

He heard something scurry by, felt the presence of something near him. He turned his head so fast his neck cracked. He scanned the room with the flashlight. It caught on one fat rat running through the zigzagging beam of light, disappearing into a corner. Another sat there staring at him defiantly. He turned it on the walls. Then the ceiling. The horror was everywhere.

He found the wood steps that led into the pit he was

252

standing in and climbed out, trying to remember where he'd entered the room. There were different halls leading off the main room – choosing the wrong one in the dark could lead him somewhere far worse than a pit of broken glass. He buried his nose and mouth in the sleeve of his shirt to stop from breathing in the stench. His radio was in the car, if he could get to it. *Why hadn't he told anyone where he was?* Mel Gibson he wasn't. He was a fool, was what he was.

He found the hallway by the pot-rack, rushed down the hall and pushed open the door, almost falling off the broken porch. Dawn had arrived in glorious splendor; slices of orange and gold erupted in the east. He kept blinking as his eyes adjusted to the light. He breathed in the fresh air. Earth had never smelled so good before. He wanted to kiss the ground.

He hobbled over to the car and grabbed his radio. 'Palm Beach 1642.' He touched the back of his pants – they were wet with blood.

'Go ahead 1642,' replied dispatch.

'I'm out here by, um, by . . . Pelican Lake, no – off Muck City and, Jesus, I don't know what street. I don't know the cross street . . .' His voice trailed off as he looked back at the building where he had just been, seconds before. Even in the warming light it was almost impossible to see, swallowed whole by trees and brush. It was hard to think.

'1642, are you requesting units to respond?'

'Yes, yes. I am requesting backup.'

'What's your 10-20?'

'Off State Road seven-one-seven – Muck City Road – east of Barfield by maybe a mile and a half, two miles. I don't have a cross street, Palm Beach. It's off the road a bit. It's a building, obscured by foliage and overgrowth. I'm gonna put my lights on so you can see me out here.' He flipped on his blue lights as he said it.

'10-4. Dispatching a unit to respond. What is your situation, 1642?'

Bryan wiped his face with his sleeve. Blood ran off his hand from his sliced palm and dripped onto his face. He searched the Taurus for a paper towel or napkin. 'Not a unit, Palm Beach. *Units*. I need units to secure the area. And Crime Scene. I need Crime Scene. It's a mess out here, Palm Beach. I have a mess on my hands.'

'Are you requesting fire/rescue, 1642?'

He shook his head. For anyone who had been in that shack it was far too late for an ambulance. 'No.'

'10-4, 1642. All available units are responding.'

The radio began to crackle with police jargon as units reported they were en route and their ETA.

He looked back at the shack he'd walked out of. He'd found what he had set out to find tonight.

He'd just stood in the heart of the kill spot.

49

Faith spotted the black Taurus in the driveway as soon as Jarrod made the turn onto Greenview Terrace. If she'd been driving, she probably would've turned around and headed back out the gates of Heron Bay. The guardhouse – that they'd just passed, complete with a guard who had waved at them – was supposed to let you know when you had a guest. That rule must not apply when the guests are cops.

'Were you expecting them?' Jarrod asked quietly, looking over at her.

She shook her head.

After Jarrod had bonded her out of jail Wednesday morning, they'd headed to Chicago to spend Thanksgiving as planned at his sister's with the rest of his family. It was a difficult trip and a difficult three days, even though they'd said nothing the whole plane ride up or back. Surrounded by family they hadn't seen since last Thanksgiving, they hadn't said much at Birgitte's, either. Faith wasn't exactly sure what Jarrod had told any of them about anything that had happened over the past year: the affair; the 'incident'; and now, the DUI. So she'd spent most of her time upstairs in Birgitte's guest room playing with Maggie when the teenage cousins tired of entertaining her, or going out for long walks by herself, trying to figure out how the hell she was going to fix the spiraling-out-of-control-mess that was her life.

While the absolute last thing she wanted to do after getting arrested, being strip-searched at the jail and completely humiliating herself, was go on a holiday trip to visit Jarrod's family and pretend everything was great, she wasn't in a position to tell him she didn't want to go. So she threw her stuff in a bag, got in the car and drove to the airport. The positive was the trip had given her a few days' reprieve from having to discuss what had happened and having to defend herself against the accusations she knew were coming about her drinking. And she would be a thousand miles away from Derrick Poole and the continuously degenerating turmoil happening in South Florida.

With the exception of Jarrod's curmudgeonly dad who only mumbled in German around her, Faith got along well enough with the rest of the family: Jarrod's mom, his sister, Birgitte and her husband Glen, and his brother Steffen and his wife, Sherry. Living thousands of miles away helped relationships stay superficial and friendly and inhibited them from developing into anything more. She helped set the table and decorate the Christmas tree Birgitte had already put up, made sure everyone's wine glasses were full at the table, and drank her own glass when no one was looking. And she tried not to worry that the hushed conversations that suddenly stopped when she came into a room were about her.

Conversation was pleasant and generic and centered around the kids and the holidays until Friday night's post-Black Friday dinner at Volare when Steffen brought up a developing story out of Palm Beach that he had seen on CNN that morning: A 'Little Shack of Horrors' had been found out by the Everglades with ties to a serial murder investigation. Apparently, a little girl and her mother from Parkland, Florida had somehow stumbled upon the killer with his last victim and were now primary witnesses in the case. *Isn't Parkland where you guys live? Have you heard of this case?* As Jarrod carefully dodged the questions, Faith had excused herself to go to the bathroom and pulled up the story on her phone. Then she'd thrown up. They left after breakfast the next day. As the plane began its descent into Fort Lauderdale she could feel the pressure change, and not just in the cabin. With each mile they drove home the clock ticked down on her mini-vacation from dealing with the fucked-up reality of it all, officially and fittingly ending as soon as they pulled in the driveway and Detectives Nill and Maldonado met them at the car door.

Jarrod ushered both detectives inside and took Maggie upstairs to her room to watch a video. Everyone took a seat at the dining-room table.

This was it. Faith's stomach churned.

Detective Nill wasted no time. 'There's been a new development,' he said as Jarrod came back into the room.

She looked down at her lap and nodded. 'I heard,' she said faintly. 'It's on CNN, Fox. It's . . . everywhere.'

'Yes. We have found a crime scene. I didn't want it to get out like that; the media picked it up on the scanners. Now we're trying to control the flow of information, because there've been a lot of calls, a lot of interest. Like you already know, we found forensic evidence in this abandoned shack that leads us to believe it was used in the homicides of Angelina Santri and possibly three other women. Maybe a fourth. There's a missing girl who we fear may also be linked to this location.'

She nodded and took a deep breath, but said nothing.

'I also heard about your arrest on Tuesday. You were double the limit. That's tough.'

The tears started. 'I'm sorry,' she whispered.

'You've been under a lot of stress.'

She nodded again.

The detective tapped his pen on the table. 'I'm gonna be

honest with you here, Faith. I'm gonna fill you in on some of the evidence we found out there, so you know what we got, what we're dealing with, and you understand where it is I'm coming from. We found fibers in this place: red and black fibers. They match the fiber patch we found in the wooded lot in Pahokee and the fibers in Poole's trunk and the passenger seat of his car. We found a lot of blood on the walls and floor that we're running tests on, but we believe it will match DNA samples we have from the dead women and missing teenage dancer. We found body parts in buckets, and we found Angelina's black boots.'

Faith covered her mouth, her eyes still locked on a spot on her jeans. It was getting hard to breathe. She knew there was no way to adequately prepare herself for what was coming.

'The building dates back to the early fifties,' Detective Nill continued. 'It was a lot of things over the years, including a restaurant, but through the seventies and eighties it was a storage facility for sugar cane, with the front room being a sort of makeshift souvenir shack. There used to be alligator-wrestling on site, cockfighting and gambling in the late seventies. The property has been abandoned since 1994. The owners picked up and moved to Wisconsin and never looked back and the place fell apart. Inside we found restraints, and a trap room that at one point in the building's history may have been used to house the alligators or roosters for cockfighting. We think it was used to hold these women before they were murdered.'

'Jesus,' said Jarrod, his head in his hands.

'I have a theory that I want to try on you, Faith. Stop me if you think I'm wrong. I believe Angelina Santri was beaten in that wooded lot across from where your car was parked that night. She fought with her attacker and ripped a piece of his shirt that was likely sprayed or smeared with her blood. She was then taken to Poole's Honda Accord and placed in the trunk, alive, but likely unconscious. As you know, we found several strands of her hair in that trunk. To prevent the transfer of blood or bodily fluids, she was likely wrapped in tarp or plastic sheeting. The person whose shirt she ripped then got into the passenger side of Poole's car, where Poole and this person drove to the abandoned shack that we found yesterday. Angelina was once again restrained, then tortured, and ultimately murdered. I'm thinking that since she was missing for over a day when you saw her, maybe she was being held there after she was abducted from the parking lot of the Animal and somehow escaped, running off barefoot into the cane fields, which explains her dirty feet. Then she found you, Faith, asleep in your car.'

Faith nodded.

Jarrod looked at her, then back at the detective. 'Wait, you said someone got into the passenger side of Poole's car. You think there's a second suspect? There're *two* of them?'

Nill didn't take his eyes off Faith. 'We were able to get DNA off the fabric patch. That DNA came from the blood spatter of Angelina Santri and from the sweat deposits of an unknown male who is *not* Derrick Poole. We're planning to execute another search warrant on Poole's house. That's why we're here: I want to know what else we should be looking for once we get back inside.'

'Faith?' Jarrod asked.

'Do you see where I am going with this, Faith?' asked the detective.

She nodded again, wiping her tears with the back of her sleeve.

'One of the bartenders at Animal Instincts places Poole in the club the night Angelina went missing,' Nill pressed. 'He wasn't alone; he was with a friend.'

'Faith?' asked Jarrod again.

'There was someone else out there with Poole the night of the tropical storm, and I think you saw him, Faith. That's my theory. I don't know why you didn't tell me about him from the get-go, but my concern now is finding him because he's a killer. He and Poole hunt women and then take turns torturing and slaughtering them in different, insane ways. My problem with Derrick Poole, the reason he's not behind bars yet, is there has so far been no hard evidence directly connecting him to Angelina's murder. All I got is you and your daughter seeing him with her when she was still alive. I got a great case, however, against an unknown subject wearing a red-and-black plaid shirt. I have *his* DNA, I have the victim's blood on *his* clothing, I have the fibers of *his* shirt all over a crime scene where I think five women have been brutally tortured, dismembered and murdered. But I need to link Derrick Poole to Angelina's murder; I need to link him to this unknown subject. I need more, because there's too much room for argument.'

She buried her face in her hands and began to sob.

Nill leaned in across the table and handed her a pocket pack of tissues. 'I know you called me for a reason the other day, Faith. I think you knew what it was you needed to tell me. I need to find out who the DNA on that fabric patch belongs to, Faith. And you're going to help me do just that.'

50

'He was in the woods,' she began, her face buried in the tissue.

'Who is he?' asked Nill.

'The other man. She went with him. I didn't think he was going to hurt her . . .'

Jarrod pushed back from the table.

Nill leaned in even closer to her. 'With all due respect, Faith, I gotta tell ya, that's not working. Even your own kid knew this Santri girl was scared out of her mind. Let me be frank here: People are having a real hard time understanding why you didn't call no one. The prosecutor, me, Detective Maldonado, your own husband. Once this gets out, if the media interest keeps up like I think it will, Joe Public is gonna have a hard time understanding it, too. And you telling everyone you didn't know no better is not jiving. 'Cause you're a nice lady. You live in a nice house, here, you have a nice husband, a great kid. You're smart and resourceful. You're a businesswoman. And your husband tells me you pick up stray dogs and take in stray sisters, so you must have a big heart.' He smiled and tapped her on the arm. 'I think I know why you keep holding back information. Your arrest on Tuesday for DUI wasn't your first.'

He opened a file folder and slid a piece of paper in front

of her. It was her criminal history. It was hard seeing it in print. She closed her eyes.

'Let me tell you the theory I have about what happened that night, Faith. You tell me if I'm getting it right. You were at your sister's, you had a few drinks, maybe more than a few, 'cause you said you were gonna stay the night originally. Then something happened, you had a fight, or Maggie was bitching about going home or acting up – whatever. You left your sister's and started to drive home when you probably should've been sleeping on her couch. I get it. You got lost and you pulled over to sleep it off and then Angelina Santri pops up at your window and turns your world upside down. Maybe you were afraid you'd get another DUI if you called the cops, huh? Is that scenario right?'

She nodded.

'You have a drinking problem,' Jarrod flatly stated.

She put her head in her hands.

Detective Maldonado shook her head at him.

'Can you describe this other man?' Nill asked.

Faith nodded, but still didn't look up. 'He was in his late thirties, maybe forties. He had a beard, but it wasn't full, it was like muttonchops. I think it was gray or light brown. He was wearing jeans and a dark shirt – it could've been plaid. It was open so I saw he had a, a, um, potbelly, even though he was thin. He had on a baseball cap but it blew off and I saw he was bald, he had no hair on his head. Maybe he shaved it, I don't know. He was average height, not as tall as Poole, maybe five ten or five eleven.'

'Wait,' said the detective. 'What kind of baseball cap?'

'It was a white Yankees hat. I saw the emblem.'

Jarrod stood up and went to the window. He ran his hands through his hair and exhaled a long breath. 'You have a drinking problem; you need help,' he declared. 'It's in your family. Maybe you can't help it, maybe it's a disease, but we have to deal with it. We do.'

She put her hands up to her ears. She couldn't listen much longer.

'You drove drunk with Maggie in the car, Faith. Our daughter was in the car. You could have crashed, those men could have . . .' His voice trailed off. 'A girl is dead, Faith—'

'It's not my family!' she screamed suddenly. 'Leave my dad out of this! It's you. Can't you see that? You're the reason I need a glass of wine at night. Or something harder while I sit there and I wait to see if you'll come home. You and that . . . *girl*. It's all I see, Jarrod! You ruined everything. Everything I thought we had. I wasn't good enough for you.'

Jarrod shook his head. 'Don't do this now,' he said quietly.

Both detectives exchanged uncomfortable glances.

'It's not my dad's fault – it's yours.' She looked at Detective Nill, wiping the tears away furiously with her sleeves. 'I wanted to tell you about the second man when we went to the police station, but I knew Jarrod would never understand. He'd look at me like he's looking at me now, like he's looked at me for the past three days: I'm damaged goods, Detective Nill. I already wasn't good enough, but now I drove drunk with his daughter in the car, and I forgot her at daycare so I'm a bad mother. And I didn't help that girl, so I'm a bad person.'

'Faith . . .' Jarrod tried. 'Don't do this.'

She shook her head. 'What would *he* think, what would *he* do, if he knew there were two men with that girl and I did nothing? I honestly didn't know what those men were going to do to her, Detective. I didn't think she was going to be murdered. But I was scared so I drove away. I was so scared. And I didn't want to be arrested in front of Maggie, so I didn't do anything. When she turned up dead, it sounded awful when Maggie said there was one man. I panicked. I couldn't tell you about the second, because I knew Jarrod would leave – he'd finally have a good enough reason. And even though I want him to leave sometimes, even though I hate him for what he did with his fucking intern – this girl who I chatted with at his holiday party while he stood right there smiling, the girl who I actually bought a pair of earrings for at Bloomingdales and had gift-wrapped for Christmas – I can't do it. I hate him for what he's done, for all the lies he's told, for all the times he's touched me after he's been with her and I didn't know – I hate him, but I can't do it alone. I'm not strong, Detective. I'm not smart, like you said before. I need him, as pathetic and demented and sad as that is. I need him. And I'm not ready to let go. So the next day I was going to tell you, when we went back to where it happened, but Jarrod was there with us, and I couldn't. After that it was too late. Every time I thought about saying something, I stopped myself, because it was too late. I called you Tuesday when I walked into that bar, but by the time you called me back, it was too late again. I thought you would find this second guy on your own. I thought this Poole would confess and tell you about his friend, and the case would plea. When Jarrod was a PD he said 90 per cent of cases never even went to trial. He always talked about his clients "flipping" and how there was no "honor among thieves". I screwed it up. I'm sorry for all of it . . .'

Detective Maldonado was the first to break the heavy silence. 'That was hard, Mrs Saunders. I know it was.'

'Faith . . .' Jarrod started. 'I'm sorry. I wish I could take it all back . . .' Maybe he ran out of words because they simply stopped.

'I'll advise you what we find at his house this time,' said Detective Nill as he rose to leave. He rubbed her on the shoulder. 'Hopefully Poole won't be out on the streets much longer.'

Faith shook her head. 'It's not about me, Detective. I thought Poole would tell you about his partner and it would all be over, that I wouldn't have to be involved any more. But it just gets worse and worse, when you think it can't, and now you say there's another girl missing.' She looked out the window, at Maggie's swing set that she rarely used and the pretty patio furniture that she'd fretted over picking the right stripe pattern on. She felt foolish that anything that trivial had ever mattered as much as it once did. 'I'm not religious, Detective,' she said in a faint, resigned voice. 'I should be; I'll get back there. But I want you to know that I'm praying now, Detective. I'm praying that this missing girl comes home safe to her family. And that I don't have her blood on my hands, too.'

51

Derrick knew something was about to happen. He could feel it in his bones. From behind his drawn living-room drapes, he peeked out his window, but saw nothing. He knew the cops were on him, though. Just 'cause he couldn't see them, didn't mean they weren't out there, pointing rifles at his head with a scope and a laser. Waiting for him to twitch so they'd have a reason to take him out. He'd spent the four-hour drive up to Ormond Beach on Thanksgiving checking his rearview, looking for that black Taurus three cars back. Then he'd spent the whole night peeking out behind curtains that smelled like boiled eggs at Gemma's ancient aunt's condo watching for that same Taurus, because it was always a Taurus and it was always black. His holiday had been ruined.

Then he'd caught the news last night and he *knew* they were out there.

They'd found the nest. Sitting on the bed in his stark La Quinta motel room, he'd watched as the crime-scene jokesters paraded in and out of his special place in their HazMat protective gear and face masks, wearing gloves and carrying out black bags loaded with . . . stuff. It had filled him with anger. He'd felt violated. Then anxious. He'd gone back to the window, looking for that fucking black Taurus in the parking lot. All night long he'd sat there, smoking cigarettes, keeping watch. He and Gemma had left before the sun was up and headed back to Boca.

They had no evidence, but that wasn't going to stop them from pinning this on him. Or focusing their scopes, waiting for that twitch they could say was a reach for a gun, and eliminating the problem they'd never get a conviction on in the courts with one pull of the trigger. He took a deep drag of his cigarette and blew the smoke through the crack in the drapes. All they had were fibers. Little snips of thread that might lead them to Profe, but they were never gonna lead them to him. Because *he* didn't make mistakes. *He* didn't shed fibers like fucking Hansel and Gretel dropped pebbles, leading the police all over the land to all the places he'd been. The fibers might seal Profe's fate – if they could ever catch him – but they had nothing on him. Nothing. Because *he* didn't make mistakes.

He rubbed his temples. His head throbbed.

Problem was, they didn't have Profe. The fucking pebbles had led them to *his* fucking car, not Profe's, and then *his* fucking door and someone was gonna need to answer, someone was gonna need to pay for those sluts' deaths even though no one gave a shit about any of them when they were alive. But the someone who was going down was gonna be him: Derrick Poole. They had called his mother and tried talking to his crazy grandma, then they'd gone to every school he'd ever attended and tried getting someone to tell them he killed animals and lit bathrooms on fire. They were trying to build a case against *him*. He wasn't so worried until he'd watched the news yesterday. And while he knew he had left nothing of himself behind, he had his doubts about fucking Hansel, which was ironic since Profe was supposed to be the mentor. He dropped the cigarette in the half-empty mug of coffee. Even if Ed had left nothing of himself behind, it was only a matter of time before the black Tauruses would be gathered outside *his* home and knocking on *his* door. Asking questions.

Gemma stood up from the couch and started for his kitchen. 'You want a beer?' she asked sweetly. 'More coffee?'

He shrugged.

'Anything going on outside?' she asked, trying to sound casual. He knew she was nervous, too. She'd seen the news.

He turned and stared at her. 'Nope.'

'Can I do anything for you?'

'You've done enough. Thanks.'

It was Fucking Gemma who had set the cops on him. She didn't know he knew that, but she was trying her best to make it up to him, anyway. She cleaned his apartment, attempted to cook him dinner, and fucked him anyway he wanted. Maybe she was scared of losing him if he found out she had a big, gossipy mouth. Maybe she was scared of him.

'I think I might get going then,' Gemma said, fingering the belt loop on her jeans.

He shrugged again and she headed into the bedroom. He left the window and walked over to the dining-room table. The mail was splayed all over it. First she had retrieved it from *his* mailbox without asking *him* if *he* wanted her to get *his* mail, then she had tossed it on *his* table, without asking *him* where *he'd* like *his* fucking mail placed. He clenched his teeth. He spotted a mailer from Mullinax Ford. He tapped his finger on the picture of a Ford Explorer.

Blondie, Blondie, Blondie. What are we gonna do about you?

That bad was on his head. Profe had wanted to kill her and her kid. String them both up and have a slow go and feed them in pieces to the gators, but Derrick didn't kill kids. He wasn't a monster. He wasn't into mommies and little girls. And what did he get for cutting that bitch a break? He rubbed his pounding head. 'I need some more aspirin,' he shouted.

How come *Profe's* ugly mug wasn't next to his caricature in the local section? How come the cops hadn't announced that they were searching for two killers, not one? He had allowed her to live, and she had sicced the cops on him. Like she was so righteous. Like she was above it all. That made him so angry it was hard to think.

He stared at the mailer. The night air was cold, the trees were dripping wet, lightning flashes erupted across a black sky. *Please don't cut me up! Please don't make me go with him! I have a baby! I won't tell anyone what you did to those girls: I promise! Don't hurt that lady! There's a kid in that car – I saw her!*

He hated when they cried. It annoyed him.

Blondie had her own secrets – and they were whoppers. He saw her slam into that stripper slut and take off like she didn't care. He knew she was bombed and probably sleeping it off when ironically the chick she'd mowed down an hour earlier had come hobbling back to her looking for help on that lonesome, deserted street, only to be turned away. Boo-hoo.

He crumpled the mailer in his hand. There was nothing that was going to link him back to the nest or to those girls. That was all Ed. The only problem he had was a drunk housewife who could possibly help the police connect the teacher to the student. He hated to admit that Profe had been right: they should have eliminated that problem before it became one. Now it was a little more complicated – for Derrick, anyway. He smiled to himself. If Blondie was fretting over grocery-shopping again for fear of running into her not-so-friendly neighbor . . . well, just wait till she met the man who'd taught him everything he knew.

'Here's your Tylenol, hon,' said Gemma, handing him two painkillers and a glass of water. She had her jacket on and purse on her shoulder. Ready to bolt.

He swallowed them dry, his eyes locked on hers. Before she could ask for permission to leave, there was a loud pounding on the door.

'Police!'

Gemma looked at him like she was thinking about opening it and he shook his head – she'd done enough damage. He pushed her aside, just as another loud bang sounded and the door broke in with a thunderous crash. Standing there was the fat detective from the stop and lineup and what looked like an army of suits and uniforms.

'Hi there, Derrick. I didn't think you heard us,' said Nill.

'You can't come in here like that!' cried Gemma. 'You can't bust in doors! You broke the door! Holy shit! What is that about?'

'Do you live here, Gemma?' asked Nill with a frown as the army marched in behind him.

'That doesn't matter! He's got rights! You can't come—'

'I didn't think so.' Nill nodded at the purse on her shoulder and then pointed at a uniform. 'I see you're headed out. Officer Kilpatrick's gonna make sure you find your way home. Bye now.'

'I've got nothing to say to you,' Derrick yelled as Gemma was led off down his front walk. Blue-gloved crime-scene techs in khakis and polos passed them on their way in. 'I have a lawyer! Talk to my lawyer!'

'Not a problem,' replied Nill, handing Derrick a piece of paper as the invading army spread out and marched upstairs to the master bedroom. 'I'm not here to talk, anyway.'

52

'How'd you know where to find it?' asked Tatiana as she took a bite out of the biggest, juiciest burger Bryan had ever seen. Mayonnaise, ketchup and mustard simultaneously oozed out every side and dripped onto her plate, along with a renegade mushroom. Bryan's stomach grumbled like a personal locating beacon sending out electronic pings, and it wasn't searching for the pile of shredded lettuce on his plate. It had been two days since the search of Poole's apartment.

'I hate the Yankees,' he replied, picking at his salad and ignoring his indignant stomach. 'I loved Jeter when he was there, but I hate the Yankees. When I was in his closet the first time, I saw it and thought, "Figures this guy is a fucking Yankees fan" and it stuck in my head. So when Faith Saunders said Yankee hat, I thought, "Hmmm . . . maybe." Now we gotta see if it's *that* Yankee hat. It was sitting right where I'd seen it, along with a bunch of other hats and sports equipment, from a lacrosse stick to football pads, soccer ball, tennis racket, none of which looked used. A little weird.'

'That is weird,' she said taking another big chomp. 'A wannabe athlete?'

'Most smart guys lacking in the muscle department who didn't make the team and hold a grudge grow up to become

271

doctors or work on Wall Street; their revenge is financial success. But I'm no shrink and I'm no profiler, Maldonado. I don't know what significance hoarding unused sports equipment has to do with this investigation, except maybe one day the guy hopes to use it. He also had all that movie memorabilia crap, too. Could be he's a two-bit collector.'

'Or a hoarder. I watch that show; they're nuts.' She shrugged. 'Maybe he has a fascination with fame. Athletes, movie stars,' she said as she slurped a thick, chocolate milkshake.

He gave up on the rabbit food and set about fixing his coffee. 'I played high school football. Thought I had a shot at playing pro. Then I went to college and was the smallest third-string cornerback on the bench. I feared for my life on the field.'

She raised an eyebrow.

He patted his stomach. 'Of course, I wasn't carrying around this luggage back then, ya know. This is from the soon to be ex-wife. It'll be gone soon, too.'

'I noticed – no fries for you, any more. No more Dove candies in your desk, either.'

'That's where they were going.'

She smiled. 'This soon to be ex of yours. Was she a good cook?'

'Nope. I did most of the cooking. She couldn't boil water, but she looked real pretty, so I let it slide.'

'That's pretty sexist. Karma comes back around in the weirdest way, doesn't it?' she asked, draining the very last drop from her shake with an annoying slurp.

'Yup. When she left me, I drowned my sorrows, not realizing how many calories it took to get good and drunk. Plus I stopped cooking, since it was just me. All the food comes in packages for two or family packs. Very depressing. I only get the twins every other weekend and on Wednesdays and they always want to eat out.'

'I did notice you lost a few pounds.'

272

'No, you didn't.'

'Yeah, I did. I didn't know if you wanted anyone to notice.'

'Well, thanks. I want to start running again, but ya gotta walk before ya run or the doc says I'll blow out a knee or an organ. I used to do half-marathons, believe it or not. Running helps me get rid of stress.' He looked down at her plate. The burger and large fries were gone. The milkshake was a dead soldier. 'I thought you were sick.' She'd missed out on the search of Poole's apartment because of a doctor's appointment. 'What did the doc say? You're not contagious, are you?'

She turned red. 'Don't make me feel guilty because you had half a salad.'

He shook his head. 'I'm envious, is all.'

She pushed the empty plate to the side of the table. 'So when the DNA comes back, if we get any off the hat, and we have a profile, what then?' she asked, ignoring his question.

'We pop it in CODIS and the FDLE database and see what we come up with.' FDLE maintained a database of DNA samples obtained from solved and unsolved crimes in the state of Florida and also from felons who were compelled to provide a DNA oral swab upon being convicted of a certain enumerated felony, which included burglary, sexual battery, lewd and lascivious behavior, robbery, kidnapping and murder. CODIS stood for the Combined DNA Index System – the national DNA database system maintained by the feds.

'And if we don't get a match?' she asked.

'I'm not waiting on one; that would be gravy. There's a good chance this guy has no record, although he might've offended before. Before Santri and the fibers, the crime scenes and bodies were squeaky clean. That tells me that either one or both of them might have had more practice making perfect before Emily Foss and Jane Doe. So we're gonna do some old-fashioned police work, Maldonado. Now that we know that Poole had a partner, we're gonna pull his life apart to find who it is. Because Poole didn't just meet some guy in a bar and they agreed to go a-hunting for women. The key is *their* relationship. For weeks I've been looking for the relationship that Poole had with all the victims, when that link might very well have actually been between his partner and the victims, which is why I never found it. Maybe the partner does the hunting,' he finished as they paid the bill and started for the car.

'So to find this guy, Muttonchops—'

'Which he's likely shaved off – a long time ago. Especially after the sketch of his buddy, Derrick, showed up on the news.'

She nodded as she climbed into the passenger side of the Taurus. 'OK. But muttonchops are pretty rare, I would think. People would remember someone who had a weird beard, right? Running a sketch might help us find him, like it found Poole.'

'I intend to run a sketch, and assuming Faith Saunders can be as detailed with him as her daughter was with Poole's description, we might get something. Problem is, we were unbelievably lucky to get a hit on a sketch with Poole – it's almost unheard of. Second, it's been over a month and I'm betting those chops are long gone, if they were ever real in the first place. They could have been part of a costume, for all I know. Third, muttonchops are not as uncommon in certain parts of this state and this country as they are in Miami. And last, Poole is not particularly social; I doubt his friend is. To find this guy I think we need to look at Poole's friends, co-workers, relatives.'

'Haven't we done that? I, personally, have memorized his résumé.'

'We washed the pot; we didn't scrub it,' Bryan replied as he pulled out of the parking lot. 'Serial killer partners are rare. It's hard to find someone who not only shares such a deviant way of thinking, but one who is willing to act on those anti-social thoughts. It's a big leap to let somebody in on your twisted fantasy for wanting to butcher a woman – it's another ginormous leap to pick up a knife and gut her. I'm not a shrink, or an expert, like I said, but historically relationships like that take a lot of trust. Think marriage, long-term friendship, sexual partners, relatives: Ray Fernandez and Martha Beck were a couple dubbed 'The Lonely Hearts Killers' who murdered twenty women; Fred and Rosemary West tortured and killed at least ten women together in Gloucester, England; Ian Brady and Myra Hindley were live-in lovers – they raped and killed five kids. Ronnie and Reggie Kray were twin brothers. Buono and Bianchi were cousins. Leopold and Loeb were college friends. Ottis Toole and Henry Lee Lucas were both friends and homosexual lovers. Lake and Ng were friends and survivalists. Bittaker and Norris, 'The Toolbox Killers', did time together in California.'

'For someone who claims he's no expert, you sure sound like you know what you're talking about. I'm impressed.'

'If we pull up everyone we can think of in Poole's past, maybe we can run those names with the victims and see if we can find a link there: school chums, names he did time with in juvi, co-workers from every job he's ever worked. Then there's social media; that's a bitch. We have his hard drive from the first search warrant. I think we need to go through it a little more carefully, look for names that continue to pop up, weird chat rooms, weird associations. Maybe cross-check that with the co-worker and friend list.'

'Ugh. That sounds like a shitload of work.'

Bryan shrugged. 'Looks like we're getting that task force. You can thank the Little Shack of Horrors for that. The press mob at the scene helped, I'm sure. Before the DNA was even back, Veerling was on the phone with the sheriffs of Hendry and Glades.' Gordon Veerling was the sheriff. 'Once the DNA came back yesterday and confirmed that the blood sprayed all over that place belonged to three murder victims – Foss,

Kruger and Santri – that sealed the deal. Now we have to find out whose foot was in that bucket. And the other . . . parts.'

Tatiana made a face. 'That was beyond grotesque. And you were in there alone in the dark . . . It gives me the shivers.'

'Aw. That's sweet – you were worried.'

She shook her head. 'It makes my skin crawl. Thank God it wasn't me in there. So whose foot is it? And . . . innards?'

'I'm thinking Noelle Langtry; we're getting a DNA sample from her mom for a genetic comparison. We can then match it to the parts we found in the shack. That will take a few more days. There could be more victims, Maldonado, but we didn't know anyone was missing so we weren't looking. What a cluster fuck.'

'Why is this guy still out walking around? Tell me that.'

'The ASA wants direct evidence connecting Poole either to the shack or to the victims. Or at least direct evidence connecting him to his partner, who she can then connect to the shack because of the fibers he shed like dog hair all over it. Romolo thinks it's still too circumstantial to make a case for first-degree against Poole. And she doesn't like to lose. If she goes for the death penalty, a life sentence means the guy got off.'

'I don't get it,' Tatiana said, shaking her head. 'I mean I do, but I don't. The guy is the last one seen with a girl who ends up dead and whose blood is found all over a slaughter-house. When does the cavalry arrive?'

'Tomorrow's the meeting with the sheriffs from Glades and Hendry. We'll meet their warm bodies then. And Amandola's giving us Genovese.' Pat Genovese was a seasoned homicide detective, two desks over. 'And you, Maldonado, ya know, if you're still up for it. Unless you're thinking of jumping ship and going back to kiddie crimes.'

'Now it's my turn to be touched. That's sweet of you to think of me. Of course I'm up to it. Do I have a choice?' she said with a short, nervous laugh. She lowered the window.

He looked at her quizzically. "'Cause you don't look up to anything right now. You look green.'

'I was remembering the body parts in the bucket and I just ate a burger. Who the hell knew there was so much evil in the world? It makes me sick.'

'And you're a homicide detective? You need a new profession, Maldonado,' he said as the light changed.

'No, it really makes me sick. Pull over.' Her head was halfway out the open window, nose in the wind, hair flapping in the breeze, like a dog.

'Jesus! Hold on!' He pulled over and she jumped out of the car, disappearing into some bushes off Australian Avenue.

The phone rang as she ran out. 'Nill,' he answered, raising the window so he wouldn't have to listen to her yack.

'Detective, it's Dave Smiga in Serology at the lab. I just faxed you your report, but I knew you wanted to hear the results right away.'

Tatiana climbed back into the car. 'You look mighty happy,' she said weakly after he'd hung up with Dave.

'You don't,' he replied.

'You can drive, now,' she said, pointing at the road. 'What? I've got a virus.'

'Really?' He eyed her suspiciously. 'Spit it out – you're pregnant, aren't you?'

'Just 'cause I'm a woman and I threw up doesn't mean I'm fucking pregnant. Your driving makes me queasy; you hit the brakes too much.' She leaned her head against the window.

'When are you due?'

She sighed. 'May.'

'Can I ask, where's the dad? Who's the dad? Is it one of us?'

'I thought you were gonna ask me how it happened,' she said with a tired laugh. 'He's a dick; he's gone. And he's not a cop. I'm doing this on my own. I can't lose this spot; I worked too hard to get it. I always wanted to be Homicide.

277

Every other girl wanted to be a vet, but I wanted to catch murderers. I'll tell the LT and the Chief when I'm headed into the delivery room, and I'll be back at my desk the following Monday. They'll never know I was gone.'

'OK, Wonder Woman. I'm not gonna blow your cover.'

'Why are you still smiling like that? Like a creepy cat who ate a canary. 'Cause you figured out I was knocked up? Good for you, Detective.'

'Nope. Although I am pretty proud of that, since you are being so cagey. I'm smiling because the lab called while you were busy yacking off.'

'Yeah? And what did they have to say?'

'Looks like we'll be combing through Poole's address book and Facebook page tonight. The DNA's back on that Yankee hat. It's the same guy that left us a piece of his shirt and sprinkled it all over that shack. The dots are starting to connect. Poole has a partner, Mama Maldonado. Now we have to find out who he is.'

53

If Bryan had any illusions that finding the connection to Poole's partner would be easy, he was wrong. Even with a task force of brains picking apart Poole's life year by year from the time he started to crawl, they were coming up with nothing. The two detectives from Hendry and Glades – Austin Velasquez and Dave Minkhaus – travelled to Deltona to interview teachers, principals, and classmates from elementary through his second year of high school, when Poole went to Haines City. They'd hoped to come back with a long list of friends that Poole had made over the years – they didn't. There were none. The task force pulled social security records and tax returns and detectives personally visited every place Poole had ever worked in the state of Florida: Walgreens, Dunkin' Donuts, Starbucks, AMC Theaters, Universal Studios for a summer, H&R Block, Ernst & Young. Fast food to college internships to career moves – there was nobody. No one Poole ever ate lunch with consistently or went out for a beer with. No one that he socialized with. Other than the names of a couple of girls he'd dated casually through work, there was nothing serious, and of the girls who could even remember him, all said there was nothing remarkable about him: quiet, reserved, shy. Forgettable. Derrick Alan Freeley Poole was the very definition of the word 'loner'.

Bryan knew the most significant authority on Poole's past would be his mother, Bethany Freeley. First he'd tried talking with her on the phone, but she'd been resistant. So he'd flown to Phoenix to interview her. He was back the next day. The woman was a clam – she wouldn't even confirm that she hadn't seen her son in over ten years. As for getting any information from grandma, Linda Sue Poole was indeed a mental mess. She couldn't remember her own name.

The geniuses in the computer crime lab were dissecting Poole's Facebook contacts – of which there were eighty-seven, and of those, most were professional associations, like every professional NFL and MLB page and fan pages for movies, TV shows and video games. Considering that most young people Poole's age had hundreds, sometimes thousands, of friends, and lived their life on social media, the fact that he didn't was troubling. Now they were busy sorting through emails and chat room visits, searching his cookies, trying to pull up his surfing history, and running his hard drive through REDS to see what files had recently been deleted or written over.

The most convenient place to hook up with a like-minded sociopath, Bryan would've thought, would've been in lock-up in sex offender therapy. Tatiana and Pat Genovese had run every guy who did time with Poole during his two years at the Orange Youth Academy, narrowing down the list to who was alive, who was incarcerated somewhere, who was out, who had reoffended, and who was presently living in the state of Florida. They had narrowed the list to thirty-nine, and were currently going through each name, marrying names with intake shots from ten years back and comparing them to the latest sketch Cuddy had done with Faith Saunders – treating each name as if he were the partner, trying to find a relationship with Poole from their end, since Poole's personal life was cloaked in secrecy. The fact that nothing had popped out yet

280

was both disappointing and frustrating. So Bryan had taken a ride up to Orange Youth to meet with the warden, Ravi Lee, who'd headed up the facility since 1999 and was there when Poole was incarcerated. In addition to looking at the facility, he wanted to look at the disciplinary records that were not kept on computer back in 2004, and interview staff who might still be working there who had known Poole.

Lee leaned back in a tired vinyl chair in his microscopic office. If this was the digs the boss gets, Bryan couldn't imagine the cubicles the rest of the staff had to work out of. The room smelled of must and old paper.

'I pulled his file after you called, Detective. So that I could review it, because I honestly didn't have an independent recollection of Derrick Poole from ten years ago. We have forty-eight boys here at any given moment. Not one bed is ever empty, which goes to show you the disastrous course our youth are on today, and how poorly parents are parenting. Anyway, I pulled his file and I do remember him, but I have to tell you that what I remember isn't bad: Derrick was a model prisoner. He got his GED here, took extra classes, including Spanish and woodwork. He got along well with staff. I've assembled for you a list of employees who worked here at the time, and outside volunteers, along with their pictures. Everyone who works or volunteers or visits on this property has to provide a photo ID and we maintain those as public records. Some of the staff and volunteers are still with us today, although most have moved on. I've also supplied you with the facility's visitor logs from the period that Mr Poole was incarcerated. Perhaps that will help.'

'Thank you,' replied Bryan as he thumbed through the staff directory. It was substantial. 'The visitor logs might be worth looking into.'

'The case you're here on is . . . um, quite disturbing,' commented Lee.

'As was the case that Mr Poole was sent here for. Model

prisoners don't make model people; that's why they get locked up.'

The warden nodded.

Nill set aside the staff directory and flipped through the volunteer folder full of pictures and dossiers. He was about to have them all brought to an interview room so that he wouldn't have to do this with an extra pair of eyes watching from across the desk, when he spotted a picture. 'Who's this?'

The warden took the thick folder back. 'Hmmm. That's Ed Carbone, he was a volunteer who taught GED classes, and tutored boys interested in Spanish. He taught Mr Poole, but I'd have to say, he was more like a mentor to the boy. He was one of the younger staff members. He was about ten years older than the kids. We don't normally like to have our staff or volunteers so close in age, but he was a positive role model for them.'

'Not so fast,' muttered Bryan as he pulled out Cuddy's sketch and held it up next to the volunteer ID. 'Where's he at now?'

'I have no idea,' replied Lee. 'Ed left about five years back. He hasn't kept in touch with anyone.'

'I'm not so sure I'd agree with you on that, Mr Lee.' He picked up his cell and dialed Tatiana first. 'Maldonado,' he said before she could answer.

'I was just gonna call you,' she said, somberly.

'I need you to run someone, find out where they are, who they are,' he started. 'I might have something.'

'We got something, too,' she replied. 'Velasquez says they just found a body in a ditch off US 27 in Hendry County. He thinks it's the rest of Noelle Langtry.'

'Damn it!' Bryan slapped the folder with the back of his hand. Dossiers and pictures spilled out and onto Lee's desk. He hadn't really held out hope that Noelle Langtry was going to be found alive, especially after the slaughter he'd seen in the shack, but it still stung to know that a beautiful little girl, the same age as his own daughters, would never come home. He stared at the face that had landed, fittingly, at his feet. 'All the more reason we need to move on this, Maldonado. I think I might've found Poole's partner. And his name is Ed Carbone.'

54

'The hat's a match; same DNA as the fabric patch in the woods,' Bryan started. 'Fibers in the car and at the shack match the patch.' He was standing in Elisabetta Romolo's office. She had not asked him to sit. She was reading something at her desk, and her Prada glasses rested precariously on the tip of her nose as she looked up at him.

'Whose DNA is it?' she asked.

'I have the profile. I think the name is Ed Carbone. He was Poole's tutor and mentor when Poole was locked up in juvi. They spent a lot of time together.'

'Where's Carbone?'

'We can't find him. He was living in an apartment in Okeechobee for the past year. Had a part-time job off the books working at a scrap-metal plant. Disappeared about two months back. No one knows where.'

Elisabetta took off her glasses. 'Besides being Poole's mentor, what makes you think this guy is his partner?'

'He dated Emily Foss. Or tried to. Hung around her at the strip joint where she worked in Miami so many times that she took out a restraining order against him and moved up to Palm Beach. He stopped coming around the club after that, and she disappeared a year later. No one knew about the restraining order up here, because it was taken out in Miami and she let it lapse. I found it running his name through FCIC. She's the link, Elisabetta. She was the first victim. If Jane Doe, the charred torso found in Glades back in 2012 is this guy's, she might have happened before he hooked up with Poole, because we couldn't find anything linking her to the shack. But the two of them murdered four girls together, maybe more.' He slid the volunteer photo and the Cuddy sketch across her desk. 'Faith Saunders identified his photo this morning. I have a BOLO out to locate him for questioning. The dots are connected.'

She nodded. 'I'll indict the DNA profile. Once you pick up Carbone, we'll swab him.'

Bryan put the pictures back in his file. 'I'm picking up Poole today. This is as good as we're gonna get on him.'

'Serial killer partners in Palm Beach. A Little Shack of Horrors,' Elisabetta mused aloud as she spun around to look outside her window at the bustle of people going in and out of the courthouse across the street. 'This is going to be huge, Detective; get ready.'

55

Elisabetta twisted the curly gray phone cord around her long, Black Pearl fingernails. She looked out the window at the beautiful marble-and-glass building across the street, which looked more like a resort than a courthouse: a grand and imposing four-story arched entranceway, a thirty-two-foot waterfall in the lobby, floor-to-ceiling windows in some of the courtrooms. The view of downtown and the water was so spectacular from some courtrooms that she hated trying cases in them because it was too distracting for jurors, who, on the best of days, had a limited attention span.

'The news outlets have been calling, Arnie. Trust me, it's going to be big,' she said quietly. 'It has all the ingredients, and it's all mine.'

'What's the name?'

'Derrick Poole. You probably heard of it as the Little Shack of Horrors investigation.'

There was a brief pause. 'Yeah, yeah. I saw something about a torture shack that the police had found down by you. No shit, that's yours?'

'I just authorized his arrest. He's a serial killer. And I'm indicting the DNA strand of his partner.'

Arnie Greenburg perked up like a flower that had just

been watered. 'Two serials? Really? How many have they killed?'

'At least three. We're waiting on DNA to confirm the identity of the fourth. And there's a fifth that we probably can't prove, but know they did.'

'That doesn't sound like a lot, you know, for a serial.'

She rolled her eyes. 'We think this is only the beginning; there could be a lot more,' she added.

'How do they kill them?'

'Different ways. They tortured the girls first, some were dismembered. Then they dump the bodies in sugar cane fields. That shack was bad. The press doesn't know how bad yet, but they want to. My office is being very tight-lipped about this, as you can imagine.'

'Confession?'

'I wish it were that easy. No. And Poole's never gonna plead; I'll be taking it to trial.'

'Where's the other guy? You said you were indicting his DNA? Do you have a name?'

'I have a name, but he's absconded. As a matter of protocol, I'm indicting the DNA profile, but the detectives are confident it will belong to their suspect, once we bring him in.' A rush of guilt came over her. Divulging confidential information on an active criminal investigation was not something she'd ever done before. 'That name will come out soon enough.'

'Who are the victims? How long have you been looking for these guys?'

'The murders stretch over the course of a year. The victims are prostitutes and strippers. Think Florida's very own Green River Killer.'

'You're about forty-five short of that title, but the partner angle is intriguing and the torture shack is fascinating. Yeah, yeah, I do remember seeing something about it up here.' He clucked his tongue a few times like a ticking clock, which meant he was thinking things over.

287

Up here. Elisabetta rolled her eyes again. Ya gotta love New Yorkers – if you can make it on the news up there, you can make it anywhere. 'It's Palm Beach, Arnie, don't forget. Crimes like that don't happen around here. Ask a Kennedy. Or a Trump.' She closed her eyes. That sounded desperate.

'Well, your competition's pretty stiff, Elisabetta. I was gonna call you about that. I found out that Rachel Cilla, the federal prosecutor who took down that sex-trafficking ring in LA last year, put her name in the hat. She's the front-runner at this point. They'd absolutely looove to get C.J. Townsend, but she turned them down.'

Elisabetta shook her head. 'No! No! No!' she mouthed at the phone. Ever since Arnie Greenburg, an old law school classmate who was a literary/talent agent at Janklow & Nesbit in New York, had called her to tell her that CNN was looking for a legal analyst to host a new crime show, it was all she could think of. And after some long, hard thinking, she'd realized it was all she wanted. As much as she wished it didn't, it bugged her that her prosecutor counterpart in Miami – C.J. Townsend, who had prosecuted the serial killer Cupid – had already been offered the job. And turned it down. No matter how tragic her tale, that woman's fifteen minutes needed to finally end. 'The witness who helped catch this serial is four years old, Arnie,' she blurted out.

'What?'

'She's four. Pigtails, blonde curls, cute as a button. Looks like Drew Barrymore in *E.T.* She was in the car with her mom and saw Poole and his partner abduct one of the women whose blood was found splattered all over a cage in that shack.'

'A cage? They kept them in cages?'

'This case is going to give me the exposure you were talking about, Arnie. What did you say, like Fairstein after Chambers, Townsend after Cupid, Guilfoyle after the Presa Canario mauling? I know its hard to predict what cases will catch the public's eye, but after ten years of prosecuting, you know which ones are hot.' God she hated how she sounded – like a used-car salesman to the prospective customer who was walking off the lot.

'Elisabetta, I don't have to tell you this – you look great on camera. You have the perfect look, just what they say they want. You're smart, you can think on your feet, you're clever, feisty and engaging. And I'm sure you're amazing to watch in trial. I'm in your corner, that's why I called you as soon as I heard about the show, but you have no name, honey. They want a name – not a person who might make a name for herself if the public thinks the case is interesting enough to follow.'

'The defendant is a good-looking, white accountant with a dark past that's gonna come out, too,' she continued. 'He tried to rape his grandmother, Arnie. His partner in these murders was a volunteer at juvi who taught him Spanish and helped him pass the GED. See what I mean? It's got it . . . well, I know it's gonna be big, is all.'

'OK. Great. I have a meeting with Woodsen next week on another matter. I'll make sure I bring you up. Let's see where your case is then.'

She nibbled on a nail. 'When are they looking to make a decision?'

Arnie yawned. 'Sorry, about that. I didn't get much sleep. They want to roll the show out next fall, so I think they want a name by early 2015.'

'It's not gonna go to trial by then. Not on a murder.'

'Oh,' he replied. There was a long pause. 'Well, see what you can do, darling, to get those headlines rolling and get your name out there. Don't compromise your case or nothing. No one wants that.'

'Of course not,' replied Elisabetta with a weary sigh, knowing full well that that was exactly what the cost would end up being. She hung up the phone, and untwisted her fingers from the cord. And she thought about something her mother once said to her a long, long time ago.

You better get your asking price, Elisabetta, because when you sell your soul to the devil, there are no returns.

56

The first time Faith could remember her father being drunk, she was five or six. Actually, the memory was of her mother yelling at her father for being drunk. He'd come home from a night out celebrating some big case he had won. It was very late. Charity had a virus, so their mom was in and out of their room every hour or so checking her temperature and Faith couldn't get to sleep. She'd heard the front door open downstairs and her dad singing some ditty in his soft Irish brogue – when he was a teenager in Dublin he'd sung in a band that played in pubs and at weddings. He started up the stairs, slower than he usually did. His shoes dragging on the wood. At the top of the landing he opened the door to her and Charity's small bedroom. The door creaked and the light from the hall backlit him so Faith couldn't see his face. 'I love you, my little ladies,' he said into the dark, louder than what was probably intended as a whisper.

'Look at you!' Aileen had snapped from out in the hall. 'It's one in the goddamn morning! I told you she was sick! What, do you not care?'

'I was celebrating!' he'd replied jubilantly.

'Patrick stop it! I'm not dancing. You're drunk. You smell like a bottle of cheap whiskey.'

291

'It wasn't cheap,' he'd answered with a hearty laugh.
'That's wonderful.'

'I was celebrating, what's wrong with that? I won my case; I get to celebrate. Jesus Christ, Aileen! Can't a man celebrate something around here? It's always so down.' He started singing again. 'You'll be fine with it when I get the check, I assure you. Everyone's happy when the money comes in.'

Her mother's voice, laden with disgust and resignation, trailed off as she'd walked back down the hall to her bedroom. 'The problem is, Patrick, you're always celebrating something.' She slammed the bedroom door closed. Her father slept on the floor of Faith's room that night, between their twin beds.

Drunkenness wasn't an event for her dad, it was a condition, a state of being. He liked his Jameson and he made no attempt to conceal his affection. He never hid his drinking or tried to minimize it. There were no mini-bar bottles hidden throughout the house, and he didn't mix his whiskey with orange juice or put a beer in a water bottle to disguise what it was he was drinking. He wasn't a fall-down, vomiting slob, or a mean drunk, or a gushy, teary emotional sot. In fact, except for a few really bad benders that she could recall, Sully acted no different off the sauce than he did on it, which meant that either he was constantly drinking, or he had a really high tolerance. It turned out that it was both.

Her father slept on her floor a fair amount. Or Faith would bunk with Charity and let her dad have her bed. She could smell the alcohol in the dark when he snored; it filled the room like a Glades Plug-In. She hated that smell – until he died. Then it actually became a pleasant part of a memory associated with him, like the scent of his cologne. Because her dad was always so mellow and happy, the worst part of his drinking was the fighting between her parents. Faith remembered always wanting one of them to just stop – stop drinking or stop yelling about it. Just stop. But as her dad's tolerance rose and he fed his condition to keep his being in the state to which it had grown accustomed, the fights grew more intense and closer together. Vivian's house became her refuge. She'd sleep over for whole weekends, and sometimes Charity would, too. Then her dad could have his pick of beds.

Aileen made her best effort to get them to hate their father for drinking. She talked about it, and about him, disparagingly, saying, 'Oh, you don't know the half of it when he's had too much, Faith. The money he's wasted, the time, the things he's done.' Sometimes she'd share some of the things that her father had done. Then the tears would start.

But Faith never felt bad for her mother. She wanted to. Charity did. She felt bad for not feeling bad, for not siding with her. Faith resented her because she knew Aileen was no teetotaler herself. She favored wine instead of Scotch, and she didn't drink as much or as often as her dad, but she drank. There were nights Faith watched her father carry her mother off to bed after she'd fallen asleep on the couch waiting for him to come home. She'd seen the empty Chardonnay bottles in the trash bin in the kitchen. They just never fought about it. Aileen would pretend nothing had ever happened.

She and Charity had vowed they would never drink. Not a drop. They would never become like them. Of course those promises were made when they were young, huddled in Charity's bed under the covers, whispering so that their dad wouldn't hear them. The smell was gross, so the taste must be disgusting. It was their fear of immediately becoming their parents upon the sip of a single drop of alcohol that kept them from tasting so much as a wine cooler by the time most of their friends had already experienced hangovers. But like fairytale characters who have been doomed by a prophetic curse would come to tragically learn at the end of the story, there is no undoing fate. Some things are meant to happen.

'How do you plead to the charges?' asked the judge. The small, chaotic courtroom in downtown Fort Lauderdale was packed with defendants, attorneys, family members. Even though the judge was speaking, there was an electric under-current of noise as lawyers whispered to their clients or exchanged information with prosecutors. A continuous stream of suits paraded past the state and defense podiums up to the clerk's desk, which was directly below the judge's bench, to check the calendar.

'Not guilty, Your Honor,' said Faith's attorney. He held his hand out to stop Faith from saying anything. 'We demand discovery, trial by jury.'

'Granted. Fifteen days, State. I need a trial date.'

'January seventh, two thousand fifteen for report, January twelfth for trial,' said the clerk.

'Thank you,' said the judge. 'Next up?'

'*State vs. David Hoyt*, page sixteen,' barked the clerk.

Her attorney gently nudged her away from the podium and led her through the well and past the state and defense tables as the next defendant and his attorney made their way up. Jarrod was waiting for them in the front row of seats in the gallery. He stood and the three of them walked out to the hall, where the hustle and bustle continued. And that was it: she had been arraigned. She felt like she'd been strip-searched again; there were just more people in the room.

'Thanks, Jack,' Jarrod said to his partner, who was her attorney. Before he'd joined Krauss and Lynch, Jack Clark had been a big DUI attorney at Greenburg Taurig.

Jack nodded. 'Let's see what they're offering. Because Faith was over double the limit, they're gonna try and be tough at first, just warning you. That's this office's strategy. Let me see who gets assigned to the case. Hopefully it's not a newbie – they like to offer state prison and make it sound like a deal.'

'Prison?' Faith cried.

'No, no. Don't worry about that. You'll get probation and community service, I'm sure. No one was hurt, there was no accident, there's no reason for prison. Your last DUI was ten years ago, which is better than less than ten. I'm just saying that brand-new prosecutors, which are the ones who handle DUIs, have something to prove, so they come out swinging. Their first offer won't be their last. This may take a few weeks to work out, is all. Don't worry, Faith.'

Jarrod reached for her hand. 'Don't worry,' he repeated.

They walked out of the courthouse, heading to their car in the parking lot three blocks over without saying a word, although he still held her hand and she held his. After her breakdown with Detectives Nill and Maldonado, Jarrod had come to her and apologized for the affair. On his knees he had sworn to her that Sandra meant nothing to him, that he didn't know why he had let it happen, that he hadn't seen her since they'd broken it off, that he wanted to move forward, not always look in the rearview, because he couldn't change anything back there. It was the perfect opportunity perhaps for her to get on her knees and join him, confess her rearview had a lot of shit in it, have a good cry together, followed by great makeup sex, and everything would be fine.

But that's not how life works. Not every fairytale gets a happy ending.

Like a frightened bird that senses a cat lurking nearby, Faith's eyes darted in a dozen different directions, trying to take in the unfamiliar surroundings of the Broward County Courthouse as they walked to the parking lot. The sidewalk was crowded. There was a long line out the entrance doors of people waiting to go through the metal detectors. The bail bondsman storefronts on 6th Street were busy with customers, as were the coffee shops and luncheonettes. The jail, as she knew, was right around the corner. There were criminals in plainclothes all around them, watching them. She felt like they were studying her. Why? Maybe they recognized her as one of them. Maybe she bore the signs of a defendant now, fresh from arraignment court. Or maybe they sensed how frightened she was, that she would make a good victim. There were so many strange faces; even walking down the street felt surreally dangerous. Derrick Poole might be under twenty-four-hour surveillance, but his partner was not. As far as she knew, detectives did not know where to find the man who they'd advised her used to be Poole's teacher. He could be anywhere, clean-shaven and in a snappy suit, his eyes hidden by sunglasses. He could be right here, walking amongst the other criminals, watching her as she obliviously ambled straight toward him. With his hand in his pocket, he could be secretly thumbing the sharp edge of a tool he'd already used on one of his victims as he approached. Then, without missing a single step, he would simply plunge the blade into her in the stomach as he casually walked on by.

She tightened her grip on Jarrod's hand as the same white van that had passed before passed a second time. She thought she might have seen it this morning when they parked. And maybe hanging around the bakery. She looked behind her, to her right, to her left.

'You OK?' he asked as they turned the corner into the lot.

She nodded.

'I know you're overwhelmed, but Jack will handle everything. He knows what he's doing. It'll be OK.'

She got in the car, wanting to say a thousand things, but opting to remain silent and study the cars.

When he was on his knees before her, asking for forgiveness, she had told him she understood, even though she still didn't. He had asked her to go to an AA meeting and she'd politely said she would think about it. Of course, inside she was thinking, 'Now? You want me to quit drinking now? When there is a pair of serial killers out there who know where we live? Who would love to see your daughter and me dead? When this horrible case is just beginning and I may have to testify? When I know that our marriage is treading into "irretrievably broken" ground? When I may have to go to prison myself? You think it's a good time to throw away the lifeboat as the ship begins to sink and everything gets sucked down with it?' But she didn't say any of those things, because he would never understand, just like she would never understand how he'd 'let something happen' with the intern. They were stuck at an impasse, with each telling the other to go ahead, but neither was moving. She might very well have a drinking problem, or she might understandably be stressed out of her goddamned mind, but this was not the time to try quitting something that helped stop the anxiety, soothed the shakes, took away the pain. It wasn't the time to quit and it wasn't the time to ask. She would cut down, yes. Like smoking, she could limit herself to a drink a day, which is what the rest of the world drank, so no one should complain. She'd done it before – when drinking became part of everyday solutions – she could do it again.

He hadn't brought it up again and she hadn't gotten bombed since. She didn't drink or smoke in front of him. To outsiders they still looked like a couple. But the emotional distance between them had grown into a chasm, with Jarrod on one side and her on the other, each watching the other pull further away as they held hands on the crater's rocky ledge. There were only two possible outcomes that she could see: either they both lost grip and were pulled apart, or one yanked the other over to their side at the last minute. Actually, there was a third scenario, she thought as Jarrod turned on the radio and the radio personality started talking about the breaking news coming out of Palm Beach.

One pulled the other off of their ledge, trying to bring them to their side, but couldn't hold the other's weight, and they both dropped into the black abyss below.

57

'On my radar tonight is a disturbing case coming out of Palm Beach, Florida,' began the talk show host with the distinctively thick Southern accent.

Faith sat on the edge of the bed in her bedroom and stared at the TV. She knew she should turn it off, walk away and read a book to Maggie or do the laundry or rearrange the shoes in her closet – anything but listen to the news tonight. And then she should go down the hall and into the office and unplug the computer to avoid the chatter that was possibly erupting on Internet news sites and over social media at this very moment. She should turn off the WiFi on her phone and cancel her subscription to the *Sun-Sentinel*. But she didn't do any of those things. Instead, she sat there transfixed, watching the train that was coming straight at her. Detective Nill's ominous warning sounded over and over again in her head.

People are having a real hard time understanding why you didn't call no one. Once this gets out, if the media interest keeps up . . . Joe Public is gonna have a hard time understanding it, too.

The news of Derrick Poole's arrest had been making the rounds all day, on both local and cable news channels. Many local stations broke into their programming to go live to this afternoon's press conference, held at the State Attorney's Office. Present at the podium were the sheriff of Palm Beach and the state attorney of Palm Beach, along with the pretty assistant state attorney that Faith had seen at the lineup – the one who was on a first name basis with Jarrod – Elisabetta Romolo. Standing behind the three were the sheriffs of two other counties, Detectives Nill and Maldonado, and a bunch of other people who wore dark suits and somber faces. The media interest had seemed to gain momentum throughout the day, as details of the investigation leaked out, the affidavit in support of the search warrant was made public, and accounts of the macabre brutality discovered inside the shack that had not previously been disclosed became known. Putting the word 'serial' in front of the word 'killers' apparently had the effect of pouring gasoline on a spark. The media's interest had indeed been ignited, and the eager reporters were busy fanning the flames trying to get the fire to jump to Joe Public.

Putting her head in the sand and not listening wouldn't stop people from saying what it was they wanted to say – it would mean she wouldn't hear it. As news of the arrest spread, Faith reasoned that she'd be better off knowing what the general temperature was before she opened her front door and stepped outside the safe confines of her house to mingle with Joe Public. At least she'd know what to wear.

'Yes, we're back in Florida, again, home to Monster Mom, Cupid, Picasso, Cunanan, Bundy, Rollings. I'm leaving some names out, because there're already too many. Now let's add a couple more. That's right – *two* more names. Police in Palm Beach County earlier today announced an arrest in the Little Shack of Horrors investigation – that's the torture chamber in the Everglades that the police found ten days ago, where it is believed multiple women were brutalized and then murdered. Twenty-nine-year-old Derrick Alan Poole of Boca Raton, Florida was arrested on first-degree murder charges in the death of Angelina Santri, the nineteen-year-old mom who disappeared after working her shift at a nightclub in Loxahatchee, Florida. Police also announced they are actively hunting for a man they believe was his partner in the murders: thirty-six-year-old Eduardo Carbone of Okeechobee, Florida.'

Video ran of a handcuffed Derrick Poole being escorted by Detectives Nill and Maldonado and surrounded by uniforms into the Palm Beach County Jail. His head was down, his face obscured by the suit jacket that he had pulled over his head. They had arrested him at work in front of his co-workers.

'Serial killers. Two of them, abducting, torturing and slaughtering women in Palm Beach County for over a year and no one seemed to notice. As the bodies piled up in cane fields out in western Palm Beach, no one sounded the alarms and said, "Hey! This might be the work of the same guy!"? Now we're learning how the pair was finally discovered and it is shocking, folks. It took the courage of a four-year-old, who had apparently witnessed the abduction of Angelina, to come forward and tell her daddy, after she saw Angelina's picture on the news when her body was discovered in a cane field. This is where I am just outraged, folks.'

It was happening. The train was wrecking right in front of her and she couldn't turn away, even though she knew she was going to get crushed. New Orleans crime reporter-turned-CNN talk show host Loni Hart had arguably, single-handedly, transformed the murder of two-year-old Caylee Anthony in Orlando, Florida from a local tragedy into a national news sensation. She had made the public hate her accused mother, Casey Anthony, referring to her derisively throughout the case as 'Monster Mom.' Faith always knew the media was powerful, that they could make a case or an issue spin one way or another, depending on the angle that they saw it keeping interest. They could take a case like the murder of Nicole Brown Simpson and make it all about race when it wasn't – it was about domestic violence and the murder of a woman and her friend by a jealous ex-husband. Faith held her breath.

'This little girl was in the car with her mother, who'd apparently gotten lost in a bad storm in the middle of the night, and pulled over to wait it out. That's when Angelina came knocking on the window begging for help. Not only did mom not help, but mom did nothing. *Nothing*, from what we are being told. I don't know who to be more angry with: The police for not noticing that women were going missing and for not forming a task force much earlier; this mom who couldn't be bothered to help or even call the police; or the men who tortured her, raped her, caged her, brutally killed her and then dismembered her. I'm really at a loss.'

A photo of Noelle Langtry appeared on the screen in the upper right corner, sharing the screen with Loni.

'Now there's a possible fifth victim: seventeen-year-old Noelle Langtry's body was found a few days ago in a cane field in Hendry County. She'd gone missing right after Angelina's body was found, but before either Poole or Carbone were on the radar of Palm Beach detectives, thanks to *that* mom. It makes you wonder if Noelle's death could have been prevented.'

A picture of Faith replaced Noelle Langtry on the screen and Faith sucked in a breath. It was from the cover of last October's *Our Town News*, the local community paper for businesses in Coral Springs and Parkland. They'd run a photo of Faith and Vivian, dressed in aprons, spatulas in hand, under the headline, *Cupcake Queens of Coral Springs: A Sweet Business, Indeed*. Vivian had been taken out of the shot, though, so it was just of Faith, smiling confidently for the camera.

'*That* mom: Faith Saunders of Parkland, Florida. She's a business owner – she owns a bakery – and she's a mom herself. Now, let me say that there's no law that requires someone to *be* a Good Samaritan. But there are laws protecting people who act as Good Samaritans from being sued later on down the road because they tried to help. That's because as a society we want to encourage people to help one another. But that's not what we have here. We have the ultimate Bad Samaritan: a woman who didn't help and didn't call the police and now two women are dead. Thank God her four-year-old had the courage to say something, or the body count might have been even higher.' Loni shook her famous red head. Her perfectly styled hair didn't move. 'It's a developing story, folks, and one I intend to stay right on top of.'

First came the reporters reporting the news of the arrest and the details of the case as they trickled out. Then the legal commentators and analysts and talk show hosts would each peek out of the comfort of their fortified stations and test out an opinion, trying desperately to find the pulse of the American news junkie and exploit it. Loni Hart had been the first to open the discussion – there would inevitably be others if the fans were working and the flames were spreading accordingly.

Faith lay down on the bed, and pulled her trembling body into a ball. This was the first time her name had been mentioned. Either the press had found it or the detectives had provided it. Detective Nill had already warned her that both her and Maggie's names would not be protected, as there was no provision in the law preventing the media from naming witnesses – even those who are children. It felt like someone had secretly videotaped her in a compromising position behind closed curtains when no one was supposed to be looking in, and uploaded it on YouTube for the whole world to see. Should she be judged by one lapse in compassion? By one mistake that she'd wished from the moment she'd made it that she could go back and undo?

Loni Hart had paraded her out on national television to be judged by the public, feeding her viewers a few select facts to whet their appetites and their anger. It was now up to the crowd to decide what should be done with her. If the people looked favorably upon her, she would be pitied: a frightened mother without a cell phone who had stumbled into a bad situation and had tried to protect her child by keeping silent. She would be viewed as another victim, who should not be condemned for the murderous acts of another.

If, however, the crowd expressed disfavor, she would be demonized like the murderers themselves, shunned by her peers, and cast out.

Faith wiped her eyes. She wished she were not alone tonight. She wished it did not feel as if the world was about to launch a war against her. She should be relieved, knowing Derrick Poole was finally behind bars. Instead, she was filled with dread at how the world outside her door was going to react come morning.

Loni Hart had cast the first stone.

Who would be next?

58

'Mommy? You OK?' Maggie stood next to her bedside in the dark room. She was tugging on her arm. The light from the TV lit her worried face, but the sound was muted.

Faith sat up and wiped her face with the tissue she still had clutched in her hand. 'I'm fine, honey. What are you doing up? Are you feeling OK?'

'You cry a lot, Mommy.'

'What?'

'I heard you crying. Why you crying?'

'I was thinking of something sad, is all. There's nothing for you to worry about.'

Maggie climbed on the bed and curled her tiny little body into Faith's, like a puppy. 'I'm cold,' she said.

Faith lay down and pulled her in close, rubbing her arm to keep her warm. She could feel Maggie's breath on her chest, where her head rested; her eyelashes tickled her skin when she blinked. She stroked her long, blonde tendrils, curling her fingers around the ends as she softly sang Sully's favorite Irish folk song, 'When You and I Were Young, Maggie'. She used to sing it as a lullaby when Maggie was a baby.

I wandered today to the hills, Maggie, to watch the scene below
The creak and the creaking old mill, Maggie, as we used to long ago

She buried her face in Maggie's hair and inhaled: The baby years were lost now, but underneath the scent of raspberry shampoo she swore she could still smell the sweet, indescribable perfume of a newborn.

Faith wanted to bottle this moment – lock it up in time and put it in a room where she could go back and experience it whenever she wanted, because it was so rare. Maggie was not an affectionate kid. She never had been. And since they'd gone to the police that awful day, she'd been even more distant with Faith, understandably, and Faith hadn't pushed for more, hoping that if she gave her space, she would come back around to trust her, like a frightened animal might. Even when she was an infant, Maggie never liked to be snuggled, preferring to be held on her tummy. Before she became mobile, rather than be carried, she liked to sit in the stroller or in the playpen. When she grew older and learned to walk, she had no time for cuddles and affection – she was too busy, her restless mind racing at all the things she could be doing, her body always rushing to the next activity.

At least that's what Jarrod said it was: Attention Deficit Disorder (ADD) or Attention Deficit Hyperactivity Disorder (ADHD), or the result of whatever Dr Michelson's catchall 'developmentally delayed' meant. But Faith had always felt responsible for her and Maggie's lack of . . . closeness. All the other mommies made having a relationship, a *connection*, with their child look easy. When she wrote her articles for *Parenting*, Faith, too, had made bonding sound natural, magical, instantaneous and eternal. The underlying message being, if a mother experienced anything different, she must be doing it wrong – including the author, herself.

She traced the outline of Maggie's ears with her fingers. She had Sully's ears – they stuck out a bit from the sides of her head.

> *The green grove is gone from the hill, Maggie, where*
> *   first the daisies sprung.*
> *The creaking old mill is still, Maggie, since you and*
> *   I were young.*

Jarrod and she hadn't been trying for a baby; that was supposed to come much later. She was shocked when she first found out she was pregnant, which, thanks to irregular periods, wasn't until she was four months along. She knew that a lot of things had happened in those sixteen weeks when she was making arms and legs and organs and brain cells. She had mistaken morning sickness for a hangover a few times. Excitement followed shock, but worry remained a constant. She didn't touch another drop for the rest of the pregnancy.

When the nurse handed Margaret Anne Sullivan Saunders over to her in the delivery room, she'd studied every inch of her pink skin, counting fingers and toes and exhaling the breath she'd held for five months when the doctors gave her a seven on her Apgar. But as she grew, and the emotional problems started – the ones that defied a definitive diagnosis – she began to wonder if there was more to normal than perfectly formed digits and a sound heartbeat. A search on Google led her to a host of websites that offered the possibility of a truly frightening diagnosis. She had heard of fetal alcohol syndrome, but that was for alcoholics, was prevalent among Indians, and the kids were born with characteristic facial deformities like wide-set eyes, a thin upper lip and a small head. Maggie didn't have the physical abnormalities, but all of her developmental delays, cognitive deficits and behavioral problems read like ingredients in a fetal alcohol spectrum disorders (FASD) cookbook: hyperactivity, attention deficit, impaired fine motor skills, speech delays, stubbornness, impulsivity, poor socialization skills. She weighed less than six pounds when she was born and had remained in the fortieth percentile for height and weight at every check-up. Of course, the broad gamut of neurological issues, developmental delays, and behavioral problems could be attributed to many other conditions, and certainly not every petite kid who had ADD or ADHD and didn't like to be hugged had fetal alcohol syndrome. Nor did it mean that their condition fell in the range of fetal alcohol spectrum disorders (FASD). Maggie's issues could be the random luck of the birth defect/disorder draw, much like what flavored personality or gave someone intellect, or caused spina bifida or muscular dystrophy. Or they could be due to too many wild nights out before Faith knew she was pregnant. There was no blood test or MRI that would offer a definitive answer. No doctor had ever suggested a fetal alcohol spectrum disorder, or asked, upon examining Maggie, if Faith drank while she was pregnant. There was no 'cure' for any of the fetal alcohol spectrum disorders; the treatment for conditions on the spectrum would be the same as what Maggie had been getting or would be receiving in the future. Her hyperactivity and ADD would be treated the same – eventually, she would likely be medicated with Ritalin or Adderall. She would be given special assistance with class-work as she got older, if she needed it. She would go to the best doctors and therapists and psychologists and have tutors and attend private school so that she could overcome her learning disabilities. There would be no point in attaching a label with a damning stigma to Maggie when the treatment would be the same anyway.

'More, Mommy,' Maggie said, tugging Faith's hair. She put her thumb in her mouth.

They say that I'm feeble with age, Maggie, my steps are much slower than then.
My face is a well-written page, Maggie, and time all alone was the pen.

She had screwed up in the having kids department. Not willfully, but it had happened. Even if Maggie's issues were luck-of-the-draw developmental problems faced by many parents, she had come from Faith's body and she felt responsible. Every day Faith had to make decisions that affected both the emotional and physical well-being of another person and she wasn't doing the best job in either department, no matter how much she wanted to, and no matter how easy the articles made parenting sound. Jarrod talked of having more children, but even before the affair, Faith couldn't face doing it wrong a second time.

It was rare moments like this that she lived for, though. That every parent lived for. When your child holds you close and you know you're her whole world and she is yours. And you know you couldn't possibly love someone more than at that very moment, because they are truly a part of you.

Faith inhaled the scent of Maggie and stroked her head. Tears of both sadness and joy ran down her cheeks. She wished she could fix what was wrong inside it. She wished she could rewire it the way it was supposed to work. Like so many things in her life, she wished she could hit a do-over button. She wished she could do it right the next time.

> *They say we have outlived our time, Maggie, as*
> *   dated as the songs we've sung.*
> *But to me you're as fair as you were, Maggie, when*
> *   you and I were young.*

Because she would, she thought, closing her eyes, her face nuzzled in her beautiful daughter's neck.

She would do everything right next time.

59

The downpour started as Jarrod pulled into the driveway. It had been threatening rain all day, and Mother Nature finally made good in a big way. He sat in the car for a minute, listening to drops the size of quarters slam against the garage doors.

He hadn't wanted to leave Faith alone tonight, but there was no getting out of the Governor's fundraiser – he'd tried. When he'd gotten the tickets last month, she'd agreed to go with him. Even after they found out her arraignment was going to be this morning, she said she still wanted to go – she had bought a new dress and everything. Then Poole had been arrested today and the media had taken off with the story and Faith had retreated to the bedroom.

He was worried about what he might find when he walked inside. Even though he had not seen her drink since the DUI, he knew she probably did. She'd said she'd think about going to AA, but without any real enthusiasm, or even trepidation, so he knew she had no intention. In their nine years together, she'd had a few instances where her alcohol consumption had escalated, in his opinion, from social to problematic and she had managed it on her own somehow, and the conversation just died out because she was OK. There had even been a lengthy period where she stopped drinking altogether. Looking back, there was always a stress factor, though, behind any escalation: She'd lost her job; she couldn't find a job. They moved. She opened the bakery. Maggie had gotten sick. He'd had an affair. There were too many stress factors happening in her life all at once now, though, for him to believe she could handle them by herself. Outside the death of her father, they were bigger than anything she'd ever had to face. She was one of the strongest people he knew, but right now, also the most vulnerable.

He headed inside. It was after midnight and the house was quiet. All the lights were out downstairs. He checked the garbage – no bottles. That was good. He exhaled. Of course, if she were trying to prove to him that she could control her drinking on her own, she wouldn't drop a bottle in the garbage or recycle bin. She'd hide it, and it was a big house.

He crept upstairs to check on Maggie first. He hadn't wanted to leave her home with Faith after the arraignment and Poole's arrest, but Faith would never agree to a babysitter while she was home. It would be like he'd hired a babysitter for her. Or that he didn't trust her with their daughter. It was such a thorny issue, and he was walking a delicate tightrope as it was, trying to balance his shaky marriage, his daughter's welfare, and his wife's mental state all on the same stick.

Leaning over her Disney princess bed, he went to give her a kiss, and his heart seized. She wasn't there. He ran down the hall to the master bedroom.

The lights were off, but the TV was on, although there was no sound. He saw a figure lying on the bed. As he drew closer, he saw it was both of them. They faced each other, but Maggie was curled up in a fetal position, up against Faith's body. Maggie's face was buried in Faith's chest, and Faith's arms were wrapped protectively around her.

He leaned against the wall and breathed a sigh of relief. Maggie never slept with them. She hated to cuddle unless she was scared, and as soon as the afflicting fright was gone, so was she. They looked so peaceful together, so beautiful, that Jarrod suddenly had a horrible, terrible thought. He slowly walked over to Faith's side of the bed. He leaned his head over and tentatively kissed Maggie's cheek – it was warm, thank God. Her arm moved as she stirred. Then he kissed Faith on the cheek, and gently brushed her hair off her face. Her cheek, too, was warm. He smiled. Thank God, again. She took a breath and then exhaled it. That's when he smelled it. Subtly, hidden under mouthwash or toothpaste or behind a soda. He felt his hope and his insides collapse.

He stood up and searched her nightstand. There was nothing. Then his. Nothing. The bathroom cabinets, under the bed, the curio, the dresser drawers. Nothing. He went into the closet and found the boot box that held old pictures and letters and stuff that had belonged to her dad, and there it was: a half-empty, 1.75 liter bottle of Absolut Raspberry. He went back into the bedroom and sat down on a chair in the corner watching the two of them sleep, swinging the crook of the bottle back and forth in his hand, listening to the liquor swish against the glass.

Faith was right: *He* was responsible for this. *He* had set off the first domino, been the first stress factor on the plate. She might have the genetic propensity to have a drinking problem, but he had done *this*, this time. Before Sandra, everything was good. It really was. Maggie was difficult, but he and Faith had a solid marriage. And he still couldn't explain why he had ruined everything. Sandra had stayed late one night to help him with a brief, and then she was just there, her ass on the edge of the desk, her face in his face. She had kissed him and he hadn't pulled away. And when her hands went to her blouse and undid the buttons he hadn't told her to stop. He hadn't moved. Instead of walking out of the room, he'd watched her unhook her bra and slip off her skirt and slide down her panties. Then she had done things to herself

311

and he hadn't moved. And when those same hands reached for the zipper on his pants, his fingers had helped hers pull it down. He had not initiated, but he hadn't resisted. They'd had sex that first time, right there in his office, up against the wall, her hands splayed across the painting of San Francisco that Faith had bought him as he took her from behind. The horrible guilt had set in while he was getting dressed and he had vowed it would never, ever happen again. But it did. Many times. He was the one who locked the door after that. He was the one who unbuttoned her blouse and slid off her panties. He didn't know why it had started, but he knew why it had continued. And even though he still felt guilty for continuing to fuck her, he was secretly looking forward to the next time he had to work late.

It took the implosion of his marriage and Sandra leaving the firm and going back to law school for him to see the damage that he'd done. It was like flying in a helicopter over a large area hit by a devastating storm: He finally saw the full extent of destruction that he had caused.

There was no going back, as he had said to Faith when he had again apologized. There was only moving forward. He had to try to fix the damage, and he had to try and repair the fallout. He owed her that. He had to make her see that she needed help so they could do this together and they could be as good as they once were.

He poured the vodka down the bathroom sink. Then he got undressed and put on his pajama pants and climbed into the bed himself, wrapping his arms around his family and holding on tight.

60

When Bryan first saw the cluster of news trucks outside the courthouse, he thought there was a hearing on the John Goodman case – the Palm Beach Polo tycoon who, on his way home from a festive night out at the Player's Club in 2010, had plowed into a college grad with his $200,000-dollar Bentley, sending the kid's car into a canal and killing him. Drama and cameras followed that man and that case around everywhere. First there was the 2012 DUI Manslaughter Trial Number One, which took too long, but finally resulted in a conviction, which didn't last too long – a juror went to jail, but the defendant didn't. Then the guy tried to adopt his girlfriend to save his millions. Then came the circus of a retrial in 2014 and a very recent second conviction, followed by more motions. Every time Goodman or one of his very expensive attorneys whined – which was a lot – there was a news camera around to catch it. That's what Bryan figured all the hullabaloo was about as he followed the morning crowd into the courthouse.

Then he got off the elevator on ten and realized that unless they had moved the Goodman case to courtroom 10F, or some celebrity was also having an Arthur hearing with Judge Cummins, all those cameras were likely there for the *State of Florida vs. Derrick Alan Poole*.

With the exception of certain serious and violent felonies, most crimes in Florida had scheduled bond amounts that a defendant could post upon arrest to get out of jail. Non-bondable offenses, however – such as murder, kidnapping, and armed burglary – required what was known as an Arthur hearing, an evidentiary hearing akin to a mini-trial, to determine if 'proof was evident and presumption was great' that a crime had been committed and that the defendant was the one who had committed it. If the state met that burden, then the judge could hold the defendant without bond pending trial.

It had been two weeks since Poole had been arrested. In Florida, except for first-degree capitol murder or juveniles being bound over for adult court, most crimes were formally charged by a sworn document called an information. Capitol murder and juvis moving up to the big time, however, were formally charged by grand jury indictment. Elisabetta was set to present Poole's case on Wednesday to the grand jury, which convened only once a month, but Hartwick had strategically set down the Arthur before then because he knew once his client was formally indicted there was no way any judge in the building was going to grant him a bond. This was his best shot at getting Poole released before trial. Because an Arthur was more than a perfunctory reading of the arrest form to see if there was probable cause, it was also a way for the defense to take a peek at the state's cards and see exactly what kind of case it had.

The Honorable Judge Delmore Cummins was a Florida native and a no-nonsense courthouse relic who had been sitting on a bench long before Bryan had gotten his badge. He was old even back then. Since Cummins was the only judge who handled Arthurs, and only on Monday and Wednesday afternoons, his calendars were always lengthy, but because he was so old and had no time left to waste, he was expeditious. He was also rather grumpy, and didn't take kindly to breaking old-style courtroom decorum – he liked to see women in skirts and men in suits and he abhorred any technology that was developed after 1985. As Bryan made his way through a gallery that was normally empty, but today was full of spectators, he wondered if anyone had broken the news yet to Judge Cummins that there were a dozen cameras set up in his courtroom.

He found Elisabetta in the well, chatting with two other prosecutors. The calendar on the clerk's desk looked thick. 'Is this for us?' he asked her quietly, looking around the courtroom.

'Apparently,' she answered as she rummaged through a file. 'We're on page sixteen.'

Bryan didn't know why he was so surprised. Ever since he'd found the shack, the press had been calling. After Poole's arrest, things had exploded like no other case he'd ever handled before. The task force had received requests for interviews and public records requests from every cable news channel there was: CNN, Fox, MSNBC. The PBSO public information officer had fielded calls from the Associated Press and Reuters, and even from London's *Daily Mail* and Germany's *Der Spiegel*. The media's hunger for gory and salacious information was ravenous. It was like someone had cut themselves over shark-infested waters. The first couple of drops of blood had aroused a few members of the herd, but the continuous trickle of blood as details of the case were leaked had caused a violent feeding frenzy, which sent sharks from all over to come searching for any scrap of information they could gather. Fact, opinion or rumor – it was all the same to them. If an Arthur hearing – normally uneventful and unattended – was attracting this much attention from the media, Bryan could only imagine what would happen when it came time for trial.

Even though he had predicted it to some extent, it was Faith Saunders who had gotten caught up in the eye of the media storm and had absorbed much of its wrath, and for that he

315

felt bad. Maybe a journalism professor could better explain the phenomenon to him, but in a world full of instantaneous news, with brutal crime and health epidemics and wars being broadcast live vying for everyone's attention, every criminal case that Bryan had ever seen command and maintain headlines had an angle – a *reason* that it appealed to the masses. With O.J. Simpson, Phil Spector, and Oscar Pistorius, he could see it was the celebrity as murderer that captivated. With Trayvon Martin and Michael Brown, it was racial injustice and the faces of innocent black teenagers. With Dennis Rader and Jeffrey Dahmer and Bill Bantling, it was the unbelievable, shocking cruelty demonstrated by serial killers and the complete randomness with which they chose their victims. And then there were the cases like Casey Anthony, Scott Peterson, Jodi Arias, and Justin Ross Harris, where there was no readily identifiable explanation for why they became household names and had their cases broadcast live on Court TV. There were hundreds more murder cases like theirs that barely got mentioned in the local section. Something about the defendants or their victims or the circumstances of a case caught the fancy of the public and somehow kept it. Bryan could see that this case was demanding that sort of fanatical attention, and although he didn't know why, necessarily, he did know that the media kept throwing whatever they could at the public to keep them fed. Once it got out that Faith Saunders had not reported Angelina's abduction, but her cute little four-year-old had, everyone from Loni Hart to Nancy Grace to Sunny Hostin had set on her. Although Bryan had once dreamed of detective rock-star status in his plans for revenge against Audrey, he didn't want to see this lady and her family destroyed as a result. It was obvious she had a drinking problem, she was scared, and she was caught up in something she never planned on getting caught up in. It was Bryan's job to take the shots, not some poor mom who had been in the wrong place at the wrong time and made the wrong decision.

316

'Were you expecting this?' he asked Elisabetta.

'No,' she replied softly. But for someone who'd handled media cases in her career before without blinking, she looked both nervous and a little excited, and Bryan didn't believe her. He wouldn't put it past Maleficent to be a closet press hound. He had his own reasons for wanting to see the case on the eleven o'clock news, after all.

She looked up from her file and studied him. 'You look spiffy. Nice suit.'

'It is Judge Cummins. I see you're showing some knee.'

'No reason to get off on the wrong foot with him. Did you lose weight or something?'

Bryan shrugged. 'Working on it.'

'Are you ready on this?' she asked.

The courtroom door swung open before he could answer.

'All rise!' yelled the bailiff.

Judge Cummins shuffled to the bench, a scowl on his ancient face as he surveyed his courtroom. It was hard to tell if he was surprised by all the cameras or if the chief judge had given him a heads up that it was office policy to allow them in his courtroom and he was just mad that he was expected to comply.

Bryan was nervous. The case against Poole was good, but far from perfect. It was circumstantial, was what it was. He wished he had Ed Carbone in custody and a sample of his DNA to compare with the sample taken off the Yankee hat and fabric, but he didn't. The task force had ripped apart what little they could find out about Carbone's life, but there was still no sign of him. Most of the information he'd supplied on his volunteer form at Orange Youth fifteen years earlier turned out to be lies, including former addresses and his work history. There was no record of him attending Volunteer State Community College in Gallatin, Tennessee, which he claimed to have graduated from. A run of his social showed he had worked as a trucker for Central Freight in Memphis, Houston and Orlando, and had been briefly married for three months. Maldonado found his ex living in Little Rock: She hadn't seen or heard from Carbone in a decade, but told detectives that he had lived in Mexico as a teenager with his mother's family and was fluent in Spanish. The owner of Abe's Scrap, where Carbone had last worked, said Carbone was a hunter and a survivalist, who had bragged of living in the Appalachians for months, like terrorist and Olympic Park bomber, Eric Rudolph, which potentially made finding him a challenge. Every state agency in Florida and the FBI were looking for him, but there had been no trace of him. It was as if the man had simply vanished.

'The court has decided to call a matter out of turn,' announced the clerk. '*State of Florida vs. Derrick Alan Poole*, page sixteen.'

Elisabetta gathered her file and strode confidently to the podium as the cameras began to roll. 'Assistant State Attorney Elisabetta Romolo, on behalf of the state.'

'Richard Hartwick for the defendant, Derrick Poole,' said Hartwick, as he approached the defense podium.

'Where's the defendant?' barked Judge Cummins.

'On his way out now, Your Honor,' replied the corrections officer.

The judge clapped his hands impatiently. 'Well, let's get on with this.'

Maybe it was a good thing all the press was here, Bryan thought as the door to the jury room swung open and a corrections officer escorted in a meek-looking Derrick Poole, clad in an orange jumpsuit and wrapped in chains.

Because with a case that was less than perfect, maybe with all those cameras watching it would make it that much harder for the judge to let a murderer go free . . .

61

Elisabetta knew how Judge Cummins was going to rule long before Detective Bryan Nill was done testifying. She had been before him enough times to distinguish his scowls from his pouts, and interpret the meaning of a raised eyebrow or a shake of the head. Once she saw it coming, she'd tried to head him off at the pass, even questioning Nill about the murders of Foss, Kruger, and Jane Doe, but Hartwick started to flip out because Poole hadn't been charged with those yet and Judge Cummins wasn't having it.

She bit the inside of her lip as her stomach churned the four cups of coffee she'd had that morning since getting up at five. Unlike some other judges in the courthouse who loved to see their cases and faces make the news, Delmore Cummins obviously did not. The cameras had really set him off. He was a retired judge who could no longer be voted off the bench, and he was too old in general to care what the masses thought, or have his rulings be influenced by public opinion. He was also cranky and passive-aggressive enough to do the precise opposite of what the people wanted or expected, just so he could show who was in control of his courtroom. When he began to lay a record, explaining the meaning of 'proof evident and presumption great', she knew it was over. Her reaction was being carefully watched, and it was important that she maintain her composure, no matter what he said. She wasn't used to not getting what she wanted, and she wasn't expecting it on this case. Especially on this case.

'The burden of proof that the state is required to show here today to hold the defendant without bond is a high one – higher even than reasonable doubt,' the judge began. 'Proof of the defendant's guilt must be evident and the presumption of his guilt must be great because the state is seeking to incarcerate him before he has been convicted of any crime. Incarceration before trial flies in the face of the most basic legal principle there is – that a man is presumed innocent until his guilt is proven beyond, and to the exclusion of, every reasonable doubt.

'Now, on to the evidence.' The judge slid his fingers up underneath his thick glasses and rubbed his eyes before continuing. 'The evidence, including the identification of Mr Poole by both Faith and Maggie Saunders, as testified to by Detective Nill, is compelling. However, the court is troubled by the two-week long delay that occurred in the reporting of the incident to the police, and the reasons for that delay. The court recognizes that one witness is a child, and that neither witness is here today, so a jury might very well access their credibility and their reasons for waiting so long to contact the police differently than this court. But looking at the evidence in the light most favorable to the defendant, this court cannot avoid considering that what was actually witnessed was not as sinister as the state wants to paint it today.

'The hair and fiber evidence found in the defendant's car is also compelling. But, unfortunately, that is the only physical evidence the state has to link their victim directly to Mr Poole. The Yankee hat, which can be linked to the crime scene by a witness, was found in the defendant's possession, but does not have his DNA on it. The individual whose DNA is on that hat has yet to be located. As far as this court is concerned, Mr Poole could well have found that hat on the side of the road and brought it back home to add to his memorabilia collection. And, finally, while the state would very much like this court to consider . . .' He paused for a few seconds, looking around at the cameras with a challenging stare. '. . . that the defendant is a suspect in other murders that might have taken place in that shack, the defendant has not yet been charged with those murders and the court can not consider them as evidence in *this* case. In fact, as the defendant has not been charged, the court has no other choice but to consider the obvious: that another person may be responsible for those homicides. Especially troubling is the disappearance of murder victim, Noelle Langtry, which occurred, as the detective admitted, while Mr Poole was under surveillance. That, in and of itself, lends credence to the defense's argument that another killer is responsible.

'Now the state may very well have enough to meet its burden at trial, but it did not meet its burden here today. The court, in recognizing the seriousness of these charges and the risk of flight that accompanies them, especially seeing as the state has indicated that this might well be a death penalty case, is setting bond at two hundred and fifty thousand dollars. The defendant is to forfeit his passport and is to have no contact with the witnesses.'

'Your Honor,' Elisabetta tried. This was beyond bad. She'd had Cummins grant bonds after an Arthur before, but not on a case like this. Not on a case where she'd invited the world in to watch.

Judge Cummins waved her off. 'The time for argument is over, Ms Romolo. And a cautionary word to both counsel for the state and the defense, since I don't know who exactly is responsible for *this*,' he said, gesturing around the courtroom. But his eyes remained locked on her. 'This court won't be a conduit for someone's fifteen minutes. This is not some reality show, people. No matter how many cameras are dragged into this courtroom, I won't be influenced by them, so don't try my patience again. Understood?'

Before Elisabetta could answer, he had the clerk call up the next case while she was still standing there at the state's podium, her case file in hand, holding back angry tears as the cameras continued to roll and the next prosecutor came up to replace her.

62

Faith stared at the happy face Vivian had drawn on her desk calendar. She felt physically sick. On the other side of the office door, she could hear the hustle and laughter of people in the bakery. The Christmas holidays were almost here and the staff were busy decorating everything in candy canes and garlands. A few weeks ago, Charity had suggested that they redesign the store layout and make it more of an Internet café, with emphasis on blended coffees and drink specialties, and that they add some sandwiches to the menu as variety. There was a constant presence now in the store, a buzz at the tables as people chatted and worked on their computers.

'Faith? Are you there?' asked Detective Nill in her ear.

She got up from her desk and walked into the bathroom off her office. 'How did this happen?' she asked quietly. She peered out through the metal mini blinds of the small bathroom window and into the back parking lot. 'I'm not understanding, Detective, exactly *why* he's being released when he's charged with murder, and after all the horrible things you found in that shack . . .'

'The judge granted him a bond, Faith. It's a pretty hefty sum – two hundred and fifty thousand – but it looks like he's going to post it. His girlfriend apparently has inheritance money. I wanted to make sure you knew – if you hadn't already heard about it.'

'I haven't watched the news, Detective.' She felt her voice start to crack. 'It's never good, the news.'

'We'll be watching him, so you know.'

Faith nodded and rubbed her temple. There was a knock on the office door.

'Faith?' It was Charity.

'I have to go, Detective Nill.'

'Of course. And Faith?' the detective said sympathetically. 'Try not to worry.'

She didn't even know how to respond to that. She'd been desperately trying to hold the pieces of her life together, like a child that has been told it's time to leave and has hurriedly gathered all her favorite toys up in her arms. There was too much to hold onto, she was carrying too much, and one by one each began to slip from her grasp. Her marriage, motherhood, her friendships, her career – they were all crashing to the ground. And worse, they were not just breaking apart, but in some instances, shattering into a million little pieces that she knew she would never be able to pick back up, much less put back together.

The knocking got louder. 'Faith? Can I come in? Why's the door locked?'

'I was on a phone call, Charity. Hold on a sec.' She wiped her eyes and took a deep breath.

Don't fall apart here. Hold it together. Hold your arms tighter, is all. Don't let go of anything . . .

She opened the office door and Charity practically fell into the office. 'Are you OK?' Charity asked.

Faith nodded. 'What's up?'

'I'm sorry to keep bugging you, but this lady insists on seeing you. I told her you were busy, but she said she'd wait.'

'OK. Who is she?'

Charity shrugged. 'I think it's about her daughter's wedding, but she only wants to talk to you. Vivian went to Costco, so I can't sic her on this lady. You look upset. Can I do something to help?'

'I'm fine. I had to take a call. Thanks,' Faith replied as she headed out the office and into the bakery. All anyone had to do was flip on the news or read the paper to know what was going on and figure why she looked so stressed out, but no one – Charity or Vivian included – actually wanted to talk to her about what was happening or what had happened the night she and Maggie had met Derrick Poole. Charity was probably hesitant out of guilt – it was her party Faith had left from, after all. Faith felt like someone had strapped explosives to her body and sent her into the middle of a busy street: Everyone was watching to see what would happen, but no one dared come too close, in case she blew up. They all took cover and offered help from afar, but there was nothing anyone could do except watch the timer tick down.

'That's her, the lady in red,' Charity said as they stepped into the crowded café.

'Can I help you?' Faith asked as she approached the woman, hoping to remember the event she was here on by looking at her face. She didn't look familiar.

'Faith Saunders?'

'Yes. My sister told me you wanted to—'

The slap came hard and fast across her face. Everyone in the café collectively gasped.

'Four weeks ago my daughter didn't come home,' said the woman. 'She was supposed to be at her friend's house, but she wasn't. She was seventeen years old. The cops said she was dancing down at some rat hole – stripping. I never knew. So I looked everywhere for her. I went to her boyfriend's house. I went to that horrible place she worked at; I even knocked on the door of the scumbag who gave her drugs and made her dance like that. I offered rewards. I *begged* for anyone to come forward with information, because if I couldn't hold her again, I wanted to bury her proper. See, I *knew* something had happened to her. I knew it right here,' she said, pounding with a clenched fist on her bony chest. 'I knew she was gone.'

'I'm sorry, ma'am, but—'

'How could you have done nothing? *Nothing?*'

'I don't know what you're talking about,' Faith cried, confused. 'Who's your daughter? What could I have done?'

'My daughter's name is – *was* – Noelle Langtry.'

Words got stuck in Faith's throat; there was nothing to say.

'You're a mother yourself. But you didn't help that girl when she begged you to help her. You left her out there to die with those men in that horrible shack with cages. You never even told the police. Even your child knew something was wrong. She knew it was wrong to say nothing . . . to *do* nothing!'

Vivian rushed in from the back. 'Whoa, now!' she said, dropping her purse and shopping bag on the floor as she raced over. 'What's happening here?' She took one look at the angry red slap mark on Faith's cheek and got her answer. 'Faith, honey, go on in the back and let's all calm down.'

'She could have been saved! *My* girl, *my* baby, would still be alive if you had said something! How can you sleep? How can you live with yourself? What if it was your daughter?'

Faith saw the button on her shirt with the picture of a smiling teenager holding a teddy bear to her face. There was an inscription on the bottom. *Never stop looking. Never stop loving. Noelle Langtry.*

Charity took her cue from Vivian. 'Miss, I'm going to have to ask you to leave now,' she said, as she tried to lead the woman to the door.

'They beat her like an animal! They cut her up and threw her broken body in a ditch. They raped her! I don't even have all of her. I don't have all the pieces.' The woman pulled away from Charity. 'How does someone do nothing?' she yelled at the stunned customers who sat watching.

Faith started to cry. 'I'm so sorry. I'm sorry . . .'

'It's not enough, ma'am! It's never enough!' shouted the mother of Noelle Langtry as she walked out the door of Sweet Sisters. 'Sorry will never be enough!'

63

Faith had smoked a dozen cigarettes and had driven around in circles – the Sawgrass over to I95 and then down to 595 and then back to the Sawgrass again – trying to calm the crazy, frantic feeling that was making her heart physically hurt. She hoped to exhaust herself both mentally and physically, like a hyperactive kid might, by driving around until the frenetic energy finally ran out and the insatiable craving in her gut that felt like an animal trying to claw its way out of her chest stopped and she went home and collapsed into bed. But no matter where she drove or how much she tried to fight the feeling off, she couldn't stop it. The physical pain from the stress was too much. She knew if she got a bottle at a liquor store, she wouldn't stop at a sip or a shot – she'd down half of it before she realized what she'd done, because it was there in front of her. But at a bar, she reasoned with herself, she could have just one. She could take the edge off the pain and the stress with just one. A taste and she would be able to breathe and she would leave. It was the responsible choice.

She couldn't remember what number vodka and cranberry she was on – if it was three or four or five. She felt horrible from the first sip, like she had cheated and liked it. That made her chest hurt more. So she'd had another. And now it didn't matter what number she was on. She just wanted to drink quietly in a corner until she didn't feel anything any more – not terrible or guilty or hurt or angry or scared or reviled. She didn't want to feel.

She had tried for so long to keep it together, functioning as best she could. Smiling when she was falling apart inside. Even when they talked about her on the news channels or talk shows or on line at the bank, she had gone about her normal life as if she didn't know what everyone was saying, as though she didn't care that everyone was judging her. She vowed to herself to make things as right as she could make them, and help the detectives and prosecutor put those murderers away. Except neither man was in jail, and while she had no control over that, she was the one who was at fault – because she hadn't come forward sooner, the case against Poole was 'shaky', as the detective had put it. She stirred the ice cubes in her empty drink with the swizzle stick. She didn't want to wallow in self-pity. She had no right. She was still alive, after all.

Sorry will never be enough.

She closed her eyes. Noelle Langtry's mother was right. No matter what she did or said, it would never be enough. It would never bring her daughter back. Faith hadn't killed Noelle, but her blood was all over her hands.

The bomb attached to her chest was ticking down. The alcohol had softened the sound somewhat, but it was still there, ticking away. Any day now it would spontaneously detonate and destroy everything around her, including all those people who had tried to take cover, watching from the side-lines. She drained the last drop from the tumbler of ice cubes and signaled the bartender to bring the check. She was still sober enough to recognize that she wasn't sober enough to drive and considering she was driving on a restricted license as it was, there was no way she would risk getting behind the wheel again. She'd take a taxi home and . . .

Jarrod. Oh God, how was she going to face him like this? She bit her knuckle. He would know she'd been drinking. That she'd had way too much. That she wasn't trying hard enough to do better. That she hadn't learned her lesson. That she had failed again.

The bartender slid another drink in front of her.

'No, I'm leaving,' she started. 'Just the tab; I need the tab. And a cab. Can you call me a cab, please?'

'Sure,' said the bartender. 'Tell me when. This is from—'

'Hey, little lady,' said the man next to her. 'Thought you looked empty. You OK?'

'Him,' finished the bartender as he walked off. 'I'll get your bill.'

Faith didn't look up. Instead, she grabbed her purse and started to dig through her wallet to find her credit card. 'I'm leaving, thank you, though.'

'You don't look like you're leaving,' said the stranger. 'You look like you need another. Can I lend an ear?'

She wiped her face with a cocktail napkin. 'I'm sorry. I don't mean to be mean, but I want to be left alone. I have to leave. I have to go home now. I'm married. My husband is waiting for me.' Her thoughts were blurring together with memories – good and bad – and coming out in choppy, slurred sentences.

He raised his hands as a form of surrender. 'No problem. That's cool. You didn't look like you was having any fun, is what I thought. No problem. If you need to talk, I'm a good listener,' he said as he got up off the bar stool to leave. 'I have my share of problems with women, trust me. We can probably learn from one another.'

She shook her head. She didn't even look at him. She stared at the fresh ice cubes settling into the red drink in front of her.

The bartender returned with the check and she slid him her Visa. 'Ten minutes,' he said. 'He'll pull up out front.'

330

Her eyes were fixed on the drink, like a dog on a squirrel. The clawing sensation was back. The creature inside of her wanted more. She tapped her fingers on the bar wishing the bartender would hurry back with her card so she could leave. Her mouth watered. The cab was on its way – one more wasn't going to drop her. She was going to have to face Jarrod, no matter what. He was going to be mad, no matter what. One more was going to help more than it hurt.

She fingered the rim and raised the drink to her lips. She closed her eyes as the cold alcohol slid down her numb throat and quenched the creature inside. 'Thank you,' she said softly.

But there was no one around to hear her. The stranger was gone, the bartender had moved on to another customer. She was in a dive bar with a name she couldn't remember in a strip mall she would never be able to find again if she tried. People were all around her, but she was alone at the bar, drinking with her demons.

64

'I got her. No worries,' said the man. The bartender shrugged.

The room was spinning. Round and round and round, like a merry-go-round out of control. Faith held her hands to her head.

'Let me help you there, little lady. Steady as she goes.'

Her legs felt like Jell-O.

'The cab should be outside,' said the bartender.

'I'll put her in it,' he called out. 'I got you now,' he said to Faith reassuringly. 'You need some air, is all. I think you had a little too much. What's your name?' he asked. He had a southern accent. Southern people were so nice.

'Faith,' she managed. The bodies in the bar and at the pool table were rushing her. She held on to the stranger's arm.

'How you feeling, Faith? You with me here?'

'I'm not feeling,' she answered – or *thought* she answered. The words weren't coming out of her mouth the way she heard them in her head. She was having problems walking. It was like she was running out of power, one appendage at a time. She feared if the stranger let go of her arm and waist she would fall on her ass. The room kept spinning and bobbing.

The door opened and she was outside in a parking lot. 'You

tell me where you want to go, and I'll take you there. You want to go home?' he asked.

She nodded. The cab was sitting in front of the bar, only a few steps away, but the stranger was walking her away from it.

'I have to go home,' she said, trying to wave at the cab but her arm was too heavy. It wasn't doing what she wanted. They were across the parking lot now, heading down an alley that led to a back parking lot.

'Just a little bit more, then you can take a load off. Take a nap if you want.'

She heard the beep of a car alarm.

'You're gonna need it,' he said. 'It's gonna be a long night, Faith.'

She nodded, because it was hard to say words any more. She was very tired. And everything was spinning. She had to lie down and close her eyes or she might be sick.

He leaned her up against the car and opened the passenger door. She looked around, trying to focus. This was not her car. This was not a cab. She suddenly felt very afraid and she knew she would soon forget her fear because she was falling asleep right there. She tried to run, but her legs no longer worked. She started to slump to the ground.

'Not yet, Looky-Look. It's nap-time in a minute.' The stranger lifted her and carried her over to the passenger seat. He was wearing tinted glasses that hid his eyes, even though it was dark out. He smiled at her with crooked teeth. 'And when you wake up, you and I are gonna have a whole lotta fun. *Que pasa?*'

65

'I'm looking for my wife. Have you seen this woman here tonight?' Jarrod said as he flashed the bartender a picture of Faith. He'd already seen her Explorer in the parking lot, and since there was only one bar in the strip mall, he knew he had to be in the right place. He looked around the sketchy bar, which had a decent crowd for a place called the Cubby Hole.

The bartender looked at him suspiciously at first, then nodded. 'Yeah. She was in here for a while. She left a few minutes ago. She had me call her a cab.'

'Thank you,' Jarrod said turning to leave.

'Oh, ah, buddy, some guy had his eye on her. He walked her out to the cab. She was in pretty bad shape. Just giving you a heads up.'

Jarrod's heart sped up and he raced outside. The cab was pulling out of the parking lot and onto Sunrise Boulevard. It quickly disappeared into traffic, heading east toward the beach. *Damn.* He looked at his cell, which was tracking her cell – that's how he'd found her. Her cell, however, was not moving. It was still in the parking lot. He looked around the U-shaped strip mall. Most of the stores were closed: A pet store, a consignment store, a Subway sandwich shop, a furniture store.

At the other end of the U was a Big Louie's Italian restaurant and a sushi restaurant, and across from the bar was a Thai restaurant – all of which were open and were probably the reason the parking lot was crowded. He zoomed in on Faith's cell. It was in the parking lot behind the consignment store and it was slowly moving.

He ran through the alley that connected the main parking lot with a cleared dirt lot across the street in the back that apparently was used as an overflow lot for the movie theater a block up on Sunrise. The lot was much less crowded than the one in front of the bar – and much darker. Surrounded by chain-link fencing, there were no street lamps or parking lot lights.

He heard the beep of a car alarm and ran as fast as he could across the street toward the guy who had just picked Faith up in his arms and was carrying her to his pickup. Her head was resting on his shoulder.

'What the hell are you doing?' Jarrod yelled angrily as he ran.

The guy didn't look back at him. 'Giving her a ride. She's wasted, man,' he called out as he went to place Faith in the passenger seat.

'What the fuck? She doesn't need a ride. She's my wife, motherfucker!'

The guy suddenly backed up away from the open door and threw Faith against the Camry that was parked next to his pickup. Her head slammed into the car and she dropped with a violent thud to the ground. He slammed the passenger door and ran to the driver's side.

Jarrod ran to where she lay, crumpled in a heap against the Camry's tire, her face pressed into the pebbled dirt. She wasn't moving. 'Faith? What the hell?' he yelled. He wanted to pummel him, pull his ass out of the car and beat the life out of him for hurting her, but he couldn't leave her. 'Faith?' he asked desperately, crouched beside her, as he tried to sit her up. 'How much have you had to drink? Talk to me! How much? Come on, honey. Come on, now!'

Her head dropped into his lap. Her eyes rolled to the back of her head. She started to shake.

'How much did she drink?' Jarrod screamed out at the stranger as he started the truck and backed it up with a screech as the tires spun out on the pebbles. A cloud of dirt kicked up and the headlights suddenly blinded him. That's when he realized that the pickup was going to run them both over. With one swoop he picked Faith's limp body up in his arms and ran to take cover between two parked cars. The pickup tore after them.

Someone screamed. He heard a voice nearby yell, 'What the fuck, guy?'

A loud bang sounded, followed by the scraping of metal. The van next to him rocked.

'Holy shit! He just hit that car!'

The pickup pulled out of the lot, leaving a thick cloud of dust in its wake.

Jarrod put his ear to Faith's mouth. Her breathing was shallow and labored. He reached for his cell.

'911, what's your emergency?'

'I need an ambulance! My wife . . . she's been drinking, I don't know how much. She's not responding; she's unconscious. She hit her head. Someone threw her into a car and she hit her head!'

'What is your location sir?'

A girl rushed up from behind the other side of the van. 'There's someone here, Phil! Are you OK?'

Jarrod heard a loud screech as the pickup presumably pulled onto Sunrise. 'Um . . . the Cubby,' he said into the phone. 'I'm at a bar, out in the parking lot. It's off Sunrise. It's a little bar. I tracked her cell here. She didn't come home and she wouldn't pick up her phone. I was worried, so I tracked her,' he rambled.

It hit him then just who was in that pickup and he dropped

the phone on the ground and cradled Faith's head in his lap. Only the whites of her eyes were visible. 'I was worried, I was worried,' he cried. 'Jesus! He was gonna kill her!'

People who had likely heard the crash and had come from the bar or Thai restaurant had started to gather on the sidewalk by the chain-link fencing. A few moviegoers heading back to their cars joined them. There was a buzz as they asked each other what had happened and the couple who had almost been hit started to excitedly tell them.

'Is she OK?' someone shouted out.

'Did anyone get the plate number?' another asked.

'I didn't. It happened so fast. Maybe that guy did,' someone replied. 'It was a pickup. That guy probably knows him, 'cause I think he was gunning for that couple. There's a lady behind the Pilot. She looks hurt . . .'

The 911 operator was saying something, but he couldn't hear her. The phone was still on the ground and he couldn't let go of Faith. 'Someone call 911, please! Tell them where we are! Tell them to hurry!' He could hear distant sirens approaching.

'They're coming, guy,' someone said, coming up to the van, breaking ranks with the gawkers. 'I called, and they said that that's Fire-Rescue responding. Is she OK? Did she get hit?'

'Did you hear that? Hold on, Faith. They're coming, honey,' Jarrod said softly, rocking her head in his lap. Blood started trickling out her nose and his eyes welled up. 'She's bleeding . . .'

'Fire-Rescue is on its way,' the man repeated awkwardly, retreating back into the throng. A few people recorded the chaos on their cell phones as more joined them.

Jarrod nodded. 'Just hold on, honey. We'll be OK. We're gonna be OK,' he whispered into her ear as he rocked her in his arms and the excited crowd watched from a safe distance.

66

Jarrod fumbled with the tremendous floral arrangement that sat on the windowsill that overlooked the parking lot of Broward General. 'You could have died,' he said quietly.

She didn't reply. She touched her hand to her burning throat. It was painful to talk.

'They pumped your stomach.'

'I don't remember that. I don't remember much.'

'You have a concussion. You were double the legal limit and you had Rohypnol in your system.'

'I don't even know what that is.'

'It's a roofie – a date-rape drug. You were drugged, Faith. Between all the alcohol and that . . .' He stopped himself. The rose he was re-arranging snapped in his hand. 'It was almost a tragedy. Worse than rape, you could have been . . .' His voice trailed off again. Even he didn't want to finish the sentence.

'I don't know that,' she whispered, turning her face into the pillow. 'You don't know that.'

He turned to look at her. 'It was him, Faith. It was Ed Carbone – the guy they're looking for, the guy you identified out there with Poole.'

She shook her head.

'Or someone sent by him to finish the job. He almost got you in the car. I was there. There's an officer outside your door right now. Detective Nil said he'll be here to interview you today, although I told him you probably don't remember much.'

'No . . .' she said, wiping her eyes.

'I tracked your cell when you didn't come home. Charity told me about what happened at the bakery. I knew you were upset and I had a bad feeling you were going to try and . . . self-medicate. I tried calling you, like fifty times, but you didn't call back. I tried texting – nothing. I reached out to talk to you, to be there for you, but you won't let me in. You won't let anyone in. You won't let *me* in.'

She rolled over into the pillow. 'I can't do this . . .'

'I can't go back, Faith. I can't. I'm sorry. I can't undo what I did. I want us to be us again. I want to get back to where we were, but I can't do it alone. And I can't do it with you drinking and shutting me out. You drink for a number of reasons, and one of them is so you don't have to deal with me. I know that.'

She said nothing. He could hear her crying softly into the pillow.

'And I know this has been hard on you, that you never wanted any of this. I know that you feel like a pariah. That mother shouldn't have said those things to you, Faith. Or hit you. No matter what she's been through, she has no right.'

'She does, Jarrod. And I can't get away from that. There's nowhere to hide.'

'You did not kill that girl, Faith. You didn't kill the Santri girl, either.' He grasped the metal siding of the hospital bed. Petals from the broken rose that he still held in his hand fell onto the bed. 'People have to stop looking for a scapegoat in this. The media has to stop making you look like the bad guy. It's not fair.'

'The roses are beautiful,' she whispered. 'I love roses.'

He sighed and stroked the bud in his hand. 'You have a drinking problem and you need help. I've found a place. It's residential. It's in a different state. You'll go in under a different name. You'll be safe.'

She shook her head.

'This is not an option, Faith: It's the only way. I can't watch you destroy yourself any longer, waiting for you to finally hit bottom so I can try to pick up the pieces of what's left of you. Because I don't know when that will happen. I keep thinking you've hit it – when you were arrested, I thought, "This is it. This is the wake-up call." But it wasn't. Now you were drugged, almost abducted, raped and murdered and I still don't think you hit it. He had you in the car. You were *in the car*, seconds from disappearing forever. Don't you get it? I can't watch any more. I can't wait for you to leave the stove on, or forget to pick up Maggie again or drive into a lake. I can't watch and I can't have Maggie watch.'

She shook her head again and moaned into the pillow, curling up into a fetal position.

He found her hand and grabbed it, squeezing it hard. He felt like he'd been on a long, long journey – part fun vacation, part business – and the train was approaching the final station, when the trip would officially be declared over. Even though the travels had been sometimes exhausting and not always what he'd thought they were going to be, there were a lot of good times and unexpected good times worked in among the rough ones, and that was what he was remembering as the conductor requested all passengers gather their belongings. An overwhelming sadness came over him. He wanted to ask her to take another trip with him, but knew it wouldn't be the same one they were about to finish. It might be better, it might be worse, but it wouldn't be the same.

'Jarrod, no. Don't send me away. Please,' she pleaded.

'I love you, Faith, I do. I have since that first night we were together. When you woke up in my bed, with your legs wrapped around mine and your head on my chest, I was glad you hadn't left. And when you did finally go back to your dorm, I missed you. God, I missed everything about you. I love the way you smell and taste and feel. I love the way you think, how you giggle, how you write. I love watching movies with you. I love watching you with Maggie and I know she is hard. I know she's been a really difficult kid and you blame yourself for that for some reason, but I love how hard you try with her. And I love how hard you try with me, with us, even after . . .' He took a deep breath before continuing and his eyes filled with tears. 'And I'll be here waiting when you get out, but I won't be if you don't go in.' He leaned over and kissed her on the cheek. 'The choice is yours; I've already made mine.'

Then he stood up, laid the rose on the bedside table next to her, and walked out the door.

PART THREE

It takes many good deeds to build a good reputation,
and only one bad one to lose it.

Benjamin Franklin

67

Elisabetta shifted uncomfortably in her seat at the state's table as Richard Hartwick stood across the well at the defense table. To say she was anxious would be a serious understatement. On the witness stand was cute-as-a-button Maggie Saunders, dressed in a cobalt blue dress and shiny patent Mary Janes, clutching a stuffed Eeyore to her chest as if it were a crucifix and the approaching Hartwick was the devil himself.

Elisabetta hated kid witnesses. She wasn't fond of kids in general – she didn't have any herself and, much to the disbelief of society and most men she dated, she was happy with that decision – but from a lawyer's standpoint, they made crappy witnesses. Terrible memories, fidgety, easily distracted – a smart defense attorney could steer their testimony in any direction he wanted to with the right questions, asked in the right tone. Richard Hartwick was many disingenuous adjectives, but he wasn't stupid.

There was a reason children under the age of fourteen were presumed incompetent to testify under common law. Although the presumption was legally gone now, the problems with child witnesses were not. Elisabetta had always expected Hartwick to make a motion to disqualify Maggie Saunders

345

from testifying. The kid was five years old; she believed in the Tooth Fairy and Santa. But just because she'd been expecting the motion didn't mean she was prepared for today's hearing. And that was the crux of the problem with child witnesses: you could prep them till the cows came home and you still had no idea what was gonna come out of their tiny little mouths when they opened them up on a witness stand. Now that Hartwick had called Maggie Saunders' competency into question, the court had to determine, 1) if she was intelligent enough to perceive, remember, and relate the events she would be called to testify about in Poole's upcoming trial, and, 2) if she could appreciate the obligation to tell the truth. If she failed either prong, she would not be permitted to testify, and if that happened, Elisabetta was screwed. The only other witness that could definitively place Angelina Santri in the company of Derrick Poole before she was murdered, and the *only* witness who could identify the still-at-large Eduardo Carbone, was the kid's mom – fresh out of rehab and currently on probation for DUI. Faith Saunders presented with her own set of ugly problems; Elisabetta couldn't afford to lose Maggie. Besides, the kid was the darling of the media. If she could charm her way into the hearts of millions of TV viewers with her powerful, compelling story, she could work wonders on a jury. If only she got the chance to tell it . . .

'Did you say you were four years old?' Hartwick began in as gentle a manner as his overbearing largeness could muster.

'Five,' Maggie answered, her eyes downcast. 'I'm five.' Elisabetta watched as Maggie looked over at where her very handsome father sat in the front row of the half-empty courtroom.

That was another concern: in the almost four months since Poole had been indicted, the case had fallen off the general public's radar somewhat, as more immediate tragedies and news stories took its place in the headlines. The circus-like atmosphere that had surrounded Poole's arrest and Arthur hearing, though not entirely gone, was certainly not as intense as it had been. The gallery was half-filled with spectators, and only two camera crews, both from local stations, sat in the front row. While it was a relief to not be under the intense scrutiny that existed at the Arthur – particularly for today's hearing – it was an additional worry for Elisabetta that the cameras might not come back. With help from an itchy Hartwick – who wanted this case over with before detectives found Carbone – she had pushed things as fast as she could push a capital murder, and she'd be beside herself if no one showed up to watch. According to Arnie, executives with CNN were holding off on a decision to see what happened with Poole. That translated to; *Let's see the Court TV ratings and then take the temperature of the public to test their opinion of the latest pretty prosecutor to come out of Florida*. If Elisabetta didn't measure up to C.J. Townsend's reputation – or worse, no one could remember her name – she was off the list and the next legal analyst headlining her own cable TV show was Rachel Cilla, LA sex-trafficking prosecutor extraordinaire.

'When's your birthday?' Hartwick continued, intentionally planting his body in Maggie's direct line of sight of her dad. 'When did you turn five?'

'January.'

'January. That was a long time ago, right?'

Maggie shrugged.

'What month are we in right now?'

She shrugged again.

'Let the record reflect the witness has shrugged. Do you know what month this is that we're in now?'

'No,' Maggie answered nervously. 'Can I get down now?'

'Not yet, honey,' Hartwick answered firmly. 'May the record reflect that today's date is March thirtieth. Do you know how long it will be before you turn six? How many months that

347

will be? How many seasons will pass, you know, like summer, winter, fall?'

'Objection,' Elisabetta tried. 'This is not relevant.'

'Goes to the witness's ability to perceive events,' replied Hartwick.

'I'll allow it. Don't go too crazy,' cautioned Judge Guckert, the trial judge.

'I can have Elsa and Anna at my birthday party if I say everything right today,' Maggie spontaneously blurted out. 'I didn't have princesses at my other birthday party because Mommy was away and it wouldn't be nice to have the princesses without her because she was sick. But we can have a second party now because she's home.'

Elisabetta winced. Hartwick smiled. Judge Guckert looked confused. 'Who are Elsa and Anna?' he asked.

'From *Frozen*,' replied Maggie.

'They're frozen?'

'No, Your Honor,' said the clerk with a smile. 'They're Disney characters – princesses. I have an eight-year-old.' The courtroom tittered.

'Ah,' said the judge. 'I get it now.'

But Hartwick smelled opportunity. 'So, Maggie, if you say everything right today, you are going to have a big party with princesses?'

'Yes,' Maggie answered, grinning herself.

Elisabetta's face turned red. 'Objection! He's misconstruing what the witness said.'

'I don't think he is,' said the judge.

Maggie was clearly confused now. 'No,' she said. Her smile disappeared.

Hartwick nodded. 'What day is your birthday, Maggie? January what?'

Maggie tried to look past the defense attorney at Jarrod again.

'Don't look at your daddy, honey,' said Hartwick sternly.

'If you don't know the answer, say, "I'm not sure." You won't get in trouble.'

Maggie's lip began to quiver. 'I don't know.' She put her face down in Eeyore's head.

'That's OK. Let's try this: What day of the week was your birthday? Was it on a Monday? A Tuesday?'

'I don't know!' she shouted defiantly.

Elisabetta stood. 'Objection! I can't remember what day of the week my birthday was on last year, Judge, and I'm not five.'

'That's why we're here, Judge, because the witness is *five*,' said Hartwick. 'As much as I'd like to, I can't cut her slack because she's so young.'

'Can we move off the birthday, then?' asked Elisabetta, exasperatedly. 'It's irrelevant. The witness has had a long day, she's already testified for the court, she's tired and counsel is exploiting that.'

'Give me a break, Ms Romolo,' shot back Hartwick. 'This little girl is the state's star witness in a capital murder case and you're seeking the death penalty. The state has skewered my client in the press, Judge, condemned him in the court of public opinion, called him a serial killer and a sadist in front of any camera she can get her pretty face in front of, paraded this kid in frou-frou dresses and pigtails in front of those same cameras to keep the public interested, and now she wants me to hurry along and wrap it up because the star witness needs a nap? This kid's concept of time and space is critical. Her ability to perceive facts and relate them back to this court is critical. What she testifies to may very well mean the difference between a man living and a man dying. If she can't recall when her birthday is, or how far off January is or what month we are in now, how can we allow her to testify about events that occurred months ago? I mean, I'm not asking her about the state of affairs in Ukraine, Judge, but I do want to make sure her answers are her own and not facts drilled into her head by an ambitious prosecutor.'

'Now counsel wants to disparage me?' shouted Elisabetta. 'I've supplied the case law; there have been witnesses as young as three who've been permitted to testify in criminal cases.'

'And as the state knows, those instances are so rare I could count them on my hand,' snapped Hartwick. 'Those witnesses were also *victims* of child abuse or sexual abuse where the identity of the perpetrator was known to the child and not at issue, unlike the situation we have here. The state's case hinges on Maggie Saunders' identification of my client and her perception of what she *thinks* she saw that night.'

'We also have Faith Saunders' testimony,' added Elisabetta.

'You're going to use this little girl to try and bolster her testimony and vice versa? Nope,' replied Hartwick, with a shake of his head. 'Each witness has to be competent to testify; they can't bootstrap.'

'All right, enough. You made your point with the birthday. Move on, Mr Hartwick,' said the judge. 'I think you're both overwhelming our little witness.'

Maggie was hunched over Eeyore, a dark, scared, confused look on her face.

'What town do you live in, Maggie?' Hartwick asked.

Maggie shrugged.

'You don't know where you live?'

'With my daddy.'

'What state do you live in?'

'I saw the bad man,' Maggie exclaimed eagerly, looking over at Elisabetta for approval.

Elisabetta turned red. She hated kid witnesses.

'The bad man?' asked Hartwick.

'At Mommy's window. But he's not here now so I won't be scared.'

Hartwick turned to look at a sheepish Elisabetta. 'The prosecutor told you the bad man won't be in court today?

That's interesting. We'll talk about what you saw when you saw "the bad man" later. I have some other questions right now: Are you in school?'

'Yes. Can I get down now?' Maggie asked.

'Not yet. What grade are you in?'

'I don't go to school. I used to go, but not any more.'

'Who was your teacher?'

'Mrs Wackett, but not any more.'

'Why don't you go to school?'

'Because I was bad. Mommy didn't come to pick me up and I cried and threw the pony.'

Elisabetta shook her head.

'Did you ever get in trouble at school?' asked Hartwick. 'You know, for doing something wrong?'

Maggie's bottom lip puffed out. 'Can I get down?'

'Not yet, honey.'

'I want to get down, Daddy!' she screamed. Her head turned in a dozen directions, like she was looking for an escape route.

'Maggie, is it ever OK to tell a lie?'

'No,' she said, shaking her head vehemently.

'How about when, say, someone is wearing something you think is ugly. Like a real ugly sweater. Would you tell that person it's ugly?'

'No. They might cry.'

'Would you tell them it's pretty to make them feel good?'

'Yes.'

'Even though you knew it wasn't true. You might tell someone what they wanted to hear because you were being nice?'

'Yes.' She rubbed her ear again. Her legs were swinging in the chair. Her eyes were darting all around, like a trapped animal.

Jarrod leaned over the railing. 'She's getting tired,' he said to Elisabetta impatiently. 'She can't do this.'

But Hartwick wasn't going to let up. He was on a roll. 'So sometimes it is OK to lie?'

'Yes,' replied Maggie.

'What happens if you lie? Does something bad happen to you?'

'Mrs Wackett tells Mommy.'

'Does something bad happen? Do you get in trouble?'

Maggie shrugged. 'I can't have dessert.'

'Do you feel bad if you lie?'

'If you lie you can't go to the treasure chest and take a toy. You're not allowed. If Mrs Wackett takes the toy back, then I feel bad and say sorry, and I get mad, because it's not fair.'

'So if you still got to keep the toy, then you wouldn't feel bad about lying?'

'No.' She shrugged. 'I want to get down.'

'Maggie, if you lied to make someone happy, would you feel bad?'

'I don't know.'

'Like telling Ms Romolo over there that you saw the bad man? You want to make her happy, right?'

'Objection!' Elisabetta stood up.

'Yes. She's got pretty hair,' Maggie answered anyway.

'Overruled.'

'Let's talk about the night you saw this "bad man". You didn't tell anyone about what you saw the night you came back from your Aunt Charity's for a long time, did you?'

Maggie tried to look around Hartwick for her daddy.

'Look at me, honey. Look at me,' said Hartwick harshly.

'Mommy was gonna be mad.'

'You have to say yes or no,' said Hartwick. 'Did you tell anyone when you first got home that something bad had happened to that lady you thought you saw outside Mommy's window?'

'Objection. The witness needs a break. She's five, for Christ sake's, Richard!'

'Overruled. Let her answer, then we'll take a break.'

Maggie put her hands over both ears. 'No!' she yelled.

'You didn't tell Daddy or your teacher?'

'No! I get down now!'

Jesus Christ – the kid was having a tantrum right here in court. Elisabetta tried one more time. 'Can we take that break now, Judge?'

'No, Ms Romolo. Have a seat,' warned the judge.

'But you said that you knew the lady was crying and in trouble, is that right?' demanded Hartwick.

'I get down now! Down! Down!' Maggie screamed, pulling at her ears.

'But you didn't tell your daddy that when you got back home, did you? How long did you wait to tell your daddy?'

Jarrod leaned back over to Elisabetta. 'You need to stop this!' he said angrily. 'She's breaking down.'

Maggie shook her head and stood up. The door in the back opened with a creak as someone slipped into the gallery.

'You need to sit down, young lady,' said Judge Guckert sternly. 'I'll tell you when you can stand up. Finish up, Mr Hartwick.'

'When you told Daddy the ride home from your aunt's house was good, you lied, didn't you?'

Maggie slammed her face hard into the witness stand ledge. The courtroom gasped. Then she did it again and again and again.

'Maggie!' Jarrod yelled.

She looked up to find her father. Blood and tears streamed down her face.

'Oh my God!' Elisabetta screamed.

Jarrod hopped the gallery railing and raced to the witness stand, but it was too late.

Maggie had already bolted off the stand and was running as fast as her little legs would take her down the center aisle and past the horrified spectators, heading for the door that was slowly closing in the back of the courtroom.

68

'This way, please,' said the secretary to Faith and Jarrod as the two of them walked hand-in-hand into the conference room at the State Attorney's Office. Jarrod rubbed her sweaty palm with his thumb as he led her in.

There were already seven bodies seated around the conference table. Faith recognized the prosecutor, Elisabetta Romolo, and Detectives Nill and Maldonado. She didn't recognize the other four men, one of whom – presumably a lawyer – was dressed in a suit. The three were obviously detectives, in khakis and dress shirts with gold badges and gun belts attached to their hips.

'Jarrod, Faith,' said Elisabetta as she began the introductions and the room rose to greet them. 'This is Gareth Williams, he's an assistant state attorney with our Homicide Unit; Gareth will be second-seating Poole's trial with me. I don't know if you've met all of the Cane Killers task force members. This is Detective Austin Velasquez with the Hendry County Sheriff's Office, and Detective Dave Minkhaus with Glades County. And you, of course, already know Detectives Nill and Maldonado, and Lieutenant Amandola.'

As she and Jarrod exchanged handshakes with everyone, a substantially lighter Detective Nill came around the table. His warm paw swallowed Faith's tiny hand. 'How're you doing, Faith? You doing OK?' he asked quietly, his voice rife with genuine concern.

That was the million-dollar question – the question everyone wanted an answer to: Jarrod, Charity, her mom, Vivian, Jarrod's family. Those were the people who'd actually asked it. Then there were the people who looked at her and pity-smiled, like they understood what she was going through and wished her the best of luck with it. She felt like everyone knew her problem, from the mailman to the teller at the bank, to complete strangers who looked over at her in traffic. Returning home was like going to a high school reunion wearing a nametag that read *Faith Saunders, Alcoholic* – everyone could read it and right away thought they knew who she was. The label defined her.

It had been a week since she'd gotten out of rehab, and Faith wasn't quite sure herself what the answer to the million-dollar question was. It should be: 'Great! I'm all better now, thanks to a restful three months at The Meadows in picturesque, serene Arizona. I have a tan and my spirit has been cleansed; I've learned coping mechanisms and I've picked up Tai Chi.' But if she was all better, she didn't feel like it. It wasn't like recovering from the flu or appendicitis, where the infection is gone or the diseased organ has been removed and you're back to feeling your old self again. The truth was, sometimes she felt worse, like a part of her was missing. Physically she felt . . . frail. And a lot older than her thirty-two years. Emotionally, an old, familiar friend had died and she wasn't allowed to even mourn her passing. Rather, she was supposed to be rejoicing with the others that *that* Faith was finally gone. She missed not being able to drink any more – she missed the taste and the smell and the soothing effect that simply raising a glass to her lips had had over her, even before the alcohol hit her bloodstream. Because, like popping a pain reliever when you have an excru-ciating headache, she knew that everything would feel better in twenty minutes. It was the euphoric state of calm she missed that Tai Chi could not replace – although she didn't dare share that thought with anyone. Faith couldn't say she felt better, even though she wanted to say it and she knew that's what people wanted to hear. So she nodded and said, 'I'm OK.' That about covered the feeling.

She smiled at Detective Nill. 'I'm OK. Wow. I almost didn't recognize you. Has it been that long?' she asked. Embarrassed by her own question, she felt her face go red. Then she looked over at Detective Maldonado's pregnant belly. 'Yes, I guess it has.'

The room laughed lightly.

'Bryan's a magic act – he's disappearing right before everybody's eyes,' said the lieutenant.

'And with Totts, the state gets two brains for the price of one,' added Detective Minkhaus.

'As you may or may not know, Faith,' Elisabetta began, her serious tone cutting off the light banter. 'Derrick Poole has filed a speedy demand, so I have a limited window with which to try him. Mr Williams and I will be picking a jury starting Monday. I suspect it will take us three to four days, although that depends on the pool of jurors we get. The case has received substantial publicity, as you well know.'

Faith's cheeks went hot again and she looked down at her lap.

Elisabetta thoughtfully tapped her pen on her notepad before continuing. 'It will be difficult to find fourteen people – twelve jurors and two alternates – who have not heard of this case, much less who haven't formed an opinion. The defense's motion for a change of venue was denied, so we're staying in Palm Beach. You're here today, Faith, so we can go over what you'll be testifying to. As you know, your testimony is critical. You place Angelina Santri in the company of Poole after we assert she'd already been abducted. And you are the only one who can identify the second suspect, Eduardo Carbone, and place him at the scene.'

'I'm very concerned about that, Elisabetta,' said Jarrod. 'Faith is back in town now and Carbone is still out there. He knows who she is; he knows where we live. He followed her – they both have, him and Poole. Carbone already tried to get at her once—'

'We don't know that, Jarrod,' replied Elisabetta. 'The identity of that man who Faith left the Cubby Hole bar with that night has not been established.'

'I know it was him,' Jarrod replied testily. '*I* know it.'

'I didn't leave with him,' Faith started to quietly say. Everyone looked at her. 'It wasn't like that. I didn't go with him. He put something in my drink.'

'Was it Ed Carbone?' asked Elisabetta, wryly. 'Was it the man you saw in the woods with Poole?'

'I didn't look at his face. And then . . . well, I don't remember anything that happened in the parking lot.' Faith wished she hadn't said anything at all. Elisabetta Romolo looked at her, read the invisible nametag on her shirt, and drew her own conclusion about what had happened that December night.

'Let's keep the people who know you're back in town to a minimum,' Detective Nill offered. 'And I'll talk to Parkland police about keeping an eye on your place. You're in a gated community, though, right?'

Jarrod raised an eyebrow at him.

'It's another level someone has to get past, is all I'm saying, Jarrod. It's a deterrent. I'll talk to the association to make sure they keep vigilant. But we believe Carbone has left South Florida. There has been no trace of him since he left the scrap yard. Interpol is looking for him in Mexico; he has family there.'

'That's why Hartwick wants a speedy trial,' added Elisabetta. 'Before we find Carbone. You were a PD, Jarrod, so you're very familiar, I'm sure, with "The Other Guy" defense. Poole is going to claim that the other guy did it – the "one-armed man", or in this instance, the unshaven, pot-bellied, Yankee fan waiting in the woods. Without Carbone in custody we can't test his DNA so we can't say for sure that that's who the Yankee fan was, and so we can't prove the connection at Orange Youth between Ed Carbone and Derrick Poole. The only way we can get that in is through *you*, Faith. You can visually ID him, and you can identify his photograph on the stand. That, in turn, will allow us to show that Ed Carbone knew and stalked the first murder victim, Emily Foss.'

'But Poole's not charged with Foss's murder – only Santri's,' said Nill. 'Won't Hartwick argue bringing in her murder is inflammatory and prejudicial?' He looked at the other detectives apologetically. 'I try not to think like a lawyer too often, but it does happen. I'd rather be prepared for bad news than surprised by it.'

'Yes,' replied Gareth Williams. 'But if we prove that it was Carbone in the woods by Mrs Saunders' visual identification, and then that Poole and Carbone knew each other from the time that Poole spent in juvi, then we can establish that they were working in concert and refute "The Other Guy" defense. Both Poole and the unidentified DNA have been indicted for Santri's murder as co-defendants, although only Poole is being tried right now. Poole can't get away from what we found in that shack. Besides Santri's, blood from Foss, Kruger, and Langtry was also found there. That's prejudicial, but if we establish the connection between Emily Foss and Carbone, that will support Mrs Saunders' visual ID of Carbone and thus the argument Poole and Carbone were working in concert. It's legal bootstrapping.'

'You make the dots connect, Faith,' said Elisabetta. 'As such, your credibility is crucial. I hate to be the one to say this, but here it is: you're not the best witness. You failed to come forward after the incident. Then you failed to divulge that there was a second suspect out there with Mr Poole. You've

358

been arrested yourself and you've recently gone through rehab for a substance abuse problem.'

'Can you cut her a break, Elisabetta?' asked Jarrod. 'She's been home a week and she got help. That says a lot. The press has been brutal to her. You don't need to be.'

'If you think I'm tough, Hartwick is going to be ruthless, Jarrod,' said Elisabetta. 'He's got a lot to work with. I'm sorry if that hurts feelings, but it's true. He's going to pounce on every lie, fabrication, or misstatement. He's going to claim Faith was drunk as a skunk out there and no one should believe anything she has to say.'

'She never wanted to be a witness.'

'Well she is,' Elisabetta said icily.

'What about Maggie?' Faith started, looking at Jarrod. He'd told her about Maggie's meltdown in court the day before, but he also said the judge hadn't ruled yet. She suspected he'd held back on the details of how bad it really was: Maggie had a huge cut on her forehead that had required fifteen stitches.

'Judge Guckert issued his ruling this morning,' Elisabetta replied. 'Maggie has been found incompetent to testify. Don't take that personally, Faith. As your husband can explain to you, it's a legal term. She broke down on the stand and it's clear she can't testify. I hate to play the bitch here, and I wish I could tell you, Faith, that if you can't stand the heat, get out of the kitchen, but I can't. This man is a serial killer. He will kill again if he gets out, whether or not he hooks back up with his partner, because it's in his nature. It's who he is. And I won't have that on my conscience. *You* are my case, Faith. It's that simple and it's that complicated. It's all on you. So let's all get to work, let's all get along, and let's put this guy on death row where he belongs.'

69

'How are you doing?' Charity asked in an overly peppy voice, like one might talk to a patient in a nursing home, as she stepped into the back office of Sweet Sisters. 'Laurie told me she thought she saw you come back here.'

'I'm OK,' Faith said, looking up from her desk. 'Who's Laurie?'

'Laurie? She's new. Started a month or so ago.'

'Oh. Well, I was gonna check on the purchase orders and inventory. You know, see what I missed and get myself back up to speed. I'm going a bit crazy at the house.'

'I did the POs yesterday.'

'You're doing the ordering now?'

Charity nodded and grinned. 'Yeah. And I learned payroll, too.'

'Wow. I'm so impressed, Char. The place looks great. It really does.'

'Thanks, Faithey; I really appreciate that you noticed. Things have really worked out here, so I hope you didn't worry too much while you were gone. I love Viv; we've gotten real close.'

Faith bit the inside of her lip. 'Good. I'm happy to hear that. I thought I might go into the kitchen and bake today, you know try something new. Maybe something that screams spring, right? Strawberry cupcakes with a lemon cream cheese and poppy seed frosting.'

'Ooh. That sounds nice. Buster is back there now with Al. Have you met him yet? Buster? He's great. Really creative.'

Faith shook her head. 'Maybe something with blueberries, then . . .' She looked at her desk. Mixed in with pictures of Maggie were pictures of Kamilla, Kaelyn and Kourtney.

Charity sipped her coffee. 'I saw the opening statements this morning on TV. Are you allowed to watch?'

'No. I'm not allowed in the courtroom until I testify. Not that I would want to be. Or that I'd want to watch.'

'Oh yeah, yeah. That makes sense. I had it on while I was getting ready for work. Are you nervous about testifying?'

'I'm OK.' There was an awkward pause. The whole conversation felt forced. Usually her and Charity could pick up right where they left off, but not today. 'How are things with Nick?' Faith asked.

'Who?' Charity smiled. 'I thought he'd be more involved, you know, Faith? I thought he'd want to see his kids and be down here in my face, trying to bring me back, but I haven't seen him. I don't even hear from him. So I got a lawyer.'

'Yeah?'

'Vivian helped me with that. I'm filing papers. It's over. Really, this time.'

Faith nodded. 'Good for you. Jarrod said you signed up for a class at Broward College?'

'Yeah. I gotta get up to speed on the computer. Even the baby knows how to work an iPad and play games. Kamilla, you know, is almost a teen. I gotta keep an eye on her; she lives on that computer. I think I'm gonna go for my associate's. It'll take forever, but that's OK.'

Faith nodded. The awkward, painful silence was back.

Charity headed for the door. 'I should get back out there. Anything you need, Faithey, let me know.'

'Thanks.'

She could hear the laughter and buzz through the walls. Three o'clock used to be slow, now it was packed. Lunch hour blended into Caffeine Happy Hours – another idea of Charity's – and then there were book signings and game nights in the new part of the store, annexed from the Feeling Lucky boutique next door that had gone out of business while Faith was away.

A lot of things had happened while she was away. One hundred and twenty days could have been three years. Maggie had learned how to ride a bike. Jarrod had won a big case. The staff – her staff – had turned over. Now it was a bunch of bakers she didn't know and baristas she didn't recognize. With Vivian's help, Charity had done the impossible: untangled herself emotionally from Big Mitts and filed for divorce. She'd started college and learned payroll and ordering. She and Vivian had become super close. The bakery had expanded and changed into a full-on café. Sweet Sisters didn't even look like the same store.

Faith chewed on her lip. It was almost as if things were better since she left.

Maggie, though, was still struggling. Her forehead was raw and ugly a week after the incompetency hearing. It would probably scar. She'd been very cautious around Faith – 'removed' was how the therapists at The Meadows had explained what Maggie's emotional reaction to Faith's long-term absence might be. For a little girl who'd always been detached, this was tantamount to taking ten giant steps back in the affection department. It was like they were distant relatives living together, not mommy and daughter. And Faith didn't know how to change that, to even get it back to where it was. *Give it time*, the therapists had advised. *Approach it slowly and get her to trust you again and trust that you won't go away again. She's scared. Kids are resilient; she'll come around.* But the therapists in Arizona didn't know Maggie. They didn't know her . . . *circumstances* . . . her

362

difficulties bonding to begin with. Faith didn't know if she'd ever 'come around', or if there would be more permanent scarring to come.

She went through her desk to see what else had been replaced while she was gone and found a picture of her and Jarrod on vacation in the Bahamas, having piña coladas pool-side. She could remember the moment the British tourist had snapped it. The very moment. Jarrod had leaned in to kiss her and she was laughing. She'd buried it in the drawer herself after he'd cheated. She ran her finger over the glass. He'd been at the facility to fly her home, a bouquet of flowers in one hand and a suitcase filled with new clothes in the other. The recovery program called for limited contact with friends and family, but Jarrod had called every night to say goodnight. And he had come out to Arizona for family week. He'd been trying. God knows he'd been trying. She wasn't sure, though, if his actions were motivated by guilt or obligation or a true desire to fix what was broken. There were many nights where she'd stared out into a vast, black Arizona desert and worried that he would turn to Sandra, or perhaps someone new, for companionship while she was gone, but she'd taken the flowers and worn the pretty new clothes and she'd leaned on him emotionally, nonetheless, in the limited way she knew how.

She looked at the desk calendar, now in April, with memos written in someone else's handwriting and Vivian's weird, funny doodles drawn for Charity, not her. She fought back the wave of jealousy and rubbed her stinging eyes before the tears had a chance to fall.

It was almost as if things were better since she left.

She felt like a ghost, floating around a few weeks after her funeral to see how life had carried on, and had surprisingly found everyone was doing quite well. Thriving, actually. And she thought, then, of her old friend, the one she wasn't allowed to grieve or mourn or miss. Four months in rehab and therapy and the only real revelation she'd had by the end was that she wasn't like the other people in there. She wasn't an alcoholic. She might say the word, because they made her say it, but she wasn't like those people. Her situation was altogether different from everyone else's in group therapy. She had not been molested as a child, or abused by her parents. She'd never drunk herself homeless or into prostitution or out of a job, or woken up wondering where she'd been for weeks. She could control herself and being part of a program of dysfunctionals had made her see that. Given her current situation, anyone would turn to drink or popping pills to cope. All she had to do was get past this trial, focus on Maggie, and work on her marriage. Once the stressful situations that made her want to drink had passed, she'd be OK. Until then, it was all willpower and self-control.

Her cell phone rang.

'Hey, Faith. It's Detective Tatiana Maldonado. I'm calling to let you know that Detective Nill will be taking the stand late this afternoon. The prosecutor expects to call you on Wednesday. I wanted to give you a heads up, you know, to prepare you.'

Faith nodded. She put the picture of her and Jarrod back in her desk.

'Faith?' the detective asked when Faith hadn't said anything. 'Are you doing all right?'

'I'm OK,' Faith replied quietly, closing the drawer. 'I'm just OK.'

70

'Do you swear to tell the truth, the whole truth and nothing but the truth, so help you God?' asked the bailiff.

Faith raised her right hand. 'I do.'

She took her seat as the jury and the spectators in the packed courtroom looked on. She'd seen the news trucks parked in front of the courthouse when she and Detective Minkhaus had pulled up, but fortunately the detective knew an alternate way in so that they didn't have to walk through the throng of cameras and reporters hanging around outside. He'd reassuringly told her they were probably there for the Goodman case, which had some hearing that morning, too, but Faith thought he was trying not to stress her out. When the elevator doors opened on nine, she knew for sure that was the case: questions had assaulted her from every angle as she walked into the courtroom, a dozen mikes were thrust in her face. She'd always believed that, unless you were a celebrity, those sort of dramatic scenes with roving packs of attacking reporters shouting questions at witnesses, defendants and attorneys, were manufactured for television. Now she knew they were not. The phone calls from the media had started after Maggie had been found incompetent, and the legal analysts and talk show hosts were back to dissecting everything about the *State of Florida vs. Derrick Poole* over their morning coffees – including, and especially, anything about her. The excitement of the crowd was palpable, even though the judge had ordered that the courtroom remain silent – there was an electric buzz in the air. All that was missing was popcorn. It was surreal. She was not the victim here, she was not the defendant. She was just some random, reluctant witness who happened to be in the wrong place at the wrong time and saw something she wished she hadn't. And it had turned into . . . *this*. She took a deep breath and reminded herself that this was just a situation; it would not – it could not – last forever.

Across from her at the defense table sat Derrick Poole and his attorney. Poole was clean-shaven today – his once long, wavy dark hair now styled in a short, classic taper, which made him look very young. He wore rimless eyeglasses and a sharp charcoal suit, white shirt and gray tie. Maybe he'd been working out, because he didn't look as lanky as he did that night, dressed all in black, wet from the rain, a crazed look in his otherwise unremarkable chocolate eyes.

Elisabetta rose at the state's table. She looked at Faith as if to say, 'It's OK. Just keep to the script. Keep to what we discussed and I'll get you through this.' The prosecutor had warned her last week at the pre-trial conference that she, personally, was going to tear Faith down on direct so that she could rehabilitate her reputation and reestablish her credibility in front of the jury. She had assured her that, while it would sting at first, by candidly having Faith explain her bad decisions, and the reasons why she'd made them, upfront, it would get the jump on the defense and take the effect of a crushing punch away from his assault. She likened it to the 'Lance Armstrong' of cancer treatments: She would have to kill her to save her. Diagnosed with Stage IV metastatic testicular cancer that had already spread to his lungs, brain and abdomen, doctors had to practically kill Armstrong with toxic chemicals to save his life. Elisabetta had noted that the man had then gone on to win seven Tours de France. It was Detective Nill who'd suggested that Lance Armstrong might not be the poster child for an inspirational analogy on rebuilding one's reputation.

As she had promised, Elisabetta took her, first, through the easy part: name, age, occupation, schooling. How long had she been married? How old was her daughter? Tell us about Sweet Sisters.

Then she moved to the night of October 19, 2014, and the questions got more personal, the answers a little more raw. Faith felt like she was betraying Charity, discussing her volatile marriage and the reason for the fight that they'd had at her party, the nasty comment Nick had made about her weight, and the reason why Faith had rushed out in the middle of the night, in a tropical storm, and in such a hurry that she had forgotten both her cell and her purse. It was disloyal enough discussing Charity's drama with Jarrod or Vivian, but to cut open her sister's personal life and watch it bleed in front of all these strangers, in front of all these cameras, and ultimately in front of the millions of Court TV watchers, made her physically ill.

Then Elisabetta went deeper. She asked about the drinking: How much had she had at Charity's? Was she drunk? Why didn't she stop at a hotel? How had she gotten so lost?

She led her to the moment Angelina appeared at her window, asking for help. Then she took her moment-by-moment through those fateful five minutes on Main Street. It was all very clinical until Faith got to the part where she drove away and never looked in her rearview until Pahokee and Angelina Santri and the man in black and the pot-bellied Yankee fan were long behind her.

Then the fangs came out. *I've got to kill you to save you, remember that, Faith.*

'Why didn't you let her in? Why didn't you call the police?

Why didn't you tell your husband? Why didn't you initially tell your husband or detectives about the pot-bellied man?'

Everything came out: Her DUI arrests. Her four months in rehab. Maggie's emotional problems. Jarrod's affair with Sandra and how, even now, she still feared him leaving her. When Elisabetta was done, Faith sat on the witness stand, cut open and bleeding herself, exposed for all to see. The most intimate, most devastating information – things she had never told another living soul before – had been divulged in a room full of cameras, and were now preserved in a court transcript that would forever be considered a public record. The cut was a mortal wound – Elisabetta truly had killed her.

Now she had to try to save her.

It started where it had ended – on a dark, deserted street in a small town in the middle of nowhere. The precise moment her life had changed forever would also be the moment that Elisabetta initiated CPR to bring her reputation back.

'The man in black that you saw pull Angelina Santri away from your window, do you see that man in the courtroom here today?'

Faith wiped the tears from her face. She didn't think there were any more left. 'I do,' she said, pointing at an unflinching, unaffected Derrick Poole. 'He's right there.'

Elisabetta nodded at Faith and offered the hint of a smile, as if to tell her that the worst was over – she was headed to post-op. She looked at the members of the jury as she announced the obvious: 'Let the record reflect then that the witness has identified the defendant, Derrick Alan Poole.'

71

'Mrs Saunders,' said Rich Hartwick rising. 'You have been on the stand for a whole day, and you've told us all some very difficult, personal information. I'm sure today is not something you ever envisioned when you left your sister's birthday party six months ago, was it?'

'No,' answered Faith. 'It wasn't.'

'Well, I don't want to rehash every detail with you – especially the more personal ones. Besides, I'm sure you've gone over those details and exactly what you were going to say here today with the prosecutor more than once, am I right?'

'Yes, I have met with the prosecutor, Ms Romolo,' Faith replied warily, looking over at the state's table.

'And you discussed extensively what you were going to say here today, right?'

'We discussed what I was going to testify about, yes.'

'And you were very forthcoming with Ms Romolo on direct about your two DUI convictions, one of which stemmed from an arrest on November twenty-fifth, 2014, only a couple of weeks after you had first gone to the police with your husband and daughter, right?'

'Yes.'

'You also testified that you recently completed a one

hundred and twenty day alcohol rehabilitation program at The Meadows in Wickenburg, Arizona, correct?'

'Yes.'

'That's a substantial time in rehab. So you admit you are an alcoholic?'

'I had a drinking problem. Had, sir.'

Hartwick nodded. 'You were very honest with the prosecutor that you had been drinking on the night in question before you left your sister's house. And that you were afraid you might have been over the legal limit to drive, correct?'

'Yes. I didn't feel intoxicated, but I was worried that, if tested with a breathalyzer, I might blow higher than the legal limit. I was worried about getting arrested in front of my daughter.'

'The one you admit you might have been driving around legally considered drunk with in the car?'

She looked down at her lap. 'Yes.'

'You've been very honest here today, even though it has been difficult revealing embarrassing information, right?'

'Yes.'

'Of course, your two arrests and your two convictions are public record, correct? Meaning, a records check with the Department of Law Enforcement would reveal your criminal history, correct? It's not like you could hide that if you wanted to, correct?'

'No. It's a public record. I was honest because it was the truth.'

'Same with your recent stint in rehab, you couldn't really hide that, either? I mean you've been gone for four months.'

'It's not public record; I chose to disclose that.'

'At the prosecutor's suggestion?'

'Yes.'

'Thank you for being honest with me right there, Mrs Saunders. Like I said, you seem like a nice lady who kind of got caught up in things the night of October nineteenth, 2014.

Wrong place at the wrong time. And now you're here. Like I said, I bet it's someplace you never envisioned being after that birthday party. And you were honest on direct when you admitted to Ms Romolo that you had been drinking at your sister's house before you got behind the wheel with your four-year-old and attempted to drive in a treacherous tropical storm two hundred miles back to your home in Parkland. Super honest. Raw honesty.'

'Objection. Is there a question pending or is Mr Hartwick simply musing?' asked Elisabetta.

'Mr Hartwick, don't muse,' ordered the judge.

'Of course, you haven't always been honest, have you, Mrs Saunders?' Hartwick walked closer to the witness stand. 'When detectives asked you initially if you had been drinking that night, you denied it, didn't you?'

'Yes. I was worried about what my husband would think if he knew.'

'Wow. You seem like a nice lady, but you weren't always so nice, either, were you?'

Elisabetta stood 'Objection!'

'Overruled. Get to the point Mr Hartwick. Let's not mudsling unless there's a point,' warned Judge Guckert.

'After Angelina Santri came and banged on your window and begged you for help and you didn't open the door and let her in—'

'I was scared. I will forever regret that decision, but my daughter was in the car!'

'The one you admittedly had driven drunk with?'

'Yes,' she replied with some difficulty.

'So after you turned away Angelina Santri, and after you had successfully driven away from these two "bad men" and you and your daughter were no longer in danger, you didn't call the police, did you?'

'I didn't have a cell phone, sir.'

'But you admit you passed establishments that were open

and that presumably had pay phones, or a phone on the premises that you could use to call the police if you wanted to?'

'Yes. I apologized for that.'

'Yes, you did. We heard that apology as well. And you admitted that you did not call the police when you arrived safely home at three a.m.?'

'I regret that, too.'

'I bet. And you didn't call the next day, or the day after that, or the week after that, even. In fact, it was when your four-year-old finally spoke up and told your husband what she had seen, that you finally went to the police, correct?'

'Yes. That is true.'

'That's a lot of excuses, a lot of regrets.'

'Yes. I have a lot of regrets.'

Hartwick paused for a long moment. 'So when it's convenient for you to be honest or nice, Mrs Saunders, you are?'

'Objection! Inflammatory.'

'Sustained.'

'I made a mistake, Mr Hartwick. I had been drinking at my sister's and I was worried I would get arrested in front of my daughter if I called the police and they thought I was over the limit. I made a bad decision. It is one that will haunt me forever. But I can't take it back. I wish I could.' She twisted the tissue in her hand over and over again.

'OK, Mrs Saunders. Everyone makes mistakes. Everyone has regrets. But you weren't very honest with the detectives when you were first interviewed, were you?'

'No.'

'You told Detective Nill that you had only seen Mr Poole with Angelina Santri. You specifically denied seeing any other person out there that night, isn't that right?'

'Yes.'

'So that wasn't a mistake, that was a lie, correct?'

'Yes. I lied.' She held back an exasperated sigh. The prosecutor had warned her the defense would ask the same damning questions over and over again with slight variations just so the jury could continue to hear her admit she'd lied. *Just temper your frustrations and answer the questions, Faith. The jury will tire of him asking the same question over and over and over again. They will appreciate your candor and patience.*

'You had, in fact been so close to the second man out there, that you could provide enough information so that a sketch artist was able to draw a composite of that man?'

'Yes.'

'And you were close enough to that second man to subsequently be able to identify him for detectives from a ten-year-old photograph, even though some of his physical features detectives admitted had changed?'

'Yes. But like I explained, my husband and I were having marital problems at the time and I was worried he'd . . . I was worried he would leave me if he knew there was *another* man out there and I did nothing to help that girl. I was already stunned that she had died, Mr Hartwick, possibly because I had done nothing, and I thought if he knew I saw two men out there and did nothing, he would leave the marriage. He would leave me. It sounds illogical now, but that's how I was thinking. And I thought I'd have an opportunity to tell Detective Nill later.'

'When it was more convenient for you?'

'When my husband wasn't around. But that didn't happen. My husband was always around. He went out to the scene with myself and the detectives.'

'So it wasn't until you were actually confronted with physical evidence by Detective Nill that there was another person out there that night who had taken Angelina that you finally fessed up and became honest?'

'I thought he would find out about the second person on his own. I thought your client would plea – I . . . I never wanted to be involved in this. It just kept spiraling out of control. And it had my whole life wrapped up in it.'

Hartwick leaned on the witness stand ledge. 'So let's get this straight: when your daughter saw Angelina Santri's face on the news and told your husband what she had seen and that Angelina had begged you for help, and he confronted you, you came forward and were honest – but not completely. And then, when you were confronted by Detective Nill with evidence of an unknown second suspect, you come forward and were honest. So the first lie was to save your daughter the embarrassment of your being arrested for your second DUI, and the second lie was to save your marriage because you were too cowardly to come forward and tell the truth the first time. And then you went through alcohol rehab – because underneath all that has happened is alcohol and while you don't admit to being an alcoholic, you do admit to having *had* a drinking problem that surely clouded your judgment and caused you to lie, but you're a better person now and we should believe you. Isn't that what you said to the prosecutor?'

'Not exactly that way.'

'So are we done with the lies? There are no more lies?'

'I'm telling the truth, Mr Hartwick. I'm ashamed of what I did and what I didn't do in the past. Like I said, I'll always have regrets. There are no more lies.'

Hartwick shook his head. 'Wrong answer, Mrs Saunders.' He walked back to the defense table and held up a piece of paper. 'Did you strike anything with your car that night? The night you were driving back from your sister's? October nineteenth and into the early morning hours of Monday, October twentieth?'

Faith felt her blood run cold.

Elisabetta and Gareth Williams huddled together. 'Objection,' shouted Elisabetta.

'Grounds?'

'We have not been presented with the evidence Mr Hartwick is holding in his hand.'

'That's because I haven't introduced it yet, Counsel,' said Hartwick with a dry smile. 'But I will.'

'Being caught unawares is not a legal objection,' said Judge Guckert. 'Overruled.'

Hartwick returned to Faith. 'Mrs Saunders, did you have an accident that night with your 2009 Ford Explorer?'

She hung her head.

'The witness will answer the question,' instructed the judge.

'There was nothing there. I looked,' Faith replied in a soft voice.

'Excuse me?' said Hartwick. 'That's not an answer. Did you strike anyone with your car on the night of October 19, 2014?'

Faith looked at the jurors. 'I hit something. I checked and got out of the car, but I didn't see anything. There was nothing there.'

Hartwick walked back over to the defense table and picked up another piece of paper. 'Angelina Santri suffered a fracture of her femur and a bone contusion, a dislocated shoulder and a spiral fracture in her left wrist. Those injuries are documented in the medical examiner's report and are consistent with a person bracing herself for impact against a motor vehicle—'

'Objection! Counsel is testifying and offering his own medical opinion!'

'It won't be mine alone for long, Judge. I am prepared to call the medical examiner.'

'Call who you want when it's your turn, Counsel,' ruled Guckert. 'Right now, don't offer a medical opinion, because you are not a doctor and you are not a witness. Next question.'

'Mrs Saunders, did you call the police after you had an accident?' asked Hartwick.

'There was nothing there,' Faith repeated, tears running down her face.

'Mrs Saunders, did you tell your husband that you'd had an accident?'

'There was nothing there.'

'Mrs Saunders, did you ever tell Detectives Nill or Maldonado that you hit someone? That you'd had an accident that night?'

'There was nothing there,' she insisted.

'Mrs Saunders, if there was nothing there,' Hartwick demanded, bellying up to the witness stand and sliding a piece of paper in front of her, 'then why don't you tell us why you replaced the damaged grille, popped a dent from the fender and two from the hood, and had two deep scratches compounded out of the hood on your 2009 Explorer at Lou's Automotive the very next day?'

72

'When Angelina Santri was banging on the window asking for help, it was because *you* had hit her and broken her leg and dislocated her shoulder and broken her wrist and *you* were now trying to drive off, wasn't it?' demanded Hartwick. Now he had pictures out from Angelina's autopsy. Grisly pictures of her leg and her hands and her shoulder.

'No! I had the accident earlier, back in the cane fields,' Faith cried. 'But there was nothing there, I swear it.'

'And when you tried to drive away, she was very upset, wasn't she?'

'Yes, but not at me. At him!' she screamed, pointing at Poole.

'She had fractured her femur. *You* fractured her femur with your three thousand pound car and you were going to leave her there. Just leave her there in the middle of nowhere.'

'No . . .' Faith whimpered.

'You didn't even call an ambulance or anonymously report your accident. Was that because you were afraid she saw your license plate and could tell the authorities?'

'No!'

'No wonder she was screaming and crying.'

'No, it wasn't like that.' She looked over at the state's table for help, but Elisabetta had stopped objecting.

'Not that you can remember, right? Considering all the alcohol you admittedly had consumed . . .'

'No! No! I didn't hit her. There was nothing there.'

'*Nothing* caused $1,200 worth of damage that you asked Lou Metorini to not put through insurance? In fact you paid him extra to finish the car before the day's end so your husband wouldn't find out, isn't that right?'

She looked around the courtroom. The tornado had picked her up and was spinning her around in the storm. She was no longer just a witness on the sidelines: she was part of the madness. She was being accused.

'You were hospitalized in December, Mrs Saunders, after you collapsed outside a bar in Fort Lauderdale. You blacked out at that time and had your stomach pumped?'

She shook her head. 'Yes.'

'You have a history of blacking out. Of conveniently not remembering things, don't you?'

And so the questions kept coming, picking her apart piece by piece, each one more and more confrontational, more and more personal, until her credibility was completely shredded. The room spun, everything around her spiraled round and round in the tornado. It was complete, controlled, perfect chaos in the courtroom and she was at the center of it. She was the only one who wanted to stop it.

There was no rehabilitating her. Elisabetta and Gareth scrambled as best they could, but the jury knew the state had been caught by surprise, and so any effect the 'Lance Armstrong' treatment might have had was rendered worthless. In fact, it had backfired. Now the jurors likely didn't trust anything the state had to tell them. And there was still a whole case to put on.

At the end of the second day of testimony, she was finally released, although warned to remain available, because she could be called again on rebuttal. She stumbled down off the stand, feeling like a victim herself, and made her way through the gallery filled with unfriendly faces who looked at her as if she were the defendant.

They had killed her, all right. The problem was, somewhere along the line they had stopped trying to save her and had left her up there to die.

73

Jarrod had not been in the courtroom when she testified. 'The rule' had been invoked by both the state and defense, which excluded potential witnesses from the courtroom. Since he'd been listed as a witness for both the state and the defense, he was not permitted to hear her testimony and the judge had banned him from watching the trial live on TV or the recaps on the news. He'd also instructed both her and Jarrod not to discuss their testimony with each other. So she didn't know exactly what he knew, but she'd figured out that he knew it hadn't gone well: the bar in the family room had been cleaned out before she came home from rehab, but now the mouth-wash was missing from every bathroom and the travel-size Listerine was gone from the toiletries bag. Same with cold medications. Even the rubbing alcohol was missing from the first-aid kit. Like she would ever drink rubbing alcohol . . .

She wanted to find her old friend. She did. She'd never wanted anything so much in her life. She wanted to resurrect her from the dead and find a bar and sit quietly in the corner and enjoy her company – think about old, fun times they'd had together, long, long, long before the nightmare that was her life now. She didn't want to talk to anyone else, but she did need to be around other people, anonymously absorbed into the décor like a picture, because it would keep her honest. It would keep her clean. She was afraid that if she got a bottle and invited her old friend in for a drink, that would precipitate the fall. She had never really feared 'rock bottom' because she didn't believe she was an alcoholic. That term defined someone who could not stop their descent because they had no control over it, and she always knew she had control. Until now. Now she feared she had no control over anything, and she feared that if she cracked open a bottle by herself at this moment, she would guzzle the whole thing until the last drop was gone. If she let that happen, she feared she would find herself in an ugly place that others might call 'rock bottom'. A place where rubbing alcohol might just be the drink of necessity.

She had enough control of herself at this very moment to know to prevent that descent, and recognize that the pressure that was coming at her from every angle was the result of a situation. A situation that could not last forever. A situation that would ultimately pass, no matter what the jury decided about the fate of Derrick Poole. Eventually everyone would forget about him and this case and hopefully her, and the situation would be resolved and she wouldn't feel this crazed panic in her chest. She wouldn't hear the ticking of that damn time bomb strapped to her chest. Once the situation had passed she could trust herself again.

From the moment Detective Minkhaus had dropped her at the house after she'd testified, Jarrod had been with her. He'd been waiting on the front steps with a can of Coke in his hand while Maggie rode her bike in the street when the detective pulled into her driveway. It was a beautiful spring day, the lawn was green, the sun had set the sky on fire. It looked like a Norman Rockwell painting: *Mom Home from Court*. At that very moment, Faith was so very, very happy that she lived in a gated community, safe from the cameras and reporters that might have tried to camp outside in the

381

street where Maggie was trying out her new bike, screaming, 'Watch, Mommy!' She'd been so overwhelmed by the apparent normalcy of the moment that she had cried. For the zillionth time that day she had cried – at what she was coming home to, and at what she might not be really coming home to. She didn't know if Jarrod knew then, at that very moment, as he stood on the steps, smiled and waved at the car, but she knew he eventually would find out about the latest lie. The judge's order wasn't going to last forever.

Inside she'd found the Listerine and Nyquil gone. But he hadn't asked what had happened during the trial and she hadn't volunteered. They had dinner and watched movies and caught up on *Breaking Bad* and *The Walking Dead*. He had stayed with her in the house for the next two days. They cooked, watched movies, baked while Maggie played in the backyard. They didn't turn the TV on and they didn't answer the phone. She didn't climb out a window and hop the guard gate to find a local watering hole.

Then Elisabetta texted him: it was his turn.

She sat on the couch after the front door closed and all she could think of was how badly she needed a drink. She tried to remember what the therapists had said. How she should handle her feelings, how she should channel her energy away from the overwhelming compulsion that ate at every rational thought. She smoked cigarette after cigarette and paced the backyard until her footprints had carved a path.

It's over, anyway, whispered a sad voice in the back of her head. It was her old friend. *He's gonna know about the car. He's gonna find out that you lied again. He doesn't trust you. He was only doing this helping thing out of guilt. To get you on your feet again so he could leave you. You made it easy for him, Faith. You made it easy for him to walk away. You gave him his reason, and that is exactly what he's gonna do when this trial is over: he's gonna walk away anyway.*

She screamed at the voice to shut up. She paced the halls of her nice house. She walked around the backyard some more. She turned on the TV only to see it was all about the Poole case. It was all about her. How her husband was about to take the stand. How the state's case was falling apart . . .

Then she took Maggie for a ride.

74

'I think it's time we consider medication, Mrs Saunders,' Dr Michelson said quietly, rubbing the back of Maggie's head as she scribbled on paper at the child-sized desk in his office. 'She's five now and coming up on kindergarten in the fall, and it would be good to find the right medication to help her cope with all the changes that are going to take place then. I know you've been resistant and so have I, but I think if we focus on her anxiety issues now and the hyperactivity, that may lessen the aggression and the tantrums. The tantrums are, as you know, born out of frustration. She feels helpless in certain situations and so she breaks down. Part of the reason she feels helpless is because of the hyperactivity. She didn't understand what was asked of her, or she didn't hear it or she wasn't focused enough to do what was asked of her. The Adderall will help her focus so that she is not so easily distracted, and so she doesn't get frustrated.'

Faith nodded. 'Yes. I want what's best for her. If you say medicating her will help her, then I agree.' Right now, at this very moment, what she loved most about the kind doctor was that he hadn't mentioned the Poole case other than to ask how Maggie had handled testifying at the competency hearing and what her behavior had been like since. He hadn't asked Faith about her stint in rehab or why she hadn't helped the Santri girl or why she'd lied on the stand. He smiled at her and behind his glasses his soft blue eyes didn't seem to judge her.

'Good. I'll write up the prescription, give you some samples and meet you outside,' he said as he walked her and Maggie out of his office and into the waiting room.

Maggie immediately ran over to the play area and Faith sat down in a chair. She'd totally forgotten about today's appointment with Michelson. She'd strapped Maggie in her car seat and gotten behind the wheel, determined to find something to quiet the paranoid whispers in her head, when the alarm on her cell went off, reminding her of the three o'clock appointment. It was a sign, she knew. A message from God. She wasn't religious, but she needed to be right now. She needed to believe in signs. She'd passed Lefty's Tavern and Falafal Wine Bar and the Publix Liquor Store and drove straight to Dr Michelson's, ignoring the angry, thirsty creature that was still shouting for her to turn into a strip mall and get her a goddamn drink.

'Mrs Saunders?'

She walked up to the checkout desk. Janet, the office manager, handed her a bag full of samples and two prescriptions. 'The doctor wants to see Maggie back here in ten days. Make sure you follow the instructions and call us if there are any problems.'

Faith nodded. She thanked Janet and tucked the prescriptions and samples in her purse and went to gather Maggie from the Supermaze table.

'No wonder her kid's messed up,' said another mother who had walked up to check in. She was not trying to whisper. 'Her mother's a lying drunk.'

'Mrs Opitz,' Janet replied in a hushed voice. 'Please.'

'Have you watched the trial? It's incredible. Have you listened to her? They should take her kid away from her. She's a horrible example of a—'

Faith took Maggie and rushed out. Ten minutes later she was at Westview Park. Maggie was surprised. And happy.

'Yay! The park! I want to play, Mommy!' she yelled, pressing her face up against the window. 'Watch me on the slides!'

As they approached the playground she let go of Maggie's hand and watched her rush into a crowd of kids. She emerged a few minutes later alone, going down the slides, then looping through the jungle gym and crawling through the tubes. Faith walked over to the benches, far away from the other moms and nannies.

The creature inside her had added a new voice to her argument. It sounded like the nasty woman at the doctor's. And there was Loni Hart and Sunny Hostin. A hundred voices had joined the chorus. Directly across the street was Evan's Fine Wine and Liquors in the Ross shopping center. Was it a coincidence that she had pulled into a park with a liquor store next door? Or was it fate?

She was so tired. So very, very tired. Tired of fighting. Tired of resisting. Tired of pretending words didn't hurt and judgmental looks didn't condemn. She watched as Maggie made her way through the network of tube tunnels, all alone in a crowd.

Then she got up and walked across the street.

75

Ed stared out the window of the stolen Ford minivan watching the little kids play in the playground. He made sure he parked it in front of a strip mall so people wouldn't think he was a kiddie pervert and call the cops. And he made sure he didn't stick around too long. Just long enough to get a glimpse of her.

Her. *El problema.* He sucked on his cigarette. Dumbass Derrick had really fucked that one up. They should have taken care of Blondie and her emotionally fucked-up kid a long time ago. They should never have let the two of them drive out of that rinky-dink town, with Derrick practically yelling 'Drive safe, now!' at the Explorer as it hauled ass on home. He should never have let Derrick bully him into letting her go, and he'd beat himself up about that every day since – even before Derrick's picture popped up in the papers and on the news, back when the dumbass was smug enough to actually say that *he* knew best this time.

No, no, fuck no. He was the professor and Derrick was the fucking student. It was always like that and it would always be. When the student starts thinking he can run the class better, then school's out. So even though Ed was pissed off and worried once it became clear that Blondie had yapped to the cops, he was happy to watch Derrick's dumbass, dumb-founded face try and figure out what had gone so wrong with his plan. Like Ed's dead mama used to say, 'It don't do me no good to say "I told you so" when life bites you in the goddamn ass 'cause you didn't listen to me, but it sure as hell makes me feel good.' The professor had to come in and save the day, give Derrick an alibi and get the coppers off of dumbass's back. Taking that young, hot, little dancer from Sugar Daddy's had been fun, although not as fun as the others, when he and Derrick had been together.

'Well look at you,' Ed muttered aloud as he took in a deep drag and watched Blondie leave the playground and head across the street, right toward him. Damn she looked tired. Spent was a good word. Haggard. Used-up. Like a frail little thing whose insides had been sucked out, walking around in fancy clothes that don't fit right no more. All he might have to do here, he thought, as he watched her come at him, is open his door and dinner would be served. Can't get much easier than that. He licked his lips. *Come to Papa, baby. Come over here, Looky-Look.* But she veered right – right into the liquor store.

Even though Blondie had everyone hating on her in the paper and shit, calling her a bad mommy and a horrible person, and even though Derrick's attorney was kicking ass in the courtroom so good that he'd probably get the dumbass off with an apology from the jury and the stuck-up prosecutor, Ed still wanted to kill the skinny bitch. Just for being her. Just for being out there that night. Just for getting away. Just for not listening. Just for blowing her God-given second chance at living. He hadn't actually talked to Derrick in months, since the shit went down, but he knew the dumbass would tell him: 'Let it be, Profe. It will all resolve itself. It'll make the ending more interesting, is all.' But Ed was old school. Ed wanted revenge so bad he could practically taste it when he ran his tongue over his chapped lips. He wanted someone to pay for the past wasted six months, for the shit life he'd been leading since his face started showing up on the news. Living in tents and under bridges. Hiding out in abandoned homes, waiting for Derrick to get out and life to get back to being what it used to be. But he was a wanted man himself now, thanks to Blondie. That was one more really good reason to want to cut her tongue out for blabbing.

Ed flicked his cigarette out the window as the door to the liquor store opened and she came out with a bag in her hand. No one's gonna miss her, he thought, watching her in his side view. Nope. She's a self-professed drunk and he'd seen it himself. Nothing more disgusting and unladylike than a girl who can't handle her liquor. Her testifying days would be forever over. She won't be identifying no one no more.

He started up the car as she hurried back across the street to her brat. He could see the little girl standing there alongside the monkey bars, desperately looking round and round for her mama who'd left her all alone to go buy booze. What a sight. Once this case was over he'd make his move – he'd go pay her a visit at her fancy house or maybe just wait till her liquor cabinet ran low on supplies and she went out bar-hopping. Unlike last time, this time there would be no mistakes.

He watched the emotional reunion take place on the playground. Mommy on her knees hugging sad-eyed kid. Boo hoo. He turned out of the parking lot. Fuck Derrick and his selective conscience that had gotten them into this fucking mess. You can't have one of those if you're gonna do what they do.

Of course, that wasn't completely true, Ed thought with a dry smile as he pulled out into the road and watched the emotional Mommy–Daughter scene play out in his rearview, the figures growing smaller and smaller until they finally disappeared from sight.

After all, this time he was gonna let the kid live.

76

'Where is it?' Jarrod demanded as he walked into the living room. He tossed aside the cushions of the couch, pulled out the end table drawers. 'Where is it?' He moved into the kitchen, checking underneath the sink and in the cabinets. Then on to the bathroom.

'What are you talking about?' Faith asked, jumping off the couch.

'You don't get it, do you? You really don't. You are watched wherever you go. There's a camera watching you wherever you go. It's gonna be all over the news! Where's the bottle?'

She backed into the sliding glass doors. 'I don't have anything.'

'You left her in the park by herself to buy yourself a bottle of booze. Now where is it?'

'I didn't drink it, Jarrod. I didn't. I bought it, that's right, but I didn't drink it.' She ran up, grabbed his face and breathed in it, then she kissed him hard on the lips. 'See? I didn't drink it! I swear! You'd taste it!'

He backed away, his fingers to his lips. 'I can't do this any more. I can't babysit you. You left her again. She's five years old!'

'But I didn't drink it! I swear!'

'Don't swear. You're not very good at that.' He ran upstairs. She heard him in the closet, rummaging around. Then he moved across the hall to Maggie's room.

'Don't fight, Daddy,' said Maggie from somewhere upstairs.

Faith paced the floors downstairs like a frantic tiger, trying to figure out what to do. Everything was happening so fast – there was no time to think. She heard him on the stairs again and looked up. He was carrying a large duffle bag in his hand and Maggie in his arms.

'No! No! Please!' she begged, running over. 'I didn't drink it! I'm sorry!'

'Not in front of Maggie. Not any more. Please, Faith,' he said as he walked past her and out through the laundry room to the garage.

He walked out the garage door and put Maggie in the car seat while Faith watched from the laundry room door, holding onto the frame for support, trying to think what to do. She could hear Maggie crying. It felt like someone was sticking a knife in her heart.

'Please, Jarrod! Please!' she pleaded. 'I'll be good! I won't drink! I won't!'

'I'll be right back, sweetie,' Jarrod said calmly to Maggie, handing her the Kindle Fire. 'I'm gonna go talk to Mommy for a minute. Watch your movie with your headphones.' He closed the car door and came over to where she stood in the doorframe.

'Please . . .'

'When you're ready to get sober, we'll be back. I'm sorry, I really am.'

'Jarrod, no!'

'You left her alone in the park,' he said flatly. 'I can't babysit you – you're a grown woman who makes her own decisions. Maggie is five – she doesn't have that luxury and I have to protect her from people who keep making bad choices. I love you, Faith, I do. I'll leave you with that. I don't know if you believe it any more, or if you'll ever believe it again. I do know I can't make you believe it, and it doesn't matter anyway. You're gonna do what you want to do. I can't watch though. I can't watch you destroy yourself.' Then he turned and got into the driver's side of his Infinity.

'But I didn't drink it!' she screamed. She raced up the stairs two at a time, stumbling on the last step, and scraping her chin on the carpet. In the master bedroom she frantically felt underneath the box spring and pulled the unopened bottle of Absolut from the hole she'd burrowed in it. She raced back down the stairs and pushed open the laundry room door with the bottle in her hand to show him, running out onto the front lawn as the garage door was closing, but he was already long gone.

77

'Ladies and gentlemen of the jury, have you reached a verdict?'

Jarrod stared at his computer screen in his dark office. Outside in the hall he heard the rumblings of the office shutting down for the day. It was six o'clock on a Friday afternoon. Most of the office staff had gone, but anyone who hadn't left yet was sitting in front of his secretary Annalee's desk, watching exactly what he was watching – the live feed from courtroom 10F.

'Is he here?' someone asked out in the hall. A nod and a point at his closed office door probably followed.

'Wow. What a crazy case. Is he still with her?' someone else asked.

A shake of the head probably followed. He had not told Annalee yet that he and Faith had separated, but the woman was very intuitive: she'd known about the affair long before everyone else had figured it out, including Faith.

'Yes, Your Honor, we have,' said a small voice off screen. The jury was not allowed to be shown on camera.

'Madam Clerk, please publish the verdict,' said the judge.

The packed courtroom fell silent.

'We the jury in the county of Palm Beach and the State of Florida, on this the fifteenth day of May in the year two

393

thousand fifteen, so hereby find the defendant, Derrick Alan Poole, not guilty of the crime of murder in the first degree in the death of Angelina Santri . . .'

The excitement simply could not be contained; the court-room exploded in murmurs and not-so-shocked 'Oh my God!' whispers.

Jarrod rubbed his eyes in his dark office. It was over. It was finally over. But he felt no relief. And it wasn't anger or outrage that he was feeling because the jury had reached the wrong verdict. It was fear.

He picked up the phone and called Vivian to tell her he'd be a little late picking up Maggie from her house. He had work to finish up.

'Have you spoken with her?' she asked.

'No. I called and texted, but I haven't talked to her. Have you?'

'Not today. I spoke with her yesterday, but it wasn't good, Jarrod. She was, ah . . .'

'Drunk?'

'I didn't want to tell you. She's had it so rough. But she has a problem and I don't know how to get her to see it. She doesn't want anything to do with me or Charity. She doesn't want to come to the bakery. She won't pick up the phone when the guard calls to tell her I'm at the gate.'

'I called the rehab. They said she has to make the realiza-tion herself. That if she doesn't want to face it yet, she hasn't hit her bottom. They said some people never do. That they never climb out. How much longer can that be for her, Vivian? Do I have to wait till she drinks herself into a coma? Or I find her dead, asphyxiated on her own vomit?' Now that Poole had been acquitted, at least there would be no more need for him to eliminate witnesses.

'I'm sorry, Jarrod.'

'I can't watch this, Vivian.' His voice caught and he started to lose it. 'It's so hard. So hard.'

'Does she know about the verdict?'

'I don't know. I imagine she saw it too. I texted her to call me, but she won't. She's probably so far gone right now, or on her way, she might not remember watching it.'

'Are you going over there?'

'I don't think so, Viv. I don't know. Probably. Maybe. No. I don't know. I'll see.'

He hung up and stared out the window of his office at the almost empty parking lot. Annalee knocked on his door about twenty minutes later to tell him she was heading out and to ask if he needed a friend.

'No,' he'd quietly told her through the closed door as he studied the cars heading toward the Sawgrass Expressway, heading home en masse to spend the weekend with their loved ones. 'I'm not going . . .'

Grief and jealousy overwhelmed him then, and he never did finish the sentence.

78

Faith watched as the courtroom went crazy. The analysts started talking, making voice-over comments, and on the bottom of the TV screen ran the newsfeed: DERRICK POOLE FOUND NOT GUILTY OF FIRST DEGREE MURDER.

She turned off the TV. There was nothing else she needed to see.

Her cell phone started to vibrate and ding. She turned the phone off. The house phone rang. And rang. And rang. Until she pulled the cord out of the wall.

There was no one she needed to talk to.

She closed all the blinds and drew all the curtains on every window in the first floor of the house and turned off all the lights. Then she headed upstairs and went room to room, doing the same thing.

There was no one she needed to see.

She headed into her bedroom and closed the door. The closet door was still open, the stack of suitcases that had tumbled off the shelf when Jarrod had grabbed his duffle bag still lay on the floor. His side of the closet still looked full – he hadn't taken much when he left.

He'll be back for the rest soon, the voice of her old friend whispered in her head. *Now that his case is over, he can be rid of you. He'll be back to get the rest of his stuff. And Maggie's, too. And you'll be all alone. It'll just be you and me.*

She put her hands over her ears to stop the voice, but it didn't help. She crawled into the closet and pulled down the suits Jarrod didn't take with him, making a soft pile. She pulled out her box of her dad's things, fingering Sully's old watch that he'd left her. She put it on her wrist. There was no need to hide a bottle in the box any more – no one lived here to hide it from. There was no need to pretend any more. She put on Jarrod's sports jacket and closed her eyes. In one hand was the half-empty bottle of something she'd brought with her from downstairs. In the other was the handgun that Jarrod had also left behind in the locked box on the closet's top shelf. She fingered the trigger. Maybe he'd left it behind on purpose.

It's just you and me, Faith, whispered her old friend as she huddled in the corner of the dark closet and raised the bottle to her lips. *I'm always here for you, buddy.*

79

Derrick mouthed 'thank you' at the foreperson. He hugged his attorney. Gemma leaned over the railing and kissed him.

'How do you feel?'

'What's it like to be vindicated?'

'Where is Ed Carbone? Have you heard from him?'

'Are you angry with the state?'

'How about the witness, Faith Saunders? Are you angry with her?'

The bailiff yelled, 'Order!' and the crowd quieted for a moment.

'Mr Poole,' the judge said somberly, 'the jury has returned a verdict of not guilty against you. You have been cleared of all charges. You are free to go, sir.'

'Thank you, Your Honor. Thank you,' Derrick replied humbly. 'Thank you.' He didn't know if anyone actually believed him innocent, but the reporters were smiling and being chummy. Their loyalties changed quickly. They all wanted a quote or to snag an interview with him. *Dateline* had already been in contact, and they were filming here today. Rich Hartwick had told him that there had been calls about a cable movie on Lifetime based on him.

This was a new beginning. He wasn't gonna run like he

was sure Profe wanted to. Run and hide and then take up together in a new town somewhere far, far away, like California. Derrick was gonna cash in on his fifteen minutes before he left town. Maybe write a book. The urges might not come back. Profe had been the one with all the ideas, after all. Ed brought out the best and the worst in him. They hadn't spoken in months and they'd made no contingency plan where or how to meet up in the event something went wrong, because they were never supposed to get caught. Nothing was ever supposed to go wrong. It never had before for Ed. He was the one with all the experience. The only fuck-up ever was Derrick's – letting the desperate housewife and her kid go. Ed would definitely hold *that* over his head forever.

He knew Profe would want to get together again, and that it was only a matter of time before he got in contact. The guy was crazy. He loved doing sick shit, thinking up sick shit that no one had ever thought of before. And he loved showing off what he could do and all the crazy things he could think up. He would want revenge first, though. The guy didn't let nothing go, like that dancer from Miami who he'd wanted to take out. She'd made the mistake of calling him a loser and he never forgot. She was the first one to go and Ed had enjoyed doing all sorts of sick shit with her, recording her screaming and then playing it back over and over again, making songs up with her screaming in 'em and using it for background noise. Derrick was no saint, but he wasn't as bad as Ed. He didn't want to be as bad as Ed. And the first person Ed likely would want to make a point with was gonna be Blondie and her little kid, and Derrick didn't do kids. There had to be a line.

Maybe the urges would never come back now. He'd maintained control for six months: Who's to say he couldn't be normal forever? That he couldn't get that incredible high from something else besides watching someone die?

'Are you going to sue?'

'Are you going to stay in Florida?'

Derrick smiled at the pretty reporters. Girls who wouldn't have looked at him a year ago. Today wasn't the day to think of tomorrow. Today was a day to celebrate.

'Come on, Derrick,' said Rich Hartwick, leading him through the mob into the congested hallway. Then down the elevator and into a lobby. He held Gemma's hand as he followed his attorney through the crowd, ignoring the shouts and questions that came at him. He watched as bystanders stopped and pointed, wanting to know what was going on. He felt so famous. He felt so *good*. Helping the three of them make their way through the raucous crowd – along with some detractors, to be fair – were two uniformed officers. Derrick thought that was hysterically ironic. If the jury had convicted him, those same officers would have been escorting him to a death row cell in Starke right about now.

Lightning lit the sky as they stepped outside the front of the courthouse. The air was cool and breezy. It was about to storm.

Across the plaza, about fifty yards away, a black Town Car pulled up.

'That's ours,' said Hartwick.

Someone opened the back door. The officers pushed the press back.

'Derrick!' a woman shouted, moving along with the crowd.

'Derrick! I'm Kathleen Hodge with *New Times*. Can we get an interview?'

'Derrick!' a girl squealed. 'Can I get your autograph?'

'This way, Derrick,' said his attorney over the tremendous clap of thunder that had sounded. 'Before it pours.'

He felt like a celebrity. It was a high like no other he'd ever experienced.

In fact, he thought, as he and Gemma moved to the waiting Town Car and the skies began to open, listening to a woman's adoring shouts of adulation might be a better turn on than listening to her screams of terror.

80

Bryan Nill stood in the back of the courtroom with his mouth agape. He was stunned. Not so much at the verdict, because he could tell early on – after Faith Saunders' cross – that the case was not going well. Elisabetta was climbing uphill everyday and the hill kept getting steeper. The dots no longer connected – they were just there – and that was all the jury needed to find reasonable doubt.

But acquitted did not mean innocent. 'Not guilty' did not mean 'didn't do it'. It wasn't the verdict that shocked him so much, because he had mentally tried to prepare himself for it. It was the reaction of the media that was so alarming. Jumping the fence at the first chance they had to ingratiate themselves with a serial killer and snag themselves an exclusive. Even the spectators seemed willing to move on already, like they'd come out of a movie theater and were going off now to grab coffee and discuss the plot. It was all a bit surreal.

His cell buzzed with a text. It was Maldonado, who had popped out a kid a few days earlier.

TM: Juries are stupid. You OK?

He typed back a simple answer: No.

TM: Come see what I made. He'll make you smile. Till he cries . . . LOL

And just like that, the world kept on keeping on. Tatiana had had a baby. He had a new gangbanger murder on his desk. His brother had asked him to come to Jersey for Memorial Day and he had to book the flight today. The twins wanted to know where they would be having graduation dinner. Within a few days, the acquittal would fade from the headlines. Within a week it would be gone altogether. Within a few months, no one besides the victims' families and Faith Saunders would remember Derrick Poole at all. The world just kept on keeping on.

He ignored a couple of calls for comment himself and walked into the courtroom's well. The state's side was empty. Elisabetta was packing up her file box. 'You OK?' he asked.

'Nope,' she said, not looking up.

Her co-counsel, Gareth Williams, had figured out to steer clear. He was at the other end of the table.

'You gonna be OK?'

'Nope,' she replied again.

'It doesn't mean they don't know he's guilty . . .' Bryan tried.

'I just couldn't prove it. Thanks, Detective. I feel so much better.'

'We'll find Carbone. You'll have a second chance at Poole with the other victims.'

She shook her head. 'Good luck with that, Detective. Hope you find him before the two of them find each other again. I wouldn't want to have to tell another mom how sorry I am that you fucked that up.'

With that she took her file box and walked out of the courtroom, and for the first time since Bryan had known her, ignored all requests for a comment.

81

VERDICT IN LITTLE SHACK OF HORRORS
SERIAL MURDER TRIAL:

DERRICK POOLE FOUND NOT GUILTY IN
MURDER OF PALM BEACH DANCER

Ed pumped his fist in the air as he read the newsfeed on the bottom of the TV screen. 'Yes!' he said, probably a little too loud. The other four people who were in the dank, smelly old man's bar looked over.

Time to go. He didn't look nothing like himself, but if this whole bullshit case had taught him anything, it was to take no chances with nosy people. Next thing ya know, someone's on the phone with the cops hoping to score a reward or some face time for being a Looky-Look. It was a great day, though. A great fucking day! He'd be able to get with Derrick soon enough. It had been so damn long – man, that was gonna be some reunion. Then they'd take their show on the road. Get the hell out of Dodge. The band was back together!

He looked at the screen as he chugged the rest of his beer. The newscast, which didn't have any sound, was now running video clips that showed the scene down at the courthouse.

Derrick sure looked like he was having a good ole time chatting it up with those reporters, with that ugly snitch of a girlfriend smiling at his side. The last conversation he'd had with Derrick, the last thing the dumbass had said to him before they'd agreed to go their separate ways for a while was, 'I think the bitch from work might've turned the cops on to me.' Ed felt the jealousy race through him like a fever. He felt it all the way down to his fingertips and he squeezed the bottle so hard he thought he might actually break it. She'd be the first to go – Girlfriend. Right after Blondie. This was no Butch and Sundance and what's-her-name threesome happening here. That's not what he and Derrick were about. He put the bottle down hard on the bar.

He was holding her hand.

He turned away from the TV, it made him so mad. What the fuck was that about, now? There was no need to play all lovey-dove boyfriend no more, Dumbass. No more need to pretend to be something you ain't, because Derrick Alan Poole was Not Fucking Guilty!

'Time to drop the curtain,' Ed muttered as he threw down a five. 'Show's over.' Maybe he'd even change the order of things and take Girlfriend before Blondie. He'd busied himself for the past four months building what was at first supposed to be a shanty Everglades hold-up for a wanted expat like himself, far away from snoops and tourists and campers and rangers and washed-up towns. But he'd made it into so much more than a place to lay his head. Maybe he and Derrick could take both of them lucky ladies to the new crib and show them around. He smiled at the thought. He hoped Derrick would like it. Even if they decided not to hang around Florida for long, they could still tidy up business before they pulled out.

Ed popped a cigarette into his mouth and lit it as he headed to the door, daring some yahoo to say shit to him about smoking in a bar. He grinned as he walked out. It was gonna be great to see Derrick. Maybe there was a way to get together even tonight. A reunion would be sweet. It was gonna be hard to hold back. There was so much he wanted to do. He felt like he'd popped a fistful of X, only better. He felt like he could do *anything* now.

'Yes!' Ed yelled as he walked out of the bar into the still-sunny parking lot. Damn, he hated summer. He fist-pumped the sky with a smile. 'Let's do this!'

82

Did she really hear that?

Faith sat up in the pitch-black closet and listened hard. She could hear rain beating on the roof. The wind whistled through the A/C vents. But that wasn't what she had heard.

She looked around the closet, her eyes struggling to make out anything and she tried to think. What time was it? What was today? She could almost feel her thoughts laboriously make their way through her brain, as if they were trudging through a thick, greasy sludge. Every few synapses or so, the thought would stop to check the route and make sure it wasn't lost. And when it finally arrived at its destination, it forgot why it was there anyway – the sludge was so slick it couldn't stick. Instead the thought slowly ricocheted around her head like a lost pinball. She shook her head to jostle the machine. Bad idea. Her head was spinning already and now she felt nauseous. So incredibly nauseous. She had to get to the bathroom. She crawled out of the closet on her hands and knees and into the master bedroom and then into the bathroom. The marble was cool on her palms. She pressed her face to the floor. It was so cold. Maybe she'd just lie here for a while to stop the awful spinning. Give those thoughts a well-needed rest. She closed her eyes.

Then she heard it again: the sound she'd heard in the closet. It was not the rain or the wind in the chimney. It was coming from downstairs.

She couldn't trust herself to stand, so she crawled back through the master bedroom and over to the door that led to the hall. She opened it a tiny crack and listened hard.

A tremendous clap of thunder sounded and she fell back on her butt.

A screechy, scraping sound was coming from somewhere downstairs. It wasn't a sound she'd ever heard before. It wasn't like the palm fronds rubbing on the window or the sigh of a settling house or the wind in the A/C vents. Those sounds were there, too, and then there was this new one. It sounded like a window had broken downstairs and the wind and rain had found its way into the house.

She felt sick again.

Then she heard crunching, like someone stepping on broken glass.

Someone was in the house.

83

'Derrick Poole?' A woman pushed her way through the cameras. She was in her thirties maybe. She wore a nice suit. She looked like a reporter. He turned to her as he was getting in the Town Car.

'I have a question, too. How will it feel to meet the devil?' she asked, with a broad smile. 'Are you excited?'

He heard the gunshot first, then he felt the pain in his gut. He stared into her dark eyes as the screaming began all around him.

'A gun! A gun! She has a gun!'

'Oh my God!'

'She's shooting!'

'He's been shot!'

People ran in a dozen directions. The crowd that had gathered around him dispersed. Gemma ran, too. He watched her run off. She never even looked back. The only one left was the woman. Even the cops were gone.

Derrick looked down at the blood that was now spreading across his white dress shirt. It was a new suit, too. He'd bought it especially for the trial. He held out his hands at the woman and saw they were covered in blood. There was a hole in his stomach.

'That was for Noelle,' the angry woman said, just as calmly as when she'd first walked up. He fell to his knees. 'But you won't be seeing her again, you fuck, because she went to heaven.'

Then she pointed the gun at his forehead and fired again.

84

They're here! whispered the voice. *They've come for you!*

Faith's whole body shook violently. He was downstairs, walking around, looking for her.

Remember the trial? said her now-panicked friend. *Remember how he told you to be quiet and you weren't? He's free now! And his partner is, too. There's more than one, Faith. That guy drugged you and tried to kill you.* <u>Drugged</u> *you. That's why you feel so sick right now. You can't think straight because you've been drugged. Poisoned. Now they're gonna come up here and take you and chop you up. Chop. You. Up.*

She heard footsteps on the stairs. She put her hand over her mouth to hold in the scream.

She crawled back into the closet and closed the door. She backed up until she hit the wall and the pile of Jarrod's suits. *The police! Call the police!* The thought finally made it through the sludge. But she had no phone. It was too late to call for help. She covered herself in Jarrod's clothes and tried to hide.

Did the murderers know that Jarrod had left her? Did they know she was all alone?

Yes, that's why they're here! answered the voice.

What would they do? Would they drag her out and finish her off here in her own bedroom?

Chop, chop, chop, said the voice. *Remember what that woman said about her daughter? 'I don't even have all the pieces . . .'*

The bedroom door opened. She could hear it. They called her name. They called her to come out.

The closet door opened. She squinted as the light from the bedroom flooded the closet. A large faceless figure stood in the doorway.

'Where the hell—'

She pulled the trigger. The muzzle flashed, and the closet exploded. Her body slammed back against the wall. Her ears rang. She could hear nothing, only the awful ringing, like a thousand church bells in her head. She sat up.

There's two of them! screamed the voice.

She looked about frantically, untangling herself from Jarrod's suits and the dresses that had fallen down on her. She picked up the gun again and aimed.

Maggie was standing over the body that was lying motionless on the floor of her closet.

Faith still couldn't hear, but she didn't need sound to see that Maggie was screaming.

85

'I still don't get how she didn't know it was her husband,' said Mike Derdin, one of the two detectives from Parkland, to Chuck Bennett, the Chief Felony Assistant from Broward County. They were sitting in a conference room at the State Attorney's Office in downtown Fort Lauderdale, along with Bryan Nill. Displayed on the table in front of them were crime scene photos.

Bryan picked up one of the pictures. It was taken in Faith Saunders' bedroom. Newspapers, magazines, clothing and children's toys lay strewn on the floor. The bedding, sheets, and pillows were also on the floor, as if the bed had exploded. An empty bottle of Ron Rico sat on the dresser along with a container of Minute Maid orange juice and a Rubbermaid pitcher. He thought of the times he and Maldonado had been out to the house – it was always so pristine and beautiful, so well taken care of. This was more than messy. Bryan had had a younger brother with an alcohol problem. That's what his apartment in Whitestone, Queens looked like when the police found him hanging in his closet. He picked up another picture. This one was of the inside of the closet. Clothing that had fallen or been pulled down from hangers sat in clumpy piles. Suitcases and shoes were strewn everywhere. Blood stained the beige carpet. Next to it was the Sig Sauer registered to Jarrod Saunders with an evidence marker beside it. Lying beside one of the clothing piles was a bottle of Smirnoff that looked empty and another evidence marker.

'They were having problems, her and the husband,' added the other detective who'd introduced himself as Tom Dunleavy.

'No shit?' replied Chuck Bennett sarcastically. He turned to Bryan. 'I appreciate your coming here and meeting with us on this, Detective Nill. I know this didn't happen in your jurisdiction, but you know this lady and her husband and the Poole case is definitely intertwined. I invited the ASA who tried him – Romolo – to join us today, but she . . .?'

'Left the office,' replied Bryan.

'That was quick.'

'She resigned the day after the verdict came in. She's moved on to greener pastures. She got herself an analyst position with Court TV. You can see her five nights a week in the comfort of your own living room, if you'd like,' said Bryan.

'Wow,' replied the prosecutor. 'Imagine what gig she might've landed if she'd won the case. So tell me about this woman. I'm doing pre-files now. I gotta figure out what to charge her with.'

'I worked extensively with Faith,' said Bryan. 'I met Jarrod on multiple occasions. If you watched the trial or read the news, you must know already that the lady has a drinking problem.'

'According to her BAC she had enough alcohol in her to keep her drunk for days,' remarked Dunleavy. BAC stood for blood alcohol content.

'She totally fucked up your case,' said Derdin angrily. 'No wonder she got blitzed. A serial killer walked free.'

Bryan looked at Faith's booking photo on the prosecutor's desk. She was a shell of the beautiful, well-dressed woman who had first come into the police station with her handsome husband and cute kid seven months ago. Sickly slim, gaunt, pale, dark circles, unkempt hair. But it was her eyes that were perhaps the most telling: The light was gone from them. Exhausted was too mild a word. She looked like she had lived a dozen lives already. He thought of what her husband had said that day of the pre-trial at the State Attorney's Office:

She never wanted to be a witness.

The woman was already beaten down by then, having had to leave her family for four months and go to rehab. She was already fragile, but they wanted another pint from her, so they'd hooked her up to an IV and sent her back in to the courtroom, knowing she was weak. Knowing she likely would not make it out of this mess. Then if it all went to shit, like it did, the blame was on her. He personally would not partake in that game any more. 'Leave the lady alone,' he said quietly, but in a tone that everyone clearly understood. 'The case was tough. Blame me. *I* fucked it up. *I* didn't have enough.'

'She claimed when the uniforms first responded that she thought it was Poole and his partner Carbone who were coming to get her,' said Dunleavy.

'But Poole was already dead!' exclaimed Derdin.

'She didn't know that till the uniforms told her,' said Dunleavy.

'Or so she says,' mused the prosecutor.

Dunleavy shrugged. 'She'd drawn all the blinds and curtains and barricaded the doors downstairs and the husband couldn't get in the house. He was coming to check on her after what happened with the verdict and Poole being murdered by Langtry's mother at the courthouse. He couldn't get in, so he broke a window. She heard it, thought it was Poole and Carbone, and hid in the closet. She was hiding in there when the husband opened the door.'

Derdin tapped his hand on the desk. 'That's what I don't get. How'd she not know it was her own husband?'

'What did you say her BAC was again?' asked Bryan.

'Point one eight seven'

414

'That's how come she didn't know it was her husband,' Bryan answered. 'He opened the door, the light's behind him, her pupils are dilated, she can't see his face and she pulled the trigger.'

'He'd left her, though,' said Derdin. 'Just the week before – after she'd testified. They were broken up. There's your motive. And he'd had an affair. We found that out too, from his secretary.'

Bryan could feel the anger in him start to swell. 'You look like you have your mind made up about Faith Saunders, Detective Derdin. So I'm gonna give you my point of view, for what it's worth. She had a drinking problem, which got worse after her husband strayed. She got involved in this case and it was a cluster. She told some lies to save herself and got caught. She drank some more and it put a hell of a strain on an already strained marriage. Her husband put her in an expensive rehab. He called her every day while she was there. Check the phone records. But this case, and the fallout after her testimony, was too much. She fell off the wagon and left their daughter alone in the park, the press picked up on it because she was the target of their wrath since the moment it got out she left Angelina Santri to die in the company of two serial killers. The husband found out about the park, took the kid and left. It's a tragedy all around. I'm surprised she didn't turn the gun on herself.'

'How is she? The kid?' asked Chuck.

'How do ya think? She saw her mom shoot her dad,' replied Derdin. 'She's a wreck. And this is on top of what she witnessed last fall. She had emotional issues before that, according to family members. She's staying with the aunt right now, and she's not talking. Not a word.'

'I spoke with her aunt, Charity Lavecki, and I tried talking to Maggie,' Bryan said. 'So did Detective Maldonado, one of the detectives on the task force. The kid got kinda close to her during the Poole case. Maggie is still pretty traumatized. She is refusing to talk.'

The prosecutor tapped his pen on the table. 'So she can't tell us what happened.'

'What's the law on this, Chuck?' asked Dunleavy. 'Can the wife stand her ground?'

The prosecutor nodded, thoughtfully. 'If she's in her home and is under the reasonable belief that she is being attacked, then, yes, she can use deadly force to defend herself and her castle.'

'But Poole was already dead, Chuck,' said Derdin. 'There was no reasonable belief he was coming to get her.'

'The belief is objective. It's a reasonable person standard,' replied Bryan. 'If she didn't know he was dead, then it would be reasonable to think he would be coming after her. And his partner, Carbone, is not dead. We don't know where he is. So it is definitely reasonable for her to believe that he might have come after her. He'd tried it once before. He has the motive to try it again: she's the only one who can identify him.'

Chuck nodded. 'That's true. How close did she come?'

'She missed his heart by an inch, doc says,' replied Dunleavy.

Chuck nodded thoughtfully.

'So she walks on this?' asked Derdin incredulously. 'Shoots the poor bastard who's coming to check up on her in his own house, claims she was too smashed to know what was going on and somehow that's reasonable?'

'I didn't say she's walking, Detective Derdin,' snapped Chuck. 'But I'm trying to see if I've got a winnable case here for attempted first. Or even attempted second. She's lucky hubby's still breathing, we can all agree on that. He's claiming it was an accident. He doesn't want to see her prosecuted. I gotta take that into account, too.'

'They all say that in domestic cases, Chuck,' replied Derdin. '"He didn't mean it" or "It was my fault he hit me." Sorry if I take what the husband says with a big, fat grain of salt. He was leaving her, he'd had an affair, he'd taken the kid, she was a social leper and she was a drunk even after he'd dropped the price of a small house on rehab for her and he felt bad. *He felt bad*, guys – that's what this comes down to. Now he feels worse because not only is she still all of the above, but because of him, she faces a few years in prison. So he's saying it was an accident so he doesn't have to feel so bad when he goes back to the cute intern. He'll still get the kid, start a new life and not feel so fucking guilty when he shows pictures of what mommy used to look like to his traumatized, mute daughter.'

'Wow, tell us how you really feel, Mike,' said Dunleavy with an angry shake of his head. 'Have a fight with the Mrs yourself today?'

'What does Jarrod Saunders want?' Chuck asked, ignoring Derdin and instead looking at Bryan. 'A lifetime restraining order? What does he want to see happen to her? Do you know?'

'He wants her to stop drinking,' Bryan answered. 'I met with him yesterday in the hospital. This isn't a domestic, Chuck. This is just plain sad. I watched this woman break down like she was decomposing, both physically and mentally. A lot of people got a lot of mileage out of her and out of this case. The prosecutor launched a TV career, late-night hosts used her for one-liners, and TV commentators analyzed every aspect of her life, including what kind of a mother she is – like any of them would have done any different under the same circumstances out there. We're all so quick to judge, but that lady didn't ask to be a witness, she didn't want the fame. This case ruined her life. The press ripped her apart, made her out to be more of a villain at times than the men who killed those girls. And people tuned in to watch by the millions. The only friend she had left at the end was the bottle, and it tricked her, too. So I feel bad. And the husband feels bad. We should all feel bad.'

The room was quiet. The other three men exchanged looks.

'What happened to vigilante mom? Langtry was her name, right?' asked Dunleavy.

417

Bryan ran a hand through his hair. 'She's looking at first, because there's no way to get around premeditated. But the State will cut her a deal because of the circumstances, I think. And she's sick; she's got diabetes and some other health issues. She'll probably plead to second and get ten in prison, or something like that. If the ASA offers her more than that, she'll probably plead NGI and let the jury walk her because we all know that any of us would've done the same if we were her and had a gun in our purse.' NGI stood for Not Guilty by Reason of Insanity. Bryan stood up. 'I have to go, boys. My twins are graduating from high school today and I gotta get there early enough to get a seat.'

'You must be a proud papa,' said Chuck. 'Two almost off the Daddy Dole.'

'Proudest Pop there is. Soon to be the brokest: They both picked out of state. I'll be doling it for four more years.'

'Then there's graduate school,' added Dunleavy with a chuckle.

Bryan rolled his eyes. 'Thanks. I feel better now.'

Everyone laughed. Everyone stood.

'You called me in here to ask for my opinion on this, Chuck,' Bryan said thoughtfully, as he slipped on his sports jacket. 'So here it is: There've already been too many victims in this case. There's no more juice to be squeezed, no more careers to be made out of this one, boys. So just do the *right* thing, Chuck: Give Faith Saunders probation. Let her get the help she needs. She doesn't need to be behind bars. None of us will be any safer for it.'

'Thanks, Detective,' said the prosecutor. 'I appreciate your feedback.'

'Like my dad once told me a long time ago,' Bryan replied as he headed out the door. '"A clear conscience is a soft pillow." Sleep well now. All of you.'

86

'You look handsome,' Tatiana said as she and Bryan took their seats in the Boynton Beach high school auditorium. 'Did I tell you that?'

'Yup. But you can tell me again,' he replied with a proud smile. 'Thank you. It's new. I cut the tags this morning.'

'I could tell. Very spiffy. What size is that jacket?'

'Forty-two.'

'No way.'

'Yes way. I'm down sixty-six and a half pounds, as of this morning.'

She shook her head. 'Damn! You're an inspiration. I still got all this to lose,' she said gesturing to her stomach. 'It's all there, like a big gloop of skin.'

'You just had a person cut out of you. Stop being so hard on yourself – enjoy a donut. And you look smoking hot – trust me. See my ex-wife over there? She is pissed just looking at you. Let me borrow the baby. That'll really drive a nail in it.'

Tatiana laughed and handed Oscar over. 'Watch his neck.'

'Damn, I remember holding two of these not too long ago.' He looked over at where Hilary and Hailey stood waiting to walk in with all the other graduates. This summer they would work at Coldstone Creamery and Chipotle. In August Hilary was headed to Penn State in Pennsylvania and Hailey to St John's University in New York. Hilary turned to look over at him and made an 'Awww!' face. Then she snapped a picture with her cell. Bryan sniffed Oscar's bald head. 'You forget how yummy their heads smell.'

'I think he just pooped,' said Tatiana, laughing. 'His face is all red. That's what you're smelling.'

'Even his poop is cool. The little dude has cool poop.'

Tatiana leaned over and kissed him then on the cheek. Her lips lingered a little bit longer than he was expecting and Bryan felt himself blush. 'Let's get her really pissed,' she whispered.

Bryan didn't know where they were going, or even if it was headed in the direction he hoped it was. Tatiana had spent a lot of time at his townhouse over the past six months and he had some new furniture now. The house didn't look or feel as empty. And it didn't sound empty when she brought Oscar over. Bryan had been there during the birth, out in the waiting room, and he'd picked up her slack at work, making sure no one said anything to her about taking some time off. He was, for the moment, anyway, considered the resident expert in serial killers and that – even with the acquittal – came with a little bit of star status, which he was totally going to use to his advantage, because he knew better than anyone how fleeting and capricious fame could be. But he was happy. For the first time in a really long time, he was happy. And he was really happy to see that the seat next to Audrey was empty. 'John Something' would not be ruining the day that Bryan could not believe was somehow already here. Eighteen years had simply flown by.

His phone beeped. An incoming message. It was an Instagram post from Hilary. He smiled. It was a picture of him and Oscar snuggling. She'd titled it: *Dad and the boy he never had.*

The band began to play 'Pomp and Circumstance', which was always a tearjerker. Bryan grinned and patted Oscar's back as the whole auditorium stood and his two beautiful girls made their way down the aisle past him to take their seats on the stage below.

87

Ed stared at the battered, oversized black wooden doors of the First Lutheran Church across the street from where he sat on a bench in the park. With shaking, dirty fingers he anxiously rolled and unrolled the paper ticket real tight, like he was rolling a joint. It was almost seven thirty, but the sun was still out, and there were people milling about in the park – some walking dogs, others stuffing their faces from the free food that Love Thy Neighbor had handed out to the homeless. Somewhere not so far off he heard the sound of little kids laughing.

He felt so damn . . . *lost*. That was the only word to describe it: lost. Empty was another good one. Hollow. It had been weeks now since Derrick had died and he still had no . . . *purpose*. Every morning he got up and told himself that this was the day he'd get his ass back in gear. This was the day he'd know what to do and he'd finally do it. Do something. Do anything. Anything besides walking around like someone had taken a knife to his frontal lobe, sleeping in cars or homeless shelters or waking up on the beach watching with scorn as the sun rose all pretty once again in the sky. He knew he was practically begging to get caught, daring some copper to start asking questions when they told him to get off the beach or he got popped for pissing in a bush or diving through a Dumpster. Then it would be all over. Someone in a uniform would recognize him when they hosed off the grime from weeks of living on the streets. Or they'd run his prints and figure it out that way. Or his blood. Or a cheek swab. They'd get a good sample of him and put it in a machine and BAM! he'd be on the ground with a dozen guns pointed at his head. One of them coppers might get an itchy finger and the next thing you knew Ed would be looking at his brains pouring out of his head on the ground next to him.

Just like Derrick.

He wiped an angry tear away before it had the chance to escape. The fact that he even cared so much pissed him off. The fact that he felt lost and empty and hollow pissed him off. The fact that some part of him would actually allow himself to get caught pissed him off. The fact that he considered going out like Derrick a better alternative to this gut-wrenching emotional devastation pissed him off the most. It made him feel weak, like some crying-ass pussy – and Ed was no fucking pussy. He loathed this feeling so much it burned somewhere deep inside. What he needed to do was take this burst of anger and fan it internally till it spread into an inferno. Then he should harness the anger and focus it and use it so he could finally get up off this bench and out of this park and do what needed to be done and move the fuck on with life.

He felt the paper uncurl in his fingers and he rolled it up tight again as he waited. People were starting to make their way into the church, one by one. Never in a pack. Never a cluster of individuals cozily chatting as they held the door for each other and exchanged pleasantries like you might see at Sunday services. Nope. Not here. Rather, each person looked over their shoulder as they pulled open the large doors to make sure no one was watching them, before hurrying inside to spill their secrets behind those big black doors.

Ed looked down at the rolled-up bus ticket to Houston that was coiled around his filthy fingers like a snake. He'd scored it from one of the homeless advocates at the shelter, after he'd told her how his mama was gonna put him in rehab back home in East End. That he had a job waiting for him when he got out of rehab and he was gonna be back with his family and his abuela and this ticket was gonna save his life and get him off the streets for good. Boo-hoo. Ed had always been a good storyteller – he was bawling himself by the time he'd finished telling the tale to the old lady with hair the color of margarine. He almost had himself believing there was somebody in Houston who gave a shit about him. That there was somebody anywhere that gave a shit about him, for that matter. But the old lady had looked at him funny when she handed him the ticket – like she either didn't believe him, or maybe like she might have recognized him. He rubbed the ticket thoughtfully. Now he wasn't sure if he should use it. He looked back up at the church doors.

Or if he even wanted to.

He'd hung around this town, this place for too long. Florida wasn't his home, it had only been a stop on the journey, but so much had happened here. Derrick had lived here. Derrick had died here. His eyes welled again and he wiped it away and smacked himself hard in the head with both hands.

How could he pick up and leave? Who would he ever be able to find that could replace Derrick? *That's* what made him want to cry like a pussy. Would he ever again be able to find someone like Derrick? No. Not happening. No way. It had taken him a lifetime to meet The One. The perfect student. The perfect partner. How do you go about doing it again? Finding someone who thinks like you and acts like you and wants to learn from you? A person you could *grow* together with. This was not a relationship that was meant to come to an end one day. This was not some marriage where you say the words, 'I do' but don't mean them when someone better comes along. It was so beyond that. It was on a different mental plane. What it was was a true partnership with a person who thought exactly like him. Thoughts that his mom had once branded 'twisted' after he told her what he'd done to the family dog. He missed the guy like he'd never missed anyone in his life. And now it was over and Derrick was gone and Ed felt completely, totally . . . *lost*.

He punched himself in the head again to drive those melancholy thoughts out. He watched as the addicts walked into the church, so absorbed in their own set of problems that it took all the strength they could muster to pass through those doors and seek help for a problem that none of them really wanted help with, given a choice. He would bet every one of them at that meeting would like nothing better than to get loaded and have no one care that they did. Unfortunately, people did care, though. Ed looked at his watch. The meeting started at seven forty-five. Most everyone was early. They lived every minute of their lives for these meetings, clinging to the inspirational anecdotes and prayers uttered behind those oversized black doors like a lifeboat, to help get them through to the next day or the next meeting – imagining their existence would get better if they just took it One Day At A Time. That One Day would come where they wouldn't still consider giving their right leg for a drink. But Ed knew from watching his own dad drown in a bottle that that day would never really come. The mythical Utopia that the lifeboat was headed for didn't actually exist, but it was the only way to get a drunk in the goddamn boat, where you could hope they'd keep on rowing instead of figuring out the whole trip was nothing but a fantasy.

The vengeful mom who'd offed Derrick was locked up tight for the moment. There was no chance in hell of getting close enough to her.

Next.

Girlfriend was long gone. The day after she'd left Derrick

to die in front of the courthouse – before a cleaning crew had even hosed his blood off the sidewalk – she'd had a moving truck at her apartment and had hauled ass out of town.

Next.

And the prosecutor was off to New York to be a star. Even though her bid to kill Derrick didn't succeed, it had all worked out for her in the end, hadn't it? Derrick was dead and she was gonna be on TV, is what the papers were saying. How he would love to take her smug face back to that shack and show her exactly what he had done to those girls. Show her how she and the fat detective had had it all wrong – the things he and Derrick did were far, far worse than what she'd probably told that grand jury . . .

The anger was back. Its hot embers were filling the hollow spaces inside of him now. Without Derrick he was just *here*. Here on this earth. Here in Florida. Here in this park. Wandering the streets like a zombie and biding his time fantasizing about taking revenge that wouldn't happen now that everyone had moved on. The Prosecutor. The Girlfriend. The Vigilante.

All but one, he thought, as he watched the slight, harried figure in sunglasses make her way up the street and into the church. She was no master of disguise – he recognized her right off.

And she was leaving soon enough, too.

He'd read in the paper that she was moving, that her house was up for sale. Once Blondie picked up and left town, he might never be able to find her again. And the sad reality would be that no one would pay for Derrick's death.

He looked around the park. Maybe it was time for him to move on, too. Getting caught doing something stupid wouldn't do anybody any good. It was near impossible to get close to Blondie, she was such a social recluse. These meetings were his only shot. And, of course, he was all too aware that if he got caught now, if it all ended, he would never have a chance to become legend himself. He'd never have a chance to meet his Second Act, if such a person did exist out there for him. Five dead girls would barely get him a mention on Murderpedia.

The bus ticket was for tomorrow morning. He had one last night to make up his mind. Twelve hours. He started to hum The Clash song: 'Should I Stay or Should I Go?'

Then he shoved the ticket into his raggedy jacket and headed across the street to the church. He knew that would help him decide.

88

The bible study room in the First Lutheran Church in Fort Lauderdale was really, really hot. Faith dabbed her forehead with the dry washcloth she'd brought with her and looked around at the others. There were people wearing sweaters. And a homeless looking man standing in the back had on an oversized coat. He tipped his curly head at her and it gave her the creeps. He looked familiar; she'd probably seen him before at other meetings. She looked away.

It must just be her. She rubbed her sweaty hands together. She was so nervous. She wiped them on the washcloth and put it back in her purse. Then took it out again. The room smelled of freshly brewed coffee. It always did at these meetings.

She looked over at Jarrod, who was seated beside her on a metal folding chair. He was rubbing her back.

'You'll be OK,' he said reassuringly. 'Whenever you're ready.'

They'd done this, her and him, a few times already. They'd come in and sat away from other people and listened to the sometimes tragic and sometimes inspiring stories of the others. Some meetings there were a lot of people in the room. At others there were only a couple. Each venue was different and Faith never liked to stay in one place, lest someone recognize her and say something. It had only been six weeks. People would forget and move on eventually. And even if they didn't, she and Jarrod and Maggie were going to. It was time to leave South Florida and start somewhere fresh, for all three of them. Jarrod liked New York. He had to take the New York bar first, but he'd already spoken with some firms and they were very interested. Finding a new home for him should not be difficult. Faith had checked out the schools on Long Island; they seemed to have good programs for emotionally disturbed and developmentally delayed children. As for Sweet Sisters, it was time to start fresh there, too. Jarrod insisted that people in New York ate cupcakes, and when she got herself back together again one day maybe she would do another start-up. Or maybe she'd dust off that manuscript and try and rewrite it. Now that she had some experience with the legal system, it would give her crime fiction voice some authenticity. Or maybe she'd just be a mom to Maggie. Her girl needed her more than ever now. And Faith needed to be needed.

She was required to go to AA meetings twice a week for the five years of her probation. Considering she should have been in jail, she was very grateful. The most she could do though, so far, was sit and listen. It was funny, because when she was at The Meadows, she could say the words they wanted to hear with ease, because she didn't mean them. But now that she meant them, she couldn't say them.

Technically, Jarrod was not supposed to be here. He wasn't supposed to attend AA if he wasn't an addict. But no one asked questions and she'd noticed that there were a few other people who brought their emotional support blankets with them. The truth was, she couldn't do this without him. She might one day in the future be able to, but right now she needed to know he was here with her. That she wasn't alone. And that he really did mean it when he said he wouldn't be leaving.

'How are you feeling?' she whispered in his ear. 'You want to go?'

He shook his head and gave her a smile and a thumbs-up. She knew he was really tired and that his chest was probably hurting, but he would never admit it. She was trying to get past everything they'd been through together, but looking at him was hard sometimes. The guilt made her cry a lot. But every day got a little better and at the end of each one he was still there. Now there was the adventure of New York to look forward to, and a future full of new memories to make. That's what got her through the tough parts. And there were a lot of those, no lie.

Today there were about thirty-five people gathered in the bible study room. No one knew her. No one recognized her, or if they did, they didn't care. They were there, she knew, because they had far bigger problems. Or were hard at work trying to fix those problems. She didn't look at anyone for too long, and they didn't look at her. They didn't call it Alcoholics Anonymous without reason.

The chairperson entered the room and walked past the rows of fold-up chairs to the front of the room where there was a small table set up. On it were pitchers of water and plastic cups. And coffee. Always plenty of freshly brewed coffee.

Vernon was his name. He was a kind-looking African American man in his fifties, with a soft face and a hesitant smile. He led the group with the Serenity Prayer: 'God grant me the serenity to accept the things I cannot change, the courage to change the things I can, and the wisdom to know the difference.'

She reached for Jarrod's hand. He squeezed it hard.

Then Vernon asked the question that had her holding her breath. 'Is there anyone here who would like to tell their story?'

It was time and she knew it. Jarrod didn't nudge her or say anything. He sat there, staring impassively straight ahead.

She stood. Her knees were knocking together, but she was standing.

'Come forward,' said Vernon, gesturing toward the podium. It reminded her of the courtroom, something she wished she could forget.

She walked cautiously to the podium and looked out at the crowd. The homeless man with the curly hair in the back was gone. She felt strangely relieved.

'My name is Faith,' she began in a small, shaky voice that she hoped one day would sound strong again. She looked over at Jarrod. 'And I am an alcoholic . . .'

EPILOGUE

Miami,
Six months later

'Counselor? You got a minute?' asked City of Miami
Homicide Detective Manny Alvarez.

Miami-Dade County Assistant State Attorney C.J. Townsend
looked up from her desk at the burly, bald, olive-skinned
detective standing in her doorway who bore an uncanny
resemblance to a Cuban Mr Clean. He actually took up most
of her doorway. 'For you, Manny, I have ten,' she answered
with a slow smile.

'You say the nicest things,' he answered, pulling up a chair.

'What are you doing around here at, what?' She looked at
her watch. 'Five o'clock on a Friday? Jeesh. How'd it get so
late? This place must be deserted.' The support staff at the
State Attorney's Office religiously cleared the halls by four
thirty. At five fifteen on a Friday it was possible that she and
Manny were the only souls left in the whole building.

'I was across the street on a motion to suppress with Judge
Shapiro that ended about three. So I headed to the cafeteria
and was enjoying a café con leche when I got a call from
the FDLE lab up in Tallahassee. Seems a lot of folks are

432

working late today. Or maybe they are for this,' Manny added, thoughtfully. 'I don't know if you're familiar with the case of the Tootsie's Cabaret dancer who went missing five weeks back. She was the daughter of a Miami-Dade commissioner who didn't know his little girl was moonlighting as a stripper?'

'Yeah, I know the case. They found her body last month, right?'

'Parts of it. Out in the Everglades, off the Miccosukee Indian reservation. It's Miccosukee land, but the Indians didn't want it, and since the City of Miami was already working the missing persons case, we kept the homicide and decided to work it with FDLE and piggy-back on their jurisdiction. The kid – Meghan was her name – wasn't killed where she was dumped, that was for certain, so the Feds didn't want it, either, although I'm willing to wager they'll probably be pretty interested now. We knew from the state of the body and lack of decomposition that the girl was definitely held for a period of time before she was killed, which was troubling. Her boyfriend was initially a suspect, but not any more. So the ME did a scrape of the fingernails and we got DNA, made a profile. All's good, right? I put it in the system and FDLE ran it through their DNA database. I also gave it to the Feds to run through CODIS.'

'And FDLE just called you? So they have a hit?' C.J. asked.

'Oh yeah.'

'That's good. Who is it? You look a little stunned, so I'm thinking you're about to drop a big name on me, Manny. It's not the commissioner himself, is it?'

'No, no. What's interesting is that I don't have a name. What I have is a match to another crime scene. In fact, this guy I'm looking for has already been indicted. Or his DNA has.'

She leaned forward. 'What?'

'And I figured that this case will probably land on your desk, Counselor, for a number of reasons, the first being it's the murder of a county commissioner's daughter – who's about to announce his candidacy for the US Senate. That makes it high profile. And second, you're the SAO resident expert on serial killers: you've tried more of them than anyone else around here.'

C.J. felt her chest tighten. 'How do you know it's a serial, Manny?'

'The DNA is a match to the indicted AWOL partner of acquitted-but-dead Palm Beach murder defendant Derrick Alan Poole. The name of the partner is believed to be Eduardo—'

'Carbone,' she finished. 'I thought he went to Mexico.'

'Everyone thought he went to Mexico, including the lead detective, Bryan Nill, who was just as shocked and troubled twenty minutes ago to hear me tell him what you're hearing now.'

'So Carbone is still in Florida then?'

Manny leaned all the way back in the chair and rubbed the back of his head. 'Apparently. In fact, I'm sure your boss is gonna be telling you that this guy is all yours, Counselor. If we can catch him.'

'Of that I have every confidence, Manny.'

'And I have every confidence that you'd do a better job than that wannabe talk show host who took a stab at it last time and missed. I hear she sucks as an analyst.'

'Thanks, Manny. Down, boy. It was a hard case. Her main witness had some problems.'

He shrugged. 'Just speaking the truth. We got a twenty-three-year-old escort from Brickell that hasn't been seen since hooking up with a Back Page date a week ago. Name is Valerie Brinley and her mom is a wreck, calling the press and shit. I'm thinking now that I got this Cane Killer guy's DNA down here in Miami all up under the fingernails of a chopped-up stripper, that this escort's disappearance could be related.' He blew out a long breath. 'I don't need to tell you how many dancers and hookers go missing every year in Miami-Dade

County alone. I'm gonna have to trawl though more than a few missing persons files and see who hasn't made it back home yet, see if anyone fits the description of what this guy Carbone seems to be looking for in a woman. Then I gotta call the County, and the Beach and see what they got in their departments. Oh boy.'

C.J. nodded. 'So he's a serial and he's still hunting. And he's in the Everglades and he's dumping by Miccosukee . . .'

Manny pulled on his thick black mustache, which was as oversized as his forearm, and leaned forward again in the chair, rocking it. 'We know from the Palm Beach case that these guys held those women in cages in that shack for a few days or more before killing them. That shack was perfect: abandoned and remote. Carbone is a survivalist according to Nill. That means he can live in extreme conditions like the Everglades for long periods of time. There are a couple of structures out west that might suit his needs. The county took down a meth lab off Tamiami Trail last year that was housed in an old mobile home in the middle of nowhere. And I'm remembering the wooden fishing shack where one of the Cupid victims was found strung up. That's only a couple of miles from the Indian reservation. I'm sure there are other places – abandoned homes, businesses, storage facilities – but those two might be worth taking a ride out to.' Manny had been part of the multi-agency task force that worked the serial killer Cupid murders. C.J. had headed up the prosecution.

'I remember that shack and that girl.' She shivered at the memory. 'That's a lot like the Palm Beach Little Shack of Horrors. It's definitely a place that this Carbone guy would be attracted to, if he found it. I would have thought it had been torn down, though.'

Manny shook his head. 'Nope. At least it wasn't last year when I was out on the reservation doing interviews on this other case I had. It's worth a trip out west to see what else has sprung up in that area. Maybe I'll make your husband take a ride with me.' C.J.'s husband, Dominick Falconetti, was a special agent with FDLE. He had headed up the Cupid task force. 'He knows the area pretty well. And I'll see if I can get a few boys with Fish and Wildlife to join us. I'm sure they know good hiding spots aplenty. I don't want to spook this guy, though. If Carbone does keep his victims alive for a while before he kills them, and he does have this Brinley girl – or any other girl or girls – there's a chance we could save them. I want to be as quiet as possible, but cover as much ground as possible. If he's still around and we lose him, he probably will flee to Mexico this time and then we'll be fucked.'

C.J. had worked enough cases in her lengthy career and brought down enough bad guys to trust the intuitive feeling that was raising the hair on the back of her neck. It was a law enforcement sixth sense that abruptly told you, after sorting through hundreds of leads that had led nowhere, that this one could be The One. It was the gut feeling, supported by intelligence, that had caused Admiral McRaven to send a team of SEALs and two Black Hawk helicopters to a remote house in Abbottabad. The abandoned meth trailer or fishing shack might not turn out to be The Place, but Manny and Dominick would find it. It was a matter of time. And her gut was telling her it could be tonight. She reached for the phone. 'You call Dominick,' she said excitedly. 'I'm sure he'll be up for it.'

Manny stood. His shiny bald head practically kissed the plastic encased fluorescent tubes that lit her dull gray office. 'Who you calling then, Counselor?'

'That detective from Palm Beach,' she replied as she started to dial. 'I have a feeling we'll be needing him to dust off his case files and take a ride down to Miami.'

ACKNOWLEDGMENTS

I'd like to thank all the people who helped me complete this project. Although *All the Little Pieces* is a book of fiction, it still required a fair amount of research, sometimes to verify even the tiniest of details. It seems that I have been thanking the same individuals since the moment I picked up the pen in 2001, and it is no wonder that they are some of my closest friends. FDLE Special Agent Larry Masterson, who always, always answers the phone, no matter what time it rings, and FDLE Special Agent Chris Vastine, who is usually with Larry when it does. Deputy Statewide Prosecutor Julie Hogan, a genius in the courtroom and my supplier of expert contacts. Marie Perikles, Assistant Legal Counsel, Office of the Inspector General, and her husband John Perikles, Miami-Dade Assistant State Attorney and Director of the South Florida Money Laundering Task Force, who, acting in concert, go above and beyond to answer my questions, including furnishing me with not just the case law but a legal brief, as well. Dr Reinhard Motte, M.D., Associate Medical Examiner, Palm Beach County, who enjoys helping me think up twisted ways to realistically kill people. Denise Seminara Pellman, avid thriller reader, kind critic and sister-in-law extraordinaire who is always excited to read one of my books and offer feedback, which any author will tell you, can sometimes be a dangerous proposition. And for my delicately honest daughter Katarina and my gingerly diplomatic husband, Rich, who were both patient enough to not just read, but then re-read and sometimes re-read again a variation not just on the same chapter, but sometimes on the same sentence. As always, I have to thank my agents, Luke Janklow, and Claire Dippel, his assistant, and Rebecca Folland who are all so supportive and encouraging, and last, but not least, my very talented editor, Julia Wisdom, whose vision and guidance helped make *All the Little Pieces* a chilling roller coaster ride of a book.